"Maisie Dobbs is a revelation." —Alexander McCall Smith

"Sometimes when you adore a series, you're terrified to crack open the next installment, fearing disappointment. Fortunately, Jacqueline Winspear's fans can rest easy." —Deirdre Donahue, *USA Today*

"A superb series." —Jay Strafford, *Richmond Times-Dispatch*

"What Jacqueline Winspear does to keep her series about the astonishing Maisie Dobbs alive and as fresh as new paint is impressive."
—Dick Adler, *Chicago Tribune*

"A detective series to savor." —Johanna McGeary, *Time*

"For readers yearning for the calm and insightful intelligence of a main character like P. D. James's Cordelia Gray, Maisie Dobbs is spot on."
—Hallie Ephron, *Boston Globe*

"A quirky literary creation. If you cross-pollinated Vera Brittain's classic World War I memoir, *Testament of Youth*, with Dorothy Sayers's Harriet Vane mysteries and a dash of the old PBS series *Upstairs, Downstairs*, you'd approximate the peculiar range of topics and tones within this novel."
—Maureen Corrigan, *Fresh Air*

"[Catches] the sorrow of a lost generation in the character of one exceptional woman." —*Chicago Tribune*

"A winning character about whom readers will want to read more."
—Associated Press

ELEGY FOR EDDIE

ALSO BY JACQUELINE WINSPEAR

Maisie Dobbs

Birds of a Feather

Pardonable Lies

Messenger of Truth

An Incomplete Revenge

Among the Mad

The Mapping of Love and Death

A Lesson in Secrets

ELEGY

for

EDDIE

A Maisie Dobbs Novel

JACQUELINE WINSPEAR

HARPER ● PERENNIAL

NEW YORK • LONDON • TORONTO • SYDNEY • NEW DELHI • AUCKLAND

HARPER ● PERENNIAL

A hardcover edition of this book was published in 2012 by HarperCollins Publishers.

P.S.™ is a trademark of HarperCollins Publishers.

HarperCollins books may be purchased for educational, business, or sales
promotional use. For information, please e-mail the Special Markets
Department at SPsales@harpercollins.com.

FIRST HARPER PERENNIAL EDITION PUBLISHED 2012.

Designed by Jennifer Daddio / Bookmark Design & Media Inc.

Library of Congress Cataloging-in-Publication Data has been applied for.

ISBN 978-0-06-204958-2 (pbk.)

19 20 21   ov/LSC   20 19 18 17 16 15 14 13

Dedicated to

OLIVER AND SARA

And Allah took a handful of southerly wind, blew
His breath over it, and created the horse.

— BEDOUIN LEGEND

For evil to happen, all that is necessary is for good men to do nothing.

—EDMUND BURKE

Once in a while you will stumble upon the truth but most of
us manage to pick ourselves up and hurry along
as if nothing had happened.

—WINSTON CHURCHILL

ELEGY FOR EDDIE

PROLOGUE

❖❖❖

Lambeth, London. April 1887

Maudie Pettit pushed the long broom back and forth across the wet flagstones, making sure every last speck of horse manure was sluiced down the drains that ran along a gully between the two rows of stalls. Night work at Starlings Brewery suited Maudie, because the grooms and drivers were just leaving when she arrived in the evening, and there was only the night watchman there, and one stable boy who slept in a hayloft over the harness room, just in case a horse was taken ill. Maudie was all of sixteen, and though an observant woman with a measure of common sense could see that she was in the final weeks, if not days, of pregnancy, her long skirts and a loose blouse topped with an old coat served to cloak her condition. Disguise was crucial, because if the guv'nor found out, she'd be out on her ear with a new baby and no job to keep the poor little scrap. Maudie had been born in the workhouse, and she was determined that not only would she not be going back there, but her baby wouldn't be born in the workhouse either.

From the time she was twelve years of age, Maudie had cleaned the stalls at the brewery every night, and then gone on to the morning shift at the pickle factory, and sometimes picked up a bit more work at the paper factory in between. She had precious few hours each day to mind her own business, but considered herself lucky to have a roof over her head and fellow lodgers who looked out for her. Jennie and Wilf were brother and sister, born in the workhouse a few years before she came into that ugly world. But as luck would have it, all three managed to live beyond the age of ten to find honest work outside. And they stuck together, eventually renting two upstairs rooms on Weathershaw Street from Mabel Hickmott, who was, as Jennie often said, "Madam by trade and madam by nature." All the same, Mabel left them alone and didn't want to know their business as long as she had the rent money in her hand on time.

"Owwwwww," Maudie bent double, clutching her swollen belly with one hand, and holding on to the brass bars of a stall with the other. The old mare, Bess, turned away from her feed and came to investigate the noise.

"Shhh, Bess, it's only the baby moving, love. You go back to your mush, go on."

The mare nickered, brushing her soft mouth against Maud's fingers. Maudie loved the mare. The draft horses at Starlings were all geldings, but Bess had been there for years, and was used to draw the guv'nor's cart when he went out to the pubs to check on business. They said that having the old mare at the stables kept the geldings in check, that she'd sort out any funny business with just one withering look across the stalls. Some of the stable lads were a bit scared of her, having felt a nip when they brushed her too hard. But Maudie always kept a treat for Bess, and would stop for a moment to run her fingers through the horse's mane.

"Oh dear God, Bess, my darlin', the baby's coming, and here I am in a manure gulley."

Maudie pulled herself up and began walking up and down again, pushing the broom back and forth, even though the flagstones were now as clean as anyone had ever seen them.

"Got to keep moving, haven't I, eh, Bess? That's what Jennie said to do, if she wasn't at home when the baby came." She blew out her cheeks and stopped to rub her back. The horse did not return to her mush, but stood watching as Maudie walked first one way, then the other.

The girl's work didn't end until midnight, after the brass fittings on the stalls had been cleaned and the floor of the harness room was spick and span. She needed the money—good Lord, she needed the money, especially if she couldn't go to the pickle factory tomorrow—so she had to carry on. She clenched her teeth to stop herself from crying out again. Then she dropped her broom and reached out towards the bars of the stall once more.

"Oh, no, the baby's really coming now."

She was alone. The stable lad and night watchman were likely playing cards and taking a nip or two of whiskey in the feed room, which was just as well. She didn't want anyone to know. She just wanted to lie down and have her baby. Taking a deep breath, she slipped the latch on the mare's stall. Old Bess stood back and nuzzled Maudie's pocket, then moved her nose across the rise of her belly.

"That's right, old love, my baby's in there and he's wanting to come out. Let me lay down with you, just for a minute. He might change his mind and the pains will stop."

Maudie piled hay in the corner of the stall, covered it with her coat, and lay atop the softness. Old Bess leaned down and nickered, her nose close to the girl's head.

"Leave me be, Bess, love. I'm all right, in truth I am."

Soon the pains became almost too much to bear, and as she felt the baby move, Maudie clutched at her underclothes and pulled back her skirts. Tears cascaded down her face; tears for the pain, tears for fear she'd be found out, and tears of terror because she might end up in the workhouse once more. Again and again she took a deep breath and pushed, and at last felt the baby's head, then his shoulders, and then, in her arms, her son, who squealed, announcing his arrival.

"Oh Bess, oh Bessie, now what am I to do? Now what? I don't know what to do." Still crying, she started to clean the baby with the sleeve of her blouse.

The mare leaned towards the baby boy squirming in Maudie's arms and began to lick his head, then his arms. Maudie lay back, astonished, exhausted, and too worn out to push the giant horse away. Then the mare looked up, her ears twitching back and forth.

"You there, Maudie? Maudie? You there?"

It was the stable lad.

"I'm here . . ." She almost faltered, and without thinking, placed her hand across the baby's mouth, for fear he would cry. Then she unbuttoned her blouse and lifted him to her breast. "Just making a bit of water in the mare's stall, if you don't mind turning your back and walking out again, Harry Nutley."

Bess was standing by the door to her stall, looking out and giving young Nutley the eye that said that if he came close, she'd go for him.

"Well, we've just brewed up, and there's a cuppa here for you, if you want it."

"Much obliged, Harry. I've just got to do the brasses and the harness room floor, then I'll be going home."

"All right, Maudie."

She heard his footsteps recede into the distance, and muffled voices as he and the night watchman continued on with their talk.

Jennie had never told Maudie what to do if there was no one to help when the baby came, but she knew she had to cut the umbilical cord. She pulled a length of ribbon from her underskirt, tied the lagging cord in two places, then the new mother leaned forward and used her teeth to separate her son from her body. She breathed deeply, looked down at the baby as he continued to suckle.

"What shall we call him, eh, Bess?" she whispered. "They say my dad was an Edwin, not that I ever knew him. Died from the consumption before he even saw me. So I'll call him Edwin. Little Edwin Pettit. Got a ring to it, eh? Eddie Pettit."

And as if the mare had understood every word, she stood over mother and child and nickered.

There are those who say Maudie Pettit was seeing things that night. They said the terror of having her boy in the stables at Starlings Brewery had been too much for the girl, and she'd had the sort of vision you hear about. But Maudie stuck to her guns, and always maintained that when old Bess leaned over them, Eddie raised his little fist and pressed it against her nose, and with that one touch from a newborn baby, the horse closed her eyes and sighed; then she turned around, pawed her spot, and lay down alongside the hayrack. Maudie said it was the mare who woke her before dawn, while the stable boy was still in his loft and the grooms and drivers had yet to arrive. The girl washed her underskirts in cold water and threw the soiled hay on the pile of stable debris at the back of the brewery courtyard, covering it with more hay so no one might wonder what had taken place. And as Maudie Pettit told it, when she walked away with her son in her arms, Bess called out to her, whinnying for her

CHAPTER ONE

❖❖❖

London, April 1933

M aisie Dobbs pushed her way through the turnstile at Warren Street station, then stopped when she saw Jack Barker, the newspaper vendor, wave to her.

"Mornin', Miss Dobbs. Paper today?"

"Mr. Barker, how are you this morning? It's very close, isn't it? Summer's here before spring!"

"At least it ain't as hot as it is over there in America—people dying from the heat, apparently. Mind you, at least they can have a drink now, can't they? Now that their Prohibition's ended. Never could make that out."

"You know, you're the only newspaper seller I know who reads every single one of his papers," said Maisie. She took a coin from her purse and exchanged it for the day's *Times*. "And there's been a lot to read this year already."

"Ever since all that business about the bodyline bowling over there in Australia, it seems it's been one thing after another—and not very nice things, either. Not that I hold with bad tactics in cricket, whether it's ours or theirs, but I'm glad England kept the Ashes all the same. Mind you, not my sort of game, cricket."

"Jack, I have to confess, I still don't know what that was all about. I never could quite understand cricket."

Maisie's comment fell on deaf ears, as Jack Barker continued his litany of events that had come to pass over the past several months.

"Then there was all the noise about that Adolf Hitler, being made Chancellor in Germany. What do you reckon, Miss? Seems the bloke's got people either worried or turning cartwheels."

"I think I'm on the side of the worried, Mr. Barker. But let's just wait and see."

"You're right, Miss Dobbs. Wait and see. Might never happen, as the saying goes. And then we'll all be doin' cartwheels, eh? At least we're not like them poor souls in Japan. I know it's a long way off, the other side of the world, and can't say as I've ever met one of them in my life—don't expect I ever will—but they say it was one of the worst earthquakes ever. Hundreds killed. Can't imagine what that would be like, you know, the ground opening up under your feet."

"No, neither can I—we're lucky we live in a place where that sort of thing doesn't happen."

"Oh, I reckon it happens everywhere, Miss Dobbs. I'm old enough to know it doesn't take an earthquake for the ground to break apart and swallow you; you only have to look at all them who don't have a roof over their heads or a penny in their pocket to put some food on the table."

Maisie nodded. "Never a truer word said, Mr. Barker." She held up her newspaper by way of a wave and began to walk away. "I'll look for the good news first, I think."

Jack Barker called after her. "The good news is that they reckon this weather will keep up, right until the end of the month."

"Good," Maisie called back. "Makes a nice change."

"Might be a few thunderstorms, though," he added, laughing as he turned to another customer.

She was still smiling at the exchange when she turned into Fitzroy Square. Five men were standing at the foot of the steps leading up to the front door of the building that housed her office; one of them stepped forward as she approached.

"Miss Maisie Dobbs?"

"Yes, that's me, how can I—oh, my goodness, is that you? Mr. Riley? Jesse Riley?"

The man doffed his cap and smiled, nodding acknowledgment.

"And Archie Smith—" She looked at the men in turn. "Pete Turner, Seth Knight, Dick Samuels. What are you doing here?"

"We were waiting here for you, Miss Dobbs."

"Well, come in then. You could have waited for me inside, you know."

Maisie unlocked the door, wiped her feet on the mat, and dropped her umbrella into a tall earthenware jar left alongside the door. The weather might be fine this morning, but she always took an umbrella with her when she left the house, just in case.

"Follow me." She turned to speak again as she walked up the stairs. "Was there no one in to see you?"

"Oh yes, Miss. Very nice young lady came to the door when we rang the bell. She said we could wait for you, but we didn't want to be a nuisance. Then the gentleman came down and he said the same, but we told him we'd rather stand outside until you arrived."

Maisie could not quite believe how the morning was unfolding.

Here they were, five men she hadn't seen since girlhood, waiting for her on the doorstep, all dressed in their Sunday best, in the flamboyant way of the cockney costermonger: a bright silk scarf at the neck, a collarless shirt, a weskit of wool and silk, and best corduroy or woolen trousers, all topped off with a jacket—secondhand, of course, probably even third- or fourth-hand. And each of them was wearing their best flat cap and had polished their boots to a shine.

Maisie opened the office door and bid her two employees good morning as she removed her hat and gloves. "Oh, and Billy, could you nip next door to the solicitor's and ask if they can spare us a chair or two," she added. "We'll need them for an hour at least, I would imagine." She turned to Sandra, who had stood up to usher the men into the room, which at once seemed so much smaller. "Oh, good, you've brought out the tea things."

"We told the gentlemen they could wait in here, Miss Dobbs."

"I know. It's all right." She turned to her visitors. "I seem to remember this lot can be particularly proud, can't you, Jesse?"

The man laughed. "Well. Miss D—"

Maisie cut him off. "I was Maisie to you when I was a girl, and I'm Maisie now. There'll be no standing on ceremony. Ah, here we are, more chairs. Thank you, Billy." Maisie smiled at her assistant as he returned with several chairs stacked one on top of the other. "Come on, all of you, take a chair, sit yourselves down and tell me what this is all about—I can't ever remember having a delegation of costers greet me, and at this time in the morning."

Sandra had taken the tray with china and a teapot to the kitchenette along the corridor, and in the meantime, with the men seated around her, Maisie perched on the corner of her desk. She introduced each of the visitors to Billy and waited for Jesse to speak. He was about the same age as her father, but, unlike Frankie Dobbs, he still worked his patch of London streets, selling vegetables and fruit from a horse-drawn cart. She knew the reason for the visit must be of some import, for these men would have lost valuable income in giving up a few hours' worth of work to see her.

"We've come about Eddie. Remember Eddie Pettit?"

Maisie nodded. "Of course I remember Eddie. I haven't seen him or Maudie for a few years, since I lived in Lambeth." She paused. "What's wrong, Jesse? What about Eddie?"

"He's dead, Miss—I mean, Maisie. He's gone."

Maisie felt the color drain from her face. "How? Was he ill?"

The men looked at each other, and Jesse was about to answer her question when he shook his head and pressed a handkerchief to his eyes. Archie Smith spoke up in his place.

"He weren't ill. He was killed at the paper factory, Bookhams." Smith folded his flat cap in half and ran his fingers along the fold. When he looked up, he could barely continue. "It weren't no accident, either, Maisie. We reckon it was deliberate. Someone wanted to get rid of him. No two ways about it." He looked at the other men, all of whom nodded their accord.

Maisie rubbed her arms and looked at her feet, which at once felt cold.

"But Eddie was so gentle. He was a little slow, we all knew that, but he was a dear soul—who on earth would want to see him gone?" She paused. "Is his mother still alive? I remember the influenza just after the war had left her weak in the chest."

"Maudie's heart is broken, Maisie. We've all been round to see her—everyone has. Jennie's looking after her, but Wilf passed on a few years ago now. The grooms down at the bottling factory, the drivers at the brewery, everyone who looked after a horse in any of the boroughs knew Eddie, and they've all put something in the collection to make sure we give him a good send-off."

"Has he been laid to rest yet?"

"This Friday. St. Marks."

Maisie nodded. "Tell me what happened—Seth, you start."

Seth Knight and Dick Samuels were the younger men of the group; Maisie guessed they were now in their late forties. She couldn't remember seeing them since they were young apprentices, and now they were men wearing the years on faces that were lined and gray, and with hands thick and calloused from toil.

Knight cleared his throat. "As you know, Eddie made a wage from the work he did with horses. There wasn't a hot or upset horse in the whole of London he couldn't settle, and that's no word of a lie. And he earned well at times, did Eddie. Reckon this was after you left the Smoke, just before the war, but talk about Eddie's gift had gone round all the factories and the breweries, and last year—honest truth, mind—he was called to the palace mews, to sort out one of His Majesty's Cleveland Bays." He looked at Jesse, who nodded for him to continue. "But horses don't have a funny turn every day of the week, so Eddie always made a bit extra by running errands at the paper factory. He'd go in during the morning, and the blokes would give him a few coppers to buy their ciggies, or a paper, or a bite of something to eat, and he'd write everything down and—"

"Wait a minute." Maisie interrupted Knight. "When did Eddie learn to write?"

"He'd been learning again for a while, Maisie. There was this woman who used to be a teacher at the school, she helped him. He'd found out where she was living—across the water—and he'd gone to her a while ago to ask if she could give him lessons. I'm blessed if I can remember her name. Apparently, he'd been doing quite well with a new customer, and it'd finally got into his noddle that if he learned to read and write he might be better off in the long run. He'd started to pay attention to money. I'd say it was all down to Maudie, pushing him a bit. In the past all he did was hand over the money to her, and she gave him pocket money to spend on himself, for his necessaries. She put the rest away for him—she always worried that he wouldn't be able to look after himself when she was gone, you see."

Maisie nodded. "I remember her being so attentive to him, always. I was in a shop once—I think it was Westons, the hardware store; I must have been sent on an errand by my mother. I was behind Eddie and his mum, and she made him ask for what they wanted, even though he didn't want to. She went stone silent until he'd asked for whatever it was, and then counted out the correct money. No one tried to hurry him along, because people knew Maud was teaching him to stand on his own two feet."

Seth Knight went on. "Well, Eddie seemed to have a little bit more about him lately, as if he'd been keeping us in the dark all along. He started asking questions about how to save his money so it was safe—of course, it was hard for him to understand, and he'd come and ask the same questions again, but all the same, he was trying. Anyway, it turns out this teacher—Miss Carpenter, that was her name—had always had a soft spot for him at school. When he turned up, that is. Trouble with Eddie, as you know, he'd always been happier around horses, so even as a young boy, when he got a message to go and sort out a horse, Maudie never stopped him. And to be honest, they needed the money, being as it was only the two of them; Wilf and Jennie were there to help out, but Maudie always said they needed everything they had to take care of themselves, especially with Wilf coming home gassed after the war. He might as well have died at Plugstreet Wood, the way the pain took it out of him, after he came home—and he was older than most of them; he wasn't a young man when he went over there." Seth took a deep breath and looked down at his hands, the palm of one rubbing across the knuckles of the other. "Anyway, going back to Eddie, he'd started to write down the odd note when the blokes at the factory gave him their instructions, and I for one think he could understand more than anyone gave him credit for. In any case, he always came back with what they'd asked him to get for them, and he never made a mistake."

There was silence for a few moments, and Maisie knew that everyone was likely thinking the same thing, that Eddie wasn't really gone, that he was as alive as the stories about him.

"Go on, Seth."

"I don't know if you've ever been in Bookhams, but them rolls of paper are massive. They come out on a belt as wide as this room, and then they go straight onto the lorries—Bookhams are going over to lorries now." He sighed and rubbed his forehead. "But they've still got a few old horses there, stabled out the back, for when the lorries pack up and won't go—which is more often than the horses went lame, and that's a fact."

Maisie could see beads of perspiration forming on the man's forehead, and the other men changed position or folded their arms. "Take your time, Seth," she said.

Seth Knight pulled a handkerchief from his trouser pocket, and rubbed it across his brow. "No one can say what happened, and no one can say the how or why of it, but Eddie was walking out of the factory floor to take a few lumps of sugar to the horses, them as are left, and the next thing you know, one of them big rolls had slid sideways off the belt and come crashing down. It was all over like that." He snapped his fingers. "Poor Eddie didn't stand a chance. Not a chance. He was crushed, Maisie. Crushed to death."

"Oh dear Lord, what a terrible way to go."

"That's not all of it—soon as it happened, the horses at the back, still in their stables, they all started going on. They knew, you see. They knew he'd gone. It was as if he was one of them. Always was like that, with him and horses."

A choked cry caused Maisie to look back towards the door. Sandra had entered the room while Seth was speaking of Eddie's death. She was standing by the door, holding the tray with shaking hands as tears ran down her face. Only months before, the young woman had lost her husband in equally tragic circumstances. Maisie nodded to Billy, who gently took the tray from Sandra and began handing out cups of tea to the men. Maisie stood up to comfort the young woman, whispering that if she wanted she could leave the office to sit in the square for a while.

Jesse Riley drank back his tea, as if it were cold water quenching his thirst. He replaced the cup on the saucer and reached down to set it on the hearth. "So, we came to see you about Eddie, thinking you'd know what to do, Maisie. Your dad comes up here from the country every now and again and he tells us, you know, he tells us how proud he is of you, and that you've brought murderers to justice." He leaned forward. "You see, Maisie, no one cares about Eddie 'cept us, and his mum and Jennie. The police didn't give a tinker's cuss about it, said it was a 'regrettable accident.' Accident, my eye. It was a deliberate act of murder, that's what it was."

"But why? Who would want to see Eddie dead?"

"That's just it," said Dick Samuels. "We don't know. But we thought you might be able to find out." He looked across to Pete Turner. "Pete's got our kitty, he can tell you about it."

Turner leaned forward to speak to Maisie. "We've had another whip-round, us and a few more costers at the market." He pulled out a drawstring bag. "We don't want you to work for nothing—you've come up the hard way and earned every penny, so we don't want favors—but we want you to find out about Eddie. We want you to find out who killed him."

Maisie was aware that all eyes focused on her. Not only the men were waiting for her to answer, but Billy and Sandra.

"Of course I will, but—" Maisie was interrupted by a collective sigh of relief. She regarded each and every person present, then came back to Pete Turner. "But I don't want your money. Eddie was dear to all of us, so it's up to us to do right by him and find out the truth of what happened to cause his death. If it was an accident, well, I'll discover why it happened, and make sure it will never come to pass again. And if he was murdered, I'll find out who wanted him dead."

At first the men smiled and nodded to one another. Then Jesse Riley spoke up.

"Maisie, I'm an old coster and it's not often I miss a trick. My mum, bless her, said that if you can't pay anything else in life, you can pay attention, and I just noticed that you said you'd find out who wanted him dead, not that you'd find whoever it was killed Eddie."

Maisie stood up. "I just can't imagine someone who knew Eddie, someone who saw him every day, wanting to do anything that might hurt him, which means that if his death was the result of a deliberate act, the person who wanted him dead might not have known him as we do. He had no means to protect himself, even as a boy. He was trusting, gentle and innocent. If he was killed intentionally, someone had a reason—and I can't imagine what that reason could be. But that's all speculation. In any case, my assistant, Mr. Beale—" The men turned to look at Billy; Maisie continued. "Mr. Beale will begin by asking each of you a good many questions, so we can get to the bottom of what you know and who you think we should be talking to. And in the meantime, here's what I want you to do—I want you to rack your brains, think of anything unusual about Eddie in the weeks and months leading up to his death. Did he have any new work anywhere? Who was he dealing with? Did he upset anyone? Was he acting, well, not like Eddie at any time? I want you to think-think-think, and tell us if you remember anything you haven't already told us about—even the smallest detail could be of use."

"Do you want us to stay here and talk to Mr. Beale today, Maisie? Until it's done?"

"Mr. Beale will want to speak to each of you for about an hour, so no, you'd all be wasting your time waiting here. Mrs. Tapley will draw up a list with a time for each of you. Come back here for your appointment with Mr. Beale—oh, and I think it's best that you don't say too much to the others down at the market; if they ask, just let them know that we're looking into it. No more than that. Best to keep as much as we can between ourselves."

Jesse Riley stood up. "But we thought you'd be working on the case yourself, Miss."

Maisie nodded. "I will be, Jesse. But Billy and Sandra know what they're doing—we've worked together on many cases, and I trust them implicitly. And while you're doing your part and they're doing theirs, I'll be on my way to see Maud Pettit about Eddie. I'm leaving now—I remember where she lives. And after that, I'll be visiting Bookhams." Maisie picked up her coat, hat, gloves, and shoulder bag. She decided to leave her briefcase, as it might seem intimidating—official people carried briefcases, people who might want to take something from you, and she didn't want to frighten Eddie's mother. "Now then, I suggest we all meet here again, perhaps tomorrow—Sandra, how about late afternoon, when the gentlemen have finished their rounds? Would you put it in the diary?"

Bidding the men good-bye, she motioned to Billy to come to the front door with her.

"You know what questions to ask them, don't you, Billy?"

"Yes, Miss. And thank you, Miss, for putting this in my hands."

"You've been with me for enough interviews to open an inquiry; you know what to do, of that I am sure. In any case, we'll go through the notes together before they come back tomorrow—we've got the rest of today to get started on this."

"What do you think, Miss? Do you reckon they're onto something. I mean, that Jesse Riley's getting on a bit, and he looks like the one who got everyone else started."

"The important thing is that *they* believe Eddie died in suspicious circumstances. They believed enough to cut into their day to see me, to turn up here in their best clothes and to risk my telling them the case wasn't solid. The fact that they took the chance, and then had the whip-round to get the funds to start an investigation—that's more than enough for me, Billy. More than enough." She pulled her umbrella from the earthenware jar, and as she opened the door she turned to her assistant. "I knew Eddie. I remember him well. He was a lovely man—always more of a boy because he never quite grew up. Which is why everyone looked out for him, especially those who'd known him from the time he was a small lad. And he had a gift, Billy, a real gift. If I hadn't seen it with my own eyes, I might not have believed it." She sighed. "If those men have doubt, then I believe it's well founded. One way or another, we'll get some answers for them. Now then, I'd better be off."

"And you turned down their money, Miss. I bet you anything they won't take your charity, they're not that sort."

"Oh, no two ways about it. They're proud—they'll try to make me take the money, and perhaps eventually I'll have to come to some sort of compromise. As far as I'm concerned, they've entrusted us to find out the truth about Eddie. I'll worry about the money later. You see, when my mother was ill, it was my father's mates down the market—and their families—who tried to help us. So I'm determined not to let them down. Now, you'd better get back up there before those boys get rowdy."

Maisie set off towards Oxford Street. From there she could use the underground railway to go across to Lambeth, but not before she'd stopped at the caff for a cup of tea. She had left the office because she wanted the men to know she had taken up the case with no delay, but in truth she wanted time to think. She wanted to remember Eddie, and to cradle his memory in her heart.

Her first recollection of Eddie was when she was just a small girl, about six years old. She was standing with her father, watching Jesse try to calm his horse, a big gray gelding with an abscessed hoof. The animal was stabled under the dry arches of Waterloo Bridge, and it seemed the limited light and a few days standing idle had conspired to upset the horse, who had nipped and kicked out at anyone who dared to come close.

"I've got to doctor 'im; if that abscess gets any worse, he'll be no good to me, and it'll be the slaughterhouse next."

Frankie nodded. "I'd send for Eddie Pettit, if I were you, Jesse. He'll sort him out."

"I've already sent my boy round to Maudie. She'll bring him, you can depend on that." He rubbed his forefinger and thumb together.

"He's worth every penny, Jess, if you don't want to lose that horse."

Maisie looked up, from one man to the other, and turned around when she heard footsteps clattering against the cobblestones.

"Here he is." Jesse touched his cap, and walked forward to greet the woman and her son.

The boy was sixteen at the time, or thereabouts, and was tall for his age. It seemed his mother hadn't managed to find castoffs big enough for him, clothed as he was in trousers that provided a goodly margin between hem and ankle, and a jacket that revealed his wide but boney wrists and long fingers. His eyes were large, and when she looked into them, Maisie thought it was like looking at the eyes of a cow or a horse. He had clear skin and red-red lips, as if he'd been feasting on berries. His hair was unruly, and he continually brushed it back with his fingers, holding his head to one side as he listened to the men. Maisie remembered his mother pressing a handkerchief into his hand, and telling him to blow his nose. "Always got a runny nose, that one." Then she smiled up at her boy, and it was clear she loved her son as no other ever would.

Jesse began to speak, but it was as if the boy hadn't heard a word, for he walked forward and took the latch off the stable door.

"Be careful, lad, he's—"

Maudie touched Jesse on the arm. "Don't you worry, Eddie knows what he's doing."

The boy stepped into the stable with calm confidence.

Sitting in the caff, staring out of the window, Maisie could see Eddie now in her mind's eye, and she could feel exactly the curiosity she experienced that day, watching the boy as he opened the door, how he seemed to change when he entered the stall. They could not see what Eddie was doing but could hear his soft voice, talking to the horse as if they were in a deep conversation. He did not shout, nor did he make a plea; he simply talked to a friend. Within two minutes, he had slipped a halter on the horse and was leading him from the stable, the horse with his head low, trusting.

"Got hot water for me to do his foot, Mr. Riley?"

"I don't believe it. Truly I don't." Riley pulled a kettle off the brazier he'd set up on the cobblestones, and poured the water into a bucket.

"Him just don't like the dark. None of 'em do, but most of the time they're too tired to say anything about it. Him's had a chance to think about it, what with his foot. And he don't want to be here anymore."

"Well, he's got to be for now. Or he'll end up on a dinner plate. Can't have a horse who doesn't work for his keep." Riley walked towards the horse, but Eddie stopped him.

"I'll do that, Mr. Riley. Best I doctor him today."

Maisie watched as Eddie cared for the horse, who seemed as soft as a kitten with Eddie there. He soaked the hoof, then dried it and applied a bread poultice, wrapping the hoof to secure the paste before leading the horse back to the stable. He remained in the stable for another five minutes, perhaps more, talking to the horse with a soft voice. Then he emerged, turning to put the latch on the door. And as he joined the men, his mother, and Maisie, the confidence seemed to ebb from him; he had nothing to say to those gathered. Jesse handed Maudie a few coins, and she nodded, and while the men began to clean up around the stables, Maisie watched mother and son walk away along the cobblestones: the small, rosy-faced woman and the tall boy, walking along in a loping gait, his arms held out at his sides, his head lowered to listen to his mother as she spoke to him. Maisie remembered thinking that he reminded her of a storybook character, a gentle giant.

Maisie set down her cup and looked up at the clock on the wall. It was almost eleven o'clock. She wouldn't be back at the office until mid-afternoon at the earliest, by which time Sandra would have left to go to her other job. She wanted to catch Sandra before she left the office, so she left the caff to walk down towards Soho Square, where there was a telephone kiosk.

"Good morning—"

"It's me, Sandra—only don't say anything. Are the men still there?"

"Just one, then another couple are coming back later."

"Sandra, I'd like you to do something for me—when Billy's finished with the interview, tell him you have to leave on an errand. Here's what I want you to do—go down to Fleet Street, to both the *Express* and the *Times*, and look up anything you can find on an accident at Bookhams Printers. Billy will be able to give you the exact date. If you've got time, you can leave your notes at the office for me to read when I get back."

"Right you are."

"Good girl. Do you have a lecture this evening?" Sandra was enrolled in classes at the Morley College for Working Men and Women.

"Yes, so I won't be home until about ten."

"And I won't be there this evening, Sandra; you'll have the flat to yourself. See you tomorrow."

Standing in front of the small soot-blackened terraced house on Weathershaw Street, where Maudie lived with her son and Jennie, brought back memories of Maisie's own childhood. She had lived in such a house in Lambeth. Her mother and father had started off with one room, then managed to rent another, and then the kitchen and downstairs parlor of the "two up, two down" house. The same had been true of Maudie and her lifelong friend, Jennie. Time had moved on and they now had the downstairs rooms as well as the bedrooms above.

"Hello, Mrs. Pettit." Maisie remembered that the woman had always been referred to as "Mrs. Pettit" out of respect for her son, even though she had never married. "I don't know if you remember me, but—"

"O' course I remember you; you're Frankie Dobbs' girl. Went across the water to work and ended up doing well for yourself—but didn't you come back here to live in Lambeth a few years ago?"

"Yes, Mrs. Pettit. I lodged at the boarding house on Solomon Street for a while." Maisie leaned forward. "I've come about Eddie, Mrs. Pettit. May I come in?"

The small woman looked at her for a moment, and pulled a shawl around her shoulders. "Well, what with this heat and that reek coming off the water, you'll catch something dreadful if you stand out here, make no mistake. Come in, girl, and sit in the scullery. Jennie's made up the fire and the kettle's on."

Maisie followed the woman along a narrow passageway to the back of the house. Jennie Robinson was taller than Maud, and was strong about the shoulders, though lean, whereas the dead man's mother seemed not only small but diminished. Now they were indoors, Maisie could see Maud had become frail, and it was hard to believe that she was sixty-two—she appeared to be closer to eighty. She took her seat alongside the black cast-iron stove as if she were cold into her bones and could not get enough warmth.

"Jennie, remember Frankie Dobbs' girl? Went into service across the water, after her mother died, God rest her soul."

"Of course I remember," said Jennie. "They always said you'd do well, what with you having a bit more up there than most." She pointed to her head.

"Any success I have is probably down to the the fact that my mother and father taught me the value of a good day's work." Maisie paused, her heart breaking for the women before her, who seemed gray and dark with grief. But she had a job to do. "Mrs. Pettit, I think I should come straight to the point."

"Sit down first, love. It'll be easier on all of us, especially if it's about my Eddie."

Maisie took a seat at the heavy kitchen table, bowed with age and pale with years of scrubbing. Jennie set a cup of tea in front of her. The women sipped from their own chipped cups, then looked up at her, waiting.

"I'll not beat about the bush. You probably don't know this about me, but I am what they call an investigator, a private inquiry agent to some, and—"

"Weren't you a nurse, in the war?"

"Yes, I was. And afterwards. Then I, well—it's a long story, but I had this opportunity, and—"

"And someone—I bet it's that Jesse Riley—thought you'd be able to find out what happened to Eddie."

Maisie sighed. "That's about the measure of it, Mrs. Pettit."

The woman took out her handkerchief, covered her eyes, and crumpled forward, resting her forehead against her hands.

"Perhaps I'd better go. I can come back another time."

"Sit there, Maisie. Just let me have my moment."

The woman soon sat back, whereupon her friend placed an arm around her shoulder.

"She's had it rough, Maisie," said Jennie. "Eddie was her life."

"I know. Truly I know. He was a lovely man, so gentle," said Maisie.

"And he had a gift. I was blessed with that boy." Maud cleared her throat. "Now then, here's what I've got to say. There's talk that my Eddie was . . . was murdered. There's them what reckon someone had it in for him, and so the next thing you know, there's an accident, only it's not really an accident. I don't know what to think, but here's what I do know—and I used to work down at Bookhams, on the rag vats, until not that long ago before the rheumatism got to me—I never heard of an accident caused by them big belts going or tipping. There was accidents, of course there was; there's always someone who don't pay attention, getting their fingers in the way of the guillotine, that sort of thing. But no one was ever crushed under a roll of paper." She paused again, looking directly into Maisie's eyes. "So if you want to look for the reason why it happened, more power to you. Every single day that's passed without Eddie, I've felt like topping myself so I could be with him up there in heaven, but I'd stay right here to see someone brought to justice."

Maisie nodded. "Then can you answer some questions for me, Mrs. Pettit?"

"*Maudie*. You're a grown woman now, Maisie Dobbs, so you can call me Maudie."

Maisie took a clutch of index cards from her bag, and a pencil. "Right, let's start with Bookhams."

"Then you'll have to start with me, Maisie, because I worked there on the afternoon shift before I had Eddie. About nine months before I had Eddie. Three different jobs I had, in those days."

By the time she left Maud Pettit's house in Lambeth, Maisie had learned several things she hadn't known before.

She knew that Maudie had been assaulted while walking from the factory to the brewery; it was dark, so she had never known her attacker—the father of her child.

She discovered that Eddie had only ever been bullied by one person, a boy who made fun of him at school. In fact, Jimmy Merton had made Eddie's life a misery, mimicking his voice, his walk, his simple way of being. She had a recollection of Merton from childhood. Her mother had warned her to keep away from the Merton children because they were all trouble, every single one of them. Jimmy was older, Eddie's age, but she still passed to the other side of the street if she saw him in the distance. Apparently, Jimmy Merton had lately come to work at Bookhams.

But of the notes she had penned while sitting with Maudie Pettit, the one that she would come back to, would underline again and again, even after adding it to the case map that she knew Billy would start as soon as his interviews ended, was the note that repeated Maud's words: "I can't put my finger on it, but my Eddie seemed to have changed lately—in the past month, perhaps more." Eddie's mother had gone on to speculate that Jimmy Merton might have started bullying him again, and she wondered if Eddie was hiding some physical ailment, perhaps a pain or discomfort he didn't want to talk about. Or if he had lost a horse. "Took it hard when a horse went, did my Eddie," Maud Pettit had told Maisie. And Maisie had nodded. Yes, gentle Eddie would have taken it hard.

CHAPTER TWO

✦

The afternoon sun was casting shafts of light through the trees on Fitzroy Square by the time Maisie and Billy took their seats at the big table alongside the window. Billy had already pinned out a length of plain white wallpaper upon which they would transcribe their notes using pencils and thick wax crayons of different colors.

"Sandra came back from Fleet Street—she left this for you." Billy handed Maisie a sealed envelope.

"Oh, good. She seems to be getting on very well, don't you think?"

Maisie had been concerned that Billy might not take to having another employee at the office, but the two seemed to have settled into working together.

"I think so, Miss. She's still looking gray around the edges, though. I reckon a young woman like her shouldn't be expected to wear her widow's weeds for a year—all that black can't be doing much to cheer her up."

"I think you're right, Billy. I'll see if I can talk to her about it. In fact, the best person to have a word with her would be Mrs. Partridge—she always speaks so highly of Sandra, and says that since she's been working part-time for her husband, she has really organized his papers beyond belief," said Maisie. "I'm so glad I found out that Mr. Partridge was looking for clerical help and was able to recommend Sandra for the position—we don't have enough work to keep her occupied full-time here, so it was a stroke of luck all around. Mrs. Partridge is so thrilled because Douglas is extremely happy with Sandra's work—which gives him more time with the family—so it wouldn't be a surprise if she endowed Sandra her entire collection from last year."

"Bit of a woman for the latest fashions, isn't she?"

"Oh, no doubt about it. Paris would go out of business without Priscilla." Maisie looked at the notes, each circled with a thick colored crayon of contrasting color. "Let's see what we've got in the way of rough edges to start nibbling at here. Thinking back to your interviews, did anything stand out? Was something said at any point that made you look up and want to dig deeper?"

Without glancing at his notepad, Billy nodded. "I've still got a couple to do in the morning, and Mr. Riley said there were a few other blokes at the market who might have a word or two to add, so I'll go down there tomorrow before the gentlemen come back here in the afternoon." He paused, tapping a crayon on the wallpaper, leaving a series of dots at the edge of the sheet. "These men didn't see Eddie regularly, not daily, as a rule, though they said they usually crossed paths with him a couple of times a week—what with all them horses down the market, it wasn't unusual for the word to go out to get Eddie over there. Mind you, this is what gave me a bit of a chill—each and every one of them said that Eddie hadn't been himself for a while. Not all of the time—he wasn't going round with a face as long as a week every day—but they said that you'd watch him walk down the road, and it'd be as if he had something on his mind. And what Mr. Riley said made sense, though at first it don't sound very kind of him, but he said, 'It was a bit queer seeing him looking like that, as if he had worries, because Eddie wasn't normally like that—he didn't have enough up there to hold thoughts for long enough.' "

"Oh dear, that does sound a bit harsh, but Jesse wouldn't have meant it badly. He thought the world of Eddie."

"He said that, Miss, and you can tell they all looked out for Eddie. Mr. Riley told me that Eddie's thoughts weren't in his head, like with most people." Billy put his hand on his chest. "He said that this is where Eddie held his thoughts, and when he saw him looking, you know, sad, he was worried that his thoughts had started weighing upon his heart, and his heart was the best of him."

"Mrs. Pettit said the same thing, that Eddie had not been himself. She wondered if he'd been feeling poorly and didn't want to tell her— he might've been worried about the money it would cost to see the doctor."

"He could've gone to Dr. Blanche's clinic."

"Of course he could, but even though there's a sign outside the clinic informing people that services are without charge, they're still often worried in case they'll be asked for money they don't have. Fear of illness putting them in the workhouse stops many a sick person from seeking help, especially someone like Eddie, who knew very well that his mother was born in the workhouse and was lucky to get out. Billy, did anyone give any idea what might have been bothering Eddie?"

"No. They knew he'd been doing a lot of work for some quite well-to-do people recently—that little stint at the Palace Mews helped word get around about him, and apparently he'd been traveling a bit farther afield to sort out difficult horses."

"Again, his mother indicated as much, and she said that at first she was worried about him traveling on the bus or the underground, but she said he'd memorized the stations across the whole railway and probably knew every single bus on the route as well as the conductors. And of course, there's that new map of the underground railway; it's made it easier to know where you're going, even though the lines on the map look nothing like what's really down there. Eddie had a good memory for the little details—I remember that about him, despite what anyone said about there not being much in his head. He just had a different way of thinking and seeing the world, I think." She made a note on the case map. "The interesting thing is that his mother doesn't know the names of some of these people he worked for."

"I suppose he wasn't the sort to keep a record of who he was seeing and when."

"That's something else, apparently he had started a little book with his customers' names, but it wasn't there when they gave Mrs. Pettit the sack of personal effects at the mortuary."

"Could it have dropped out?"

"Or it might have been taken." Maisie looked at Billy. "Look, here are the notes I made after I visited Eddie's mother. I've circled the items that need to go on the map, so if you can do that, I just want a minute to look over what Sandra's left for me."

Maisie sat at her own desk and began to read through observations written in Sandra's neat, precise handwriting. For speed she had used pencil, but Maisie noticed that in her work at the office she generally used a marbled fountain pen, a gift from her late husband's parents when they learned she planned to attend night classes. Sandra had indented each new note with a tiny star, and she had underlined any point she believed to be of particular interest. One of those points in turn piqued Maisie's interest: No union membership had been allowed at Bookhams since the company was bought by John Otterburn. Otterburn was the owner of daily and weekly newspapers throughout Britain, in particular the *London Daily Messenger*, a newspaper that had garnered a wide readership in the past three decades. The newspaper owner's opposition to union membership was well known, along with his belief that Bolshevism would "buckle commerce and lead to the downfall of the British Empire." Despite powerful unions in the print and allied trades, Otterburn had kept organization of workers out of Bookhams—and men who needed work didn't argue.

From Sandra's meticulous notations, she learned that Otterburn had visited Bookhams himself following the accident, promising a full inquiry and an investigation into safety procedures at all Otterburn factories and offices.

In one newspaper report, it was said that Eddie's presence was "tolerated" by staff, who felt sympathy for his condition; a manager was quoted as saying, "Luckily for him, on account of his impaired mind, he wouldn't have felt anything when that roll hit him."

"What a callous thing to say!" Maisie thumped the desk as she put down the notes, pushed back her chair and proceeded across the room to the case map. "It says in a column in the *Express* that a manager at Bookhams reckoned Eddie wouldn't have felt a thing because of his 'impaired mind.'"

"That's nasty, Miss."

"I wish I knew his name, and that's a fact."

"Anything else?"

"Bookhams is owned by John Otterburn."

"The bloke who owns all the papers? Millionaire, ain't he?"

"Yes, he's a very rich man. I believe his family were from Canada, and seeing as there's a considerable timber industry there, it should come as no surprise that the Otterburns made a lot of money in the paper business. In any case, I know where I can get more information about him."

"Viscount Compton?"

Maisie nodded. "I'll ask him tonight."

Billy gathered the pencils he was using and looked down, his cheeks showing a blush of pink. While he was aware his employer was "walking out" with James Compton—who was not only heir to Lord Julian Compton but had also assumed complete responsibility for the family's interests in timber and construction in both the British Isles and Canada—even the smallest hint regarding the depth of their relationship caused Billy embarrassment. He preferred not to know about his employer's personal life.

"Of course, Miss. He would have some important information for us, I daresay," added Billy.

Maisie tapped a pencil against the table. "And I want to know what happened to Eddie's notebook. I'll talk to Mrs. Pettit again tomorrow, and let's ask the men if they know who was first to reach Eddie's body after the accident. At some point that notebook—if he had it with him—left his person. I want to know who has it now."

"Right you are, Miss."

"According to the early reports, the conveyor was working properly, so why did the roll of paper fall? What caused the 'inexplicable' accident?"

"What shall I do next, Miss?"

"Let's finish this job first, see where we are and if anything leaps out at us. Then here's what I want you to do—but wait until after my visit to Bookhams. I want you to have a word with some of the employees, ask around as if you're looking for work, that sort of thing. Find out about the union situation. I daresay there's a local pub where a number of the men go after work."

"Oh, I get your train of thought—an accident would give union organizers a bit of weight, even if Eddie wasn't strictly a worker."

"It crossed my mind. It is unusual for a paper factory not to have a union presence. I'm not sure about the level of bearing it has on the case, but it certainly paints a picture of the owner as being a man who wants nothing to do with collective bargaining of any sort—he wants to retain control at all times. In any case, I also want you to find out a bit more about a fellow named Jimmy Merton—apparently he was about the same age as Eddie and made his life rather difficult when they were children. According to Maud Pettit, he came to work at Bookhams recently, and might have taken up where he left off with Eddie."

"If there's one thing I can't stand, it's a bully."

"Me neither. In any case, as I said, I'm going back to see Mrs. Pettit tomorrow morning. I didn't want to push things too far today, but I want to see if I can inspire her to remember who Eddie was working for on a regular basis. And I want to find the teacher who was helping him. All Maudie knew was that she lived across the water—that could be anywhere north of the river."

"Right then, Miss. I'd better get cracking."

Maisie smiled at Billy. He had seemed on edge at the beginning of the year, but seemed calmer the past month or so.

"Baby sleeping through the night yet?"

"At last, Miss. And I think we're all grateful to her for that. Bobby asked me the other day, 'When's our little Meg going to stop screaming in the night, Dad?' I had to laugh." He looked at Maisie. "And I know I don't say it much, Miss, but it makes all the difference being in that house. The boys don't have them chesty coughs all the time now, and I swear Doreen is looking more like her old self. We go back to Shoreditch every few weeks, regular, to see our Lizzie's grave. We smarten it up a bit, leave some flowers. We tell her we haven't forgotten her, that we still love her. And we tell her all about Meg, and how much she looks like her big sister."

"As long as Doreen doesn't overdo it, she'll be fine. I take it she's still seeing Dr. Masters."

Billy nodded. "Once every three months now, as from the beginning of the year. My mum helps a lot, so we make sure there's not too much on her shoulders. But she's doing very well with her dressmaking, you know—got it all set up in that big front room. We don't go in there as a rule—not used to having that much space, to tell you the truth, so we mainly stay in the dining room or the kitchen, and the front room is kept for best and for Doreen. Funny that, saying the words 'dining room' and knowing we've got one."

Maisie smiled. "I'm glad it's all falling into place."

"I tell you, all this news makes us think twice about going to Canada when we've got the money put by. I mean, they've had a big railway strike over there, and all the same goings on we've got here. But you never know."

Maisie nodded. "Just see what happens in time, Billy."

"That's all you can do, ain't it, Miss?"

James Compton was now living at the Compton family's London home, a grand Ebury Place mansion house that had recently undergone considerable refurbishment. The house had been mothballed for some time, and it was Lady Rowan who decided that James had been living at his club for long enough; a man in his position should have a London residence. It was also the house to which Maisie had come to work in service when she was just thirteen years old.

That Maisie and James had love for each other was without question. Whether that love would lead to marriage was the subject of much conjecture in both the Compton household and among Maisie's friends, Priscilla and Douglas Partridge. Maisie's father was happy to stand well back and remain noncommittal on the subject. Frankie Dobbs had always wanted to see her "settled," but kept his counsel. For the moment, Maisie was happy to continue with the relationship as it was, though it was becoming more apparent to those who knew the couple that James was less than content with the status quo.

Now Maisie sat in her motor car, an MG two-seater tourer, which she had parked in the mews behind the mansion. She did not get out of the vehicle because it still took every ounce of her courage to enter the house. In the months of their courtship leading up to completion of the mansion's refurbishment, James had been a frequent visitor to Maisie's flat in Pimlico. She had taken out a mortgage to purchase the property a couple of years earlier, but was able to settle the loan following the death of her longtime mentor, Dr. Maurice Blanche. Apart from a few smaller bequests, Maurice had left Maisie his entire estate, honoring his esteem and, indeed, his love for her; he had come to regard her as a daughter. Paying off the mortgage had been one of the very few expenditures she made on her own behalf.

She liked the arrangement as it stood with James; it suited her. But since he had taken up residence at 15 Ebury Place, Maisie was not quite so comfortable. It wasn't that she didn't know the house—indeed, at the request of Lady Rowan Compton, she had once returned to the mansion to live in rooms there for over a year before purchasing her flat. No, this was different, and while she sat in the MG as the damp evening air replaced the day's warmth, seeping into the motor car to cling to her clothing, she realized she knew exactly why those feelings of discomfort had assailed her.

Though she had the advantage of a good education and had

worked hard to earn a respected name in her profession, she came from poverty. She had been a maid in this very house. It was Lady Rowan who, in 1912, had discovered the young domestic servant reading in the library in the early hours of the morning. Recognizing the girl's intellect, Rowan had turned to her friend, the esteemed psychologist and forensic scientist Maurice Blanche, for advice. So began the relationship—and the opportunities—that formed the woman Maisie would become. Maurice directed Maisie's education, the intensity of her studies leading to her winning a place at Girton College in Cambridge. She suspended her education to enlist for nursing service in the war, returning later to complete her studies, and then to work with Maurice as his assistant.

Since inheriting Maurice's fortune, it seemed to many of those who knew Maisie that she had taken on the mantle of wealth with confidence; however, it was likely only her father and, perhaps, Priscilla, who suspected that Maisie was now experiencing something of a struggle. She had purchased a few items of furniture for her previously spartan flat in Pimlico, and there had been some painting done on The Dower House—the home Maurice had purchased years before on the Chelstone Estate in Kent—but otherwise she had spent no money unless it was on others. There had been the investment in a semidetached house in Eltham, which she now rented to Billy at a peppercorn rate—she would have loved to give him the house as a gift, but she knew much embarrassment would have been caused to the very proud man. She had helped Sandra where she could, assisting her with the cost of classes she attended in the evenings, and she had already planned to pay for her to attend Birkbeck College—her explanation being that it was in her interests to promote the education of her staff. She felt that in this one act she was repaying a debt. Lady Rowan and Maurice Blanche had paid for her first two terms at Girton, before she gave up her studies to serve as a nurse in France—though when she returned to complete her tertiary education, she had won a scholarship.

Now she was parked outside the house in which she had once been a maid, where she had first entered via the side door that led into the belowstairs scullery. And now she was walking out with the master of the house who, she knew, had come to expect her to be his consort when guests arrived for supper or when a party was held. It was as if, in her flat, she could imagine her life had not changed. She could cook supper. They would sit by the fire and talk. And in truth, if she admitted it to herself, she could control how much . . . what? She rubbed her hands across her face, tired. Yes, she could control how she felt. She could pretend that Maurice's generosity had not made everything different. There was part of her that wanted to retain the need to exercise thrift, to consider every purchase with care. It was the part of her that did not want to let go of her beginnings as she became more established. The bequest had changed all that. She was a woman of property, of wealth, and the days of want had slipped away into the past. Maurice had trusted her to accept the legacy with integrity. She knew others considered her conduct exemplary—there had been no mad spending sprees, after all—but inside there remained an element of fear. She was afraid she might lose touch with her past, and in so doing lose herself.

Maisie walked up the front steps and rang the bell to summon the new butler, Simmonds, who, she thought, must have been lurking on the other side of the door, waiting to welcome her into the newly decorated entrance hall. The hall and broad staircase before her were now flooded with electric light that brought the old house alive; indeed, since its redecoration, Maisie thought the mansion was like an old lady who had discovered her girlhood again. She had even heard one of the maids saying that all the mansion needed was the laughter of children to add some life to the household. It was a comment that gave Maisie pause.

"Is the Viscount home yet, Simmonds?"

"No, mu'um. He telephoned with a message to say that he expects to arrive at seven o'clock. He asked that you should decide at what hour dinner will be served."

"Let's say eight o'clock, shall we? We'll have drinks beforehand, at about half past seven."

"Very good—"

"Simmonds, please, do call me Miss Dobbs. I know this isn't what you're used to, but I've asked before and I really do not care to be addressed as 'ma'am' or 'madam' or 'mu'um.'"

"Right you are . . . Miss Dobbs. I shall remind the staff."

"Thank you. Now, I think I will go to my room."

"I've asked Millicent to run a bath for you, Miss Dobbs."

"How thoughtful," said Maisie. "Especially after a long day."

"Indeed." The butler gave a short bow.

She wanted to tell him there was no need to bow before her, but that would have meant more embarrassment. "Well then, I'll go up," she said, and walked towards the staircase.

James had insisted upon Maisie having her own rooms at Ebury Place, though when she stayed at the mansion, they lived as man and wife; his own rooms were adjacent and accessible through a dressing room. As far as the new staff was concerned, Maisie was mistress of the house, and though the more junior members had no idea that Maisie had first come to the property as a servant herself, she suspected it would only be a matter of time before that snippet of intelligence worked its way up from Chelstone Manor, the Compton estate in Kent.

She breathed a sigh of relief upon reaching her rooms—which had been decorated in colors reminiscent of The Dower House.

"I wish this wasn't so complicated," she said aloud, as she half-threw her briefcase onto the bureau in the corner.

"I beg your pardon, mu'um?"

"Oh, sorry, Millicent. I didn't realize you were there."

"Just adding a bit of lavender oil to your bath, mu'um."

"Millicent—"

"I know, sorry—Miss Dobbs."

"Thank you—and thank you for the lavender oil; your thoughtfulness is much appreciated. That will be all for now, Millicent."

As Maisie soaked in the hot bathwater, she leaned back and allowed her thoughts to skim across the events of the day, as if she were watching a picture show. In her mind's eye she reconsidered the expressions of those she had spoken to. The men, a little embarrassed when asking for help from a woman they'd known as a child. There was the fragile bereaved mother, herself no more than a girl when she'd given birth to her son, and who had been aged beyond her years by work, worry, and now grief. She thought she would try to take Jennie aside to ask some questions, and she thought again about Eddie. Tweaking the tap with her toe for more hot water—the new boiler in the cellars under the house had worked like a charm, so in winter the radiators were always hot when they were supposed to be hot, and the water was piping whenever one wanted a good long bath, whatever the time of year—Maisie felt an ache. She had felt the same pain when she was a child, watching him walking along the road, or when he came to the house to mix a poultice for Frankie's horse. "I don't know what he does that's different, but when that boy makes a poultice, it does the trick in half the time," her father had said.

She suspected Eddie must have suffered the sting of loneliness, a sense of separation that lifted only when he was with horses. Was his death simply a matter of a terrible accident? Or was there something more to be uncovered? She knew from experience that following even the most innocent passing, something always came to light that was not known before. Thus she would have to tread with care, for she knew that in her desire to be of service to men she considered to be the giants of her childhood, it would be easy to interpret the inexplicable as something more insidious.

She remembered once asking her father how it could be that Eddie's presence calmed an intemperate horse.

"Well, Maisie, there's them who reckon it's on account of him being born in the stables, and his mother having to take him to work with her when he was just a baby. It was as if he knew he'd have to be quiet around them right from the beginning, or she would've lost her job. But later on, I thought about it and I reckoned it was to do with the horses themselves. You see, they don't think about yesterday, or what's happening tomorrow, they just want to know what happens right now and if they'll be safe, looked after. And Eddie was like that too—he'd forgotten a lot of yesterday by the time today rolled around, and he didn't take on tomorrow before it got here, so they were the same—they took it all as it came, and when he was with them, they knew his mind wasn't anywhere else. I've always thought that calms a horse, if they know you're right there with them."

Despite Eddie's shyness, he'd always had a hail-fellow-well-met attitude about him; he trusted people. Indeed, it was as if to mistrust would take more from him than he could give; so he carried with him an innocence, a simplicity found in young children. If he had changed in the past month, then something had happened to damage that innocence, and along with it the gift of being able to meet the next moment as if the last had not happened.

Darling, are you there?"

"Just a minute." Maisie stepped out of the bathtub, toweled her body, and slipped into a deep-blue dressing gown.

"Hello, darling. I've missed you." James stood in the doorway, then came to take her in his arms. "I don't know about you, but I've had one of those days."

"Me too. I told Simmonds that we'd dine about eight and have drinks about half past seven—how does that sound?"

"Nothing too formal, I hope."

"If you didn't want formal, James, you shouldn't have taken on staff and a butler."

"I know—I didn't realize how much I was getting used to quiet suppers at your flat or a visit to Bertorelli's."

It was over a supper of roast lamb with mint sauce, Jersey Royal potatoes, and green beans, that Maisie asked James about John Otterburn.

"Otterburn? Of course I know him. I don't see him regularly, but we keep in touch. In fact, funny you should mention him—look here, an invitation arrived today. The Otterburns are having a supper do at their London house. I was going to send apologies, but, well, would you like to go?"

James knew Maisie did not care for suppers with London "society," though at the same time, she had been trying to get used to the fact that such occasions were an important part of his business calendar.

"Yes, I think I would like to go. Who else might be there?"

"Not sure, probably a government minister or two, some authors, newspapermen. You never know with Otterburn. He likes to put the cat among the pigeons sometimes."

"Do you like him?"

"I do quite like him, actually. He's a formidable businessman and he has a real knack of being in the right place at the right time—good at procuring businesses, people, and things to make the people and the businesses work very well together."

"Did he inherit his company?"

"His father was a newspaperman who went on to buy the local paper in the town where they lived, somewhere just outside Toronto, I think. John inherited as a young man, then he made the paper turn a profit in a very short time—and sold up in pretty short order. He took the proceeds and came here, to London, though his first newspaper purchase was in the West Country. Then he sort of moved around like one of those newfangled Hoovers that the staff are using—he vacuumed up newspaper after newspaper, then sold some to get a toehold in London. There was no stopping him then, so his interests encompass the whole business of newspapers, a book publisher, and raw paper production. The Compton Corporation has contracts with Otterburn to supply timber by-products for paper manufacture. The interesting thing is, he still refers to himself as a newspaperman."

Maisie nodded, brought her knife and fork together and picked up her wineglass. "So, taking into account the many pies in which he has a finger, would it follow that he has some strong associations with politicians and the like? You said there might be a few government types at the party."

James nodded and reached to pour more wine for Maisie, but she shook her head. He topped up his own glass—the staff had been dismissed so that the couple could eat supper in peace.

"He generally rides every morning in Hyde Park, and I would say that twice each week there's some important city man or politician riding out with him. Some men talk on the golf course—Otterburn's a horseman."

"Is he really?" Maisie leaned forward.

"Yes, in fact I heard Winston Churchill was seen out with him early one morning last week, cantering across the park as the fog was beginning to lift, like a couple of cavalrymen."

"Churchill? I thought he was persona non grata in London these days—didn't your friend Nancy Astor say, '*Churchill is finished*'?"

"She's never been my friend, though I still get invitations to those dreadful soirees of hers—you almost have to sneak in your own wine under your jacket, and heaven knows why she invites me. My mother knew her at one point, but frankly she couldn't stand the woman. Never mind Churchill being finished, there are many saying that Nancy has well and truly had her day." James paused. "Why the interest in Otterburn?"

Maisie shrugged. "Not sure yet, although someone I knew when I was a child was recently killed in one of his factories—Bookhams, the paper factory in Lambeth."

"And don't tell me, you're looking into it, just in case the circumstances are suspicious. And are they?"

Maisie took a last sip of her wine. "Perhaps." She smiled. "I don't know whether you've room after the lamb, but I've heard your new cook has prepared a sort of meringuey pudding with raspberry sauce. Very popular in Paris these days, so I've been told."

"Deft change of subject, Maisie. But seeing as you've asked, let's try that pudding."

Maisie looked around, to see if Simmonds might be waiting outside the door.

"You can use the bell behind you to summon Simmonds—that new electric system cost a fortune to put in," said James.

Maisie avoided his eyes. "Oh, I'm sure he'll be back in a minute."

James sighed and half-threw his napkin on the table as he pushed back his chair. He stepped past Maisie and pressed a button on the wall, which was situated within easy reach of her place.

"There, that wasn't too hard, was it, Maisie?"

The door opened and Maisie smiled at Simmonds as he entered. A footman cleared the plates and cutlery from the table.

"We'd love some of the pudding, please, Simmonds." She was still flushed from James' rebuke.

"Of course, mu'um. 'Pavlova,' cook calls it—and it looks very good indeed."

"Lovely. Thank you."

As Simmonds turned and left the room, James placed his hand on Maisie's. She smiled in return, but felt a pressure upon her chest, almost as if she could not breathe. And she knew that if she were sitting with dear Maurice, he might have asked her, "What happens when a person cannot breathe?" And she would have had to reply, "They suffocate."

CHAPTER THREE

❖

The Bookhams paper factory was located close to the Albert Embankment in Lambeth, between Salamanca Street and Glasshouse Lane. Not for the first time in recent weeks the MG had failed to start, which meant that Maisie risked being late. In the past, Sandra's husband had been her mechanic; however, since his death, after which his employer had eventually closed up shop, she had not taken the car for regular servicing and repair—and there always seemed to be something under the bonnet to attend to. Now the MG remained in the mews behind Ebury Place while she used the underground railway. As she made her way past the warehouses on Salamanca Street, Maisie was annoyed at the motor car, and annoyed with herself. She wanted to go back to her own flat this evening, and now it seemed she would be spending another night at Ebury Place. And she realized her annoyance came, not as a result of any serious discord in her relationship with James, but from a thwarted desire to be back under her own roof where she did not have to face—*endure* would be a good word, she thought—the rituals of life in the mansion as its de facto mistress. The MG's refusal to start—she suspected it might have a corroded plug—demanded she face up to the fact that if the courtship continued as those in their circle thought it would, her life would be dominated by the household's rituals from dawn until dusk, and in truth she wasn't sure she could warm to it, though she enjoyed being with James. Most of the time.

"Watch out, love—you want to be careful creeping round 'ere!" A husky voice called out to her, and at once she saw a bale of old rags being winched up from the back of a lorry towards a door high above the ground. "If that thing goes, you'd be squashed like a fly, make no mistake. Look where you're going."

Maisie stepped back and walked to the other side of the road. "Sorry." She could hardly make herself heard over the screech of the winch. "I was—"

"Daydreaming," the man interrupted her. "You was daydreaming. Can't do that near the factory, or you'll be in trouble."

"Can you tell me where the entrance to the office is?"

The man waved towards an alley some yards along the street. "Go down there. Door on the right, says 'Office.' Ask for Mr. Mills."

Maisie nodded her thanks and went on down the street, turned into the cobblestone alley, and found the entrance to the offices of Bookhams Paper. She rang the bell to the right of the door and waited, looking through a window of frosted glass threaded with wire to see if anyone was there. Soon a young woman came down the stairs and opened the door.

"Can I help you?" She was about thirty years of age, dressed in a pleated navy-blue woolen skirt that skimmed the top of her calves, a white blouse with a loose bow at the point of a V-neck, and a long woolen cardigan. Her hair was pulled back in a low bun, and she wore round spectacles.

"Thank you, Miss—"

"Miss Marchant. I'm the secretary here. Are you here to see Mr. Mills?"

"Yes, I am."

"Your name, please?"

"Miss Maisie Dobbs. Here's my card," said Maisie, taking a card from her pocket and handing it to the woman.

Marchant glanced at the card, then looked Maisie up and down, from her plain navy-blue court shoes to the robin's-egg-blue hat with a navy band and bow at the side and the matching blue gloves with dark pearled buttons at the wrist.

"Hmmm, he never said he was expecting anyone. Anyway, come with me—and be careful to shut that door behind you; it sometimes comes open again and there's a nasty smell wafting in from the river, what with this warm weather taking us all by surprise this year."

Maisie closed the door and rattled the handle to make sure it was closed, then followed the woman up stone steps impregnated with the smell of disinfectant. The walls were painted in a cream gloss, and at the landing a large sign informed visitors that they had entered "*Bookhams Paper, Serving the Printing, Publishing and Sanitary Industries.*"

The landing opened out onto a large office, at the center of which was a small typing pool surrounded by several other private offices, each with a frosted-glass door framed with heavy oak. Miss Marchant instructed Maisie to wait. There were no seats for visitors, so she stood by the wall, facing the backs of three young women whose fingers danced over their typewriter keys. The secretary knocked on a door with a sign in gold lettering: "Mr. Bernard Mills, General Manager, Bookhams Paper." And underneath, again the legend, "*Serving the Printing, Publishing and Sanitary Industries.*"

With the secretary now standing in the open doorway, Maisie saw Bernard Mills look up from his desk in her direction. He shrugged his shoulders, then nodded. Maisie feigned interest in the notice board behind her, which bore a sheet of paper entitled "Milk Roster," followed by a list of employee names. According to the schedule, today it was the turn of Miss Cheryl Beekin to fetch milk for tea.

"Mr. Mills will see you," said Miss Marchant as she approached Maisie. "He's only got about a quarter of an hour to spare—we've important visitors coming to the factory later on this morning, so we're busy."

"That's perfectly all right. Fifteen minutes is all I'll need today."

The secretary looked at Maisie as she said "today," but said nothing as she led her to the manager's office. After introducing the visitor, Miss Marchant left the room, quietly closing the door behind her.

Mills was a man of average height, possibly only two inches taller than Maisie, who was considered tall for a woman. The top of his head was bald in a perfect circle, surrounded by thick black hair threaded with gray, which led Maisie to think he would need only dark brown robes to take on the persona of a monk. The sleeves of his white shirt were held up with gaiters above the elbow, and he wore pin-striped trousers and waistcoat. He seemed surprised when Maisie extended her hand in greeting.

"Good morning, it's very good of you to see me, Mr. Mills."

"Hmmm." He cleared his throat as he took her hand to shake while holding her card with his other hand. "Not at all, not at all, Miss Dobbs. Sit yourself down."

The office was on the small side, only about twelve feet square, but against each wall there were filing cabinets and bookcases with ledgers and catalogs of paper samples. A pile of paper samples teetered on the desk, surrounded by open files and an array of pens and pencils.

Once seated, Mills checked the time on his pocket watch and looked up at Maisie. With his left hand he rolled the end of his waxed mustache as he spoke.

"Now, what can I do for you?"

"Mr. Mills, I am a friend of Mrs. Maud Pettit, who as you probably know is the mother of Mr. Edwin Pettit, who lost his life in a recent accident here."

Mills sucked in his breath, looked down, and shook his head as he put both hands on the desk and pushed back his chair.

"Oh, no, I can't talk about that. Orders from above. Lawyers, and all that. Can't discuss it at all—and certainly not with a—" He looked at her card again. "Investigator."

Maisie remained seated. "I'm not here to question you in a way that would compromise your position, Mr. Mills. Rather, I want to bring some degree of peace to a grieving mother—I am sure you understand."

"Well, of course. We all feel very sorry for her, and as you know—" He looked up at Maisie, as if to ensure she *did* know. "We had a collection for her here at the factory, to help cover her costs at the Co-op, with the funeral and what have you."

"And very much appreciated it was, too. But I wonder if you can help me, Mr. Mills, to get a picture in my mind of what took place on the day Mr. Pettit died. I'll obviously be careful in terms of how I recount the story to Mrs. Pettit, but—how did the accident happen?"

Mills shook his head. "I don't know, truly I don't know. If the guv'nor finds out I've talked to you, I'll lose my job."

"Then we'll pretend I'm a prospective customer. Could you show me where it happened? It would really help Mrs. Pettit very much to learn more—she worked here herself as a girl, you know, before it was taken over by Mr. Otterburn."

"All right then. Look, come with me and I'll take you along the corridor—there's a window overlooking part of the shop floor where the accident happened."

Maisie followed Mills along a corridor which she could see ended at a staircase leading down to the main factory floor.

"The pulping is done next door; we've got about fifty women in there shredding rags for boiling in the vats, and we also take paper that's already been used—it pulps down again. The quality of the paper needed dictates the rag and timber content of the materials used—for example, the newsprint has a lot of wood in it. But we also produce high-quality papers for stationers and what have you as well as the rolls for the print industry."

"And they come off the conveyor over there." Maisie pointed to the rear of the factory.

"They're checked on the belt, then straight out onto the loading ramp for delivery—either to Fleet Street or the stations for newspapers up north and down in the West Country."

"Where did Eddie come into the factory—from that door over there?"

Mills nodded. "He usually stopped to see the ladies first, to see if there was anything they wanted him to go out for. He would come in with a tray he'd made up, like one of them usherettes at the picture house. There'd be smokes, sweets, that sort of thing, and he would make a bit of money on them. And then he'd run the errands—he never had to write anything down you know. I could never get over it, how a dim soul like him could remember all that, but he did."

"Really?" said Maisie. "Then when he was done, would he leave the same way?"

Mills shook his head. "No, as a rule he'd leave through those doors to the loading ramp. You see, once you're through there, you only have to walk across the courtyard and you're in the stables. It's not full these days, on account of the lorry deliveries, but we still keep a few, just in case. You never know when one of them engines will go. Mind you, I reckon they'll get rid of the horses any day now, have 'em put down."

"Put them down? Why?"

"The owner says it's time to move into the modern age completely, rather than hanging on to the past—exact words, mind. In fact, the brass are expected soon. Factory's going to be brought up-to-date, so they all want to sniff round. It was on the cards anyway, doing away with the horses, but the accident has chivvied things along."

"Can't something be done? I mean, you can't just kill a working horse."

"There's many who think the same way as you, Miss Dobbs, myself included. But it won't just be us, you know—all the big factories are doing away with horses, and it'll be the railways next, mark my words. The horse is a thing of the past—and there's so many of them, all over London, you can't put them all out in fields, so they have to be done away with. But Eddie made their day when he went out there. He always had a treat for them, you know."

Maisie was thoughtful as she looked at the workers scurrying back and forth, at the magnitude of machinery before her—iron girders and scaffolding supporting pulleys and wheels, with ladders going up and down, and a gantry above, for the men to check load and balance. At once a siren was sounded, reminding Maisie of the foghorns that called, one after the other, up and down the river in the dead of a pea-souper night. Workers stood back, and soon a conveyor belt at one end of the factory began moving; clunking and screeching as if there weren't enough oil in the world to silence each turn of the cogs underneath. Maisie thought it looked and sounded like a giant bicycle chain straining against the pull of a steep incline, and tried to imagine what might have happened on the day of the accident. The conveyor seemed solid enough, but she could see how even the smallest locking of the cogs could jolt it out of true, so that the rolls of paper became unbalanced, perhaps causing one to lift up and eventually fall. She had not seen such machinery before, but it looked to her as if the whole contraption had been designed for smaller bales and should perhaps have been replaced to accommodate a heavier, more cumbersome load. She wondered if profits from larger bales had been so attractive that new investment had been delayed in the interests of the owner's accumulation of wealth.

She covered her ears, and in time rolls of paper with a diameter the height of a man began to shunt along towards the loading ramp, where they seemed to lumber onto the waiting lorries like animals to slaughter. She looked at her watch.

"Was this about the same time that the accident happened? Eddie would come in about now, wouldn't he?"

The man nodded. "Yes, it was about this time." He did not look at Maisie, keeping his eyes on the moving rolls of paper. Two men stood on the gantry looking down upon the paper rolls as they moved along the conveyor belt; more were watching from below. In an instant one of the men above waved to a man by the wall, who pulled a lever; the belt shuddered to a halt. The men clambered from the gantry down onto the belt and, using long iron poles, together levered one of the rolls, then climbed back to their places.

"What happened? Why did they stop the rolls of paper?"

"One of them was slightly off, so they manipulate the belt to get it on track again. It's an easy job, and it's the rules that no one goes down onto the belt while it's moving."

"I see." She paused as the machine lurched into life again and the rolls of paper continued on their way. "I've been trying to imagine how one of those rolls came down."

"Freak accident, Miss Dobbs." Mills turned away from the window, and held out his hand for her to return along the corridor towards his office. "The belt buckled, reared up off the cogs, is what we believe, then it snapped back into place again, so we couldn't find anything wrong with it when it was checked—and it was looked at thoroughly, mind you."

"Hmmm. But with those men down below, I'm surprised no one could have pushed Eddie out of danger or alerted him in some way."

"That's a new procedure, on account of the accident. Everyone not directly involved in making sure the paper is on the belt has to keep away now, as soon as that horn goes off."

"And what about the men on the gantry? Is that a new procedure?" Mills shook his head. "No, they've always been there."

"Who was there on the day Eddie died?"

"Oh, I can't give you that information, Miss Dobbs. They've both been thoroughly questioned regarding their observations, and no fault has been attributed to their actions."

"Couldn't they have stopped the belt if it was going out of control? Couldn't the man who sounded the horn have been alerted?"

"All new procedures, Miss. We can't bring back Mr. Pettit, but we can make sure no one suffers in the same way again. Perhaps that will comfort his mother a little." He looked at his watch. "Now, if you don't mind, Miss Dobbs, I really must be getting on. This is a place of work, after all." Mills paused again. "May I suggest you contact the firm's solicitors for further information? And please let Mrs. Pettit know that we think of her, here at Bookhams. Eddie might not have been an employee, but he was well liked around the factory, and we're very sorry that he was caught up in the accident. Terrible thing, it was. Terrible."

Maisie thanked the man, and had turned to leave when she stopped, and faced him again. "Oh, Mr. Mills, just one more thing, if you don't mind. In one of the newspapers a manager was quoted as saying that Eddie wouldn't have felt a thing when the roll of paper fell onto him, given that he was backward. Do you know who might have made that statement?"

"Well, first off, that wasn't reported in an Otterburn paper—not that you asked, but I wanted to make that clear. Secondly, I know the report you're talking about because I read it myself, and we looked into it. I can tell you it wasn't a manager here at Bookhams. We reckon the newspaperman went down to the pub—on the corner, at the end of the road—and talked to the blokes who work on the floor. One of them must've made the remark, or whatever was said was twisted. You know what these reporters are like; anything to add a bit of excitement."

"But, why would anyone say such a thing, even a reporter embellishing a story? I thought Eddie was well liked here."

"And so he was, but well liked doesn't mean liked by all, does it?"

"Did Eddie have enemies?"

"Oh, I wouldn't say he had enemies, but you always get people who take advantage of someone like Eddie being around, and they push a joke a bit too far. They make themselves seem bigger by showing up the weaker ones."

"And who would you say is like that at Bookhams?"

Mills shook his head. "I couldn't say, Miss Dobbs. I'm management. The men keep themselves to themselves. They don't include me in anything not directly connected to their work."

"Does that have anything to do with the fact that there's no union activity here?"

"I can't talk about company policy regarding organized labor, as I am sure you know. Like I said when you first arrived, I think you should be talking to Bookhams' legal counsel."

"And if I wanted to do just that, to whom should I speak?"

"Sanders and Herrold, at Lincoln's Inn. Mr. York Herrold."

"York Herrold? That sounds like a newspaper, not a man," said Maisie. "No wonder he's the company's legal counsel."

Mills smiled. "I'm told he was named after where he was born. York. In any case, he's very sharp, but approachable. Not like some of them. He can answer all the questions that I can't—or shouldn't have." A horn sounded on the factory floor again. "Now, if that's all, Miss Dobbs."

"Yes. Thank you for your time. I am sure the fact that I have been here to see you will give Mrs. Pettit a little peace of mind."

"Indeed. Please give her our kindest regards."

Maisie had just reached the door at the bottom of the stairs when footsteps behind her on the concrete caused her to look back. "Miss Marchant—don't worry, I'll close the door behind me."

"No, that's all right," said the secretary. "I mean, well, I'll see to it, but that's not why I ran after you."

"Did I leave something?" asked Maisie.

The young woman shook her head. "No. I overheard part of your conversation with Mr. Mills and I wanted to talk to you." She paused, looking back up the staircase before bringing her attention back to Maisie. "I liked Eddie, Miss Dobbs. He was a good man—more like a boy, really. He reminded me of my brother; he was like that too, you know, a bit slow. He was older than me and died a few years ago, when he was thirty-six. Very gentle person, he was, and I have to tell you, I do miss him. Always cheerful, and a sweet man, just like Eddie Pettit."

Maisie smiled and put her hand on Miss Marchant's arm, for she could see a welter of emotion rising in the woman's eyes. "I'm so sorry you've lost your brother, Miss Marchant. I knew Eddie when I was a child. Everybody I know held him dear, and he tried so hard to be useful, to be part of society. It's fortunate that both men had families who cared for them; otherwise they might have been sent away from an early age."

"That's what my mum always said. 'No one's taking my boy away to sit and rot in an asylum.' Our Brian could read and write, you know, and it was all down to my mum. She wouldn't give up on him." She cleared her throat and pulled at the hem of her cardigan. "Anyway, what I wanted to tell you is that Eddie had been pushed around a bit by some of the men. A new bloke started a few months ago, name of Jimmy Merton, and he's what you might call a hard nut. I don't know why people listen to him, but they do. He started nipping at Eddie—at first he acted like it was a game, you know, and that it was just a bit of harmless joshing. Then he seemed to get a little crew around him. It was surprising, really, because some of the other men—not those in Jimmy's crowd—would talk about organizing at Bookhams, and they asked people from the union to come down. But Jimmy would say his piece against it and get stroppy with anyone who had a differ-ent opinion. He would go on about how the unions were only out for themselves and that he was against it—he could get nasty with it, too. I was in the pub after work with some of the women here—sitting in the corner for a quick drink before we went home on a Saturday—and I heard them talking." The woman sighed and shook her head, press-ing her lips together for a moment as if to quell her emotions. "And I saw him having goes at Eddie—Ed sometimes dropped in to see the landlord, who'd have a bit of work for him. That Jimmy always got up to his mischief when the men who would stand by Eddie weren't there to see it happening."

"And you said his name was Jimmy Merton?" asked Maisie.

"Yes. Bit of a boxer on the side, he is. Every night he's in a boxing gymnasium upstairs at one of the pubs over on the Old Kent Road; that's where they all go to throw a few punches. I can't remember what it's called, though."

The sound of a door slamming came from the direction of the offices above, and Marchant looked up the stairs. "I'd better get back to work. I just wanted to let you know that Eddie'd had trouble with that Merton and some of his mates, and I reckon it made him miserable. He wasn't looking himself lately."

Maisie reached out and touched the woman's arm again. "Miss Marchant—do you think Eddie's death was an accident?"

She sighed. "I really don't know. If I said, 'Yes, I do,' I'd go home feeling as if I'd told a lie. But if I said I thought it was deliberate, I think I'd feel the same." She sighed. "The only thing I know is that it wasn't right. None of it. I must go now, or Mr. Mills will start docking my pay."

The woman ran up the stairs, patting her hair as she went. Maisie stood for a moment, then left the building, pulling the door towards her until she heard the loud click that signaled it was closed completely. She retraced her steps until she came to the pub on the corner. It was called The Lighterman, the sign above depicting two men unloading a Thames barge. Billy could pay a visit to the pub; he might find out a thing or two there, thought Maisie. A few shillings invested in buying a drink for some of the men from the paper factory could prove to be a worthy investment.

That Maud Pettit and Jennie had been friends together at the Union Workhouse, along with Jennie's brother, Wilf, was well known.

And that the three had worked hard—two or three jobs each, with hardly any respite—was testament to their resolve never to return to the dank place where they had met. The workhouse was not as full of the dispossessed as it had once been, but it was rumored that poverty caused by the depression had caused an increase in the number of men, women, and children living within the redbrick Victorian buildings. The men were not idlers, and the women had been as busy as they could, but the shifting sands of fortune had pulled any semblance of stability from under their feet and they had fallen on times harder than they could have imagined—thus the workhouse had once again become the shelter of last resort. Maisie shuddered when she thought about it, and considered the conditions that must have existed when Maudie was a girl—no wonder she had worked so very hard to give her son something better.

"Jennie, I wonder if I could bother you and Maud again?" Maisie smiled as Jennie answered the door to the house on Cornwall Road.

Jennie's face was drawn in a way that might have seemed pinched had she not smiled readily when she opened the door. Maisie remembered being told, when she was a girl, that Jennie had once tried to starve herself to death, such had been her despair in the workhouse. Her body had never recovered, and despite reclaiming the will to live, her frame always seemed to need a bit more flesh on the bones.

"We're not doing anything else important today, though I should warn you that Maud is a bit tired. Come on, she's in the kitchen. I've just put the kettle on to boil."

"Thank you, Jennie."

For the second time in as many days, Maisie walked back to the kitchen, where Maud was sitting in a low chair alongside the stove; the fire door had been left open and a blanket drawn around her shoulders, despite the warmth outside. She looked up as Maisie entered, and made as if to stand.

"Afternoon, Maisie girl, I didn't expect—"

"No, don't move on my account, Maudie, you just stay where you are. I'll draw up a chair."

Maisie pulled one of the wooden kitchen chairs closer and sat alongside Maud. She thought the chairs had once seen service in church, for at the back of each was a holder for a Bible or hymnbook. Jennie went through the motions of making tea as Maisie began to speak again.

"Maud, I just thought I'd drop in to see how you are."

"Not much of a change from yesterday, or the day before. The house is so quiet without him. Not that he made a lot of noise, even as a little boy. But you just know when someone's there, don't you? You can feel them in the house, as if—oh, I don't know, I'm an old woman rambling—but it's as if your heart knows that their heart is beating somewhere, and everything's all right. I know if Jennie's here the minute I wake up in the morning, or whether she's gone down to the dairy or the shop."

Maisie took Maud's hand. "Maud, I want to ask your permission, if I may. I want to go down to the Co-op, to talk to the undertaker before Eddie's laid to rest."

Maud Pettit turned to look at Maisie. "You want to see Eddie, don't you?"

"Yes . . . yes, I do. If that's all right with you."

The woman looked at Jennie, who was closing the stove's dampers to cool the hot plate. Jennie looked away; it was Maud's decision.

"Yes, you can go to him. Jennie will write a note for you to give to Mr. Gibson, the undertaker, just so he knows who you are."

"Thank you."

Maud turned back again and reached out to Maisie. "It's me that should be thanking you, after all. You can make sure he's passed over, that he's not lingering here in this world, frightened to go to the next." The woman took a deep breath as if the air in the room were evaporating. "They always said that about you, Maisie. That you and your mother could see things that others couldn't."

Maisie felt a shiver go through her. "Oh, Maudie, that was just talk, and I'm sure it started because I was an only child, and because my mum was so ill. She was in great pain at the end. Dad spent every penny we had, and a lot we didn't, for the doctors, and for special medicine to help her bear the worst of it. They said the powders would make her see things that weren't there, and they were right about that. I was on my own with her a lot at the time—Dad was working all hours to make extra—so I suppose people thought all sorts of things about us. But I'll say a prayer for Eddie—that's what's important."

The Co-op chapel of rest was housed in separate premises at the back of the main shop. She explained the purpose of her visit to Mr. Gibson, and watched as he perused the letter penned in Jennie's shaky hand.

Gibson, far from looking like an undertaker, had the build of a well-fed docker. His jacket and trousers—both made of black cloth, but not matching to an extent that the word *suit* could be used to describe the ensemble—appeared to strain at the seams. He was rosy-cheeked and seemed a merry soul, which Maisie thought commendable. She had met many men in his position, and had always thought they resembled Dickens' Uriah Heep.

"Come this way. We haven't put the lid on yet. There's always the chance that the next of kin might want a last-minute look." Gibson sighed. "And I should tell you, Miss Dobbs, that the body is covered in a sheet from the neck down. His mother gave us a nice pair of trousers and a clean shirt for him, but with his injuries, it wasn't as if we could dress him. Funny, though, his head looks as if nothing happened to him. It was his body that took the brunt." He cleared his throat. "Not that I would imagine a nice woman like yourself taking liberties, but I would ask that you don't pull down the sheets covering his remains."

Maisie nodded and was led into a room with several empty and two sealed coffins with flower wreaths on top. There was one open coffin containing a body.

"He was in a cold locker until this morning, so there's more of a blueness around his face than you might usually see, though they're never exactly flushed, the dead. Would you like me to stay here, Miss Dobbs?"

"No, that's all right."

"Right you are. Some of the ladies don't like to be alone with them, you know."

Maisie smiled. "My father always says that it's not the dead who can hurt you—it's the living you've got to watch."

Gibson laughed. "Never a truer word said, in my book. I talk to them, you know. And I've never been followed home, that's a fact. Now then, I'll be in the office when you're finished." He turned, and the door clicked shut as he left the mortuary.

Maisie stood alongside Eddie Pettit's open coffin and looked down at his face. As described by Gibson, several layers of thick white sheeting covered his broken body, and she, too, thought it miraculous that there was barely any damage to his face, which seemed strangely child-like. Only a bruise just above the left eye and some grazing to the cheek suggested an accident. She was glad that Maud had been able to visit her son in death soon after the tragedy, when his face still bore a hint of life's bloom. His heart, that part of Eddie that Maisie thought to be the very best of him, had been crushed.

During her apprenticeship, Maurice Blanche had mentored her to spend time with the dead, if at all possible. She had learned that in quiet contemplation there is respect for the one who has passed. Given their task—that of discovering the truth behind an untimely death—such an interlude served as a reminder that a human life had been lost, and with that, there was much grief. He instructed her that in an urgency to uncover the truth, the human factor must never be neglected. And in one of her first lessons as his apprentice, Maurice had taught Maisie that the dead had secrets to reveal, if only one has the vision to see them.

Maisie lifted her hand and rested it on Eddie's forehead, as a nurse might bring comfort to a feverish patient. His rich brown hair no longer shone, and she noticed gray at the temples, which seemed incongruous juxtaposed with his barely lined face. The eyes had been closed, but the lips were slightly parted, as if it would only take a slight nudge for him to breathe again. She sighed and spoke in a whisper. "What have you held from us all, Eddie? What was going on? I know you were keeping something to yourself." She stood still for a moment, then with her hand brushed back his fringe. She wished she could lift the cover to take his hand in hers, but was respectful of his broken body. "You were afraid, weren't you? Was it Jimmy Merton? Had he been after you?" Maisie drew back her hand and pulled a chair to sit next to the coffin. She closed her eyes, rested her hands on her knees, and quieted her breathing as she began to still her mind. She remained sitting in this position for several minutes, finally taking a sharp breath as if she had been woken from a deep sleep. Opening her eyes, she looked around the room almost as if she were familiarizing herself with her surroundings. Once more she stood next to the coffin, and once more she rested her hand on Eddie's forehead.

"I'll make sure we get to the bottom of why this happened to you. And I'll look out for your mum—she won't know want, so don't you worry. Godspeed, Eddie, love. You're in safe hands now, dear man."

At once it seemed as if the air in the room changed, and Maisie turned towards the office.

"All done, Miss Dobbs?"

"Yes, thank you, Mr. Gibson. I appreciate your time."

"Well, none of them are going anywhere today, are they?"

She smiled as she turned to leave. "Oh, you never know. Some wait a while before moving on."

Gibson stood by the window and watched Maisie walk along the street and turn the corner. He met all sorts in his line of work, and on this occasion it didn't surprise him at all to walk into the mortuary and find that it felt a little warmer than it had an hour or so ago.

CHAPTER FOUR

❖❖❖

Maisie returned to the office to find the costers already seated and sharing reminiscences with Billy.

"I can go for hours on the streets south of the river and I won't see a motor car anywhere—only the horses. All the breweries still swear by them, and the bottling factories. Got right of way, they have, so other traffic has to let 'em pass." Jesse Riley held his audience, pouring tea from his cup into the saucer to cool it down before lifting his saucer to his lips. He took a sip, then saw Maisie. "Oh, sorry, Maisie, I'm forgetting my manners."

"Miss—let me get you a cuppa." Billy stood up and brought Maisie's chair into the circle.

"Thank you, Billy—and don't you worry about me, Jesse. If that tea's hot, then you drink it from the saucer. As I've said before, you don't need to stand on ceremony here—this is where I do business; it's not a palace."

Maisie knew that if the men were at ease and relaxed, their recollections and comments would come with greater fluency. The habits of the market might not suit some of the company she kept when she was on the arm of James Compton, but this was her domain, and within reason, she liked her clients to be comfortable enough to be themselves.

"Let me tell you what I've been doing since we spoke yesterday." Maisie recounted her visits to Maud Pettit and to Bookhams—though she did not give complete details. She knew these men, and understood it wouldn't be beyond the realm of possibility for them to jump to conclusions and take the law into their own hands.

"And I went along to Haddon Road School and spoke to the headmaster. As you said, Eddie's teacher was Miss Carpenter, but she left when she married—and that was a long time ago. She's now Mrs. Pauline Soames, though no one could tell me where she might be living now."

Seth Knight cleared his throat. "We reckon she might live on this side of the water, towards Camden Lock. Pete here remembered Eddie saying something about going to the library there. Seeing as he could've gone to a closer library, it stands to reason that she might live in that neck of the woods and gone with him—or something like that."

At that moment, Billy returned to the room with a fresh pot of tea. "Sorry about the wait, gents. Mrs. Tapley is a bit better at the tea than me." He handed a cup to Maisie.

"She's a bit easier on the eyes, too, mate," added Dick Samuels.

The men laughed. *Good*, thought Maisie. They were at ease.

She thanked Billy, then turned back to the men. "But Billy here is the man to track down Mrs. Soames," said Maisie. "Did you hear what Seth had to say about Camden Lock, Billy?"

"Clear as a bell." He pulled up his chair again. "I'll get onto it as soon as the gentlemen leave."

Maisie smiled. "Now then, have any of you recalled anything new since yesterday? Any memories been jogged?"

"Well, I didn't set much stock about it at the time," Archie Smith began. "But last night as I was running Gussie, my old horse, through the passage out to the back, I remembered seeing Eddie at the market—must've been, oh, about six weeks ago—and he had this notebook he was writing things down in. We told you about that, eh?"

Maisie nodded. "Go on, Archie."

"Well, it was a right nice little book, none of your cheap stuff. Had a spine, and 'Notes' written on the front in gold letters. I mean, it wasn't top of the line, but like I said, it wasn't bottom of the heap. Anyway, I mentioned it to Ed. I said, 'Nice little book you've got yourself there, eh?' And he says, 'Bart gave that to me.' I was just about to ask, 'Who's Bart?' when old Bill Flackley came over for a jaw about the moldy old oranges coming in from the docks, and that was that. Last I saw of Eddie that day, he was helping out a copper with a lame horse—they all knew Eddie, them coppers."

"Bart?" asked Maisie. "Did anyone else ever hear Eddie talk about Bart?"

The men shook their heads, looking at one another as if hoping someone would say, "Oh, Bart—well, that must be . . ." But it was clear that no one knew Bart or had heard of him before.

Maisie made a notation on an index card while asking another question. "You've all said that there was something about Eddie that was different in the weeks before his death. A secretary at Bookhams mentioned the same thing, so I can't help but come back to it. Can any of you put your finger on exactly what you could see that was different? Was he sad? Happy? Did he seem unwell? What do you think?"

Jesse Riley rubbed his chin. "It was as if he had something on his mind. And Eddie was never like that—your dad always said Eddie's gift was right here and now, and that was the beauty of the man. It was as if—"

"I'll tell you what it was like," Seth interrupted. "It was like one of them fairy tales they tell you when you're a nipper, you know, where a witch comes along and casts a spell, making everyone afraid of their own shadows. Well that was Eddie, going about as if someone had waved a wand and changed him all of a sudden."

"And no one knows what happened?"

"Might've been that bleeding magic notebook, if you ask me," offered Dick Samuels. "Reckon it all came at the same time. He never lost his way with the horses, though, even with whatever was going through his mind that was bothering him. Never more content than when he was with the horses, Eddie."

Maisie and Billy talked with the men for another ten minutes or so, though no more specific information was imparted.

"Have you spoken to your dad, Maisie?" asked Archie Smith.

"Not yet, Archie, though I'm planning to see him soon."

"You probably don't remember this, girl, but your dad knew Eddie better than anyone outside of Maud and Jennie. In fact, when Eddie wanted a haircut, that's where he went—around to where Frankie kept Persephone, underneath the railway arches."

"Dad cut Eddie's hair? I don't understand." Maisie leaned forward.

"Well, you weren't to know, were you? I doubt if Frankie talked about it, on account of Eddie being afraid of the scissors."

"What do you mean? I'm sure I saw Eddie using scissors or a knife to cut a bandage, that sort of thing."

Jesse shook his head. "No, what it was, I reckon, was that Eddie didn't like the flashing in front of his eyes, so close to his head. It was that sharp metal, that clicking—hated it, he did. When he was a lit'lun, it was all Maud could do to get the boy's hair cut—Eddie could have a temper on him at times, no two ways about it. It was your dad who sorted him out. He told Maudie to bring the boy around to the stable and he'd cut his hair. Frankie knew, you see, it was as if he understood straightaway; he knew two things—that Eddie wouldn't play up with a horse there to watch him, and that the boy didn't like that sharp metal close to him. So your dad put a blindfold on Eddie, and cotton wool in the boy's ears, and then he'd sing all the while he was cutting, so the sound of the snipping and the metal on metal wasn't so bad. And it went on like that until your dad left—but that's why he came up on the train every couple of months: to cut Eddie's hair."

Seth laughed. "Bet you thought it was to see us lot!"

Maisie smiled and shook her head. "The things you don't know about your own family."

"You can always trust Frankie Dobbs," said Jesse.

"Yes, that's something I know." Maisie stood up and shook hands with each man in turn. "Billy will come down to the market and leave a message with one of you when we've got something to report. I think it's best we just get on with it now—don't worry if you don't hear anything for a few days; it sometimes takes a while to get to the heart of an investigation. But send a message immediately if you remember anything—as I said before, even the smallest detail can help us."

The men filed out, with Billy escorting them to the front door and out into the square. He came back into the room as Maisie was collecting the teacups.

"What do you think, Miss?"

Maisie set the cups and saucers on the tray with the teapot and looked up at Billy. "I think we have to find Pauline Soames, and we also have to find out who this Bart is. And I have to talk to my father—it seems he knew Eddie better than most."

"Funny, that, about the hair," said Billy, taking the tray from Maisie.

"Not really, when you think about it. Eddie was scared by things that were too much for his senses to absorb. The scissors close to his head was probably more than he could cope with, and scary for a person who felt emotions so keenly. And there was something about this notebook that I believe had the same effect on him—it was too much for him. Far too much."

Billy nodded. "And that bloke Archie Smith, what did he mean about running the horse along the passageway?"

Maisie laughed. "Unless you'd seen a coster when he's finished for the day, Billy, you wouldn't know this, but a lot of them can't afford stables, so they keep the horse at home if they've got a bit of a yard at the back. They take off the harness, lead the horse to the front door, then slap him on the rump so he trots along the passageway, past the kitchen and right out the back door to the yard. By that time the horse is good and tired anyway, so all it wants to do is eat a bag of oats, a flake of hay, and have a good night's rest."

"Well I never; me an East End boy, born and bred, and I never knew that."

"And if you had Eddie Pettit around, you never needed to pay for doctoring, either," said Maisie.

"So, you want me to look for this Mrs. Soames?"

"Yes, find out where she lives. I reckon she must be about sixty-five or thereabouts by now. And you might start at a library within walking distance of Camden Lock. Don't go to visit if you find her—just bring me the details. And the other task is to nip along to a pub called The Lighterman; it's just past Bookhams, at the end of the street. The workers get in there after the day shift has finished. It's probably best if you give the impression that you're looking for work, so you're asking around to see if anyone knows of vacancies at the factory. Money is passing hands all the time these days—men who can barely feed their families are parting with cash they've borrowed just to get a word in the right ear for a job, so you might need a few pounds." Maisie opened her bag and pulled five crisp notes from her purse. "Here—I know it seems like a lot, but I've heard the foremen down the docks are rubbing their fingers together for no less than five pounds to pick someone out of the line for work. And I'd rough those notes up a bit if I were you—you don't want to look as if you just came from the bank."

Billy took the money. "Makes you sick, don't it, Miss? How there are men out there—working men, union men—taking advantage of the poor blokes who are down on their luck."

"It does—but I don't mind parting with money to find out why Eddie had changed in recent weeks, and why he was scared."

Maisie walked to the window and looked out across the dusky square. The day's warmth was diminished now, as a chill damp air seeped up from the river and along the streets. She thought about her flat, knowing that if she were alone, she would doubtless set off for Chelstone that very evening—but not if she couldn't get the MG to start. James had suggested she buy herself a new motor car, but she'd replied that all the time the MG was running without too much maintenance, it was good enough for her. She looked at the clock on the mantelpiece. If she went back to the flat and packed an overnight bag, she could be at Victoria by seven, and with a bit of luck she would arrive at Tonbridge station in time to catch the last branch-line train to Chelstone; she could walk from there to her father's house. She wondered about James, knowing he would be disappointed not to find her at his home, but at once she knew that, not only did she need to see her father, but she had a great desire to be on her own for a while. As she considered her thoughts, she placed her hand on her chest.

Yes, she needed to get away from London, from Ebury Place, if only for a day or so. She craved the fresh country air. She wanted to feel her lungs filled with one deep breath after another.

She picked up the telephone and dialed the Ebury Place number.

"Simmonds, good evening. It's Miss Dobbs here. Would you take a message for Viscount Compton for me? Lovely, thank you. Please inform him that I've had to leave town for Chelstone and—no, Mr. Dobbs is in good health, thank you, Simmonds, but I have to see him on a matter of some urgency. I'll most likely catch the early train on Thursday morning. Yes. Thank you very much."

Later, seated in a warm first-class carriage, lulled by the side-to-side motion of the train as it made its way through London down to Kent, Maisie knew that she might fool Simmonds, and even James. But there was never a chance of fooling Frankie Dobbs.

Long way to come at this time of a night. Couldn't you wait until the morning? Mrs. Bromley will be upset when she knows you've stayed here at my cottage and not up at the house—it's your house now, Maisie, and Mrs. Bromley takes great pride in looking after you while you're there. You might let her do a bit more for you, and—"

"Dad—please don't. I just wanted to stay here tonight, in my old room. Now, if you would only move up to The Dower House—"

"I thought I'd made myself clear, Maisie."

Maisie sighed. "Yes, you did. I'm sorry, Dad."

Frankie said nothing as he poured scalding water into a brown teapot and slipped the lid into place. He wrapped a woolen tea cozy around the pot and set the pot on the kitchen table with two large mugs, a spoon, a jug of fresh milk, and a bowl of sugar. Finally, Frankie sat down opposite his daughter.

"Choked me up when I found out about Eddie." Frankie turned his head and pulled a handkerchief from his pocket. He pressed the cloth to his eyes, then faced Maisie again. "Terrible way to go, I'm sure."

Maisie nodded. "They all came to see me, you know. The lads."

"What do you reckon?"

Maisie shrugged. "If something's amiss, I'll find out what it is. Certainly, there are some unanswered questions. I thought you might be able to help me, Dad—you knew Eddie as well as anyone."

She uncovered the teapot, stirred the tea, and began to pour the strong brown liquid into the mugs. Frankie wiped his eyes again.

"The thing you have to remember about Eddie was that he walked along a very narrow path. He didn't like surprises, and anything new worried him; took him out of himself—but all the time he was inside himself and knew what was expected of him and how to go about his day, Eddie was a happy lad. He knew his mum, he knew Jennie and— bless his soul—old Wilf. He knew who he trusted at the market, and though he was nervous when someone new asked for him, as soon as he was in with the horse, you wouldn't've known there was any tightness in him—when he was worried or out of sorts, Eddie could get very tight in his body. I remember when he was a boy, he'd get these turns when it seemed as if his whole body had gone like a board, with his little hands clenched. Maudie used to gather him up and hold him like he was in a vise, and soon he'd calm down. She learned how to cope with it, and he learned a bit about what made him unhappy—like I said, it was a narrow road, but as a man he knew not to stray, if you get my meaning." Frankie sipped his tea, set the mug down, and sighed. Maisie said nothing, and soon her father continued talking.

"With Eddie it was get up in the morning—same time every day— have his bowl of porridge and a cup of tea, always in the same cup. Then he went off to his jobs, one after the other. Maudie would go with him the first couple of times if he had a new customer, just to make sure. But I give the woman her due, she made him stand on his own two feet. I remember her saying to me, 'Frank, when I'm gone that boy's got to look after himself, so I can't mollycoddle him. I know what sets him off, and as long as I don't push him too far, I reckon he'll learn enough to do without me when my time comes.' Poor Maud don't have to worry about that now. I s'pose there's a blessing there, because in truth I could never see Eddie getting on without Maud, and that's a fact. And I feel terrible for saying it."

Maisie reached out to hold her father's hand. "I'm sure there are those who've thought the same—which is probably one of the reasons Eddie's death wasn't investigated properly, as far as I can see." She paused. "Look, Dad, I hate to have to ask you all these questions about him, but I didn't know you'd been cutting his hair for most of his life until the men told me about it—which means you must have seen him in the past couple of months."

Frankie nodded. "Even during the war, when you were over there, I went up every now and again to see him and Maud, and to cut his hair. It was easier when he was younger and I had the old horse, but by the time I'd come down here to live, well, he'd got used to me and trusted me."

"What happened to Eddie in the war? I always thought he was called up but they took one look at him and let him go."

"That's more or less what happened, though he did his bit. He went to work over on Hampstead Heath, just for a while, looking after the horses. The army'd requisitioned thousands of horses—as you know—and the Heath was one of the places where they'd gathered a lot of them. So Eddie ended up as a groom. He never went to France of course—he wouldn't've lasted a minute before he went off his head. But apparently there was one officer who realized that as long as Eddie knew what to do and he did more or less the same thing every day at the same time—and that's what the army does, anyway—he was a good worker. They kept him nice and peaceful, just working in the makeshift stables, but he was discharged when the regiment left." Frankie shook his head and smiled. "I heard a story that, one time, there was all these army blokes, supposed to know their horses, and not one of them could make these horses what'd just been brought in pull a gun carriage. Eddie comes along and looks at the horses, then vanishes for a few minutes. He comes back with a bell, and as soon as the horses heard that bell, off they went. See, Eddie knew they were horses what'd pulled the buses—they went on a ring and stopped on a ring, and it was only Eddie who'd tumbled it."

Maisie smiled back at her father, remembering Eddie at the work he most loved. "So when you last saw Eddie, how was he?" she asked.

"Must've been about five or six weeks ago. I went up on the train to Charing Cross, then walked up to the market—you'll remember, because I popped round to your office afterwards for a cup of tea before I went to catch the train home. Eddie was there, so I sat him down round the back of one of the sheds and cut his hair for him. We had our usual chat—he never was one for a long conversation, Eddie. He'd talk about the same things he always talked about; and if he was looking after a new horse, he'd tell me about it." Frankie smiled, remembering.

"Nothing out of the ordinary then."

"I suppose not, no—well, there was something that made me wonder a bit at the time because it wasn't anything he'd ever commented on before." Frankie looked at his daughter. "I don't know why it didn't strike me more at the time, because, now I come to think about it, it wasn't like Eddie—you know I told you about his narrow path? This was off the path."

"What did he say?" Maisie poured more tea into the mugs.

"He started off talking about birds, how he sometimes watched them flying. And I could imagine that, you know, him standing by the river, watching birds swooping down. Then all of a sudden, he started talking about aeroplanes. Just a mention, about things that fly."

"You're right, that doesn't sound like Eddie at all to me."

"He said he'd like to fly, because he'd been drawing aeroplanes."

"Would he have seen an aeroplane?"

"You do see one go over every now and again, and there's always something in the papers—them aviator types like Amy Johnson and Jim Mollison; photographs of folk in overalls leaning against the steps going up to their ship. I've sometimes been in the village and seen one go over, and everyone comes running out to look, so perhaps he saw one—and you know Eddie, once a thing captured his imagination, he'd keep on about it."

"And did he—keep on about it?"

Frankie shrugged. "I s'pose that's another funny thing. He made mention of an aeroplane, and then never said another word about it; just went back to the usual about horses, repeating himself, like he did." Frankie looked out of the window, as if imagining Eddie Pettit, then turned back to Maisie. "You going to the funeral?"

She nodded. "Of course. Will you come up?"

"I'll come on the train—in fact, I could come back with you. Thursday morning you reckon you're going back? Early train? Yes, I'll come. I wouldn't miss seeing the boy off, and there'll be a lot of lads from the market there, paying their respects. And from Lambeth, from the old streets. Gentle soul, Eddie. Loved by a lot of people, he was."

"Stay with me at the flat, Dad." Maisie reached out to hold her father's hand.

"I might do that, love. Let me see how I feel—at my age, you want to sleep in your own bed of a night."

Maisie moved to clear the mugs and teapot. "Oh, that's true for all of us, I think."

With her back to him as she washed the mugs and rinsed the teapot, Maisie wouldn't have seen her father's expression. Had she turned, she would have seen a father who wanted to inquire about her comment, but decided it was best to leave well enough alone.

M aisie remained at Chelstone until early Thursday morning, when father and daughter left the Groom's Cottage when it was still dark and caught the milk train to Tonbridge, and traveled from there to Charing Cross. Frankie insisted upon going to the market first, so Maisie gave him a key to her flat and went on her way to the office. Sandra was at her desk when Maisie arrived.

"Good morning, Miss Dobbs." Sandra looked up from her typewriter and smiled. "Nice day again, isn't it?"

"I only hope it lasts," said Maisie. She took off her jacket, which she hung over the back of her chair. She placed her hat on the mantelpiece and pushed her gloves into her briefcase, then sat down at her desk. "I came up from Chelstone this morning, with my father, so I'll be leaving earlier today—tomorrow's Eddie Pettit's funeral; it's in the late morning, so I'll be out for a few hours. Are there any messages for me? Has Billy been to Camden Lock yet? Or Bookhams?"

"Mr. Beale was at the market for a fair time yesterday, talking to the men again, and he interviewed a few more; then he had a letter about one of the other cases, so he had to attend to that. He went over to Camden Lock this morning to make inquiries, and then he'll get down to the pub down the road from Bookhams by opening time. I would imagine he'd go home from there rather than come back to the office." Sandra paused, flipping over a page in her notebook.

"And there was a message from Viscount Compton; he asked if you would telephone him."

Maisie nodded. "Yes. Indeed. Thank you."

"I'll make a cup of tea then," Sandra busied herself with the tea tray and left the room.

Maisie sighed, picked up the telephone and dialed the number for the Compton Corporation. Upon being put through to James Compton's secretary, she learned that James was engaged in a meeting with a client but would return her call at the earliest opportunity. She thanked his secretary and placed the receiver in its cradle, whereupon the telephone began to ring.

"Fitzroy—"

"Miss, it's me."

"Billy—is everything all right? You sound breathless. Are you calling from Camden?"

"Yes, in a telephone box round the corner from the library." Billy coughed. "'Scuse me, Miss. I thought this weather would make it easier on my chest, but it's sort of damp and sticky out and it goes straight to my lungs. And what with all these flowers coming out and giving me trouble—that market started me off yesterday, I'm sure of it." Billy coughed again and Maisie could hear him struggling to breathe; his lungs were damaged by poison gas when he was a soldier during the war. Wheezing, he continued. "I reckon I've found out something really interesting, Miss."

"Go on, Billy, but take another breath—you shouldn't have been running. You know it strains you."

"Well, anyway . . ." He dismissed her concern. "I went to a couple of libraries—I told the librarians that I was an old pupil of Mrs. Soames' from when she was a teacher, and I wanted to talk to her about one of my mates who'd passed on and who she'd remember from the old days. At the second library, they knew her and said she was a regular, and one of them remembered seeing her with a man in his forties, they thought. One of them said he seemed a bit slow, so I reckon that must've been Eddie Pettit."

"Good—did they tell you where she lived?"

"No, they didn't want to give her address—and wait for this bit."

"What did they say?"

Billy coughed again, and Maisie wondered if he might be coughing up blood, which she knew could happen at any time, but especially when there were changes in the weather.

"Take your time, Billy," she added.

"I just need to lean my head over a bowl of scalding hot water with Friar's Balsam when I get home, that'll help me out. Anyway, here's what the second librarian said; she said she didn't want to give me the address, due to Mrs. Soames being away. Apparently, she's a widow, so she lives on her own, but here's the thing—Eddie's old teacher left London about a couple of weeks ago to stay with a sister who lives in Sussex, on account of the fact that she needed to get away from London because she's grieving, having lost her son."

"Her son died? And probably a few weeks ago? That's—"

"That's one of them coincidence things, that's what it is, Miss. But I haven't finished. Turns out she has two sons, but one went off to Australia about five years ago—he's an engineer or something like that. It was the other one who died, in an accident. Drowned, he was, in the river."

Maisie shook her head. "Drowned? Did they have any details?"

"No, just that they'd heard he'd fallen late at night from Lambeth Bridge—might've been the worse for wear, by all accounts."

"Billy—what was his name?"

"Bartholomew Soames. Everyone called him Bart, apparently. He was a newspaperman, a journalist. Only he didn't work for just one paper, but would write his stories and then sell them to whichever paper was interested."

Maisie was silent as she considered this new piece of the puzzle.

"Miss?"

"Good work, Billy. Look, your chest sounds awful. I think you should go home for the rest of the day."

"I'll be all right, Miss. I just want to try a few of the shops, see if I can find out more about Mrs. Soames, and I'll pay a visit to the Lighterman over near Bookhams before I go home."

"Be careful, Billy."

"Don't you worry about me, Miss. I'll be all right."

CHAPTER FIVE

❖

M aisie!"

Maisie started as she answered the telephone, and held the receiver away from her ear.

"Maisie, I've missed you." James Compton's voice was so loud, the line echoed. "Did you really have to rush down to Chelstone in such a hurry?"

"Yes, I'm afraid so, James, and I'll be staying at the flat this evening—my father's in London and we've a funeral to attend tomorrow morning."

"Oh, yes, of course, that man who was good with horses, I remember now." There was a pause, and James' voice changed. "When will you come back to Ebury Place, Maisie?"

Maisie coiled the telephone cord around her fingers. He sounded like a wounded child; she felt as if she were being drawn into placating him in some way. "Well, how about Saturday afternoon? We could drive out to Richmond."

"We've a party on Saturday, an invitation from Duncan and Rose Hartman. Remember? It's his fortieth birthday, so there will be dancing until the small hours, then breakfast served at four in the morning to round off the night. And don't forget there's the Otterburn supper coming up next week too."

"Oh dear, yes, of course."

"You don't sound very enthusiastic."

Maisie stood up straighter and smiled. "No, not at all—it's just that I'd forgotten all about the Hartmans. I'm sure we'll have a lovely time, James."

"I think Priscilla and Douglas are going too."

"Oh, I wouldn't doubt it! Priscilla came back from a visit to Paris a couple of days ago, so she's bound to have a new gown or two to show off." Maisie smiled. She looked forward to seeing her friend.

"In my eyes you'll always be the belle of the ball, Maisie."

For a second, Maisie didn't quite know how to respond. "That's very sweet of you, James."

"It's true."

Maisie glanced at the clock. "So, I'll see you on Saturday, about lunchtime. Richmond in the afternoon, and the Hartman do in the evening."

"I'll see you then, my love."

"Yes, see you, James."

Maisie sighed as she replaced the telephone receiver, feeling the call's tension ease. Though she hated to think about it, she wasn't sure what had happened in the relationship, but this feeling of suffocation, which began as just a passing sensation, was growing. Now every conversation felt stilted, and she found herself questioning feelings she'd had for James and her own declarations of love. She picked up the telephone and dialed Priscilla's number.

"Darling, how are you?" Priscilla was effusive in her greeting.

"I'm well—how was your trip to Paris?"

"Absolutely divine! I adore my toads, but sometimes there is simply too much maleness in this house and I have to get away. Mind you, two or three days in Paris on my own and I've had enough of that, too, though I had a wonderful time choosing a few more dresses for summer. You should come with me next time—there's more to a shopping trip than a quick dip into Derry and Tom's for a new woolly cardigan, you know, or to Debenham and Freebody during the January sale."

"Shall I pay you a visit? How about later tomorrow afternoon? I've a funeral to go to in the morning, but I'd love to see you."

"Oh, dear Lord, please, don't come in that black dress again, Maisie. Do promise me you won't drag out that miserable-looking garment for another airing in company. I swear, if I see that thing again I will scream. Either change before you get here, or buy a new black costume to wear to the funeral."

"I'll just change before I come over."

"And James?"

"What about him?"

"Oh, Maisie, that doesn't sound very promising."

"See you tomorrow afternoon, Pris."

"I'll have refreshments ready. About four then?"

"Yes, about four. See you then."

Maisie set down the receiver and sighed, then looked up to see Sandra staring at her.

"Sandra?"

"I just wondered if everything's all right, Miss Dobbs."

"Yes, of course it is. Now then, I expect you'll have to be leaving soon, to go to your job with Mr. Partridge."

The young woman shook her head. "No, Mr. Partridge has given me time off while he works on something else—and he's paying me! I don't mind, because I can catch up with reading for my studies. But it's really generous of him, not a lot of people would do that."

"Douglas Partridge is a man of generous spirit—I am sure it's the quality that attracted Mrs. Partridge."

"They married after the war, didn't they? He does well for a man with only one arm, and who can't walk without a stick."

"They met in southwest France, actually—both trying to get away from their memories, if truth be told. They were married some thirteen years ago—yes, it was, because their eldest is now twelve. And he and his two brothers are growing like weeds. Anyway, I'm sure Mrs. Partridge will tell me more about her husband's exciting new job."

Sandra slipped a sheet of paper into the typewriter and smoothed it against the platen. "Oh, I doubt that, Miss Dobbs. I think it's something he's doing on the QT."

Maisie was about to ask what Sandra meant but could see she had spoken without thinking and was oblivious to the curiosity such a comment might inspire.

Maisie stood at the side of the road with her father to watch the hearse carrying Eddie Pettit pass along streets he'd walked as a child. Drawn by two gleaming jet-black Friesian horses, their manes braided and with black plumes attached to their browbands, the hearse was followed by costermongers driving carts and pushing flower-filled barrows, by a few mounted policemen, and by horse-drawn drays from Starlings Brewery, the leatherwork and brassware of their harnesses polished to a shine. When the cortege passed, Maisie held on to Frankie's arm, and they stepped out to join the procession to St. Mark's Church, where Eddie would be laid to rest.

As they stood in the church, Maisie looked at Maud Pettit during the reading of the lesson, and could see grief enveloping her small, vulnerable frame. She leaned on Jennie, who looked tired but stood tall—and while watching, Maisie wondered what those early years of motherhood had been like for a young girl with not two ha'pennies to rub together. How she had worked, and what a struggle it must have been. And how comforting to have her old friends, Jennie and Wilf, to help support the young boy in his early years.

"Best be going now, love." Frankie waved to another man he'd known in his days at the market, and began to walk away from the churchyard.

Once again Maisie slipped her arm through his. "Will you stay at the flat again this evening?"

"No, love. I should be getting back."

"All right, but look, I'll come to the station with you."

"You've no need to—" Frankie looked up as Jennie walked across the churchyard towards them. She was holding something in her hand, waving it as she called out.

"Maisie! Maisie, wait a minute." Jennie pressed her free hand to her chest as she approached, dressed in an old but well-ironed black skirt and jacket, with a brooch pinned to her lapel. A black cloche was pulled down on her head, with a small patch of black decorative net covering her face. She pushed back the net.

"Nice send-off you gave him, Jennie." Frankie removed his cap as he spoke.

"No more than he deserved, God love him." She turned to Maisie. "I found this yesterday. We'd already done a bit of clearing in Eddie's room, but to tell you the truth, it was too much for both of us, so we sort of left it. I was turning the mattress yesterday and found this underneath. It's his pay book. Maud always told him he had to try to write down what he'd earned, so he could keep an eye on his money. He wasn't very good at writing his numbers, but Maudie nagged to get him to keep it all in his little ledger. Anyway, this one has the details for this year so far, and it's got the money he earned in his last few months. I might be able to find more of these, but as you can see, when he came to the end of a book, he added it all up, then rubbed out everything he'd written and started all over again, with the amounts earned that year listed before the new earnings." She opened the book. "Look at this first page, it goes back five years, according to the list of numbers, but as you can see—" She flicked the pages in front of Maisie. "As you can see, the pages are all gray now because he kept rubbing out the numbers and names so he could write new ones in."

Maisie took the notebook and squinted to read the thick, deliberate, but almost illegible hand. She turned page after page. "He didn't do too badly, with all these jobs, did he? And you're right about what you said when I came to the house—he was working a bit further out, and for some wealthier people. He'd upped his prices for them, too." As she turned the pages, Maisie realized she was looking for a particular name, and was somewhat disappointed when she couldn't find it, though it would have been a surprise all the same. Then several pages before the notations ended, Maisie stopped.

"Oh."

"What is it, Maisie?" asked Frankie.

"Oh, nothing, nothing." She turned to the woman beside her, who was now kneading a handkerchief with her fingers and looking down so that no one could see her face.

"Are you all right, Jennie?"

The woman nodded. "I'll come round. I've got to keep my chin up, what with looking after Maudie. But we're broken without our Eddie. We'd always looked after him, you see. He was the sun in our lives, even though he wasn't right, and he could be a handful—remember that, Frankie?"

"Oh, yes, I remember, Jen."

"But we miss him."

Maisie nodded. "May I keep this?"

"Of course you can, love. If it helps you, then you keep it." She paused and rubbed her eyes with the handkerchief. "We might have laid our Eddie to rest, but there'll be no rest for us until we know the truth about what happened to him. Now then, this will never do—I'd better get back to Maudie."

Father and daughter watched her walk away.

"I don't want to miss my train, love—look at you, you're miles away," said Frankie. "I know that look—there's something on your mind."

"What? Oh, sorry, Dad. Yes, let's get on."

They turned to walk in the direction of Lambeth underground station; Maisie had every intention of seeing off her father at Charing Cross Station.

"Anything useful in that book?"

Maisie shook her head. "I don't think so, but I'll go through it again—I need to know all I can about Eddie."

"Right you are, love. With a bit of luck we'll get to the station before that big old cloud over there breaks open."

Maisie unfurled her umbrella, just in case.

N ow it was raining hard, a rain that caused a shadow of steam to rise from the path ahead when it struck the warm pavement. As Maisie quickened her step, water splashed into her shoes and up around her ankles, leaving her stockings with black pockmarks at front and back. Stepping across puddles, she entered the square, and as she approached the former mansion house in which her office was situated, she could already see Sandra looking for her from the floor-to-ceiling windows in the first-floor office. She waved as soon as she caught Maisie's eye, turned from the window and was opening the front door to meet her as Maisie reached the steps.

"Miss!"

"Sandra, whatever is it? You're white as a sheet—what's wrong? What on earth is wrong?"

"Oh, Miss Dobbs—it's Billy."

Maisie felt a cold sweat envelop her body, and at once it was as if Sandra had spoken to her from within a long tunnel. "What's wrong with him? Where is he?" Her own words seemed to bounce back to her.

"He's in St. Thomas' Hospital. We've had the police here this morning already. He was found not far from that pub, The Lighterman, by some workers coming onto the early shift at the factory; he was in a bad way. The police say he'd been set upon, beaten up, sometime last night."

"What?" Maisie slipped past Sandra and ran up the stairs. "How is he? What about Doreen? Why didn't she telephone me when he didn't come home? What—"

Sandra followed Maisie into the office. "Miss Dobbs, if you'll pardon me for interrupting, but I've got answers to almost everything. That Detective Inspector Caldwell was here and told me to tell you this, and—"

"Caldwell? He's with the Murder Squad." Maisie picked up the telephone receiver, but realizing she didn't quite know who to call, she returned it to its cradle.

"That's what he said. 'I'm with the Murder Squad, not the Not-Quite-Dead-But-Might-Be-Soon Squad.'"

"He can be a sarcastic piece of work, Caldwell."

"I think he was shocked, to tell you the truth," said Sandra. "He told me he'd always liked Billy, so when the call came in and he got word of it, he went straight over to St. Thomas' and sent a driver and a woman police constable to Eltham to collect Mrs. Beale. Then he came here, to see you. Everything's under control, Miss Dobbs."

"But what about Billy? What happened to him?"

"He's still unconscious, but the police are waiting to interview him when he comes round—they had to operate on him as soon as they got him to the hospital. He's got a nasty concussion, a thick black eye, several broken ribs and they kicked him in the legs—his poor wounded legs." Sandra put her hand to her mouth.

Maisie gathered up her bag and moved away from her desk. "Right, I'm going to the hospital. And then I'm going to find out who did this to Billy. In the meantime, Sandra, I'd like you to find out everything you can about a man called Jimmy Merton."

"Miss—I wouldn't go down to the hospital if I were you."

"Why ever not? I must go to him—I have to make sure he receives the very best medical care." Maisie put her hand to her forehead. "And could you telephone Mr. Andrew Dene—he's a consultant now, so he's known as 'Mister' not 'Doctor.' He lectures at St. Thomas' Medical School several times each week, and he surpasses anyone else in his field when it comes to wounds of this sort—he's an orthopedic surgeon. He knows Billy, and he'll bring in a good neurosurgeon and a vascular expert. Tell him what's happened, tell him I'd like him to see Billy—and tell him that Billy must be well taken care of, and all accounts may be sent to the office, to my attention. Now then, I must go."

Sandra reached out and put her hand on Maisie's arm. "No, Miss Dobbs. Please don't." Tears had filled her eyes. "You see, Caldwell warned me—he said that Mrs. Beale wasn't of sound mind when she heard about Billy, that she's sort of gone off again. She's very emotional, and she's blaming you, shouting that it's all your fault, that if Billy wasn't doing this job, then he wouldn't be in this state, and that they were better off in Shoreditch, until you interfered and made them move, and—"

"But she wanted to move, Sandra." Maisie grasped the back of a chair to steady herself. "I wanted to help them—I . . ." Tears filled her eyes.

Sandra held on to Maisie's arm, her grip tentative. "I know that, Miss Dobbs. But like I said, Mrs. Beale is very emotional at the moment, and she's, well, she's gone back a few steps."

"I still think I need to go down there. Doreen has always trusted me—I can talk to her."

"I don't know that anyone can talk to her, Miss. When Caldwell told me about it, I took the liberty of giving him the name of her doctor—Dr. Elsbeth Masters, the one you arranged for her to see, who helped her so much. I think he's telephoned her, and she's spoken to the ward sister on duty at St. Thomas', and they've given Mrs. Beale something—but I don't know if now is the time to go."

Maisie closed her eyes and, not for the first time, felt herself yearn for Maurice's counsel. She had mourned his loss, and she had grieved for him, but the ache of missing him lingered—who was there to turn to now that he was gone? Where was that wisdom to draw upon? She heard Sandra leave the room, the light rattle of crockery signaling that she had gone to the kitchenette to prepare a mug of tea.

"What shall I do, Maurice? What can I do for Billy? For Doreen?" Maisie asked her question into the nothingness that now seemed to envelop her. And she waited, leaning forward as if to hear a voice in the distance.

Minutes later, she felt as if she had been woken from a light and troubled sleep when Sandra touched her shoulder and held out the tea.

"There, Miss. That'll make you feel better. It's been a shock all round, the news."

Maisie nodded. "Thank you, Sandra." She blew ripples across the steaming tea and sipped. Drawing back, she looked at Sandra, who had pulled her own chair closer. "I'll wait a while, and then I'll go to the hospital—I must, Billy's my responsibility. I'll telephone Dr. Masters to ask her advice, then I'll go."

"Right you are, Miss Dobbs. And I'll telephone Mr. Dene, and I'll find out what I can about Jimmy Merton. Do you reckon he's responsible for this, Miss?"

Maisie shook her head. "I did what I had taken pains to stop the gentlemen from doing—I jumped to a conclusion without evidence, because I want someone brought to book for the attack on Billy. Merton might have something to do with it, and he might not—but I do know he was a thug who had made Eddie's life difficult in the past, and I would bet without a shadow of doubt that he's a regular in The Lighterman."

Following a brief telephone conversation with Dr. Masters, Maisie thanked Sandra for taking care of matters at a difficult time and left the office. Still in a daze, she walked to Tottenham Court Road and hailed a taxi-cab to take her across the river to St. Thomas' Hospital. If Doreen had been given medication as instructed, she would be calmer. But she knew that Doreen—for whom the same daily round was crucial to her well-being—would be seriously affected by the sudden news of the attack on her husband, especially following a night of worry, when it was likely her fear had led to a paralysis of action. And Billy's aging mother, though sensible and strong, would have found it difficult to deal with the younger woman—a woman who, though happy with her baby, might be suffering from the ups and downs of new motherhood. Masters had cautioned Maisie to "tread carefully."

The taxi-cab dropped Maisie outside the austere exterior of St. Thomas' on Westminster Bridge Road in Lambeth, across the river from the Houses of Parliament. She lingered a while, trying to compose herself for what she might encounter within the walls of this venerable old hospital. It had been in its present location since the end of the Crimean War, when Florence Nightingale had been consulted on the move from Southwark, where the hospital had been situated since its founding some eight hundred years earlier. Nightingale had decreed that ceilings in the new hospital should be high, and wards must be light-filled and airy, so that patients might feel better and be at less risk of infection.

Maisie felt small as she walked those long, high-ceilinged corridors towards the men's surgical ward. She had been informed that Billy was now in a side ward on his own, and that a policeman was currently with him, as was his wife, for whom a small camp bed had been rolled into the room. Apparently, Elsbeth Masters had warned the ward sister that they might have a significant problem to deal with if Mrs. Beale could not remain with her husband. Maisie acknowledged her fears as she continued walking, hoping that Billy might be awake, hoping that his injuries might be overcome in time, perhaps soon. She felt she might have made a terrible error in her belief that in helping Billy and Doreen to move into a new house in Eltham, far from the slums of Shoreditch, she was doing the right thing. If what Sandra recounted was true, perhaps she had overstepped the mark—yet Doreen had been so very pleased with her new home, hadn't she? Maisie sighed, straightened her shoulders, and went up a staircase to her right, then along another corridor. She reminded herself that Doreen was deeply emotional, and that such fluctuations had a poor effect on her well-being, on her ability to cope with even the smallest task. Billy's condition would have brought back memories of losing their beloved daughter, so she would be deeply troubled and—Maisie knew this—barely responsible for her words or actions. But despite her own medical training and her understanding of the wounded mind, Maisie felt the mantle of guilt heavy upon her shoulders.

A policeman was outside the door when Maisie arrived. Caldwell, who was sitting next to Billy's bed, looked up and waved her into the room.

"Miss Dobbs. He's just come round, though he goes in and out, but he's been telling me a bit about what happened."

Maisie rushed to Billy's side and took his hand. His head was swaddled in white bandages, and his face swollen, with deep purple eyelids he seemed unable to open.

"S'all right, Miss. I can't see you, but I know you're there." Billy croaked the words, and began to cough.

Maisie looked around for a water jug and glass. "Where's the—"

Caldwell caught her eye and shook his head, pointing to a sign above the bed. "Nil by mouth."

Maisie sat down on the opposite side of the bed and looked at Caldwell, with Billy between them. Caldwell shook his head again and pointed to his stomach. He didn't need to say anything—Billy could not take fluid due to the possibility of internal injuries.

"I was a nurse, I should have known better," whispered Maisie.

"I did exactly the same thing—it's natural."

"What, Miss?"

"Nothing, Billy—we were just wondering who did this to you."

Billy smacked his lips together. "I'm dry, Miss. Can't hardly talk. And they've got this Christmas tree here pushing water into my veins, yet where I need it is in my mouth."

"I'll talk to the doctor, see what we can do." Maisie paused and was about to ask if he remembered anything, when his breathing changed.

"He's gone again," said Caldwell. "Goes in and out, like I said. I've been here half an hour so far. He can only tell me that he can't remember anything—well, he remembers ordering a half pint of light and bitter, then he started talking to some of the lads from Bookhams. That's not to say that there wasn't a lot more talking done, but that's where his memory stopped. I had to question a bloke last week, got himself in a motor accident, and his last memory was having his breakfast that morning. Funny, that."

Maisie nodded and whispered. "I've asked a friend of mine to see him—he's a senior consultant here, and he'll know who to bring in."

"Always down to who you know, eh, Miss Dobbs?"

"What do you mean?"

At that point a shrill scream pierced the air. Maisie turned and saw Doreen outside the door to Billy's room, her open mouth and bloodshot eyes distorted by the glass as she screamed again. Maisie could see the panic in her expression. The door rattled as Doreen tried to enter the room but in her distress had difficulty coordinating her movements until, with a final turn and push, the door opened and crashed back against the wall and Doreen stumbled in, her hands held out before her. She ran at Maisie, who caught her wrists, and as Doreen began screaming, trying to beat Maisie with her fists, the constable and Caldwell restrained her.

"You did this! All he thinks about is doing his best for you, and this is what happens. 'Do this, Billy, Do that, Billy.' And off he goes, like a lamb to the slaughter for his Lady-bloody-Bountiful. What was he doing in a place like that, my Billy? Look what you've done to him, just look. He was better off working as a caretaker than for you. I rue the day he ever met you—never mind about knowing you in the war and you saving his life. Look where that's got him now. And we were better off in Shoreditch—now we're beholden. And look where it's got us, look . . ."

Spent, Doreen Beale slipped to the floor, her legs caught under her. The two men reached down to help her to her feet.

"Leave her be. Just leave her be." Maisie sat on the floor next to Doreen and put her arms around her, holding her as tight as she could. She felt the thin, bony shoulders and elbows through her clothing, and the depth of sorrow and pain as Doreen sobbed. "There, there, just you cry, Doreen. There, there." Rocking back and forth, Maisie felt herself rubbing her cheek against the woman's hair, and she felt the weight of her vulnerability, and how that burden must have been so hard for the family to bear.

"I thought they were doing so well now," she whispered to Caldwell.

"They probably were, Miss Dobbs." The detective knelt down beside Maisie, his voice far more tender than she might have given him credit for. "But this is a serious matter, and what with her having a new baby and all . . ." His voice trailed.

"It's just not fair. They've gone through so much. No family should have to endure this . . . this . . . suffering."

"But it happens. I see it all the time. There's some people who seem to be dealt the wrong hand, and it's just one thing after another." He signaled to the policeman to help Doreen to her feet; it was as if she were a deadweight, with no thoughts to inform her limbs. "Come on, let's get her over to that camp bed before sister comes down the ward breathing fire and wondering what the racket's all about. PC Henley, as soon as we've got her settled, you go and find the staff nurse, see what they can give her—she's half with us and half not, so she needs some help."

With Doreen settled and the constable sent to summon the staff nurse, Maisie turned back to Billy. It was clear he was aware of what had just happened, for as she took his hand again, a single tear emerged from each swollen eye and trickled across his bruised cheeks.

"I'll find out who did this, Billy. I'll find out," whispered Maisie. She felt the pressure of acknowledgment in Billy's fingers.

Once in the corridor, Maisie and Caldwell stood aside to allow the staff nurse to pass; clasped in her hand was an enamel kidney bowl with two large metal syringes.

"Miss Dobbs, I heard what you had to say to Mr. Beale, about finding out who did this, and I must caution you—you are not to try to find out anything. This is a job for the police, and, quite frankly, I don't want to come visiting you in this hospital, or any other hospital for that matter, and I don't want to be seeing more people looking like that." He nodded towards Billy.

"But Detective Inspector—"

"Now then, we're on the same side here." He gave a half-smile. "I've told you before, I don't mind them dead, but I can't stand to see all that wounding on a person still drawing breath, so I don't intend to make a habit of it. As far as I'm concerned, Mr. Beale is the victim of an attempted murder, and I will be looking into it."

"I think it's to do with Eddie Pettit's death. Do you see? It might not have been an accident at Bookhams."

Caldwell said nothing, the only sounds a soft moaning from the room, where drugs were being administered to Doreen, and the tap-tapping of his foot on the tiled floor.

"All right, I'll give you the benefit of the doubt. But I've got to be careful, you know. Why don't you and I have a cuppa together on Monday morning and compare notes. Will that suffice for now?"

"Yes, it will. Thank you."

Maisie shook hands with Caldwell and turned to go back into Billy's room to have a few words with the staff nurse.

"Oh, Miss Dobbs," said Caldwell. "Remember, Mrs. Beale's a sick woman. Don't set too much stock by what she said in there."

"Thank you, Detective Inspector. The thing is, I think she might be right. Perhaps I have taken advantage of Billy. I've made errors of judgment, and the fact that a good, kind man is lying in there so badly injured is down to me. Now I have to sort it all out."

"Just be careful you don't make it worse, that's all I can say. See you Monday." Caldwell turned and walked away.

Maisie was about to step into the room when the staff nurse came out.

"No more visitors, madam. I think there's been enough excitement around here for one day. I don't know what Matron will have to say about it."

"What will happen to Mrs. Beale?" Seeing the nurse's hesitance to speak, Maisie added, "I was a nurse in the war—and just afterwards, at a psychiatric hospital—so I have some understanding of the situation. I arranged for Mrs. Beale to see Dr. Masters, who has been advising on her state of mind."

The nurse chewed the inside of her lip, as if debating how much to reveal; then she sighed. "Oh, that'll have been the last straw, that little outburst in there. We've done our best, what with the nature of her husband's medical condition—it's almost unheard of to bring in a bed so a family member can stay. We only ever think about that for the little ones, but even then it's rare. But we thought he might go after the first operation, to release pressure on the brain."

Maisie gasped. The nurse appeared not to notice.

"I know our registrar has already been on the telephone to that Dr. Masters," added the staff nurse. "And an ambulance is expected any minute to take her over there, to the psychiatric hospital."

"Oh, dear—what a mess. She's a mother, and her baby—" Maisie shook her head. "Not to worry, I'll sort it out. I'll look after the family."

As she was about to leave, Maisie turned once more to the staff nurse.

"I wonder, do you have Mr. Beale's personal effects?"

"Yes, they're in the office—usually they're only handed back to the patient when they leave, or next of kin if the patient's deceased."

"I'm Mr. Beale's employer, as you know, and there were some items in Mr. Beale's possession that belong to my business. Could you make an exception for me to see the items taken from Mr. Beale when he was admitted?"

The nurse motioned for them to walk along the corridor.

"Follow me," she instructed Maisie.

She stopped for a moment in the sterilizing room, where the kidney bowl and syringes were left on a table to be put into the autoclave, then led Maisie along another corridor, where she stopped outside an office and asked Maisie to wait. Two minutes or so later, the door opened, and the staff nurse emerged with a paper sack. Billy's name was on the front.

"These are the things that came in with him—you can have a quick look while I wait."

Maisie opened the bag and emptied the contents onto a small table outside the office. There was Billy's watch—a gift from Maisie—along with a clean handkerchief, a pencil, about three shillings in change, the keys to his house in Eltham, and a small plain brown-paper-covered notebook.

"I'd like to take this—if I may?"

The nurse nodded. "You'll have to sign for it here." She handed Maisie a list that had been inserted inside the bag along with the contents.

Maisie signed for the notebook, thanked the nurse, and asked to be directed to a telephone kiosk.

"There's one by the door, just as you leave—it's on the right."

"And may I call later for a report on Mr. Beale's progress?"

"Of course, but try to telephone before afternoon visiting hours—it gets very busy here, you know."

S andra picked up the receiver after only one ring.

"Sandra, it's me."

"Oh, Miss Dobbs, I've been on the edge of my seat, waiting here for you to telephone. How's Mr. Beale?"

"Very poorly, Sandra. He's sustained some serious injuries, though I won't know exactly until Andrew—Mr. Dene—sees him. Did you get a message through?"

Maisie held the wooden concertina door open with her foot and, holding Billy's notebook to the light, flicked through the pages as she spoke.

"Yes, and he called back and said to tell you that he expected to examine Mr. Beale later today, and he'll be in touch with you as soon as he's spoken to the doctor who's been treating him so far."

"Good. Now, Sandra, I wonder—I'd like you to do something for me."

"Anything you ask, Miss Dobbs. I want to help."

"Billy's mum has been left with the boys and the new baby. Can you go over there and give her a hand? She's very independent, but she's also a realist, and she'll know she needs help; she's getting on in years and those boys are good boys, but they might be getting upset without their parents and I am sure they can be a handful if they start playing up. They've been through a lot, so, if you wouldn't mind . . ."

"I'll leave straightaway, Miss. I can nip home to pack an overnight bag and be on my way. I know where Billy lives, so rest assured, you don't need to worry. I'll see what I can do about baby milk on the way—the chemist at Boots will be able to help me."

"Thank you, Sandra—oh, and take whatever you require from petty cash. You might need to go out for extra groceries. In fact, telephone the local shop and have them delivered, it'll make things a bit easier. There's a telephone installed at the house, though I think they only use it when I call and Billy answers. I am still wondering why Doreen didn't telephone me when Billy failed to come home."

"She probably forgot, Miss. People do that, when they're not used to having something. I know of a woman who had a telephone put in, and when she spotted a fire in an empty house across the street in the middle of the night, she ran up the road to the telephone box, forgetting she had one at home."

"I can believe it—especially if Mrs. Beale was getting more and more emotional as the night went on. Or perhaps she took something to make herself sleep, and didn't panic again until the morning, when she realized he wasn't home. Anyway, Sandra, will you call me later? You'll probably get me at the flat. Let me know how you're getting on?"

"Like I said, Miss, don't worry. I'm the eldest in my family—I know how to look after them."

Maisie held back tears that welled up again. "Bless you, Sandra. I'll talk to you soon."

Outside the telephone kiosk, Maisie looked down at a page in the notebook she had dog-eared during her conversation with Sandra. While still in Camden, and before he'd made a fateful visit to The Lighterman, Billy had discovered not only an address for Eddie Pettit's former teacher, but the name of her sister, Mildred Taylor, who apparently lived in Brighton. Though there was no full address, Billy had noted "Shell Close" with a question mark alongside, and had taken the trouble to add that his information came from a Mr. Cooke, the shopkeeper in Camden who knew Mrs. Soames, and who had been tasked with receiving her mail from the postman and keeping it until her return. He had also noted a woman's name—Eve—with an arrow pointing to the name "Bart."

CHAPTER SIX

❖

Maisie considered the time. It would take her a good two hours or more to reach Brighton on a Friday evening, so how on earth would she find Mrs. Taylor in the last few sociable hours on a Friday, or even on Saturday morning? She could, however, telephone Caldwell—perhaps he could help, enabling her to make an early start in Brighton on Monday, if she left on Sunday. But, on the other hand, that might not be the best idea. She leaned back in her chair, aware that she was shuffling obligations in her mind, that she was trying to work around the Hartmans' party. If she had been alone, without James in her life, she would go to Brighton this evening. She would leave right now. But that one move would cause a row, a fissure that would take days to heal and leave them both wounded. It would be yet another one of those silly arguments that had started cropping up between them. Perhaps the investigation could wait. Would anything be changed by her acting now, except that it would allow her to feel as if she were doing something in the aftermath of the attack on Billy? She tapped her fingers on the desk, picking up the telephone receiver twice before putting it down again. Then it rang, causing her to start.

"Hello."

"What, no reciting of the telephone number? No 'Maisie Dobbs, at your service'?"

"You never give me a chance to make a formal greeting anyway, Priscilla."

"I would, if you were at my house. Where are you? I've been waiting for ages."

Maisie looked at the clock.

"Oh, dear. I'm sorry, Pris—we've had an emergency here and—well—it's been very difficult."

"Are you all right?"

"I am, but Billy's not—he was beaten up last night and only discovered early this morning. He's already had an operation to relieve pressure on his brain, and he's terribly ill. His wife has taken a slide backwards into the abyss, and—frankly, it's all my fault."

"You're not being a martyr, are you? Is it really your fault?"

"Yes. It is. And I have to do everything I can to help."

"Come over, Maisie. We'll have a cup of tea and talk about it."

"Tea?"

"I'm trying harder to change my ways. The trouble starts when I put a cube of ice in a glass, so if I go immediately to a cup requiring a hot liquid, step one on the slope down to a cocktail or two is eliminated."

Maisie looked at the clock again. "Priscilla, look, I'll have to put off our get-together; there's so much to do—I'll telephone early next week."

"You're about to rush off somewhere, aren't you?"

"Yes. I've just decided to go down to Brighton—I'll be back tomorrow lunchtime anyway, to see James."

"And how—"

"I have to hurry now. I can't use my motor car, it won't start, so I'll have to get the train from Victoria—it'll probably be quicker anyway. I'll be in touch, Priscilla."

"Maisie, is there anything I can do? If not for you, then for Billy's family?"

Maisie was about to decline the offer when a thought occurred to her. "Could you spare Elinor? Perhaps for a few days? She's a trained nanny, and with both Billy and Doreen in different hospitals, Billy's mother is alone with the children, including a young baby. I've sent Sandra to help over the next couple of days, but—"

"Consider it done. Do you have a number for the house? I will telephone, speak to Sandra, and sort it all out for you. This is something I can take charge of without too much ado. Marshaling children and nannies is something at which I excel—have no fear."

Maisie read out the number. "And thank you, Pris. I really—"

"Now, don't start to grovel. Let me just get on with it and rise to the occasion. By the way, I was about to ask but you cut me off—how's James?"

"Another time, Pris, I have to go."

As she ended the call, Maisie wondered if this organization of the Beale family's children and Billy's mother might be just the sort of thing to set Doreen off if she knew about it. But what else could be done? She couldn't leave hard-of-hearing Mrs. Beale with the boys and a baby, not in a new house where, as far as she knew, they hadn't had much of a chance to get to know the neighbors. Things would have been different in Shoreditch, of course.

Maisie stood for half the journey to Brighton on a train crammed with commuters returning to a burgeoning suburbia on the outskirts of London. It wasn't until the train reached Croydon that she managed to claim a seat. When the station first opened, the town's population was under fifteen thousand—now it numbered several hundred thousand people, with most of the growth due to the increase in railway services offering a fast means of travel into London. As she watched workers and shoppers disembark at Croydon station, Maisie thought half the town's population must have been on that very train.

Arriving at Brighton station in darkness, Maisie took a taxi-cab to a small whitewashed hotel along the seafront, predictably named "Sea View." Many guesthouses had only recently opened in readiness for Easter and the summer season, though some were looking tired, as if from the sheer effort of remaining in business at a time when few people had the funds for holidays by the sea. The taxi-cab driver had been true to his word and dropped her at a hotel "good enough for a lady traveling on her own." He was also helpful, informing her where she could find the street she was looking for, so she asked him if he could collect her at nine the following morning; she would require his services for about two hours, after which she planned to catch a train back to London at eleven.

"I'll pick you up in the morning, then. My name's Sid Mayfield—tell Mrs. Hicks in there who brought you; it never hurts to let her know. And thank you for the work, madam—it's still been a bit slow, even with the nice weather."

Maisie paid Mayfield and stepped out of the motor car. A woman at the window, a green-and-yellow scarf covering hair set in curlers, waved to the driver, then smiled and motioned to Maisie that she was coming to open the door.

"Good evening, madam. Windy old night out there. You've come in late—here until Monday, are you?"

"Just until tomorrow morning, thank you."

Maisie felt warmed by her busyness, by her chatter, and, not least, by the fire in the drawing room grate, visible from the entrance hall, its soothing flames countering the chill coastal air outside.

"I'll have a fire lit in your room and a hot water bottle in the bed before you turn in. I don't have a proper supper this evening, on account of the time of year, but I can do a beef barley soup—will that do?" The woman paused only long enough for Maisie to draw breath to answer before she went on. "Now then, here's my rate for the night, and if you wouldn't mind signing my book here. Cash in advance, if you don't mind, Miss—?" She seemed to press her chin down into her neck when she asked for payment, and Maisie thought the expression could become confrontational with ease, if a customer tried to negotiate payment terms.

"Dobbs. Miss Maisie Dobbs. Soup would be lovely—and if you've enough hot water for a bath, I would be grateful. In any case, let me pay you now." Maisie reached into her shoulder bag and took out her purse. Mrs. Hicks seemed relieved as she pocketed the coins.

"A hot bath—of course—I pride myself on my establishment. Let me show you up."

Mrs. Hicks led the way upstairs, the seams on her stockings clearly visible, zigzagging along each lower calf, as if she had dressed in a hurry. She escorted Maisie to a room decorated in unmatching chintz fabrics; the overall impression was of a garden of roses left to grow wild. Wind rattled against French windows, beyond which a small filigree balcony allowed guests to enjoy a Channel view in summer. Mrs. Hicks drew the rose-bedecked curtains and turned to Maisie.

"There, we don't want any drafts, do we? Let me take you along to the facilities."

The bathroom was spacious, heated by bulbous brown radiators that were warm, not hot to the touch, and with a towel rail in front.

"I'll leave you to yourself then. Supper in half an hour? Will that do?"

"Lovely, thank you, Mrs. Hicks."

In her room once more, Maisie unpacked her overnight bag, took off her coat and hat, gathered her towel, and made her way along to the bathroom, where a girl was kneeling next to the claw-foot bathtub with her hand under the tap.

"Mrs. Hicks said to run the bath for you, madam."

"That's all right, I can do it myself now. Thank you."

As soon as the girl left, Maisie turned the key in the lock, tested the heat of the water with her hand, and allowed the tap to run a little longer before stepping into the hot bath. She lowered herself into the water, hoping its heat might soften the ache left by the day's events. Cupping water in both hands, she rinsed her face and leaned back against the enamel tub.

Maurice had spoken to her, more than once, about the importance of seeking distinctions when asking others to describe their feelings, or when trying to identify emotions in the self. At first she had not understood, and now, her eyes closed, she recalled the moment, the conversation when he said to her, "To just say, 'I'm sad,' isn't enough. To gain greater understanding of the situation, of yourself or another, you must search for a word that better describes the moment. Sometimes we say we're sad when we would be better served by using the word *melancholy*, for example. Sometimes anger can be more accurately described as *frustration*. The distinction helps us identify a path through the maze of emotion—and emotions can be debilitating, can paralyze us if we allow them power, and we do that when we fail to be precise. It's rather like accruing knowledge of your enemy so that you can defeat him. So, Maisie, how do you feel?"

"Guilty," said Maisie aloud, and with only a second's hesitation.

She scooped more water onto her face and rubbed her eyes. "I feel responsible, and I feel guilty. I feel inept. I feel inept in my work and I feel inept when it comes to James." She splashed her hand down into the water. "I feel as if I am doing everything bloody wrong, and half the time I can't get enough air in my lungs, otherwise I would probably scream!"

"You all right, dear?" a voice called from the other side of the bath-room door. "Your supper's ready when you are."

"Thank you, Mrs. Hicks. I won't be long," Maisie called back. She felt annoyance building within her and acknowledged, too, her rising temper. She wanted to be out of this guesthouse, away from the busy-body woman with her curlers and chins, her payment in advance and her overbearing pride; and she couldn't wait to get home to her flat again—home to the place where she could do what she pleased, when she pleased. She couldn't do that at The Dower House—there always seemed to be someone taking account of what she was about, and when. If she asked the gardener to do something different—plant a new shrub, for example—it was more than likely that Lady Rowan would remark on the new development. It was never exactly a nega-tive comment, but an expressed opinion all the same. "Mr. Buckle told me you'd asked him to plant wisteria at the front of the house. You're not taking out Maurice's roses, are you?" Then there was her father. He always knew when James was with her, and when he wasn't, and of course, the fact that he was courting Mrs. Bromley—Maurice's housekeeper, whom she'd asked to stay on when the house became hers—meant he probably knew more than he let on. She realized how much she minded him knowing. She minded him worrying that she might have settled for something less than a commitment from James, though she knew it was she who was faltering when it came to the question of a promise. And what was a commitment if not a promise?

"Guilty. That's what I am. And I have to put everything right." Maisie lifted herself out of the bath, clasped the warm towel to her body, and readied herself to go down to the dining room for supper. She hoped the well-meaning but tiresome Mrs. Hicks would leave her in peace.

The proprietress must have been starved for company, or simply happy to have a paying guest on a gusty Friday evening. She pulled up a chair and talked, jumping from one subject to another, as Maisie ate the soup, occasionally dipping bread into the brown, hearty broth as she nodded her head, agreeing with whatever the woman said. Maisie thought she seemed like a talking machine, needing only a word to keep her going.

"I said to Mr. Jones, the butcher, I said, 'My customers want the very best, you know. It might only be a simple stew, but it will be the best stew—tasty and fresh.' And he told me, he said, 'Madam, I like serving a customer who has high standards.' And that's what I have here, high standards."

"Yes, I can see—"

"Now, there was this one couple, came in a week or so ago. Not a wedding ring to be seen, and I said to them, I said—"

And so she went on until Maisie pronounced the soup the best she'd ever eaten; in fact, it had made her so content she really had to turn in for the night.

A welcoming coal fire warmed the room, and a scuttle had been left so that Maisie could make up the embers before she went to bed. Her evening practice of meditation had been abandoned of late, and she realized that she felt the absence of the deliberate quiet it offered. In this stilling of mind and body it was as if she became rooted, and in that time she could plumb the depths of more than simply her own experience to answer questions. It often felt as if she had opened a vein of thoughts that were new to her, yet at once timeless, and she was served well by her practice, not least in the calm it bestowed upon her.

She sat for some time on the floor, her legs crossed, her eyes closed, and her hands one on top of the other in her lap with thumbs just one rice grain's width apart. When she opened her eyes, it was as if she had been sitting for just a moment or two. Later, as she lay in bed, her eyes heavy as she watched flames lick around small red-hot caverns created by the burning coals, Maisie remembered something Maurice had said to her a long time ago.

"This work, Maisie, will touch you in many ways. In delving into the secrets held by the dead, by the living, and by those who have come to harm and caused harm, you will learn much about yourself. You will be challenged by this knowledge, and will be drawn to self-examination and—perhaps—recrimination. On the one hand, this is not without merit, and can offer a depth of understanding not previously available to you. But be warned—your allegiance must first be to your client, to those whose lives are touched by your work. There will be time enough afterwards to allow yourself the luxury of self-inquiry. When you are working on a case, that is to be the focus of your attention. You are the engine that drives the investigation, you are not the destination—attend to yourself only as required to reach that destination. Now, is that clear?"

She had answered that it was clear, though she had come to understand, sometimes painfully, that clarity developed slowly, and she had learned that particular lesson anew with each case. Now, in the darkness, with the sound of waves crashing across the seafront beyond the chintz curtains and filigree balcony, Maisie knew she had to deal with her guilt, with her mistakes, and she had to remember that the investigation was about gentle Eddie Petitt's death. Her duty was not only to those left heartbroken by his passing, but to truth itself. And tomorrow she would visit another bereaved mother who had lost her son.

T hem waves came in last night, eh, Miss Dobbs? Keep you awake, did they?" Sid Mayfield opened the passenger door for Maisie, ensuring that the hem of her coat was tucked inside before closing the door and taking the driver's seat. "I did us a favor last night, after I dropped you off. When you told me the name of the lady you were looking for, I went to the pub at the end of the road there and I found out the exact—the exact, mind—address, so we're in luck, eh, Miss?" Mayfield turned to face Maisie and smiled, revealing several missing teeth.

"That is good news, Mr. Mayfield. That being the case, I hope we won't be too early."

"It might take us about twenty minutes, half an hour to get there, as it's just outside the town—on my way home, so don't you worry, I didn't go too far out of my way last night."

"Thank you."

Maisie understood why Mrs. Hicks and Sid Mayfield were a good commercial team but wondered how either one of them managed to get a word in edgewise, given the chatter that both seemed to thoroughly enjoy. Mayfield's running commentary began with a summing up of the last season, and how they were hoping for a bumper spring, summer, and autumn. He talked about the shows coming to town—they were much better when he was a boy, mind, what with the old music halls still doing well; about the pier amusements—not what they were in his day; and about the number of motor cars queuing up to get into the town on a summer's day—too many, and the roads not big enough to cope, and where were they all going to park, anyway? Having only responded with comments such as "Really?" or "Well, I never," or "And then what happened?" Maisie was relieved when they reached Shell Close, the street where Mildred Taylor lived. Mayfield stopped at the end of the road.

"It's number six, Miss. Shall I wait here, or outside the house?"

"Definitely here. I'll walk the rest of the way. I might be an hour or so—or I might even be back in two minutes, you never know."

Mayfield walked around to open the passenger door, and Maisie stepped out, her briefcase in her left hand, her right hand firmly holding her hat in place.

"You want to keep your hand right there, Miss Dobbs. You don't want to go chasing that hat down the road."

Maisie smiled and went on her way.

Shell Close comprised a series of Victorian semidetached houses, each with a front door and bay window, and a path on one side leading to the back of the house. The path to the front door of number six was flanked by splashes of color from spring flowers, and of buds promising an even more colorful garden in summer. The door, painted in a matte maroon color, was half-paned with stained glass formed in the shape of a bouquet of lilies. In recognition of this embellishment, a sign attached to the brickwork bore the name "The Lillies." She lifted the brass door knocker and made three sharp raps.

From the depths of the house she could hear voices; then a woman walked towards the door—Maisie could see her shadowy outline approaching through the glass. The door opened.

"Mrs. Taylor?"

"Yes." The woman smiled, her eyes revealing relief that it was a woman who had come to call, though she seemed somewhat wary nevertheless.

"My name is Maisie Dobbs. I wonder if I might see your sister, Mrs. Soames." She reached into her document case. "Here's my card. I'd be grateful if you could tell her that it's about Mr. Edwin Pettit—my family were his neighbors in London, when I was a child."

The woman took the card, half-closed the door, and went back towards the kitchen. Maisie could hear the murmur of a conversation kept deliberately low; then Mrs. Taylor came to the door again.

"Come in, Miss Dobbs. We're in the kitchen, if you don't mind."

She stepped around Maisie and led the way past a front parlor and a dining room, to the spacious kitchen with an open range and a steaming kettle above the hot plate. Not a plate, cup, saucer, dish, or item of cutlery was out of place.

Pauline Soames rose from the table to greet Maisie, the calling card still in her left hand. Both Mildred Taylor and Pauline Soames were dressed in plain skirts and blouses, each with a cardigan buttoned to the neck, and each wearing small pearl earrings. And though Mrs. Taylor was just a little heavier, it was clear the women were twins. Maisie thought they probably did not plan to dress alike, but in the way that there is a depth of communication between siblings so close, it no doubt caused them some amusement when they came down in the morning to find that they had chosen almost identical clothing.

Before Mrs. Soames could speak, however, her sister had revealed herself to be the more dominant of the two.

"I suspect you know that my sister here has suffered a most difficult bereavement, losing her son only a year after her husband died. Did you know that, Miss Dobbs?"

Maisie tempered her voice to meet the occasion. "Yes, Mrs. Taylor, I knew about Mrs. Soames' recent loss, although I wasn't aware that Mr. Soames *senior* had passed so recently." She turned to the bereaved woman. "I am deeply sorry. I know this is not the best time for me to visit, and I wouldn't be here today if it were not a matter of some import. I wanted to talk to you about Eddie Pettit, if I may." Maisie paused; Soames nodded, her eyes welling as she reached for her sister's hand.

"I come from Lambeth, Mrs. Soames—in fact, I went to the same school as Eddie. You'd married and left by the time I started school, otherwise you'd have been my teacher too."

"I loved teaching at that school, Miss Dobbs. I was always being asked why I went there to teach—people made it seem as if little urchins from Lambeth with not a pair of shoes between them weren't deserving of an education." She continued speaking in a way that suggested she was putting off whatever question might come next. "Not that it was easy, no, not in a million years, but you know, in every child there's a spark, and you just have to find that spark and you can light the fire. I loved it when I found that spark—made it all worthwhile. But of course I had to leave when I married, it was the rule."

"You found the spark in Eddie, didn't you?"

"Oh yes. There was a lovely light about Eddie Pettit—an unworldliness you didn't see much in those parts. The other teachers said it was because he was nothing more than the local idiot, that he didn't have it in him to know anything. But to me the guilelessness of the boy—his innocence—was the very thing that held promise; a lot of the knowledge the other children had was not the sort you like to see in a child—poverty, a good whipping every night at home, going out to work before they came to school or after school. No wonder so many got into trouble. Not all parents were like that, of course—there were some strong families on the streets of Lambeth; poor, but responsible with it."

Maisie allowed the woman to speak freely without interrupting. There was time enough to pepper questions into the conversation; for now she wanted only to gain her trust.

"You're spoken of highly to this day, Mrs. Soames. I know Mrs. Pettit thought the world of you, for what you did for Eddie."

"Oh, a remarkable girl, Maud Pettit. Exceptional, when you consider what she came out of. She was very anxious for Eddie to learn to read and write—probably the only parent ever to come up to the school to see me. An old head on young shoulders. As far as many of them were concerned, the school was just a way-station for the children until they went out to work—twelve years old and one day you're in school, the next you're working at Bookhams, or Starlings, or the pickle factory, or on the river. Or you're not working at all."

Mildred Taylor cleared her throat to speak. "My sister is very involved in trying to change the school leaving age, you know. And in bringing more opportunity to the run-down areas. Very political, aren't you, my dear?"

Pauline Soames nodded and smiled at her sister, then turned to Maisie. "What can I tell you about Eddie?"

"I understand you'd been giving him lessons in the past few months. When did he come to you?"

Soames sighed. "It must have been last summer—perhaps the end of the summer, I can't quite remember." She leaned forward towards Maisie, placing her elbows on the table and setting Maisie's card in front of her. "What you should know is that Eddie was both simple and a bit more complicated, all at the same time. You knew him, so I believe you might understand exactly what I mean—though you're a good bit younger than Eddie." She paused again. "His mother had always pushed him to do more—and though that wasn't exactly bad, I sometimes thought she didn't need to press him. You see, for example, she wanted him to note things down—his hours, his earnings, his customers—yet she of all people knew that Eddie just remembered these things. He could tell you to the farthing how much money had passed his hands between this day and that day. He knew the names of his customers and their addresses—once he'd got over the initial problem of going to wherever they were, of finding his way there and back. But I suppose someone had suggested to her that there might be those who would take advantage of Eddie, so she started to nag him to write it all down. And I think that in her concern about what might happen to him when she went, she began to pass on that worry to him—Eddie told me she'd told him he needed to learn his letters properly, because he had to look after himself when she was dead and gone. Now, that's all very well—she wouldn't be the first anxious mother to chase after a child—but it just added a thread of concern, a weight Eddie found hard to bear." She shook her head. "You see, Eddie was a boy—and man—who had to travel light, if you know what I mean. Everything had to be simple, or the spark would just . . . would just . . . it would just go out."

Maisie nodded. "I've heard you were a wonderful teacher, Miss Soames."

"I missed it very much when I married. But then, later, I had my children, and found joy in teaching them, too."

"May I ask, what did you think when you first discovered that Eddie was dead?"

Maisie noticed Mildred Taylor squeeze her sister's hand, giving a slight shake of her head. The former teacher nodded. She would answer.

"I was shocked beyond belief. It was as if something very dear had been taken from this world. You see—and I know how this might sound, but I will say it anyway—there was that innocence about Eddie, and I know I'm repeating myself, and I would imagine many have said the same thing—but when I think of Eddie, I think of him as if he were a flower blooming amid the rocks and stones. Lambeth can be a dark place, and indeed, unless you've got a bit of money put by, there seems to be such a darkness going on in the world these days. But Eddie, in his simplemindedness, had a light about him. He didn't grasp good and evil, he only knew his world, what was expected of him, and the love of his mother, of her friend Jennie, and let's not forget, every single horse he ever laid a hand upon." She rubbed her throat and in silence rose and stepped over to the tap. As she ran water into a glass, her hands were shaking; when she turned back to Maisie, she leaned against the sink for support. "This may sound strange, and perhaps not easy to grasp, but it's as if we who knew Eddie have lost something precious. We've lost that lovely simplicity that he brought with him wherever he went—and I suppose it's fortunate that there are people who had that instinct about him, though they might never have put words to the sense of it." She sipped her water.

Maisie nodded. "You're right, Mrs. Soames. I've been talking to the men at the market who knew Eddie, and they've said the same thing, though without your eloquence." She paused for a moment. "They came to me because they believe that Eddie's death was no accident." She paused again, picking over her words as if making her way across a rushing stream on stepping-stones. "You have my card, Mrs. Soames. You know I am an investigator, and because of where I come from, and because I knew Eddie, the men have asked me to look into the circumstances surrounding his death. I have made a promise that whatever the cause, whether it was an accident or a deliberate act that led to his death, I will find out what happened to him. That's why I want to ask you about Bartholomew."

"Polly, you don't have to answer Miss Dobbs, you know." Mildred

Taylor folded her arms. "She's not the police, and she's very nice, but I don't want you pulled this way and that by an inquiry agent. You've been through quite enough already."

Pauline Soames refilled her water glass and took her seat once more. "That's all right, Milly. It'll probably do me good." She turned to Maisie. "Please, go on, Miss Dobbs."

"Tell me about Eddie and Bart—they knew each other, didn't they?"

Soames nodded. "Yes. Eddie had set his mind to finding out where I lived, because he wanted to learn to read properly. He knew some words, and he could express himself to a point, but he wanted to show his mother that he could accomplish the task of reading and writing. I'd always had a soft spot for him—you can probably tell—so I said I would, and that he should come to my house once a week, and I'd also give him some homework—just a bit. Bart came to visit one day when Eddie was there. In fact, I'd told him about Eddie, so he must have known he would be there. Bart was very gentle with him, yet didn't talk down to him. No, he spoke to him man to man, but made allowances for him. Eddie seemed to really appreciate it, and took a liking to Bart. In fact, Bart would help him with his lessons, which bolstered Eddie a bit, you know, another man reading with him. And Bart took an interest in Eddie's work, asked about what he did, how long he'd been doing it, who he worked for. He even bought him a lovely notebook with gold lettering. And though Eddie was shy with my son at first, he became quite chatty—well, chatty for Eddie. I think it gave him a boost in confidence, to tell you the truth."

Maisie traced a pattern on the tablecloth with her finger. "Did Bart see Eddie at other times, do you know? Or did they meet only at your house?"

"Oh, I can't say. I would imagine not—but there again, they might have, though Bart never mentioned it. As I said, Bart treated Eddie like an equal, so he might have seen him again and never thought to tell me."

Maisie drew breath, knowing she must navigate troubled waters. "Your son died in a tragic accident, I understand. Do you know what happened?"

"Pol—"

"I'm all right, Milly. I told you." Soames turned again to Maisie. "My son fell from Lambeth Bridge in the dark of night. I was told he'd been seen drinking in The Prince's Tavern on the other side of the water, and that he was the worse for wear when he set off to go home. There was a thick smog that night, and they believe he lost his footing and managed to pitch himself over the side."

"And what do you think?" Maisie did not look away as she asked the question.

Pauline Soames returned Maisie's gaze, though her thoughts seemed distant.

"I have my doubts, Miss Dobbs. I have my doubts. My son had stepped on a few toes in his time—he was a thorough and inquisitive journalist, and he had a way of sniffing around in places where people were up to no good. He didn't like working for the newspapers, because he said they were always kowtowing to someone, somewhere, and that the big nobs were in the pockets of even bigger nobs. So I have tormented myself with imaginings, I must confess. But at the same time, he was courting another writer by the name of Evelyn Butterworth, and though it had nothing to do with me, I do believe they were living under the same roof, and that it was probably not a very calm union—or whatever it might be called, so you never know . . ."

"Living in sin," said Mildred Taylor. "You can call it living in sin."

"No, Milly, that's not what I would call it, though I would rather they were courting and planning a wedding. But listen to me—talking as if it might happen any day now, when it won't ever happen now." Soames pulled a handkerchief from her skirt pocket.

"Do you have an address for Miss Butterworth? I would like to speak to her."

Pauline Soames wiped her eyes before answering. "I'll jot it down for you when you leave."

"Indeed." Maisie noticed that both sisters had looked at the kitchen clock, and she imagined them as children, Polly and Milly, identical twins in identical clothing. "But perhaps a couple more questions—if that's all right?"

"My sister's getting a bit tired, you know—she's been under a lot of strain."

"I can see that, Mrs. Taylor. I'll be very quick." Maisie leaned towards Pauline Soames. "What can you tell me about Jimmy Merton?"

The question was met with a heavy sigh. "I always liked to think I could find something good to say about every child I taught, no matter what their upbringing, no matter how the cross they bore might have affected their character and made them less than likable—but I never, ever met a meaner person than Jimmy Merton. He was trouble from the time he came into the classroom—if he came into the classroom—until the time he left. I breathed a sigh of relief on those days when I took the register and he wasn't there to answer to his name. I should have reported him to the school board inspector more often than I did, but most of the time I simply kept quiet because I dreaded seeing him walk into my room."

"I understand he was cruel to Eddie."

"He was—but what always surprised me was the fact that many of the children stuck up for Eddie. They'd tell him to clear off if they saw Jimmy coming, and though it was more than they dare do to square up to the bully, they helped Eddie when they could—as did the teachers. But you have to remember that with Jimmy, it was all he knew. He was beaten at home. All the Merton children were beaten by that father—so was his mother. The brute left her with a black eye when she was eight months gone with the youngest. That's who Jimmy learned from. The streets could be a difficult place to grow up, but the likes of the Merton family made it all the more dark for everyone." The woman rubbed her hand across her forehead. "I'm sorry, Miss Dobbs, what with not sleeping properly since my son died, and the wind last night, I am very tired."

"And I shall leave you in peace. You've been most kind, Mrs. Soames." Maisie paused, leaning forward to take the woman's hand in her own. "I thank you for your time—and for the way you helped Eddie. He was much loved, and you gave him respect, for which his friends are most grateful—they know how you took him under your wing."

Mildred Taylor touched Maisie's shoulder. It was time for her to leave. Without saying another word, Pauline Soames scribbled an address for Evelyn Butterworth and pressed it into Maisie's hand. Maisie thanked her and allowed her twin to escort her to the door. Mildred Taylor bid their guest good-bye, but before Maisie could turn and walk away, she added, "You did all right for yourself, all things considered, didn't you, Miss Dobbs? You look more like a gentlewoman than a girl from the streets. I thought it was only Charlie Chaplin who came out of Lambeth and did well for himself."

Maisie looked down at her hands as she pulled on her gloves. "I was lucky, Mrs. Taylor. I was very, very lucky. Thank you for your time—you've both been very kind." She placed her hand on her hat and set off along the path to the street. She turned to look back and wave once more, aware that the woman had not retreated into the house but was watching her. Mildred Taylor had been joined on the threshold by her sister, and Maisie had the impression that they were rather like characters from a storybook, or subtle caricatures on the back of a set of playing cards—indistinguishable sisters, one mirroring the other with her pleated skirt, her blouse and cardigan buttoned to the neck, the delicate pearl earrings, and both raising their hands at the same time. One a bereaved woman. The other her protector, the one who—without realizing it—in her manner had told Maisie that there was more to learn, that Pauline Soames—doubtless the younger of the two—had more to tell. And she was afraid, though Maisie suspected the woman was not sure who it was she should fear.

O ff to the station now, are we, Miss Dobbs?" Sid Mayfield held the door open for Maisie to board the motor car.

"Yes, please, Mr. Mayfield. I should be in good time for the next train up to Victoria."

"Plenty of time—you'll be up in London by noon at this rate."

"That's good. I'll be in trouble if I'm late."

"Uh-oh—that sounds dodgy to me."

Maisie laughed, then settled back in her seat while Sid drove towards the station. Tuning out the buzz of chatter as the taxi-cab driver went on about this and that—about the Saturday train service, and whether there might be a delay, because you never knew with trains—Maisie considered the meeting with Mrs. Soames in her sister's kitchen. The former teacher seemed to have a compassionate understanding of Eddie, and though there had been similar descriptions of him, each time someone else talked about Eddie, a light shone on another facet of his story; they were variations worth considering. Bart Soames was doubtless a kind man, generous with his time as far

CHAPTER SEVEN

❖❖❖

D arling, you must be exhausted." James pushed back his desk chair as Maisie entered the library. "I hope you've saved some energy for our outing."

Maisie gave in to his embrace and held him in return. She had expected him to be angry, put out that she had not been at Ebury Place the night before. She suspected he had buried his dismay with the intention of carrying on as if nothing were bothering him.

"Don't worry, I'll get my second wind. But I do have to place a couple of telephone calls before we leave for Richmond—and I must change my clothes."

"I'll leave you in peace then—would you like a bite to eat now, or shall we pull in at a pub on the way?"

"Yes, let's stop somewhere." Maisie lifted the telephone receiver, then called to James before he left the room. "Oh, James, what time shall we leave for the Hartmans' this evening?"

"About seven."

"Seven. All right . . ."

"Look, we don't have to go out this afternoon, not if you're tired."

"Of course we'll go. Let me make my telephone calls, then I'll take only a few minutes to change."

Maisie placed her first call to Scotland Yard, where Caldwell informed her that Billy had shown signs of improvement, and that Dr. Dene had visited again and given fresh instructions for the injured man's care.

"He knows what he's doing, that Dene," said Caldwell.

"Yes, I know." Maisie tried not to sound impatient with her questioning. "Do you have any more information on who the attackers might have been—and why they set upon Billy?"

"We're working on it; should have more on Monday."

"Right you are, Detective Inspector." She paused for a second before pressing another query. "I wonder, do you have a good liaison set up with the river police?"

"Certainly do, seeing as London's waterways are a convenient place to dispose of the recently bumped-off."

Maisie cringed. Recently bumped-off? Caldwell certainly knew how to construct a phrase when he liked. "I just wondered—"

"Yes, you sounded like you were wondering."

"I just wondered if you might have heard about a recent drowning, a man named Bartholomew Soames."

"Soames. I'll see what I can find out. To do with the death of Eddie Pettit?"

"The son of his former teacher. He died recently, suspected suicide. And he'd been quite friendly with Eddie, apparently."

"Let's not read too much into it," said Caldwell. "These things can send us off along the wrong path."

"Yes, I know that's only too true," said Maisie. "But I appreciate your time all the same, Inspector. I expect I'll be in touch again on Monday."

Maisie ended the call, waited for the signal to dial, and placed a call to Billy's house in Eltham. After eight rings, a breathless Sandra answered. "Hello!"

"Sandra, you sound overwhelmed."

"Not overwhelmed, Miss, but busy. I've got the boys sorted out, and I'm just about to feed the baby. Mrs. Partridge is sending Elinor over this evening, and I am sure she'll be better with little Meg here."

"What are the boys doing at the moment?"

"Making mud pies in the garden."

"Hmmm, enough said. I'll be there in about three quarters of an hour—we'll take them for a ride in the motor and wear them out."

"Only if you've time, Miss. I'm sure it would take their mind off things—they miss their mum and dad, and they're not the sort of children to sit quietly with a book."

"I see—they've been playing up a bit. I'll see you soon—and thank you, Sandra."

Maisie replaced the receiver as James came back into the library.

"Um, James. Slight change of plan today."

"I'm not sure whether to smile or frown. Where are we going?"

"First, to Eltham, to pick up Billy's boys. We'll take them for an outing in the motor—perhaps somewhere to walk or kick a ball around—then we'll find somewhere for tea and cakes afterwards. It'll do them a power of good."

"And you'll feel as if you're doing something for Billy."

Maisie nodded.

"Well, let's go then," James swept his hand towards the door.

"Thank you, James."

"As long as we're back in good time—we don't want to be late for the Hartman party."

Maisie thought the afternoon with young Billy and his brother, Bobby, had not only been good for the boys, but for James and herself. Playing with the children at the park had brought a lightness to the day for all concerned, and took her mind off her worries about her feelings for James or his expectations of her. He had graciously accommodated her desire to help the Beale family, and it had all been for the better. Now, as she opened the door of her wardrobe at Ebury Place, Maisie considered that perhaps their relationship was best enjoyed without scrutiny. And it occurred to her that she was so used to turning over everything in her mind, as if each thought were an intricate shell found at the beach, that she had never truly known the value in simply accepting things as they were. She couldn't help wondering if James could do the same. They might both benefit from a less intense analysis of their relationship.

Maisie flicked through a series of garments, taking stock. She was not one who would automatically consider several new evening gowns a necessary purchase for the season's social engagements, which meant she was usually pleased to receive any crumbs of unwanted couture falling from Priscilla's table; Priscilla was more than generous with clothes she had tired of, and Maisie never too proud to turn them down. Priscilla was an inch or two taller than Maisie, and a little broader across the shoulders—indeed, she had heard a woman at a supper in December referring to Priscilla as "that rather outspoken Amazon." Maisie usually took the clothing to Doreen Beale for alteration, glad that she could send some work in her direction. A pale gray silk dress seemed perfect for the evening party; it was not quite ankle length, with three-quarter-length sleeves, loose-fitting, and embellished with an embroidered band just above the hip in a lighter shade of gray. The layers of silk skimmed across her skin, clinging in places that rendered the dress both modest and sensuous at the same time. Yet as she was dressing, Maisie could already feel the dread rising within her. She was now equal to most of the guests in wealth and had no cause to feel inferior to any one of them. Feelings of inadequacy from earlier years had been replaced with something else—a sense that a sumptuous party during a time of great want was not quite the right thing to do. In truth, though, a social occasion such as the one she and James would attend this evening might be seen as frugal when compared to the parties of just eight or nine years earlier, parties she would neither have been invited to nor wanted to attend.

"Ready then?" James stepped from his dressing room, handsome in a black dinner jacket, starched white shirt, and bow tie. He was fiddling with cuff links bearing the Compton family crest when he looked up, saw Maisie, and stopped.

"You look quite stunning," he said.

"Here, let me help you, James." Maisie smiled. "You're all fingers and thumbs."

"It's playing with those boys—my heart's still racing from the exertion."

"Perhaps we can leave the party early," suggested Maisie. "Surely there will be so many guests, no one will notice if we sneak out before the small hours roll around."

"The Hartmans usually put on a good spread, but let's see how it goes. You're the one who's used to stealing away in the dead of night."

They smiled at each other and James took Maisie in his arms. "Everything will be all right, Maisie."

She nodded, knowing he was not referring to the party, but to the often sharp words that had crept into their exchanges of late.

The tall redbrick Knightsbridge home of Duncan and Rose Hartman was bubbling with guests by the time they arrived. An expansive foyer led to a drawing room with tall ceilings and large bay windows looking out to the street on two sides, and it seemed the men in their evening attire and women in many shades and hues of silk and satin moved in whirlpools, circling into conversations here before moving on to another group over there. A band played on a dais in the entrance hall, serenading partygoers with the latest jazz numbers, while those who were a bit peckish could choose from a bounty of food laid on in the dining room. Though the event was formal, there was to be no sit-down meal; clearly the hosts wanted their guests to mingle, chatter, laugh, and dance the night away, rather than find themselves locked in conversation with the person on either side of them.

As Maisie and James squeezed and wove their way through the foyer, a voice could be heard above the music, calling Maisie's name.

"Maisie! Maisie—over here!"

"Priscilla!" Maisie excused her way through the guests, feeling James in her wake, his hand at the small of her back as she reached Priscilla and her husband, Douglas.

"Would you believe it? I would say the whole of London has turned out for this party—I cannot imagine what might have overcome Rose to take on such a thing. I would be exhausted just thinking about it."

"Remember our New Year party at the end of '31, my dear? You didn't do so badly then, did you?" Douglas reached out to a passing waiter who was struggling not to lose his tray, and took two glasses of champagne with his one hand. "Not so fast, sonny," he called to the waiter, who was about to walk away.

James took another two glasses. "Thank you—but do pass this way in about fifteen minutes, won't you?" he said to the waiter.

"Ten will do nicely," added Priscilla.

The group laughed, toasted one another, then seemed to need a breath before conversation continued.

"Thank you, Priscilla, for sending Elinor to take care of Billy's children," said Maisie.

"Believe me, she will get them sorted out. I call her the Welsh terror. She and Sandra have worked it out between them: Sandra will stay until Monday morning, to give Elinor a hand, then Elinor will be there until Billy's wife returns to the house." Priscilla looked at Maisie and took another sip of her champagne. "Just tell me how you'd like to play your hand—I can have Elinor leave just before Doreen arrives home, or be there to help her out for as long as she's needed."

"I'll let you know, but I think having her leave before Doreen arrives home is best."

James and Douglas were deep in conversation, leaning towards each other to better hear themselves.

"Perhaps if we went into the dining room, it would be a bit easier to talk for a while, before the dancing really begins," said Priscilla.

"Good idea," said Maisie.

Priscilla tapped her husband on the shoulder and pointed towards the dining room. He nodded and the four nudged and shimmied their way through the throng. Maisie felt herself begin to relax when they reached the relative quiet of the room, with its high ceilings, paneled walls, and expanse of thick green carpet. At the far end, lush olive-green velvet curtains had been drawn to provide a backdrop to the broad table bearing the evening's feast. At one end a footman carved steaming slices of roast beef, while another served a selection of vegetables, and yet another poured gravy. As soon as a couple or a group of guests reached a table, a footman was waiting with wine. There were salads and breads, condiments, salvers of shellfish kept cool on mountains of shaved ice, and cold cuts fanned out on platters. Some guests preferred to stand, clustered against the wall while balancing a plate heaped with delicacies, a glass of wine, and conversation.

"Let's sit over there," said James, nodding towards a table set for four.

"My feet are rather killing me already," said Priscilla.

"In the choice between comfort and style, my wife will choose style every time," said Douglas.

"I never thought I would hear myself say this, but I think I might like to leave this party earlier than usual, my love—I cannot hear myself think out there," said Priscilla.

"Maisie probably feels the same, don't you, darling?" James rested his arm along the back of Maisie's chair.

"I've had a busy week, and of course, we went over to see the Beale boys today, so we're both quite worn out," said Maisie.

"Now you know what it's like! When the toads are asleep and quiet, I breathe a sigh of relief and slump into the chair—even with the amazing Elinor," said Priscilla.

"So make the most of the peace and quiet now, you two!" Douglas raised his glass to James and Maisie, and leaned to kiss his wife on the cheek.

Maisie was quick to change the subject. "How's work, Douglas? Priscilla tells me you're contributing regularly to the *New Statesman* now."

Douglas nodded. "Thank goodness! And my latest book has done well—though I think rather eclipsed by Winston Churchill's, which seems to be in all the bookshops."

"Oh dear, I feel rather a Philistine," said James. "I think I've missed that one."

"Came out not that long ago," said Douglas.

"Even I've dipped into it," said Priscilla. "It's a collection of essays, some of them written in years past. Oh dear, what's it called? Now my memory's going." She frowned as she looked at her husband.

"*Thoughts and Adventures*," said Douglas. "It's well worth reading— I'll send a copy to you, James. I bought the book and then received another as a gift."

"Thank you—look forward to reading it," said James.

"Is there another book on the horizon, Douglas?" Maisie took a sip of champagne; her interest in Douglas' work was genuine.

"Oh, I've been taking a little time to myself, and with Priscilla and the boys, so I've given Sandra a bit of time off. It's been all work and no play for a while—not what I planned at all!"

The group laughed, and it seemed that all too soon they were discovered by their hostess, who herded them out of the dining room to enjoy the dancing. Priscilla and Douglas were swept along by the tide of people, and Maisie soon lost sight of them among the guests. As others moved on into one of the many reception rooms at the Hartman residence, to talk, to dine or to dance, the crowd seemed to have thinned.

"Shall we have a dance or two, then call it a night?" said James.

"Yes, let's do that. How about this number? Think you can keep up with me, James?"

"Always." He took her left hand in his, placed his right arm around her waist, and led her onto the dance floor.

t was after midnight when they arrived back at 15 Ebury Place. She thought about the party while applying cold cream to remove the light dusting of rouge on her cheeks. It was the brief conversation with Douglas that she reflected upon, for she had a distinct feeling that her best friend's beloved husband was lying to her. Of course, it might not be a significant lapse of truthfulness, but it bothered her all the same. She liked Douglas very much. He was a person of profound dignity, one who measured his words with care and gave thought to those issues that troubled him, and he always seemed to reach a balanced view of a given situation. She knew he adored her friend, and that alone stood for a lot in Maisie's book. But why would Douglas not tell the truth? Hadn't Sandra said he had taken on a new assignment of some sort? She thought about it, then told herself that it was absolutely nothing to do with her—and frankly, she had enough to worry about at the present time. But the sense of a lie niggled her all the same.

was so glad when Elinor arrived on Saturday night—you wouldn't believe it, she sorted those boys out in next to no time, and had the baby fed and asleep just like that." Sandra snapped her fingers. "And she charmed the old lady, who—would you know it?—had a Welsh granny and knew a few words of Welsh, so that endeared them to each other, Billy's mum and Elinor. Did Billy ever tell you that, about his mum? That she had a bit of Welsh in her? Mind you, it wouldn't surprise me if he didn't know. Anyway, Mrs. Partridge is a gem to have sent Elinor round. Apparently she's going over there herself this morning—I can just see the looks on the neighbors' faces when she pulls up in front of the house in that bright-blue posh motor of hers."

Maisie noticed that she had barely arrived at the office before Sandra began her account of the last few days, as well as the week ahead. "And I'm in for a busy time of it after all, what with my work for college and everything else," continued Sandra. "Mr. Partridge has started working on a new book—he telephoned me right here this morning. As I told you, at first he didn't want my help, but now he says he's got a lot to do, and it's very important. He also said it's confidential, but I don't suppose he meant you, being as you're all friends. Anyway, I have to look after his other matters—correspondence and what have you—so he can get on with it." She looked up at Maisie. "And I've had an idea."

"What's that, Sandra?" Maisie replaced the telephone receiver in its cradle. She had begun to place a call to Scotland Yard, but Sandra's expression more than her words caught her attention.

"I've been thinking," said Sandra, "and here's what I've come up with: I know Billy was trying to find out information on what happened to Eddie Pettit, and who might have wanted him harmed, and I thought I might be able to do it instead, on account of him being in hospital."

"No, Sandra. I can't have you snooping around Bookhams, not in light of what's happened to Billy. It's too risky. I will have to think of another means of assessing what's going on there—if anything is going on at all. We also have to consider that the attack on Billy might have been random, and nothing to do with Eddie Pettit's death."

"But listen, Miss—"

"Sandra—no. You're valuable to me here and now, and you're more than busy, anyway. The very fact that Billy was set upon in such a violent manner is cause for deep concern, and it's my job to get to the bottom of it without risking harm to anyone else's life. Now then, let that be the end of it." Maisie paused and rubbed her neck. "Oh dear, I am sorry, that sounded so ungrateful. You are an asset to the business, Sandra, and I have such an admiration for you—perhaps I should tell you that more often. You've gone through a loss in the past year that might have broken a lesser person, and I cannot allow you to do anything that might jeopardize your well-being."

Sandra was silent for a few seconds, drawing breath as if to counter Maisie's instruction, and then seemed to think better of it.

"All right, Miss," she said. "I'll just get on and type these reports. And what do you want me to do about these three smaller cases that Billy was working on?"

"Let's talk about those when I've had a chance to look through his notes." Maisie looked at Sandra and saw how keen she was to be of service. "Perhaps there's something you can take over for him." She remembered an old saying, that if you gave a job to your busiest employee, you could expect it to be done properly.

"Right you are, I'll do a good job. I promise."

Maisie nodded. "Yes, I know you will. Now, let me just make this call to our friend at Scotland Yard." She picked up the telephone receiver and dialed.

"Detective Inspector Caldwell."

"Could have set my watch by you, Miss Dobbs. First thing in the morning, and there you are—like clockwork."

"Happy to be of service, Inspector." Maisie smiled. After a very shaky start, when Caldwell was promoted to take the place of Detective Chief Inspector Richard Stratton, they now enjoyed something of a rapport, if one marked by the odd sarcastic comment or two. However, she had learned to counter like with like and had discovered that he was actually warmer when a little friction entered the dialogue. It was as if it were a game to be played, and he rather enjoyed the challenge.

"Right then, the river police." He paused. "Did you know, by the way—and here's a bit of history for you, Miss Dobbs—that our esteemed brethren, the river police, otherwise known as the Thames Division, were the first police in London? Interesting, that, don't you think?"

Maisie sighed. Caldwell was unusually loquacious this morning. "Actually, that's something I know. My grandfather was a lighterman, so he was on first-name terms with a few of them."

Caldwell went on without acknowledging Maisie's comment. "Funny blokes, though. Ask them how they are, and they start to tell you how many jumpers they've dragged out of the drink during their shift, dead or alive, as if it's a game of catch. Not my idea of a day's fishing, I must say."

Maisie felt herself getting a little impatient. "Did you discover anything about Bartholomew Soames?"

"Yes, I did. He was a jumper. Drunk himself silly, then whoops, over the side of Lambeth Bridge, straight into the murky waters of London's most famous river, held with great affection by us all."

Maisie rolled her eyes and waited for Caldwell to continue.

"But I do have the name of the constable who tried to revive him, and if you go down to the Embankment—I'll give you exact directions—you'll find him there at about half-past ten. And do report back to me, won't you?"

"Of course—and thank you. I appreciate your assistance in this matter." If Caldwell thought Bartholomew Soames' death important with regard to either the attack on Billy or the death of Eddie Pettit, he would surely not have allowed her to meet the police constable.

"Whatever helps, Miss Dobbs. We're still on the case of Mr. Beale's attack and hope to make an arrest in the not-too-distant future."

"You do?"

"Can't say anything yet, but I might be able to let you know more when you telephone in after you've seen Constable Dawkins, Thames Division. He'll be mucking about on his boat at Waterloo Pier, the floating pontoon. And don't worry, he'll recognize you—I've told him what you look like."

"Oh dear."

"Yes. I said, 'Worried-looking woman with a hat pulled down over her eyes, but nicely turned out. Usually carries a briefcase.' You don't see many ladies carrying document cases."

"I don't think that's quite true, but anyway, I am sure we'll find each other."

"I'll talk to you later, Miss Dobbs."

"Yes, indeed."

Her second call was to Priscilla, to make arrangements to meet for afternoon tea at Fortnum and Mason, following Priscilla's visit to the Beale household. She would have liked to ask Priscilla not to overwhelm Billy's mother with her ebullient and commanding manner, but as her friend was being generous with her time and her sons' nanny, she considered such concerns best left unspoken.

"Sandra, I'm going out shortly. I'm to meet a certain Constable Dawkins of the Thames Division at half past ten, then I want to see if I can locate a woman named Evelyn Butterworth, so you'll probably be gone by the time I'm back here in the office. I want to see Billy if I can, and—oh dear, this will be difficult—Doreen as well. She rather hates me at the moment, but I want to assure her that all is well with her children."

"She'll get over it, Miss Dobbs. It's the shock, that's all. Shock can cause you to say and do terrible things."

Maisie nodded. "I suppose we've both been in that situation."

"Yes, Miss. I suppose we have." Sandra smiled. "Oh, Miss Dobbs. I wanted to remind you that I'll be moving out of the flat on Saturday afternoon—you'll have your spare room back again. We've paid the deposit on a flat on the other side of Gower Street, us girls, and the landlord said we can take our things over as soon as we like."

"Sandra, forgive me, I'd forgotten all about your move. Look, can I do anything? Can you manage? Let me—"

"No, thank you all the same, Miss Dobbs," Sandra interrupted. "You've done me a huge favor in allowing me to stay when I had nowhere else to go. I'm on my feet now, and I was lucky to meet the other women my age, and all of us looking for lodgings. We're pleased as punch about the flat—especially me, as it's not that far to walk here, and of course with Warren Street station so close, it doesn't take me that long to get over to Mr. Partridge's office. And it's not as if I have much to move anyway—so no thank you, I can manage it all on my own."

"Well," said Maisie, reflecting Sandra's smile, "it's just as well I'll be away then—at least I won't get under your feet. But let me know if you need anything at all, won't you?"

"Thank you, Miss Dobbs—you've been kind enough already."

Sandra went back to her typing while Maisie hesitated for a moment, then continued assessing the cases Billy was working on. She decided that two inquiries of no particular urgency could be handed to Sandra, and one she would take care of herself—an investigation on behalf of the owner of a small company where a member of staff had absconded with funds from a bank account; the member of staff was the owner's nephew, hence a desire not to alert the police. A short telephone call to the client would buy her some time, and she hoped to attend to the assignment while working on the fast-expanding case of Eddie Pettit.

Maisie pulled out the case map that she and Billy had begun for Eddie. She added new notes and, using the colored crayons, looped names together and circled questions. It was Maurice who had introduced Maisie to the process of building a "case map" when she was his assistant. A length of paper was drawn across and pinned to the table—the reverse side of a wallpaper offcut proved to be a cheap but ideal material for the job—and as more information was gathered, it was laid down on the paper in a nonlinear fashion. With the assignment forming the center of the map, new knowledge, thoughts, and hunches were added as they became apparent, sometimes in the form of a sketch, sometimes in words marked in red, green, or blue. "We must spark the imagination, Maisie, for the solution to any case is often the one that seems most unlikely, or so obvious that we can easily pass it by on the way to another thought that we consider to be the most brilliant deduction of the day. Everything must be added, even if we think we will embarrass ourselves by revealing what is going on in our minds—the most amazing facts can be revealed by our fictions, you know. We must be creative in our thinking."

Maisie smiled as she recalled Maurice's words, remembering the early days of their work together, a time when there was the excitement of a new case, yet before she was required to bear all responsibility. Maurice had been careful, adding more weight to her remit only gradually so she would not be overwhelmed at a point in her life when she was so vulnerable. He had understood that she had been as shell-shocked as any man who had been to war, though she had denied such an affliction. She had pushed back the memories, the visions that assailed her at night and drove sleep away when a terrible wakefulness enveloped her. At times she wondered how far she had come; the abyss was certainly at a greater distance now, though on occasion she felt as if a downdraft of random recollections was trying to drag her towards the brink again. The demons might be knocked down, but they weren't necessarily out for the count.

She tapped her red crayon on the edge of the map. *Eddie Pettit, Bartholomew Soames.* She wrote the names and linked them in red. She sat back and added *Bookhams,* followed by *Otterburn.* And then, a few inches away, she scribbled another name with a question mark and circled it. *Douglas?* Why had Douglas Partridge come to mind? She had been trained to look for anomalies, her senses alert to contradictions and coincidences—but didn't people often make comments that were out of alignment with something they'd mentioned before? She thought back over the past days. What was it Sandra had said? *He's working on something important and new.* And then at the party, Douglas more or less told her that he wasn't working on anything of note. Perhaps she was making too much of it. Was her anxiety to get to the bottom of Eddie's death taking her down misleading paths? She drew a series of question marks.

In time everything written on this map would be funneled into a solution. There was always a moment when order came to the case, when everything seemed to fall into place and an explanation for all that had come to pass rose up and unfurled like a bud coming into blossom. But she was nowhere near that moment. There was still much to be done, much to discover—and to understand.

Maisie buttoned her lightweight navy-blue jacket and pulled her cloche down further against cooler air coming off the water. Remembering what Caldwell had said about her hat, she pushed it up a little and paced back and forth close to Waterloo Pier. She held down her skirt to counter a gusty breeze that had blown along the Embankment, and had to pull down her hat again in case it was carried off. She was glad she wasn't the only woman striking various poses in her attempt to retain both hat and modesty.

"Miss Dobbs?"

Maisie turned to see a young man in police uniform.

"Yes—you must be PC Dawkins." She smiled, and decided to remove her hat; another sharp breeze caught her hair, which she struggled to keep out of her eyes.

"Come with me," said Dawkins. "There's a bloke with a van serving tea along here. We can talk out of this here wind. Not that it's cold, but it gets on your nerves—I know, I'm in it all day."

Maisie nodded and followed the constable, stopping alongside the van from which a gruff and gray man served tea across a counter lowered from the side of the vehicle. An iron brazier filled with hot coals had been set up on the pavement. Dawkins was right, it was not a cold day, but there was comfort in the fire's warmth.

"There you go, you stand there. Tea?" asked Dawkins

"This is on me—I'm grateful to you for seeing me. Would you like tea and a bun?"

"Very nice, Miss Dobbs. I'm a bit hungry on account of being on duty since early morning. And we've had a few jumpers, too; one of them—"

Maisie held up her hand, smiling as she remembered what Caldwell had said about the river police . . . *they start to tell you how many jumpers they've dragged out of the drink, dead or alive.*

"I'll just get the tea, Constable, before we're blown along the street."

Returning to their spot close to the brazier, Maisie handed a cup of tea to the policeman, on top of which she had balanced a plate with a buttered currant bun. "There you are, a little sustenance to keep you going."

"Thank you, Miss Dobbs," said Dawkins.

Maisie gripped another cup of tea in her other hand and took a sip as she stood shielded by the van. "That's better." She looked up at the tall, gangly young constable and judged him to be in his mid-twenties. "You must be perished when you're on the night shift, out there on the river for hours at night in the cold."

"Oh, it's not too bad, we've got warm clothes for the really bitter nights in winter, and that's when I take a flask of something hot out with me. I tell you, I sleep well when I get home, since I've been doing this job."

"Even having seen a few jumpers in the course of a shift?" asked Maisie.

The constable nodded. "You get used to it. In a way. Some are accidents, there's the odd murder, but most of them jump. And you get all sorts—the man who lost everything on the stock market, the woman who's lonely because her husband died in the war, or—this happened a few weeks ago—a woman who'd lost her sons in the war, all of them, and then when her husband passed on, she just didn't want to live anymore. Sad, that one. Made me think of my mum, because my father died at Gallipoli. I make sure she's never lonely, that there's always one of us going round, taking her out."

"You're a good son, PC Dawkins." Maisie took another sip of her tea. "What can you tell me about Bartholomew Soames? I understand you were the one who pulled him out."

"There's generally a couple of us on the boat, but I saw him and got my mate to keep the boat steady while I pulled him in—we've got this hook we use. It was a really cold night and, funnily enough, we'd got to him not long after he jumped." He bit off a chunk of his currant bun, chewed, and swallowed. "I needed that, Miss Dobbs," said Dawkins before continuing. "We got him out quickly, and wrapped him up in a blanket—we have a special drill, so we can get them out sharpish. Most of them are dead, and he was not far off. I tried to save him, but it was clear he was a goner—talk about blue. And I could hear he was trying to talk to me, so I leaned down to listen, and told him I was there, and could hear him. But his breath—that man must've downed a bottle of whiskey before he went over, probably trying to pluck up the courage to do it—some of them are like that, they either drink too much at the pub and fall in on their way home, or they drink to get drunk quickly and hope it takes them into the water and away, if you catch my drift." The PC clutched his white mug and looked towards the brazier's glowing coals.

"What did he say? Anything you could distinguish?"

"He said, 'Tell Eve . . . tell Eve,' then he coughed, caught his breath—one of his last—then he said something I couldn't make out; his voice was very quiet, what with all that water."

Maisie nodded. "So Mr. Soames didn't say anything else that you could hear."

The police constable looked down at his feet and shook his head. "No, nothing else. He just drifted off. People don't realize how cold that river can be, even in hot weather. It can kill you in seconds, at night especially—that's if you're not hit by a barge."

"I should have asked Detective Inspector Caldwell about this, but do you know who conducted the postmortem?"

"No, none of my business, that."

Maisie drank the remains of her tea and looked over towards the constable's mug. "Finished?"

He nodded.

"Would you like some more? Or another bun to take back to the pier with you?"

Dawkins shook his head. "No, thank you, Miss Dobbs. I'd better be getting back in any case, though I'm officially off duty now."

Maisie passed the mugs back to the old man who had served her, and as she turned, she saw PC Dawkins walking away at a brisk pace. "*Oh no you don't,*" she said to herself, and ran after him.

"PC Dawkins," she said, coming alongside him. "Gosh, that air can take a layer of skin off your lungs when you run, if you're not careful." She placed a hand on her chest, as if out of breath. "You never gave me a chance to thank you for your help."

Dawkins shrugged. "That's all right. Glad to be of service."

Maisie looked at the young man and leaned forward so that he had to look at her in return.

"What is it that you're afraid to tell me, PC Dawkins?"

The policeman sighed and looked around him, then back at Maisie. "That man, in the water, he said something else, but I was told—word came down very quickly through my sergeant—to keep quiet about it and not say anything to anyone. No one threatened me as such, but I reckon I could lose my job."

"If they sack you, I'll take you on. Don't worry about your job, PC Dawkins. It's the truth that counts."

"That's what my mum says. 'Tell the truth, son. We might not have much, but we've got our pride, and you can't go far wrong in telling the truth.' Mind you, she doesn't do my job."

"What did Bartholomew Soames say to you?"

"He said those other things, but the first thing he said, when I pulled him into the boat and turned him over, was 'Pushed. Pushed me.'"

"And what were you told?"

"I was told by my sergeant to just get on with it. That there are always jumpers who say that sort of thing because they don't want their relatives to know they committed suicide." He paused and scratched his cheek. "And the other thing—and I know this sounds strange—but he didn't sound drunk, this Bartholomew Soames. I mean, I'd pushed on his chest and there was whiskey coming up along with that rotten water, but it was as if it hadn't gone very far down here, inside." The constable pressed his hand against his chest, then tapped his head. "It wasn't up here. It was like the drink hadn't had time to get to his head. And that's funny, to me, because the ones who fall or jump are usually well gone—and despite what people say, a bit of cold water doesn't suddenly make a drunk think straight. This man was all but dead, but he was thinking straight. It was just that he was in such a bad way, couldn't get the words out."

Maisie looked up at the tall policeman, who at once seemed more boy than man. And for a second an image of Eddie came into her mind's eye and she wondered when childhood ended and the life of an adult began, and if there wasn't always, somewhere, the child inside.

"I thank you for your honesty, PC Dawkins. Your mum would be proud of you if she knew." Maisie opened her briefcase and took out a card. "Don't leave that around where anyone can see it, but let me know if you have any problems with your job."

"You know a few high-ups, don't you?" said Dawkins.

Maisie laughed and held out her hand. "If you can call Detective Inspector Caldwell a high-up, then I suppose I do."

"He is to me."

"Then that's good enough. Thank you again, Constable Dawkins. You've been most helpful."

Maisie turned and walked away, stopping once to look back. Dawkins was still standing there, looking at the card; then he folded it with care and placed it in his pocket before pulling up his collar and stepping forward into the wind.

CHAPTER EIGHT

❖

B illy was asleep when Maisie arrived at St. Thomas' Hospital, though she was able to speak to a police constable outside the private ward where he had been placed at police request. The policeman informed her that this would be his last day, and that Mr. Beale would be moved to the public ward tomorrow as there was no need to keep him sequestered; danger to him had been assessed and it was believed there was no further risk, that the attack was random and unlikely to be repeated.

Maisie could see the sense in this decision and agreed. Being situated in one of the main wards—where there would be nurses moving to and fro, the sound of hospital business and men talking to each other—might be good for Billy, stimulating his mind. He liked to show off his sense of humor, and he liked to be among others, so the move might well accelerate his recovery.

From St. Thomas' she traveled to another hospital, the psychiatric institution where Doreen had been taken while her mind was still so unsettled due to the attack on Billy. With more than a little trepidation, Maisie made her way to the office of Dr. Elsbeth Masters, with whom she had worked many years before and whom she had consulted on Doreen's condition during her last and most serious breakdown.

Elsbeth Masters was known not only for the excellence of her work with acute psychiatric cases but for her personal eccentricity. Born and raised in British East Africa, she was known to describe her childhood as being a time when she was "at one with the wild." She preferred to forgo footwear whenever possible, and was often to be seen kicking off her shoes, sometimes even in the midst of her rounds. A nurse would pick up the discarded shoes and follow Dr. Masters, ready to pass them to her when she realized she was in her stockinged feet and was wondering where she had left the heavy brogues she favored. Now in her later years, she was peppered with the freckles of age and intense exposure to the sun in her youth. Maisie had known the doctor since she'd returned to nursing and the care of shell-shocked men following her own wounding in the war. Masters was now in charge of Doreen's case.

"The trouble is, Maisie," said Masters, "this all happened—the attack on her husband—during a very vulnerable time for Mrs. Beale. Granted, she was well on her way to recovery, but I had been most concerned about the pregnancy in the first place—it's too simplistic to assume that she was trying to recreate the child she'd lost, but on the other hand, her state of mind and the distress accompanying loss rendered her worthy of continued observation. And she was doing quite well, but as I am sure you understand, that doesn't mean the mind can take on the huge responsibility that comes with caring for an infant—by the way, do you know what's happening with the children?"

"It's all in hand. My friend, Mrs. Priscilla Partridge, has sent her nanny to look after the boys and the young baby. She's an efficient young woman, well able to bear the weight of responsibility in this case. And of course Mrs. Beale senior is there and can help, though she couldn't have taken on all three children alone."

Masters nodded and looked at Maisie directly; she was known for her compassionate yet often brutal honesty. "She won't see you, Maisie. In her state of mind, Doreen Beale needs someone to blame, something concrete to attack in order to release the anger and despair, so she's holding you responsible. Of course, that will, hopefully, change, and I will make sure she knows the children are in very good hands."

"She's right—I am responsible. I asked her husband to go to the place where he was attacked, so it's up to me to put things right. "

Masters continued to meet Maisie's eyes without deflecting her attention as she listened to Maisie. She slipped off her shoes—as was her habit—and rested one foot on top of the other.

"If you step out of yourself, Maisie, you will see what you're doing."

Maisie frowned and shifted in her chair. "Dr. Masters, I really don't know what you mean."

"I'm not your doctor, Maisie, but I knew you years ago, when you returned from convalescence following your wounding in the war, and since we rekindled our professional dealings with each other, it has not gone beyond my notice that you have struggled." Masters picked up a pen and tapped it on the desk. "There's nothing wrong in wanting our lives to be ordered—it makes things a bit easier if we can do it—however, I sometimes sense that you walk a very narrow path."

Maisie felt as if her voice might not work if she opened her mouth to speak. She had a sudden awareness of repetition. Hadn't someone—was it her father? perhaps Jesse or Seth?—hadn't someone spoken of Eddie walking a narrow path?

Masters continued. "The man who has been mentally affected by war can be a controlling person, setting boundaries so that, for example, every event in the daily round happens at a certain time. Even the smallest thing outside the accepted rhythm of the day can cause a complete upset in personality; a late delivery by the postman, perhaps, or something not working—let's say the plumbing springs a leak, that sort of thing."

"But I'm not like that. I have lots of things go awry in the course of a day."

"Yes, I'm sure you do. Yet I would wager that you keep a very tight rein on what happens in your personal solar system, even though you are a woman of some means—and can thus let others do things for you—and you are successful in your profession. Let us look at the way in which you assist your employees. In 'helping' them, you're affecting their lives, making decisions on their behalf that they might not have made for themselves or might come to at a different time."

"I was only trying to make life easier for them, Dr. Masters. I have the ability to assist, and I wanted to see Billy and his family settled, and to . . ." Maisie faltered.

"And what else? Who else have you been trying to help? How might you have been trying to make the lives of others conform to your view of the world?"

"I think that's rather strong. I have the resources to help my employees and friends, so—"

"Step back, Maisie. I am sure you think you are well on your way to putting the past to rest, and certainly you give that impression. However, I sense—and I know that's not a medical term, but I am a different kind of doctor, as I am sure you know—but I sense that you are overly protective of yourself, that you have perhaps too strict an idea of what you should and should not be doing."

"I—"

"Consider it, that's all I ask." Elsbeth Masters held up her hand. "I'll say no more as I may be on the wrong track, but there could be something there for you."

Maisie nodded. She did not want to upset her professional relationship with Masters, but at once she felt as if she wanted to run from the place. Instead she spoke as if the dialogue concerning her state of mind had not taken place.

"Might it be possible to let me know when Mrs. Beale is to be discharged? I would like to have Elinor—the nanny—leave the house before she arrives home, to avoid additional distress."

"Of course." Masters slipped her shoes back on and stood up to say good-bye. "And do drop in to see me again, Maisie. We women in the professions must stick together, eh?"

Maisie smiled, said she would keep in touch, and turned to leave, though she could still feel a tremor in her limbs as she walked from the hospital; it was a physical sensation that began the moment Elsbeth Masters had challenged her.

As she left the hospital, she stopped to lean against the wall and rubbed her forehead, for she thought a headache might be coming on. A man approached to ask if she was all right, and she assured him that all was well, she was just a little warm. She was reflecting upon her own actions, weighing them up as, one by one, they seemed to line up in her mind, waiting to be considered in light of the unexpected judgment against her. She had tried hard not to push Billy and Doreen into the house, waiting for them to take her up on the offer of a cheaper rent in a much better area. And it *was* a much better area—look how the boys were so much healthier, and how the family had more room. She had encouraged Sandra to continue her education, and had brought home details on Birkbeck College and other places the young woman might aspire to attend. Was that controlling, especially as Sandra was doing so well now? Offering her lodging at the flat until she was on an even keel in the wake of her sudden widowhood was a natural extension of a desire to help—after all, the girl had stayed there before. That was all *caring*, surely, not control.

Maisie began walking again, and as she straightened her back and stepped out with purpose, she decided that Masters had taken the wrong tack; that in caring for her patient, she had focused on Maisie without due cause. It occurred to her, briefly, however, that her father might agree with the doctor. But hadn't she drawn back from trying to get him to move to The Dower House when it was clear he really didn't want to? Of course, it would be better for him if he moved; any daughter in her position would have done the same thing.

As she made her way to the bus stop, Maisie tried to distinguish the feeling she had when Masters had said that there might be "something there for you." It was a phrase used by Maurice, when he had observed a trait in her that she hadn't seen herself. Invariably, at some point, she caught up with him and was able to view her actions through a stronger lens, and as a result felt as if life had expanded around her in some way. She wondered what had inspired Masters to confront her, why she had spoken her mind in so candid a fashion. Maisie had felt discomfort, yes, but something else had happened. For the first time since Maurice's death, she felt . . . tightly held, as if Elsbeth Masters' honesty were enveloping her with caring, even as she challenged her actions.

Number 1 Shelley Street, the address given for Evelyn Butterworth, proved to be a narrow, modest, end-of-terrace house divided into flats, not far from King's Cross station. Though it was not in a particularly good area, someone had tried to make a garden, but soot from the trains rendered the district gray and tired, and even the sunshine failed to cheer the street. Looking up at the house, Maisie noticed that the curtains on the third floor were quite bright. She had never seen fabric in such a myriad of colors, and wondered if it had been hand-dyed to achieve the vibrant effect. She thought this might be the flat rented by Bart Soames and his lover.

A series of names had been written on paper and slipped into brass holders at the side of the door. To the right of each name a bell pull was provided, though with rust and dents, the system bore signs of age and mishandling. Maisie pulled the two-fingers'-width handle next to Evelyn Butterworth's name—she was indeed on the top floor—and a bell sounded faintly within the house. As she waited, Maisie noticed that Bartholomew Soames was not listed at the address, and wondered if his name had been removed already, or if their status as an unmarried couple had something to do with it. No one came to the door. Maisie pulled again, then after a moment or two gave the door a light push. It opened onto a small square entrance hall, in front of which a staircase led to the upper flats, with the door to the ground-floor flat just visible beyond the staircase. A bicycle was resting against the wall, which she assumed belonged to the ground-floor resident.

Taking care not to make any noise, Maisie made her way up several flights of stairs, and was soon standing in front of the door to Evelyn Butterworth's flat. She knocked and was surprised when the door creaked open—it had not been locked and had given to her touch with ease. Looking about her, Maisie stepped into the flat. A small kitchenette was situated to the right, with a dresser painted in red and cream. At one point the dresser had apparently displayed a collection of china, but now shards of crockery were strewn across the linoleum, and the dresser was pulled back from the wall. Maisie stood still for a moment, listening for noise to suggest she was not alone, but could hear nothing to indicate there was company waiting for her.

A WC with washbasin was to the left—the mirror above the sink was broken. And when she entered the main room, she could see that it had been left in some disarray. Papers and books were scattered all over the floor, a sideboard had been overturned, and upholstery—in the same riotous blend of color as the curtains—had been ripped from the armchairs. Pictures had been pulled from the walls, glass broken, and the contents pulled out, perhaps to see if something was hidden. Maisie had just begun to step forward when she heard voices behind her.

"There she is!"

At once she felt her right arm almost ripped from her shoulder and pulled up behind her back.

"Let me go!" Using her left elbow, she jabbed back to make contact with her attacker's torso and heard a woman scream behind her.

"That hurt!" said the woman, wrenching Maisie's arm higher.

Someone pulled off her hat, grabbing her hair.

"Let's get a look at her."

With her head wrenched to meet her arm, Maisie was in great pain, but not so incapacitated that she could not see that she was now surrounded by four women, as well as the woman holding fast to her arm and hair. She was strong, of that there was no doubt.

"Would you *please* let me go!" said Maisie.

"Not so fast—who are you? Why are you here?" A woman who appeared to be in her early thirties, with jet-black hair and red lips, glared at her, hands on hips.

"My name is Maisie Dobbs. I am here to see Miss Evelyn Butterworth. There was no answer to the bell, but the door was unlocked." Maisie coughed, her neck extended, making speech difficult. "I—I came up here, and the door was open. I had just walked in—" She began to choke, but the woman behind her did not release her hold. "I was looking to see if Miss Butterworth was here, and perhaps hurt—and then you grabbed me."

Maisie began to choke again, but this time she kicked back her right leg, hooked it around her assailant's ankle and set her off balance. As the woman released her hold, Maisie turned, using her right elbow to bring home another jab. Soon the woman holding her was on the ground. Another woman stepped towards Maisie, but she held up her hand.

"Just stop! All of you, come to your senses and stop this nonsense." She rubbed her arm. "And you can get up. I didn't hurt you half as much as you hurt me, so don't pretend, it doesn't become you."

The women seemed stunned, as if, having come into the flat with all guns blazing, they were now not sure what they should do.

"Which one of you is Evelyn?" Maisie wiped her forehead and pushed back her hair.

The woman with the black hair and red lipstick spoke up, and as Maisie's attention was drawn to her, she realized her clothes had been chosen to match her hair and makeup; she was wearing a scarlet jacket and black skirt. "I am," said the woman. "Look, what do you want here? Can't you see someone has turned over my flat?"

"Of course I can see what happened. Do you think anyone doing this would be so stupid as to return, when they've made a pretty good job of looking for whatever it is they're after? They may have made a mess of your home, but this is a professional job. They've gone through everything thoroughly. I'm surprised the carpets aren't pulled back and the floorboards torn up. In fact, I would bet that they were fairly systematic in their search." Maisie cast an eye around the five women, who were now all standing in front of her, staring. She thought they were likely all in their thirties, and suspected that, with the exception of Evelyn, they were probably all spinsters, living in a women's boarding house, ekeing out a living working in offices or as teachers; perhaps there was a librarian among them, a waitress or shop assistant. Though ostensibly alone, without a spouse, they had each other for company, for entertainment, and to turn to when troubled.

Evelyn Butterworth sighed. "I came home from the college where I work—I teach English, but not full-time—and found my flat like this." She held out her hand. "I was so shocked, scared, I ran out. I went to the tea shop and found my friends—we were supposed to be meeting anyway, about the women's pensions march." She turned to her friends. "Alice, Marjorie, Penny, and Kate. I brought them back here. Safety in numbers. And then we saw you."

"And did you see anyone walking away as you approached the house? Anyone in the area lately who you haven't seen before?"

"Who are you?" asked Alice.

"Maisie Dobbs." She reached into her briefcase and took out five calling cards, giving one to each of the women.

"Investigator and psychologist? What do you do?" The woman introduced as Penny looked up, frowning.

"She's looking into the death of a man named Eddie Pettit, aren't you?" said Butterworth.

"Ah, you've had a chance to speak to Mrs. Soames," said Maisie.

Butterworth nodded. "Yes, she said you'd visited, that she gave you my address."

Maisie looked around the flat, then at the women. "Look, I'd like to speak to Miss Butterworth in private, if you don't mind."

The women looked at Butterworth. She nodded her assent. "That's all right, girls. I'm pretty sure I'm safe here now."

There were kisses among the women, a squeeze on the arm, and offers of a sofa to sleep on for as long as she needed. Maisie felt at once alone in the room. Beyond Priscilla, there was no one she could call upon to talk about, well, anything really. There were no long-standing friendships and no new ones either. She had enjoyed evenings at the flat when Sandra was with her—a bit of laughter as they listened to the wireless, or a deeper conversation if Sandra wanted to discuss an aspect of her academic work. At once Maisie felt bereft of the sort of sisterly confidence so freely enjoyed by Evelyn Butterworth's friends.

"See you later, Evie," Alice called out as she pulled the door closed behind the group.

"See you, Al—and thanks again."

"Oh, just a minute! Alice!" Maisie opened the door. Alice waited at the top of the landing.

"There's a locksmith just up the street. I passed the shop on the way here; it's on Euston Road. I wonder, would you drop in on your way, and ask if someone could come round to fit a new lock here?"

Alice smiled, clearly confident now that she was leaving her friend in good hands. "Yes, of course. I'll tell them it's urgent."

"Good. Thank you."

Maisie closed the door behind her.

"Evelyn—may I call you Evelyn?"

"Just call me Eve. That's what most people call me."

Maisie smiled. "Right then, Eve, let's go into the kitchen. I think they left a couple of chairs in there without completely destroying them, though I don't think you've any china."

The woman's eyes watered. "That china belonged to my grand-mother. It wasn't posh or anything, and to tell you the truth, I didn't really like it, but it was hers. I lived with her for most of my life, after my parents went."

"I'm sorry," said Maisie.

"Oh no, they didn't die. They just left me and went off. Makes me wonder whether they had any more children and just left them when they got fed up with them, like they did with me. They were on the stage, you see; trod the boards with a music hall troupe. My gran always said that my mother—her daughter—was a bit of a gypsy, and I suppose she was."

Maisie pressed her lips together as she regarded the crestfallen woman. "Look, if we've time when we're finished here, let's go out and see if we can get you some more crockery." She stopped for a few seconds, recalling Elsbeth Masters' words earlier, realizing she was beginning to direct another person's life again. "That is, if you want to stay in this flat."

"I'll stay—it's cheap enough, and a new lock and a chain will do the trick. As you said, I don't think whoever did this will be back in a hurry. I don't have what they want, anyway."

"And what do you think they want, Eve?"

"They want Bart's notebooks. They want his papers, his books, anything he wrote in or kept with words."

"Who are 'they'—have you any idea?"

The woman shrugged and picked up a piece of broken china, running her fingers along the patterned edge. It had once been a cup, and Maisie could see a brown stain on the inside, where much tea had been poured over the years.

"I don't know."

Maisie walked further into the kitchen, picked up two chairs, and arranged them so that she and Evelyn could look out at the houses opposite and the street below, and not at the many broken things behind them. Once they were seated, she did not speak, allowing the woman her moment of silence. Maisie understood that the shock of seeing one's home violated was a deeply emotional blow. But this woman had also lost the man she loved, so must feel as if she were falling without chance of her descent being broken.

Evelyn Butterworth was a striking woman, her jet-black hair in tight curls about her head, rouged cheeks, and scarlet lipstick that seemed to render the red jacket even more exotic. Maisie noticed that even her footwear was red, with a single strap of grosgrain ribbon across the foot and a bow at the side to hide the buckle. The tips of the shoes were mottled with tar and dust from walking; here was a woman who would not allow the weather—good or bad—to thwart her very personal style.

"Eve, I think the first thing we must do is go through the flat, square foot by square foot. We'll make a pile of anything that cannot be restored or mended, and I am sure we can find a rag-and-bone man to come in and clear the lot. But as we go through, I want you to tell me if you're aware of anything missing—for example, the sideboard has been turned over, so if there were photographs on top and they're not there now, we can assume the intruders took them."

Evelyn Butterworth nodded. There would be plenty of time for Maisie to talk to her in the hours ahead, or even tomorrow or the next day, if conversation had to wait that long. She knew the process of sorting through the mess would serve as catharsis of sorts, an opportunity for Evelyn to go through the ritual of leave-taking, a farewell not only to everything that was destroyed, but to the life she'd had with Bartholomew Soames, for surely so many cherished items—from a cup to a chair—must remind her of him. Maisie well understood the woman's need to remain in the flat despite the destruction around her, for she hadn't yet said good-bye to the man who had lived there with her. She had noticed the cheap gold band on Evelyn Butterworth's left hand, a token that must have persuaded the landlord they were a married couple.

For several hours, Maisie and Eve Butterworth knelt down, picking up books with torn spines, collecting pages from a half-finished manuscript belonging to Eve, and making a pile of splintered wood and torn fabrics in the middle of the room. They carefully removed photographs from shattered frames, placed unbroken items in the corner, and brushed down clothing pulled from the wardrobe, which they righted and put back in place. As they were placing jackets, dresses, trousers, and shirts back on hangers, Maisie felt tears prick her eyes when she realized that Bartholomew Soames' lover had not let go of his clothes, which already seemed to have the musty smell of one who was here not so long ago, but was now gone.

They swept the floors and dusted the windowsills, and they shook the bed linens and remade the bed. Eve went out to see if the local shopkeepers had some old boxes to spare, and when she returned with half a dozen boxes of various sizes, they filled them with broken crockery and glass, torn fabric, splintered wood and crumpled papers. As Maisie lifted a box to put it outside the door, Eve stopped her—she wanted to keep a single fragment of her grandmother's tea service. The floor was soon swept and those items in the kitchen that remained in one piece were stowed where they belonged.

In the midst of their endeavors, the locksmith arrived and Maisie asked questions about the types of lock available and was shown a selection. She chose the strongest to be fitted, along with a chain on the inside of the front door. She also asked if it might be possible to fit one of those fish-eye holes so that the lady in residence might see her callers before opening the door. The locksmith returned to his shop and came back to the flat with the necessary hardware to fit the tiny glass.

Finally the task of clearing up was complete, and when Maisie went downstairs and out onto the street with a final box of rubbish, she flagged down a trader passing with his horse-drawn cart. It was dark, but the carriage lights illuminated the man's face.

"Want to earn yourself a bit extra this evening, sir?" asked Maisie.

"You calling me sir? Blimey, I ain't been called sir for a long time." He pushed back his cap and scratched his head. "And we don't mind if we do make a bit extra, do we, my boy?" He nudged the young man next to him.

Maisie described the job, and soon man and boy were going back and forth from the curb to the cart, loading up the boxes. When they had completed their task, Maisie pressed several coins into the man's hand. He turned to the light and looked at his payment.

"Very generous too, madam." He touched his cap once more. "You want anything more doing, you just let me know—I come by this way every night, about this time."

Maisie thanked him for a job well done, and returned to the flat. She soaked a handkerchief under the cold tap and wiped her face and neck. Evelyn did the same and they stood back and looked at the results of their work.

"I think this is the cleanest this flat has ever been, to tell you the truth," said Evelyn. "Bart hated me cleaning—he said he could never find anything if I tidied up."

"Yes, it's nice to have some order to a home, isn't it?" She flushed as her words again reminded her of Elsbeth Masters' admonition earlier in the day. "Now then, I think you should lock up and we'll be on our way. I can have a taxi-cab drop you at your friends' home. I think it might be best if you stay elsewhere for a couple of nights at least."

Evelyn Butterworth gathered her jacket. "Yes, I think you're right." She took a long look around the room before turning to leave. "Funny how everything can change," she said. "Just like that."

En route to her friends' flat—Evelyn had informed her that several women shared the accommodation—Maisie asked about Bart Soames' belongings.

"From what you said as we were clearing, it seems they didn't take much at all. What about Bart's work?"

"Oh, well, he didn't work from home. Well, that's not true; he would bring notebooks back in the evening, and he would go through something he'd written, but as a rule he worked at an office—I'm sorry, I thought I'd mentioned it."

"But I was under the impression he was no longer with a newspaper," said Maisie.

"He wasn't. But after he started working for himself, he said it was difficult to work in the same place where you live, especially as our flat was so small—just a glorified bedsit really, with a separate kitchen and lavatory."

"Where did he work, then?"

"There's a studio for writers, so he applied for a desk there, and that's where he worked, and he didn't have to pay much as it was laid on for nothing."

"No rent? Who paid for it, then?"

Eve Butterworth wiped a hand across the taxi-cab window to rub away condensation, and looked out into the darkness. The task of clearing the flat had clearly drained the bereaved woman. The old had been destroyed and the new was yet to come, and as Maisie knew only too well, the limbo in between was akin to a desert, a place where one stood with nothing while waiting for the road ahead to become clear. And it might be some time before a fresh opportunity, a new job, another love, or a different way of life would make itself known.

"Eve—do you know who sponsored the writers?"

"Um, yes. Sorry, I was miles away. It's a large studio, not far from Lancaster Gate—the first floor of one of those mansions that looks out over Hyde Park. It's owned by a writer. Bart told me that as he's quite successful and obviously got a bit of money—the property belonged to his family—the man wanted to contribute to the lives of other writers, especially as many have a difficult time making ends meet. And Bart certainly had a bit of trouble in that regard; my wages from teaching at two schools kept us. The trouble was, it didn't give me much time to do *my* writing, though I've had some articles published in women's annuals." She paused, holding on to the strap above her as the taxi swung around a corner. "Anyway, the studio is divided into small working rooms, and there's a waiting list to have one. As luck would have it, Bart didn't have to wait long before he was assigned a desk there, so that's where he's been writing for some time now. There's a telephone installed on the landing—you have to pay, but it means that if you're a journalist, you don't have to run out to the street if you need to get in touch with someone."

"Have you been over to the studio since Bart died?"

She shook her head. "No, but I've applied to take over Bart's desk. He was the only newspaperman there, the others are all poets or authors; there's a biographer and a man writing a book about the planet Mars. The man who owns the property doesn't have anything to do with the running of it. The writers are supposed to keep it clean themselves, and the one who's been there the longest keeps the waiting list—I was hoping I could jump the list, being as I was Bart's, well . . . friend. Anyway, it's very pally there, a sort of salon. There's a general seating area with armchairs and a fireplace, and the writers take it in turns to buy coal in the winter, so you can read of an evening in comfort—in fact, you can do everything but sleep there."

"That sounds just the ticket for you, Eve." Maisie paused. "Look, if you don't mind, I'd like to go with you to visit Bart's room and to check his desk. I didn't have time to explain in any detail earlier, but as Mrs. Soames told you, I'm investigating the death of a man who was known to Bart; in fact, Bart became his friend and was trusted by him.

There's a chance that something about Eddie Pettit will be among Bart's papers."

Eve looked at Maisie. "I never thought of that. I met Eddie once. He was a very sweet man, wasn't he? Bart's mother was helping him with reading, and I was over at her house, with Bart. That's how Bart met him, when she was giving Eddie a lesson." She smiled. "I don't know if anything came of it, but Bart told me that Eddie Pettit had given him a real gift."

"What sort of gift?"

She shrugged. "I don't know, but Bart was a reporter, and there's only one true gift you can give to a reporter, and that's a really big scoop." She leaned forward and rapped on the glass between the driver and his passengers. "Just at this corner, please."

As Eve Butterworth stepped out onto the curb she opened her purse. Maisie shook her head. "I can pay when I get home. Not to worry."

"Thank you, Maisie. And thank you for all your help. I just wish we could have found something that might have helped you in the flat."

"Oh, I think you've helped enormously. Now, remember, you have my card. Please get in touch with me if anything occurs to you. And I know someone with some old furniture I can send over, if you like."

"If you can spare anything, I would be grateful. But I'll see what I can find secondhand—there's a lot more people trying to sell their belongings off cheap these days."

Maisie smiled. "Eve, I almost forgot. The studio where Bart went to write—do you know who the absent owner is?"

"Yes. His name is Douglas Partridge. You might have heard of him. Bart never met him, but apparently his wife is considered one of the best-dressed women in London, so they must have money."

Maisie took a deep breath. "Yes, I do believe I have heard of him.

Thank you, Eve. Now then, you need to go inside and put your feet up, and I have to get home. I'll sit here in the taxi until you're inside the front door."

Evelyn Butterworth thanked Maisie again as she stepped onto the curb. Maisie watched her walk to the door of the building and ring the bell. As she pulled her red jacket around her, she could feel the woman's aloneness, an all-too-familiar demeanor she had witnessed in so many women when she was a nurse. The wives and sweethearts of wounded men would come to the hospital, and when the extent of their lovers' injuries were realized, it was as if they could see the rest of their lives before them. They would either be caring for a man almost destroyed by war, or they would be widows. And sometimes when the loved one died of those wounds, Maisie would see that moment of relief in the young wife's eyes, when she understood that her beloved husband's passing had released her—but she also saw the veil of lone-liness as it came down around the woman whose hand clutched the still-warm hand of a love gone forever. Evelyn Butterworth wore that gray veil, despite her colorful garb, despite the bright red lipstick and rouge, and her intention to stay in the flat she had shared with her lover, Bartholomew Soames.

As the door opened, Evelyn turned to wave one more time, and once she was inside, Maisie leaned forward. "Fifteen Ebury Place, please."

"Right you are, madam."

Maisie sat back in the taxi-cab and thought about Bart Soames and Eddie Pettit. A cold shiver went through her as she saw the case map in her mind's eye, the threads of color linking the names and events, an inquiry that had already taken her from the dark streets of Lambeth and a man who could barely read, to the studio of those who wove words together and created poetry. And in her heart of hearts, she faced up to something she had not wanted to believe, that Eddie had been a pawn in a bigger game; a game he was not equipped to comprehend. A game in which it seemed her best friend's husband might have played a part, a part he hoped to conceal from her. Or did he?

CHAPTER NINE

❖

Maisie had only just stepped into the entrance hall at 15 Ebury Place when James came downstairs, calling to her.

"Maisie, I thought something dreadful had happened to you. I telephoned the flat in case you were there, and when you didn't come home at your usual hour—though heaven knows what that is anymore—I wondered if I should get in touch with the police."

James was dressed in trousers the color of charcoal, with a soft, white Vyella shirt and a navy-blue silk cravat at his neck. His blond hair with threads of gray at the sides was combed back with a side parting, and at once it struck Maisie that he seemed older than his years; closer to his father, Lord Julian.

"I was helping a young woman who'd had her flat broken into. Her—" Maisie hesitated. "Her husband died a few weeks ago and I had to see her about something, but when I arrived she was in rather a state. There was no telephone on the premises or nearby, and it was clear she needed help."

"Had her flat broken into? And how did her husband die, may I ask?"

Maisie handed her coat to the butler, her cheeks blazing. James had confronted her as if the servant were not there, listening. This, thought Maisie, was a perfect example of the chasm opening up between them—she was humiliated at being spoken to in front of someone she had never considered to be anything less than an equal, despite his position in the household, whereas James did not even appear to think it necessary to temper his comments in front of the man. She smiled and thanked Simmonds, who caught her eye for just a second. Maisie thought she saw the faint cast of a smile in return.

"I think we'll go straight through for drinks, if that's all right," said Maisie.

The butler inclined his head. "Right you are, Miss Dobbs. At once."

He left with her coat, and Maisie looked back at James.

"Let's have a drink before supper and I'll tell you all about it, if you like."

James seemed mollified, and as if he had caught himself acting poorly, he came to her, took her in his arms, and kissed her on the cheek.

"I'm sorry. I was just worried."

Maisie nodded. "Really, there was nothing to worry about."

Once settled in the drawing room—James with a whiskey and soda and Maisie with a small cream sherry—she gave him an abbreviated version of the story, to the effect that she had called at the address not far from King's Cross station just moments after the woman had discovered her flat in a state of disarray. Given the young widow's emotional response to the violation, Maisie had remained with her to help clean the flat and to accompany her to a home shared by some women friends.

"Did she call the police?" asked James.

"No, and frankly there was precious little to be garnered from a search of the flat—it would have been listed as just one of so many burglaries in London today." Maisie paused. "Did you have a good day, James?"

He shrugged. "The usual sort of things. All a bit boring, to tell you the truth."

Maisie nodded, twisted the stem of her glass in her hand, and looked up at the man who was her lover, the man whom she knew wanted to marry her, but who would not ask because she had not given him reason to think he might be accepted. He was waiting for her to come to him, as if he were standing at the far end of a large field, and she were meandering her way across, stopping to look at anything that drew her attention along the way, and likely at any moment to strike out in another direction. And for that she felt an ache of guilt, because James was a good man, a sensitive man who had fallen in love with her, and she had believed she loved him, too. Doubt, the parasite, had become embedded in her heart, and increasingly she was aware of the differences between them, rather than the elements of character and experience that allow a man and a woman to see themselves reflected in each other.

"James, are you happy in your work? Do you feel as if you've had a hand in a job well done at the end of the day?" asked Maisie.

"What sort of question is that? I don't stop to think about it, Maisie. I just get on with it." James stood up, walked to the drinks tray set out earlier by the butler, and poured himself another whiskey. Maisie felt herself take a breath when she saw the large measure he'd allowed before adding soda. James turned back to her. "If I win a contract or pull off something big—buying at a good price, selling at a higher price—I certainly smile about it. But that's my job. I have the family corporation to run. I don't expect it to be a picnic. As I said, I just get on with it."

Maisie took care in framing her question. "That's not quite what I meant. Let me ask you this: If you weren't working for the Compton Corporation, what would you be doing?"

"That's just plain foolish, Maisie. I don't have a choice."

"But if you did. What would you do?"

James slumped down into the chair, and Maisie was dismayed to see his eyes water; he looked down at his drink and ran a hand through his hair. "I would be out. I would not be in an office, and I would be somewhere . . . oh, I don't know. I just don't know. I think I would probably be a farmer, so that I could only see land, land, land around me." He appeared to be warming to the question. "I'd love to live in Canada again, but not in Toronto—somewhere else in Ontario, or in Alberta, or somewhere out in the prairies. Yes, that's where I'd like to be a farmer—a million miles away from everything. But this is what is expected of me, so . . . so this is the sort of talk that gets us nowhere." He looked up at her. "And I'd miss you, Maisie." He paused. "Is this what you want, Maisie? It's my turn now. What do *you* want?"

She had talked herself into a corner. Was this the time for honesty? And if it was, then what would she say? That she loved him, but did not feel she could live his life? But at the same time, was she ready to let him go? Was she with James because she feared being alone? Had it come to that? Were they, in fact, suffocating each other? And was this the time to bare their souls, or were they both too vulnerable for the conversation that must follow?

At that moment the door opened and Simmonds came in to inform them that supper was ready in the dining room.

James smiled, put down his drink, and embraced Maisie. "As long as you want me, Maisie, I'll be here. That's all that matters."

She smiled in return. The moment was gone, the opportunity whisked away by time and chance. They had ventured out with their hearts towards honesty, but had scurried back to protect their feelings, and now they must follow the protocol of life in the mansion. Supper was ready. Time to eat, then time to sleep; to wake, to start another day. Maisie wondered if it wasn't such a bad thing, this call to dine. She wasn't sure of her feelings, but felt confident she knew exactly what she didn't want. Yet at the same time she could not quite articulate what she *would* have in her life. And at that moment, she yearned to be able to share her confidence with Maurice, just once more. He would have known exactly what questions to put to her. Hadn't he always said that the power of the question was in the question itself? He'd taught her that one must let a question linger in the mind as one might savor wine on the tongue, and he'd cautioned that a rush to answer could diminish all chance of insight. Indeed, if one continually avoided questions by trying to answer them immediately, such impatience would become a barrier on the path to greater knowledge of oneself.

The evening passed with light conversation, and they were both grateful for an element of humor as James told a story and Maisie laughed.

"You never really said that, James!"

"It just slipped out before I could stop myself." He lifted his glass of wine, took a sip, and held on to the glass as he continued. "And the man is one of our best clients. My father, who was at the luncheon, looked at me as if he had brought a six-year-old along to a grown-ups' party—haven't seen that look in years. I wish I could say since I was six, but I fear I've seen it more than a few times since then."

James seemed as if he might slip into melancholy again, so Maisie described walking along the Embankment, and how the wind gusted so much she thought she might be lifted off her feet. "I felt like one of those silly women you see in a picture-house comedy, grasping my hat, the wind lifting my skirt. Had I a few yards of string, I would have tied my clothes down with it."

"I would have paid good money to see that!" said James.

There was laughter once again.

Maisie went on to describe the pontoon used by the river police, though did not explain her reason for being there. "I don't know how they do that job," she added. "Even on a warm spring day, it can be quite cool down by the water, so it must be freezing on a winter's night." She shivered, though the evening was mild.

There was a moment of silence, then James spoke again. "Oh, just to remind you, the Otterburn dinner—it's this week. And we've also been invited down to their estate in Surrey for Easter, a Friday to Monday. They live more or less on Box Hill, actually; beautiful for a hack across the downs—would you like to come? There's also the hunt, probably one of the last of the season; I'd love to go, if there's the opportunity. I know I couldn't persuade you to follow on a mount, but you could spend a few hours in their library. I understand they have a smashing collection, some very old books there."

"Let's see—it really depends upon how the next couple of days go, and how Billy progresses. I know it's a bit informal, but would it be all right to let Mrs. Otterburn know on Wednesday?"

"I'm sure it would, can't imagine why not." James drained his glass and poured himself more wine. Maisie shook her head when he reached to refill her glass. And at once she saw a picture in her mind's eye, of James on horseback in a field of wheat, the golden crop reflected in his windswept hair and smiling eyes. It was an image as clear as day, and she felt as if he had left her. The vision—daydream, whatever it was—seemed to be a portent of possibility, and Maisie thought that perhaps she should encourage James to step out towards the life he yearned for. Surely the Compton Corporation had groomed someone to assume responsibility if it had come to pass that James had died in the war. Wasn't there a great-nephew or second cousin of Lord Julian Compton's who worked for the company?

Supper was soon over. Coffee was served in the drawing room, after which James took Maisie's hand and led her upstairs. She leaned on his shoulder, feeling competing emotions: a warmth of affection and a level of confusion. She would miss him, that much she knew. But she also knew she must encourage him to follow a path he could see but was afraid to step towards. As she turned over the possibility in her mind, she felt a weight leave her chest, felt her breathing come with more ease than it had in weeks. Maisie hoped that one day, when the time was right, she could do what she must without arguments, raised voices, or too much heartache. Hadn't she forged a friendship with Andrew Dene, a past love who had also wanted to marry her? And she had been the first to congratulate him on his marriage and subsequent fatherhood. Perhaps it could be like that with James.

James had arranged for a mechanic to come to the mews behind 15 Ebury Place, where the mansion's motor cars were kept. A diagnosis of the MG's engine ailments was made and repairs duly completed. The motor car, apparently, would not let her down now, no matter how damp or harsh the weather, or how high the temperature might rise.

"So far, so good," thought Maisie as she made her way to the office. An earlier light rain shower had given way to bright sunshine, which seemed to bring the fresh green leaves on the square's trees into sharp relief. Steam was rising up from small pools of water on the road, and it promised to be another fine day. Evelyn Butterworth was due to telephone around nine-ish, and Maisie hoped she could arrange to collect her and then go together to the writers' studio where Bart Soames had a desk. Having parked the MG on Fitzroy Street, she walked in the direction of the office. A police vehicle parked close to the front door caused Maisie to start.

"Now what?" she said, under her breath, stepping with care across the slippery flagstones.

Only the driver was in the black vehicle, so she assumed Caldwell and his assistant had gone up to the office. She was a little late; she hoped Sandra had arrived. As she opened the front door, it occurred to her that the visit might be in connection with Billy. She ran up the stairs and into the office.

Detective Inspector Caldwell was sitting at Billy's desk, drinking tea, his assistant in a seat opposite him. They were discussing whether a British woman who had married a foreigner should register as an alien—an item of news in the papers that morning. Maisie caught the tail of the conversation.

"Well, what I think is, why marry outside of your race, anyway? Aren't there enough British men for you girls?"

Sandra's back was ramrod straight. "Well, actually, Detective Inspector, if you took notice of the population numbers, you would see that there aren't enough men—there is currently a surplus of women, which means an unmarried woman of, say, my age, stands only a one in ten chance of finding a husband. That's nine women alone. And I don't see why you should lose your nationality, just because your husband is Russian or Dutch."

"What if he's German?"

"What if? We're not at war anymore."

"Not yet, young lady."

"Looks like I arrived just in time to stop another war," said Maisie. "Good morning, Sandra. Is the revered inspector here causing trouble?"

Sandra blushed. "No. Just a bit of conversation about the news today."

"At least we were spared football, cricket, or more on the bowling controversy." Maisie spoke while taking off her coat. "To what do we owe the pleasure of your company, Inspector? When I first saw your motor, I thought you might have unwelcome news of Mr. Beale, but as I ran up the stairs and heard your voice, I realized you wouldn't be quite so cheerful had it been so." She took a chair from behind her desk and sat closer to the policemen. "How is he? I visited again yesterday, but couldn't see him."

"Your Mr. Beale is making good progress. In normal circumstances, you would be able to see him later, but his wife has lodged a complaint with the police—she may be in hospital herself, but she can still do this—and you are to keep a good distance from the Beale family." He looked down at his hat as he ran the brim through his fingers.

Maisie felt her hands begin to shake. She tried to remain composed. "I understand. Yes, I—I understand. I am held responsible, and that is only fair. Billy is my employee and he was working for me when this happened."

"I'm sorry, Miss Dobbs."

"That's all right, Inspector. I would ask one thing, though—would you keep us apprised of Mr. Beale's progress, and when he's well enough, please tell him I am anxious to have word of his recovery? Please also tell him that he is not to worry about his children, that they are safe and well, especially the baby. I am sure this will all be resolved soon, and the family will be reunited."

"There *is* some good news, but I thought if I gave it to you second, after the bad news, you'd feel better."

"Good news? I hope so, I could do with some already, and it's only Tuesday morning."

"The man we believe to have been Mr. Beale's attacker has taken his own life. The guilt probably got to him. Not only that, we believe he was responsible for the accident which killed Edwin Pettit."

"Jimmy Merton?"

"That's him. You came across his name while you were doing your homework, didn't you? Frankly, he had the lot—the motive, the opportunity, and in the case of Mr. Pettit, he had a grudge."

"Yes, he'd always been one to bully Eddie." Maisie was thoughtful, her mind not completely on the conversation.

"Bit of a hard nut, and with previous. The reason he'd been off the streets for a while was because he'd been spending time lolling around at His Majesty's pleasure in the highly palatial Maidstone Prison, but as soon as he was back in Lambeth, he found Eddie again. And though we're not sure how he did it, we think he must have had a hand in Eddie's death—at the very least, he didn't save him when he had the chance; he just watched it happen. According to a witness who's come forward, the conveyor belt—the one that carries the bales of paper—buckled up when a bale began to wobble. The witness said that as far as he could make out, Merton—who was up on the gantry—didn't do a thing to stop it, didn't even try to prevent the accident. Our investigation has led us to believe the machinery might have been overburdened, causing a vibration that in turn made the conveyor buckle—Merton could have seen his opportunity to actually cause the accident, knowing that Mr. Pettit would be badly injured, if not killed. When your Billy came along, the fact that he was a stranger was likely enough to set off Jimmy Merton, who had a bit of a short fuse. We believe he didn't mean to do as much damage to Mr. Beale as he did, but Merton is—was—the sort of man who never knew when to stop. It's a surprise he topped himself, that much is true—he's more the sort who'd do a runner. But his conscience seems to have caught up with his actions, so he hung himself from Lambeth Bridge."

"Lambeth Bridge? That's becoming a rather popular place for suicide, don't you think?"

"Easier than some—you wouldn't want to try to put a noose around the girders on Tower Bridge, would you? You might fall and kill yourself." Caldwell grinned.

Maisie shook her head. "Oh dear . . ."

"You've got to laugh about it sometimes, Miss Dobbs. It's the only way to get through the day in this job."

"Thank you for coming, Inspector. I was planning to go to the hospital again today, which might have caused a problem. And now I have some news for Mrs. Pettit."

"About this business of restraining your access to Mr. Beale—I'm sure it will sort itself out." Caldwell put his hand on her shoulder. It was an uncharacteristic move, and one that might once have caused Maisie to step back, but instead she appreciated the good intention in his gesture.

"Thank you, Detective Inspector Caldwell. I'm grateful for your support."

Maisie closed the door as Caldwell and his assistant departed, and turned to see Sandra looking at her.

"What is it, Sandra?"

"You don't think it was Jimmy Merton, do you, Miss Dobbs?"

Maisie walked to her desk, pulled the chair back into its place, and sat down, resting her hands on her blotting pad. "I think it's a bit more complicated. I like to see a quick solution as much as the next person, but it seems that this has been swept into the dustpan and tidily dispatched with too much ease and congratulation on the part of the police. And I can't deny, I would have liked to talk to the man myself, but that won't be possible now." She picked up a pencil and ran it through her fingers. "No, there's something missing. Probably almost everything Caldwell says is right—I don't doubt Eddie died as a result of Jimmy Merton either causing an accident or not stopping an accident when it was about to happen—but what about Bart Soames? Or the fact that his girl—wife, whatever she wants to be known as—had her flat broken into? Which reminds me, Sandra—did you know Mr. Partridge owns a property at Lancaster Gate which he allows cash-strapped writers to use?"

"I knew he had some property over that way," said Sandra. "I've seen some correspondence come in about it, you know, very ordinary mail regarding the water or the gas bill. I take the bills—all his bills for the property, actually—and I list them for him so that at the end of each month he has all the due invoices in front of him."

"That's interesting. Do you know if he ever goes there?"

"No, I don't think so. As I said, I don't know much about it except where it is. But I believe the writer who's been there the longest lets Mr. Partridge know of any changes, or if something needs mending, like a window, if it's broken."

They were interrupted by the telephone ringing. The caller was Evelyn Butterworth, who said she had been summoned to the school where she taught—they'd sent another teacher around to the flat where she was staying—as they were short-staffed that week. She would telephone Maisie when she was available to go to Bart's studio—possibly in a day or two.

Maisie replaced the telephone receiver and asked Sandra to let her know directly Evelyn Butterworth called again.

"I should go down to the market to see the gentlemen." She pushed back her chair and was reaching for her coat, which was on a hook behind the door, when the telephone rang again. Sandra answered, jotting down a name before asking the caller to hold the line just one moment.

"It's a Mr. Dawkins for you. Said you'll remember him from Waterloo Pier."

Maisie reached for the receiver just as the caller pressed more coins into the slot to extend the call.

"Are you still there, Mr. Dawkins?"

"Yes, thank you. Is that you, Miss Dobbs?"

"Yes, it's me."

"This is PC Dawkins, Thames Division."

"I gathered it was you. What can I do for you, PC Dawkins? At least it sounds as if you're still in employment. When my secretary said, 'Mr. Dawkins,' I thought something untoward had happened."

"I'm still in a job, but something untoward *has* happened—well, I think it has."

"Can you speak now? Or would you like to meet?"

"Better get it over with now. I don't want anyone to see me talking to you, just in case they know who you are."

"You're taking a risk, so be careful."

"I know. But I just don't like what's going on."

"What is it, PC Dawkins?"

"A man took his own life, along the water. I reckon you might have heard about it—his name was Jimmy Merton."

Maisie caught the telephone cord and began twisting it through her fingers. "Why do you think I might be interested in him?"

"Just occurred to me—after all, he was found hanging from Lambeth Bridge, where that other man went in. And in my opinion, most people who want to do away with themselves along the water choose one of the other bridges—the Albert is very popular, although we do get quite a few over by Blackfriars Bridge, what with it being close to the courts."

"Tell me about the man, if you don't mind. You said he was found hanging."

"It was me and my mate what found him. We couldn't call for assistance at the time, so my mate had to hold the boat steady while I cut him down and lowered him in."

"That must have been difficult for you," said Maisie. She wondered at the effect of seeing so many suicides on one so young, and at once she was glad that at least he had never been called upon to go to war.

"The thing is, Miss Dobbs, I've been thinking about it, and I don't reckon he took his own life. I daren't say anything, because they like it cut-and-dried here, no doubts. And the CID, when they came and had a look, they said they could see he was dead and that it was by his own hand, and that it would be an in-and-out job for the pathologist."

"What evidence do you have that it wasn't by his own hand?"

"There was marks on his face—mind you, granted, it could have been where the body was hanging and got bashed about a bit. But the other thing is, I really don't know how he would have got down there, to rig up the noose. He was sort of partway under the bridge, not hanging from the top, where you'd stand to look down the river. I mean, he could have climbed down, but I don't think so. I reckon it was done by boat—I think he must have been dead already. Then someone came along, put up a rope, and then hung him there, so it looks for all the world like he did it himself. And of course, the marks on his neck, on account of him swinging back and forth, couldn't be told apart from any other marks."

"So, are you saying he had wounds consistent with someone who had hung himself, but he would have had difficulty in setting up the suicide in the first place? From your description, it sounds as if he's more likely to have fallen and drowned in the attempt. Is that the measure of it?"

"That's it, Miss Dobbs."

Maisie was about to pose another question when the constable spoke again. "And if you wondered, I don't want any money, and I'm not working for anyone. I just don't feel right about it, that's all. There's some things being ignored, and I didn't join the police force to ignore a criminal act."

"Good for you, young man. What will you do now?"

"I'm leaving this lark. I know there's no jobs about, but I'll do any-thing, anywhere—and don't worry, I won't be coming to you for work. No, I've had enough of the crime business, even if I am on the right side. And this river is bleeding cold of a winter's night, and it stinks to high heaven in summer. The corpses smell a lot worse as well. I think I might like to get out of London altogether, get down to the country."

"Do you know anything about gardening, PC Dawkins?"

"Funny you should ask that. My mum has a little patch; I go out there to work every day, keep it neat and see what I can grow. I should've been a country boy."

"Look, let me give you this address in Kent. It's a place called Chelstone Manor, and the head gardener is a Mr. Avery Buckle. Tell him I recommended you—it doesn't guarantee anything, but he might be able to give you an apprenticeship at some point. You catch the train to Tonbridge, then a bus or the branch line to Chelstone. The station master will direct you to the manor from there."

"Thank you, Miss Dobbs."

"And thank you, PC Dawkins."

"I'll be off then."

"Oh, and young man—watch your back. Until you leave the force, just watch your back, and take care."

Maisie leaned over Sandra's correspondence tray to replace the telephone receiver.

"That sounds dodgy, Miss Dobbs."

"It does a bit. But the man gave me some interesting information, without doubt—and he's an honest policeman, so I trust him." She put on her coat, hat, and gloves. "Slight change of plan. I'm going down to Lambeth Bridge, then on to see Mrs. Maud Pettit. I don't think it'll do me any good to go back to Bookhams at this stage, but I intend to drop in at the market to see if Seth and the men are there—they should be back from their rounds by then. How about you? Is everything clear on Billy's cases?"

"Yes, I should have a final report on one of them tomorrow morning."

"Tomorrow morning? Well done. Remember to put in a chit for your overtime—and I'm sure you're working overtime, Sandra." Maisie paused as she reached for the door handle. "Oh, and tomorrow I'd like you to help me with the case map—perhaps you can spot some connections where I can't. It's always better with two pairs of eyes on the task."

A dirty wet mist hung over the water, and though the sun might have broken through clouds outside London, there was nothing but a slight round paleness in the sky where the sun's glow should have been. She pulled her coat around her as she walked to the center of Lambeth Bridge and rested against the wall to look down the river towards the Houses of Parliament. The new Lambeth Bridge had been opened only the previous summer by the King, and though already tarnished in places by the elements, it was still resplendent in red paint chosen to match the color of the leather benches in the House of Lords. In one direction she could walk to Lambeth Palace, the London home of the Archbishop of Canterbury since the thirteenth century, and in the other she could cross to Millbank, then along towards Westminster Bridge, painted green in honor of the House of Commons. She smiled. Maisie loved this London, as much as it grieved her to see the poverty, the desperate need of people in Lambeth; at the same time, there was a fierce grandeur about the factories, about chimney stacks fired by the hard work of an ordinary, working-class population. She loathed the inequity of it all, that the final profit went to those who hardly gave a thought to the workers who toiled, their skin thick with dust, oil and sweat—yet she also knew that without those who had never known want, there would be no work at all.

Perhaps her own prejudices were part of the reason she and James were floundering in a relationship that seemed to start well, so easily had they moved from being friends to lovers. If they were to part now, surely the ripples of broken expectation would affect much in her life—from her father's position as Chelstone Manor's head groom, to her closeness with Lady Rowan Compton, James' mother, who had taken to treating her as if she were the daughter she had lost. How might they all react to such news?

Maisie looked down into the river, at the dense mass of water working its way towards the Pool of London, and from there out to the marshes, and then on to the North Sea. A dredger slipped under the bridge, then a barge and a tug in succession. This was the Thames as a working waterway. This same river would entertain pleasure-seekers at Henley or Marlow, and supply fishermen close to its source, but here it was an ugly mistress—a thick gray killer if you slipped into her clutches. Maisie leaned over the side of the bridge to look down, and wondered how desperate one might have to be to climb down towards the water,

CHAPTER TEN

❖

Jennie's face lit up when she opened the door to see Maisie standing on the step.

"Come in, Maisie. Come in. We were just talking about you, weren't we, Maud?"

Maisie stepped into the passageway. "Oh, so that's why my ears were burning." She smiled at Jennie. "Shall I go through to the kitchen?"

"Off you go, love. She's in her chair by the fire. She does feel the cold, you know; even has a hot water bottle on a summer's night. I just walked in the door a little while ago, from my cleaning job down at the pickle factory."

"You're still working there, Jennie?"

"Until I drop, probably. Mind you, Maudie and me, we've been careful with our money, and Wilf left us a little. And now Maud has earnings that Eddie saved up, we should be all right when it comes to the time I can't work anymore, though I hope to keep at it for a few more years yet. The rent on this place hasn't gone up in a long chalk, and we've been lucky because when we first came here, the three of us, we could only afford rooms upstairs, but now we've got the downstairs as well. Nice enough, for a couple of old girls, eh?"

Jennie chivvied Maisie into the kitchen, and as she entered, Maud held out her hands.

"It's nice to see you, my love. Fancy you coming back here on account of our Eddie."

Maisie took the woman's hands, and was surprised at the strength that seemed to be returning to Maud Pettit.

"You sit down next to me, Maisie. Tell me what you've been doing for my Eddie."

Maisie rubbed Maud's hands as she began to speak, looking back and forth between the two women as she explained that Jimmy Merton had been found dead, an apparent suicide.

"The police believe that, one way or another, Jimmy was responsible for Eddie's death, that even if he didn't create the circumstances for the paper bale to fall, he never made an attempt to help Eddie. They think he might have just wanted to scare Eddie, or intimidate him in some way, but it went too far. They had questioned him a couple of times, but couldn't really pin anything on him, though they were working with possible witnesses—the fact that he killed himself has convinced the police that Jimmy was their man."

Maud Pettit nodded, slowly, her gaze on the windowpanes, where dust had collected against the glass outside.

"Kettle's boiling. I'll brew us some tea," said Jennie.

Maisie thanked Jennie, her voice barely more than a whisper. These were people for whom a cup of tea was balm for the shock of bad news; perhaps a death, an accident, the loss of a job or a roof over one's head. The more desperate the word that came—from a neighbor, in a letter, from the bailiff or the police—the stronger the brew and the sweeter it was to the taste.

"What do you think, Maisie?" asked Maud. "What do you think of these policemen and what they've said about Jimmy Merton?"

Maisie looked down at her hands, then back at Maud to answer her question. "I don't know, to tell you the truth. But here's what I do think—that they're probably right that Jimmy Merton had a hand in Eddie's death, and for that he's paid a price. And I think we must be thankful because now we know."

"An eye for an eye and a tooth for a tooth, ain't that right, Maudie?" Jennie began pouring the tea, her hand shaking.

"It's a terrible thing, all the same," said Maud. "Two boys growing up here on these streets, you'd think we'd all stick together; after all, we're all in the same boat. We should be looking out for each other, not one trying to kill another. It's a terrible thing, terrible."

"Yes, it is." Maisie began to choose her words with care. "But now you can rest, can't you? You know how Eddie died, and you know that, however wrong it all was, the piper's been paid his due. Now you can mourn, and you can remember Eddie with all the love in your hearts, because he touched so many people—and he brought comfort to the horses; he loved his horses, didn't he?"

"Yes, he did. He loved them and they loved him back."

Jennie brought a cup to Maud, holding on to the saucer until the woman had it in a secure grip.

"I won't stay, Jennie," said Maisie. "I must be getting along. I'm going up to see Jesse, Seth, and the men up at the market—I want to catch them before they go home. They'll want to know the news too, and I daresay you'll be seeing Jesse soon, Maud."

"Oh, he'll come round to see us. You'd better keep that kettle on the boil, Jen."

Maisie said good-bye to Maud, who made her promise not to be a stranger.

"It does us good to see a young face about. Two old women like us, we could do with a bit of life around here, especially now Eddie's gone."

She saw grief in the woman's features, and gave her word that she would keep in touch.

At the door Jennie squeezed Maisie's shoulder. "I know you're busy, Maisie, so don't feel you have to visit. Maud's just feeling a bit lonely. She's afraid, you see, of being on her own. Not that I'm planning to go anywhere." She put her hand to her forehead. "I keep meaning to ask you—was that notebook of Eddie's any help?"

"It's a help, Jennie, but I'd still like to find the one with all Eddie's customers and their addresses listed. It hasn't turned up."

"I've racked my brains and nothing fell out," said Jennie. "But I'll keep looking. Take care, young Maisie. And thank you. Thank you for coming over with the news."

Maisie said good-bye and walked along the road to where she'd parked the MG. She started the engine and for a while sat in the idling motor car, looking about her. She was one of the lucky ones, and there were few. The outcome could have been so different. She felt as if she were in debt, that there was something to be repaid, and she thought she could start with Maud and Jennie. Perhaps she could ensure their security in the house, or have some alterations done to make it more comfortable for the two women as they aged. Despite what Elsbeth Masters had said, she thought it was the right thing to do.

Having set the motor car in motion, she made her way on towards the West End, but a wave of fatigue seemed to envelop her as she negotiated the lorries, horse-drawn carts, motor cars, and weather. And at the same time she felt a pang of guilt. She had told the truth, that Jimmy Merton was dead, and that the police believed him to be responsible for Eddie's death. The weight she carried within her came from a growing sense that Eddie's death was just the tip of a very different iceberg.

M aisie stood on the edge of the market, watching porters running to and fro, and costers clearing up after a busy day. The ground was spattered with dropped fruit and vegetables, and street urchins waited to be thrown a few "specks"—damaged fruit unsuitable for sale—or to be given a coin or two for running an errand. Maisie was pained to see so many of the children running in bare feet and threadbare clothing. She thought she would talk to Andrew Dene; in Maurice Blanche's last will and testament they had been given a responsibility to ensure the continuation of the medical clinics he'd set up in the poorest areas of London. Perhaps they could add a distribution office to provide discarded clothing to the poor, or she could allocate a certain amount to add new children's clothing each year; perhaps C&A's would give her a discount, if she asked someone at the store. She hated to see children so wanting.

She spotted Jesse lifting a box of cucumbers and stepped out in his direction, waving when he looked up.

"Mr. Riley! Jesse! Over here!"

Riley touched his flat cap, and began walking towards her. On the way he called out to a man walking across the market.

"Fred, could you have a scout round for Seth, Archie, Pete, and Dick? Tell 'em we've got a visitor and they're wanted over here." He smiled as he approached Maisie. "I didn't think we'd see you here today, Maisie."

"I've some news for you, Jesse."

"Better wait for the lads. Here, come over this way; they've more chance of seeing us if we wait on the corner."

Soon the other men joined them, making their way past barrow boys and porters, everyone pushing, shoving, and running to bring more produce to the stalls or to load up for deliveries.

"Why don't we go over to Sammy's, eh? He won't mind us taking up a table while we talk."

Pete led the way through the throng to a small café on the opposite side of the market. The owner waved to the men as they came in.

"Just want to sit down for a minute or two, Sam," said Jesse. "All right with you?"

"Trying to impress the lady?" said Sam, sweeping back gunmetal gray hair that had flopped into his eyes as he worked.

"You know who this is?" called Jesse. "Frankie Dobbs' girl. Remember Frankie? Went down to the country when the war started. He still comes up this way now'n again. This is his Maisie."

Maisie waved to the café owner. She recognized him when he looked up, and remembered being told he was from Malta, though she recalled that when she was a child Sam had jet-black hair, always oiled and in place.

"Maisie? Maisie the little girl who loved my ice cream?"

At once she could almost taste Sam's special hazelnut ice cream, a crunchy confection that slid across the tongue, so rich it made her eyes water with each spoonful.

"Oh, now I remember you, Sam—you made the best ice cream in London."

"You want some, Miss Maisie? Still make it, 'specially for you!"

"No, thank you." She shook her head. "I'm here to talk to the gentlemen. But I'll come back for a cornet when I have time to sit and savor the taste—so remember me, won't you?"

The man laughed, waved, and continued to clean his small café.

"Got some news for us, Maisie?" asked Pete.

"I have. Yes." She stopped speaking for a moment, watching the men. Pete leaned forward, but Seth and Jesse sat back, their arms folded. Archie and Dick both folded their arms as well. She went on. "I heard from the police that Jimmy Merton was found dead, apparently by his own hand. He'd hung himself from Lambeth Bridge."

"Bloody hell," said Pete, looking back at the others.

Seth shook his head while Jesse looked out of the window, then back at Maisie.

"Merton was under suspicion anyway," said Maisie. "The police said they couldn't pin Eddie's death on him, but they believe he either caused the accident, or at the very least he didn't make any attempt to help Eddie. And that wasn't the end of it. My assistant, whom you met—Mr. Beale—was attacked when he left The Lighterman after conducting inquiries. He was left for dead and is now in St. Thomas' Hospital. He's out of the woods, but still very ill. Jimmy Merton was fingered as the attacker. The police believe Merton knew he could face the gallows for Eddie's death, if guilt could be proved—and he doesn't exactly have a sterling record. At the very least, he could have been sent down for a long time for the attack on Billy, for which there were apparently witnesses. The result was that he took his life to avoid the gallows or prison."

"Well then, he got what was coming to him." Jesse looked at the other men. "I've no sympathy for him. It's a shock—I never expect the likes of Jimmy Merton to do away with himself, but you never know what goes on in a man's head, especially his sort. But I'm not sorry to see the back of him. I don't think any of us are."

"Can't say as I disagree, Maisie. I don't like to speak ill of the dead, but I never liked the bloke. He was bad all the way through, that one. Good riddance, that's what I say," said Archie.

The men nodded in agreement.

"Will your Billy be all right? Will he be able to go back to work, do you reckon?" asked Seth.

"I don't know, Seth. I—I'm not allowed to see him at the moment. I'll probably know soon, though."

"Strong lad, that one," said Dick Samuels.

"But you could see he'd been wounded in the war," said Pete Turner. "And did you hear his chest, when he spoke to us down here in the market? He'd been gassed, you can always tell 'em." Pete looked from Jesse to Maisie. "What about his family? They going to be all right?"

"Yes. I'll make sure they want for nothing."

"And you—what about you?"

Maisie smiled. The men had no knowledge of the way in which her circumstances had changed, that she was not only a working woman but one who had considerable wealth.

"I'll be all right, don't you worry about me. I can take care of them."

"That's all right then." Jesse frowned for a second or two, then looked at his friends. "Well, lads, we'd better get a move on. Reckon we should go round to see Maudie, don't you?"

There was agreement all round, and Maisie made her farewells, called out good-bye to Sam, and went on her way. She would have liked to feel as if her investigation was coming to a close, that she had given her clients exactly what they wanted. But there were too many loose ends. The police may have filed the case away, but for Maisie there were still pages flapping in the wind.

The office was silent at the end of the day. There were a few messages from Sandra, but nothing urgent. She picked up the black telephone on her desk and dialed the number for the Compton Corporation. James was not available, so she left a message asking him to telephone her at the flat, later. She did not care what James' secretary might think. For the moment, she just wanted to be alone. She was gathering her belongings when the telephone started ringing.

"Fitzroy five-six-double-zero."

"Maisie, where on earth have you been? Come over for a cocktail, now. I insist."

"Pris—oh dear, I know I promised, but I've been busy."

"All the more reason. I'll drink tea if it makes you feel better."

"All right, give me a few moments to tie up some odds and ends here, and I'll come over before going back to the flat."

"The flat?"

"Yes, it's my home, and I want to go back there this evening."

"Oh dear, hit a nerve there, didn't I? I'll expect you by half past six then. All right?"

"I'll be there, Priscilla."

"I don't even like the way you said 'Priscilla.' Something must be terribly wrong. Half past six, not a moment later. And never mind the tea, I prescribe gin and tonic. Bye!"

Maisie rubbed her forehead. At least she had done two good deeds for the day. She'd given a young man the possibility of work to which he might be suited, and she'd taken news to Maud Pettit that her son's murderer had paid a price for his actions. Billy's family were taken care of; and if all went well, she knew Billy would contact her as soon as he was in better health. In the meantime, she would keep her distance from the Beales, though she thought she might ask Sandra to visit Billy on her behalf.

The door of the mansion in Holland Park was flung open by Priscilla's eldest son almost as soon as she pulled the bell.

"Good heavens, how you've grown! You'll soon tower over your mother," exclaimed Maisie.

Thomas Partridge, who had recently celebrated his twelfth birthday, blushed. "About an inch or so to go." He leaned forward and kissed her on both cheeks. "Hello, Tante Maisie. We've missed you."

Soon they were joined by Timothy and Tarquin, who, Maisie thought, were also shooting up like vines.

"Is Uncle James coming?" asked Tarquin. All the boys were mad about flight and aeroplanes, and the fact that James had been an aviator in the war had given him extra points as far as the boys were concerned.

"Sorry, just me this evening."

There was a collective sigh of disappointment.

"Oh, for goodness sake," said Priscilla as she approached, her arms outstretched to shepherd her sons in the direction of the staircase. "You three toads can just go to the playroom and do whatever you boys do in there, but if I hear one scream, one 'I'll kill you' or the sound of a ball being whacked against the wall, you can rest assured there will be another sort of whacking in the works."

The boys ran off, and Maisie rolled her eyes. "Just as well I know that you wouldn't lay a finger on them, isn't it?"

"I do a very good line in threats, though. Come on, to the drawing room. I've been so terribly good for so long that I've been looking forward to my cocktail this evening. Join me?"

"I think I might."

"Oh dear. Now I know there's trouble."

Priscilla led the way to the drawing room. Maisie took a seat on a leather chesterfield and looked out at the garden while listening to the sound of Priscilla dropping ice into glasses, pouring gin, and then a brief swish as she added tonic water.

"There you are, mother's ruin." Priscilla handed a glass to Maisie and, kicking off her shoes, seated herself at the opposite end of the chesterfield, her legs to one side. She rubbed her feet.

Maisie sipped her drink and sighed deeply as she leaned back.

"All right, out with it. I have the distinct feeling that all is not well with your love life."

"Not exactly," said Maisie. "But if you don't mind, I wanted to ask you something. About Douglas."

"That's one way of getting out of telling me what's going on—mention my husband so I just have to know immediately what on earth you might want to know."

Maisie rubbed her forehead, her fingers still cold from holding the chilled glass. "I'm curious about how well Douglas knows John Otterburn. I mean, I know he must know him—but to what extent? Does he work for him?"

"Douglas has written for all the big newspapers at one time or another, so he knows Otterburn, and our paths have crossed socially—we were invited to tomorrow's bash, actually, but had to decline in favor of a supper with one of Douglas' old army chums and his wife. They went off to live in Greece after the war. Bit like us; they had to get away from it all."

"But do you know if he's working for him at the moment?"

"I couldn't say, though I think he might be beavering away on more than an article. To tell you the truth, I don't ask questions about his work. If he chooses to show me something or ask me for an opinion or just moan that he can't quite get something right, I do what I can—read, say what I think, or listen. I couldn't write my way out of a paper bag, so I fear I can't really be very constructive in my assistance."

"Why do you think he might be working on more than an article?" asked Maisie.

Ice rattled in the glass as Priscilla stirred her drink. "Years of practice in the art of being married to a writer. I know it's something important, and that he's not saying much. The last time he started a book, he did the same thing—it's as if he was going into a cave to thrash things out with someone. Fighting with the words, I called it once. He sometimes works at home—his lair at the top of the house—but as you probably know, he also keeps a small office not far from here."

"Does he ever use the studio at Lancaster Gate?"

"So you know about that?" Priscilla picked up her drink. "Not that it's a secret, but Douglas doesn't have much to do with it on a day-to-day basis. It's part of an estate left to him by an uncle—very handy too, if you're a writer. He wanted to help other writers who aren't quite so fortunate as to have the space to work in peace—perhaps they live in a flat and have children at home, something of that order. But go there himself? Never. He said he wants to help support those writers, not do their work for them or be there in an advisory capacity. I don't think he ever sets foot in the place. There's an overseer for the building—as well as the studios, there are residential apartments on the upper floors—and one of the writers takes care of administration of places and the waiting list."

"I see. So you think he's writing a book?"

"He'll tell me soon, when he's wrestled the first chapter or two. And he'll also be working on his articles and essays. He likes to write different sorts of things, and sometimes at the same time—he says it keeps him on his toes."

Maisie nodded. "And has he ever mentioned a man called Bartholomew Soames?"

Priscilla stirred her drink again and took a sip before setting the glass on a side table. "Doesn't ring a bell. Do you want me to ask him?"

"No. No, please don't. It's best left alone, and I'll ask him if need be."

"What's going on, Maisie?"

Maisie shook her head. "I don't know. Not yet."

"Knowing your work, I do hope there's nothing frightening going on to do with Douglas."

"No, not in the way you think. I just happen to be working on a case that involves a writer—Soames—so I thought I'd ask. And as for what Douglas is working on, well, Sandra just happened to mention that she was busy with some important work for him at the moment."

"Your questions are very specific, though, Maisie. I think you're fobbing me off."

"I just wondered how well he knows John Otterburn—that's at the heart of it. And the young man in question had a desk at the studio, so the two names came up a few times. That's all." Maisie felt she had asked too much and hoped Priscilla would accept her explanation. "And I'd be awfully grateful if we could keep this conversation between us. I know that's a lot to ask—after all, he is your husband. But I wouldn't want my questions to be of a concern to him when he's so busy."

"I see. Well, as long as you don't think he murdered anyone!" Priscilla stood up, holding up her glass. "Another one?"

"I'm only a few sips into this one."

"I'll just have another half-glass, and lots of ice." Priscilla stood up and went to mix another drink.

Maisie watched as Priscilla stood beside a sideboard of dark wood and mirrored glass, the top reflecting bottles and an ice bucket, as if the designer had intended the effect to resemble a kaleidoscope.

"So, tell me," said Priscilla, pouring gin into her glass and holding it up to check the measure before adding another splash. "What's going on with you and James? To tell you the truth, I've been expecting a joyous announcement of forthcoming nuptials."

"That's far from on the cards."

Priscilla took her seat once again. "But everything started so well, and he's a very nice chap—the boys adore him."

"Yes, he's lovely—kind and solicitous. But we seem to be arguing over all sorts of silly things. And some not-so-silly things." Maisie sighed, set her drink on the side table, and ran her fingers through her hair. "And we're just different. I thought it might not matter so much that our roots are poles apart, but it does matter, and it seems to be becoming quite significant. I've been suffocating at Ebury Place, and I've come to see my flat as a retreat."

"Do you spend much time at your house?"

"My house?"

"Oh, for goodness sake! The house that Maurice left you . . . ? The Dower House . . . ?"

"At first I did, because there was a lot to go through. But now—no, not really."

"I see."

"What do you see, Pris?" asked Maisie. "What do you see that I can't see?"

"I'm going to have to be blunt with you."

"When haven't you been blunt, Priscilla?"

"Not as often as I would like. I've been watching you since Maurice died, and I believe you've found it harder than you think, having the responsibility of wealth and property."

"I have Maurice's lawyer to advise me," said Maisie.

Priscilla shook her head. "That's not what I mean."

"What do you mean, then?"

"Look, this is just what I've seen, what I've noticed during the past months, since your inheritance. You seem to be spending an awful lot of money on trying to make other people happy. You've essentially bought a house for the Beales in all but name; and, admittedly, you've trod very carefully so as not to offend, but you've set them up and have barely asked for rent since they moved in. And then Sandra—bless her, she's a lovely, intelligent girl and she's been through a lot, but I know you're paying for her education and her books and everything that goes with it. That's without your contribution to Maurice's clinics, over and above the trust he'd set up so that the work may continue. And there's been other things—I won't go so far as to say you've been spending money like a drunken sailor, because you don't direct it at yourself, but it's as if you feel you're having to apologize for having the money in the first place, and you're trying to get rid of it so that you can be comfortably strapped for cash again."

"Priscilla, that's unfair!" Maisie stood up and began to pace. "I mean, well, if you're thinking like that, look who—look who acted as a guarantor for me to obtain a loan for the flat? Eh? You thought I wouldn't find out?"

"How on earth—?"

"I discovered that you'd had a hand in it when I went to pay off the mortgage—which is something I was able to do with the money left to me. And I'm only doing what you did for me."

"Oh no, Maisie. It's not the same—and for goodness sake, sit down, will you?" Priscilla raised her voice. "You're making my head spin."

Maisie sat down. Priscilla continued.

"Look, you are my most precious friend; you're like a sister to me. You are dear to my heart, and I knew that even if you found out, you wouldn't hold it against me."

"But what do you mean, 'It's not the same'?"

"I mean that this . . . this controlling of other people's futures won't get you any thanks, you know. In fact, if you go on like it, coming to the rescue all the time, you could make more enemies than friends." Priscilla paused, then stood up. "Oh, bloody hell. I'm going to have the other half of that G and T, and I might just make it a very large one." She continued talking while pouring another drink, throwing ice cubes into the glass in a manner that almost caused them to bounce out again. "The fact is, people like a *little* help when they need it, usually because there's a means to pay it back—perhaps not in the same way, with money, but with a task completed, something like that. If you give people more than they can ever repay, you run the risk of resentment, because then they feel beholden." She sat down again, but closer to Maisie. "I know this is hard, and it's only my opinion, but I've seen it happen. I would bet anything that in time there will be repercussions from the recipients of your largesse. Those people you've helped might distance themselves, or they might decide it's easier to stop seeing you at some point. You leave them with such a debt, and no one likes to feel in debt. There are ways of helping without doing everything—otherwise you take away the opportunity for them to be proud of something they've achieved."

"But I couldn't leave Billy and his family where they were, not with the boys always ill, and them cramped with Billy's mother in that small house."

"Small by whose standards?"

"They were so happy to be moving."

"Of course they were," countered Priscilla. "But give people time to settle, and the obligation begins to weigh on them."

Maisie bent forward and pressed her hands to her eyes. "I just keep doing everything wrong. I feel as if everything I touch is falling apart in my hands."

Priscilla placed her drink back on the side table and put her arm around her friend. "It's all to be understood, Maisie. I may not have your insight, but I know when I see something out of kilter, and I think that's what's happened to you, but in a subtle way. Everything good has a dark side, even generosity. It can become overbearing, intimidating, even humiliating—and no one likes to think someone else is pulling the strings, do they?"

"Oh, I've made such an idiot of myself. I wish Maurice had left the money to someone else, someone more capable."

"He did the right thing, Maisie, but it is a change in circumstances you weren't prepared for—and I think you've done a remarkable job, really."

"I should keep my nose out of other people's business."

"Well . . ."

Maisie sat upright. "But I do know one thing, and that is, James and I, we're on different paths. We have different expectations of what might be and of each other. I think we're at the end. I just feel it."

"Now then, now then. The sky isn't falling in, Maisie. You've just got to buck up, take care of your business, take care of your estate, and, above all, take care of yourself. I bet this upset with James is just a storm in a teacup, truly I do. The course of true love ne'er did run smooth."

Maisie finished her drink. "The fact is, Pris, I don't think we are each other's true love. I think we've simply been very good company for each other, and we've probably helped each other realize that we still know how to love."

Priscilla looked at Maisie for a moment. "I do wish you would just give it some more time."

"Anyway," said Maisie, coming to her feet, "we've that Otterburn supper tomorrow, and perhaps a Friday to Monday with them, over Easter. We've some other social engagements on the horizon, so we'll get through them and see where we are."

"Yes, dear friend. See where you are. Don't be hasty in your decisions."

The two bid farewell on the threshold, Priscilla holding Maisie just a few seconds longer than usual. She was aware Priscilla had remained at the door as she walked down the steps to her motor car; and as she turned at the end of the street, she looked back and Priscilla was still there, watching as she drove away. She thought she might feel light-headed following the strong cocktail, but as she negotiated traffic back to Pimlico, she felt alert, her thoughts clearer than they'd been in a long time. She was surprised at how easily she had articulated her situation with James; she could see in Priscilla's eyes a hint of realization that the intermittent discord was not a storm in a teacup. And yet she was even more surprised—mortified, in fact—by the way in which her friend's words had echoed the conversation with Elsbeth Masters. But Priscilla's summing up—one phrase in particular—resonated in a different way: "Everything good has a dark side, even generosity . . . *and no one likes to think someone else is pulling the strings, do they?*"

For some reason Eddie Pettit had come to mind when Priscilla spoke, and it caused Maisie to wonder if someone had been pulling his strings, which might explain why he had been so unlike his usual self in the weeks before his death. And she thought the puppeteer in question might have been Bart Soames, and she was determined to find out why.

the shelter constructed with care had come down and she had to start all over again. The bequest from Maurice was the gust that had swept through her card house, and though it was a most beneficial inheritance, and she at least had a solid foundation upon which to construct her place of belonging once again, at the same time she was left wondering who she might be now and in the future. James was right to turn the question back to her: "What do *you* want, Maisie?"

Once upon a time that might have been an easier question. But now? What did she want for her life to be considered well-lived? How could she honor both her past and at the same time take on a future that offered so many more opportunities than she might ever have imagined? She thought of Maurice. What had contributed to his wisdom? How had he gained the knowledge he'd brought to every case, every conversation, every challenge? The water was growing cold, but Maisie wanted to follow this train of thought to its destination. Who did she want to be, in this new life? She had resources now such as she had never dreamt of having, and she knew—more than most—that with money came freedom and restriction, both. *To those whom much is given, much shall be expected.* She understood this: that she wanted to be worthy of Maurice's legacy. She wanted to serve, and it seemed she was adept in only one endeavor at the moment, and that was as an investigator. She had, she admitted, made quite a mess of trying to sort out the lives of those closest to her—the words of both Elsbeth Masters and Priscilla had cut her to the core, but she had to admit to herself that they were right. She'd made some dreadful mistakes. And it was true, she had put a lot of effort into her world being just so: into controlling and organizing; mending this, making up for that; and she'd done more of it since being given the keys to Maurice's money. It had bolstered her, it had made her feel safe, in a way, when she was able to change the circumstances of those around her who seemed to be careening towards disaster. At times it was as if the gods of perfection were holding her to account. Perhaps that was due to the war, or to the battle inside her.

The water was too cool now to bear, so she stepped out of the bath, toweled dry, and pulled on her dressing gown. Sitting in front of the gas fire, she rested her elbows on her knees and held out her hands to the heat. Though she had calmed her thoughts—those recollections that would so easily skirmish within her—she couldn't deny that part of her was still at war with her past. Again she asked herself what Maurice had been exposed to throughout his life that might have contributed to his strength of character and to the deep well of knowledge he seemed to have at his disposal. She smiled as an image of her mentor came to mind, sitting in the chair alongside the fire at Chelstone, pipe in hand, his eyes upon her as he asked her a question, then counseled her to take her time, to chew it over while he poured another malt whiskey and savored the warmth. Could his knowledge have come from all the questions he'd put to himself?

As she lay in her bed, before her eyes became heavy with sleep, Maisie made a list in her mind of the elements she believed had contributed to the qualities she most admired in Maurice. That he was well educated was without doubt, and he had done much to ensure that her own education was as deep as it was broad. He was well read—and his library was at her disposal. That he had loved was understood; he had never given her details, but she knew he'd had the love of women and had loved in return. He had gained professional acclaim. He had served those less fortunate. And he had known the world, in his day spending time on every continent, immersion into the lives of others in far-flung places contributing to his understanding of humanity. Ah yes, there was something: Maurice had traveled. Maisie, for her part, had been to France. And she had been to war.

But war was more than a place; it was a monster, a thing at once alive and dead and predatory, and it could be the root of a newfound hell anywhere. Like a new island born of volcanic eruption, it could even create havoc before fully formed. Yes, war was a country, and she had been there.

The offices of Sanders and Herrold on Chancery Lane were situated close to Lincoln's Inn Fields, in a Georgian stucco building with high arches and heavy oak doors. Maisie's footsteps echoed on flagstones as she entered, and a porter asked if he might help her. She informed the porter that she was there to see Mr. York Herrold, and had been told by his clerk that he was not in court that afternoon and would see her at her convenience. If the man detected a lie, it was not revealed in his expression. Holding out his hand as if he were a policeman directing traffic, he explained to Maisie that at the top of the staircase she should turn right through the black door and the clerk would assist her. She thanked him and went on her way.

The clerk, a man wearing gray pin-striped trousers, a black jacket, a crisp white shirt with a wing collar and a black tie, asked if he could help.

"I am here to see Mr. York Herrold regarding the matter of Mr. Edwin Pettit's untimely death at Bookhams Paper in Lambeth. I am a representative of the deceased's mother and I have been referred to Mr. Herrold by the general manager at Bookhams."

The clerk, who had not given his name, cleared his throat. "Quite. I'll see if he can spare you a few moments. You should have telephoned first, you know. He's a very busy man."

"Which is why I so appreciate your help," said Maisie. "And not to worry, I can wait until he's available. I've brought something to read."

Without being invited to do so, she seated herself on a bench and looked at the clerk. "I'll just sit here while you talk to him then."

The man cleared his throat again, opened another door leading to a buttermilk-painted corridor with a burgundy-colored floor runner, and left Maisie for some moments before returning. The door opened once more, and the clerk held it back for her to proceed. "He'll see you now, Miss Dobbs. First door on the left, but let me show you in." This time the man whispered, as if he were in church.

"Thank you," said Maisie, her voice at a normal pitch.

The clerk closed the door behind him, then knocked at another door, painted in the same rich shade of cream, before entering the book-lined room.

"Miss Dobbs to see you, sir."

"Very good, Williams." A tall man, younger than Maisie had expected, came from behind the carved oak desk to greet her. "I'm glad I was here when you called. A stroke of luck." He shook her hand. "Do sit down."

Maisie had anticipated a crusty old lawyer, not someone who seemed more of a high flyer, with his confident smile and ready greeting. York Herrold was probably around her own age, with dark hair and features set off by the requisite dark clothing. A barrister's wig hung over the back of his chair, and a gown had been placed on a hook on another door.

"I see you looking at my wig—yes, I know I should put it away carefully, and Williams will tut-tut-tut about it, but there you are. It makes my head itch and brings me out in a rash on my forehead, so I can't wait to be rid of the thing when I leave court. But of course you're not here to talk about my wig problems, are you?"

Maisie at once felt herself on guard. Here was an ambitious man, a man who was used to disarming those he questioned. Was that why John Otterburn had chosen the firm to represent his business interests?

"No, I'm here to ask a few questions that you may or may not be able to answer, about the death of Mr. Edwin Pettit at Bookhams Paper."

"Very tragic. And I believe the man thought to have caused the accident has taken his own life. Yes, it's sad all around. But how can I help? As the owner's counsel, we ensured that Mrs. Pettit received a sum to help with funeral arrangements, though as you know, Mr. Pettit was not an employee and, frankly, should not have been on the premises. We have assisted the company in the process of instigating new rules regarding access to the factory by nonemployees, and as you know—because you've been to the factory, according to the manager, Mr. Mills—there are now additional safeguards in place so that such an accident will never happen again." He smiled at Maisie. "Factories are dangerous places, and it's a painful truth that it often takes an accident such as this to have the engineers and so on look again at the various processes and procedures to see what might be done to stop it happening in the future—tragedy as the mother of invention, if you will."

"Quite. But that's not exactly why I'm here, though I'd like to come back to the plight of Mrs. Pettit."

"Go on," said Herrold, his face giving away nothing of his inner thoughts.

"I'm curious to know why Bookhams took on a known criminal in James Merton. The man had previous convictions and seemed to wield a certain amount of power, especially when it came to preventing union activity in the factory. I wonder if that was sanctioned by the company? I'm here because, as the company's legal representatives, you would have had a hand in development of policy regarding organized labor, I would have thought."

Herrold took a moment to answer, clearly formulating his response with care, then he smiled again. It was a sudden smile, put on as if it were a mask.

"Miss Dobbs, I fail to see what any of this has to do with you, or with the death of Mr. Pettit, or, indeed, his mother's needs at the present time."

This time it was Maisie's turn to smile. "Fair enough, but speaking of his mother's needs, with the discovery of Mr. Merton's guilt, a guilt that led to his death, one can conclude that a flawed yet obviously trusted employee—especially if he was tasked with the obstruction of union activity—not only may have had a hand in the death of Mr. Pettit, but at the very least might have prevented his death, or could have offered assistance when he was dying, which he didn't. Now, Mrs. Pettit has been left in a precarious financial position, given that her son was the breadwinner in the family—indeed, he had worked for Mr. Otterburn in another capacity, I believe, assisting with his horses—so my visit here is to negotiate a . . . a settlement, I think is the word. Yes, a financial settlement to ensure she is not compromised by want."

"Well, I—frankly, Miss Dobbs, I—" Herrold stuttered.

"Yes, you do know what I'm talking about, Mr. Herrold. And I suggest you discuss the matter with your client. I am sure he will be more than willing to accommodate Mrs. Pettit, given the fact that her son died a terrible death at one of his most important factories." Maisie stood up. "I'll give my name and telephone number to Mr. Williams, so you can contact me when you have a figure in mind. We'll haggle then, shall we?"

She held out her hand, and saw that Herrold was beaming his confident smile once more.

"I will be in touch, Miss Dobbs." He rang a bell and the door opened almost at once, giving the impression that Williams had been on the other side, like a faithful dog waiting for his master's summons.

As Maisie reached the door, Herrold spoke again. "Well done, Miss Dobbs. I have to admit, very well done."

Maisie smiled in return, nodding to Williams as she passed him in the corridor. She remained long enough to give the clerk her address and telephone number, and departed the offices of Sanders and Herrold, ensuring she thanked the porter as she left the building. John Otterburn would no doubt hear about her visit within a few moments, and she wondered if he would comment upon it when they met at dinner. It did not matter. Maisie had decided that instead of simply writing a check herself, she should try to squeeze some money out of Otterburn via his lawyers. It would mean a great deal to Maudie, and at the same time, Maisie might discover something of use. The fact that the ploy had worked so easily, that Otterburn's representative was so quick to consider her request at just the mention of possible criminal activity, gave her pause.

A plain correspondence postcard from Eve Butterworth was waiting at the office. The message informed Maisie that she was available to visit the Lancaster Gate writers' studio on Thursday morning. Using a similar postcard to reply, Maisie said she would pick her up outside her friends' flat the following morning at ten o'clock.

Two new customer inquiries and a sit-down with Sandra to compare notes on work in hand saw another couple of hours go by. Caldwell telephoned at noon.

"Afternoon, Miss Dobbs. Got some news for you."

"Is Billy all right?"

"Doing much better, sitting up and talking—in fact, as far as I can tell, he's talking rather a lot."

"That is good news." Maisie put her hand on her chest. "I am so glad, I cannot tell you how much."

"We were able to have a word with him this morning, just dotting i's and crossing t's in this Merton business, because that's one thing I want to get right off my desk. Anyway, he'd like to see you—afternoon visiting tomorrow, if you'd like to go in. He is considered fully capable and his wishes make the previous instruction from Mrs. Beale null and void."

"I'm so glad. How is she? Do you know?"

"Being discharged tomorrow, late morning, so I would suggest your little helper over there at the house should leave first thing."

"I'll make sure it's done. Thank you, Inspector."

"By the way, here's a bit of police gossip. You know that lad I put you in touch with—PC Dawkins?—well, he's vanished off the face of the earth."

"What? What do you mean?"

"Left a message that he was sick of the smell of the river and being on the water, so he just upped and left. Couple of the lads went round to his house and his mum said he'd gone out as usual that morning. She was dead surprised."

"Aren't you worried? Is there an inquiry in progress?"

"He'd been talking about going off, apparently. Told a couple of the other lads that he was always aching in his bones, what with the damp and all, and he said he didn't really like the work. And off he went."

"His mother must be sick with worry."

"She is, but we reckon he'll get in touch soon—or he'll be back when he realizes that there's hardly any work to be had, wherever he goes." He paused. "I just wondered, seeing as you spoke to him recently—any idea where he might've gone?"

"Inspector Caldwell, I'm concerned for his safety. Of course I don't know where he's gone. And are you sure he's just left to go off to find work elsewhere?"

"The note says as much, and he hasn't been missing twenty-four hours yet. Mark my words, he'll be back soon enough, though the police won't take him on again. No, we need men with a bit more about them; not shirkers afraid of a bit of wet."

"So you wouldn't mind a shift or two on a cold night out on the water."

"Not blimmin' likely!"

Maisie left the office earlier than usual, arriving at Ebury Place to prepare for the evening's outing to the dinner party hosted by John Otterburn and his wife. James arrived home within an hour of Maisie, and swept her into his arms when he came into her room.

"I almost came over to the flat last night, I missed you so very much, Maisie."

She smiled. "Oh, I had my usual bowl of soup. You were better off here, having a good meal."

"No, not really. I rather miss our evenings at the flat." He shrugged. "Perhaps it was a mistake, opening up the house."

"Your mother was right, James. A man of your position needs a home in London, not to be living at a club," said Maisie. "And you've breathed life into the old house."

"It's alive when you're here with me."

James held Maisie close, and she was filled with confusion again. How might it be, she wondered, if they were married? And with that question she felt the air leave her lungs and her breath become shorter. She pulled away.

"We'd better get ready, don't you think? This one's an early supper, so we don't want to be late."

"Right you are, General!" James turned. "Let's have a glass of champagne before we go."

"Lovely idea."

Maisie, you look smashing, as always."

Maisie looked down at her dress of heavy silk in the same violet-blue as her eyes. "It's another one of Priscilla's, gratefully accepted."

"She probably had to give it to you—I can't see that suiting her half so well, not with her chestnut hair. It gives you an air of intrigue—all dark colors reflected."

"Oh dear, I do believe you're in a poetic frame of mind this evening." Maisie was glad they were in a light mood, almost as if it were the early days of their courtship. She hoped there would be no discord this evening.

Following a quick glass of champagne, they were soon on their way to the Otterburns' Park Lane mansion. As they reached Hyde Park, James reached across and took Maisie's hand.

"Be careful, James, you're supposed to be watching the road." She had noticed that James often waited for a nighttime journey to broach a troublesome subject, when the rhythm of the motor car conspired with the shadowy darkness to ease what he anticipated might be a difficult conversation.

"I want to ask you something, Maisie."

Maisie felt herself tense. "Yes, James. What is it?"

"Look, I've been thinking a lot about your work lately, and I have to admit I've been getting more and more worried. This business with Billy rather floored me, and I think—if you don't mind my saying—I think it's the thick end of the wedge. I want to ask—no, in fact, in respect of our . . . our relationship . . . I believe I must insist, if that's not too strong a word—that you give it up. Or perhaps not do so much or don't accept these risky assignments. You asked what I really wanted, and I realized I want you to step back a bit, not only for your own safety, but for us. I mean, look, what is to be achieved by taking on these jobs? And this one has been for a simple man who died in an accident."

"What? Did you just call Eddie a simple man?"

James ran a hand through his hair. "Look, that came out all wrong—but at the same time, please, Maisie, let's be honest; from everything I've gleaned—not that you tell me anything about your work, not the details, I have to find that out myself—but from all I know, he was not quite all there, was he?"

Maisie thought her head might burst as questions formed in her mind—and a rising anger caught in her chest when she thought of what James had said.

"The only thing that matters is that he was a human being. In fact, he was the most innocent of human beings, James, and those men who came to me for help deserve everything I could do to bring peace to the memory of Eddie Pettit. I don't have to explain any of this, James, but let me ask—what do you mean, you have to find out yourself? Am I the subject of an investigation?"

"No, not at all. I mean, well—"

"James, I will not spoil our evening, and I will not give you cause for embarrassment at the home of John Otterburn. But you can drop me at my flat after we leave, and then be on your way back to Ebury Place.

I won't be the subject of an investigation because you don't like what I do. Have you someone snooping on me? Is that it? Well, that would certainly be one for the books."

"Maisie, don't take it like that. There's no investigation; I've just been paying attention, that's all. Really, I only wanted to let you know that I worry about you, that I'm concerned."

"Then it's best if you don't know what I'm doing, or when. Then you won't worry, will you?"

"You're being unfair. Most unfair. You're not a bachelor girl anymore, you're a woman who is loved, and I think I have some say in your well-being."

"Think of that next time you want to screech off somewhere in your Aston Martin, or go with your friends to watch motor racing. It cuts both ways, you know."

"But, Maisie—"

"I do believe we're here."

James cruised the motor car to a halt alongside the main entrance to the grand house, and a footman came to open the passenger door. Maisie took his hand and stepped from the vehicle, then waited on the top step for James, who buttoned his jacket as he approached her.

"I love you, Maisie."

She sighed. "I know you do, James. And I understand how you might feel. But my work is part of me. Now then, let's compose ourselves and go in. This can wait for another time."

At first glance, Maisie judged there to be about thirty people invited for supper, all of them clustered in the drawing room while footmen zipped to and fro with champagne and canapés. Maisie recognized several politicians, as well as two or three actors and a writer whose name she couldn't quite remember. She recognized Winston Churchill, who was in conversation with an American whom she suspected was a man of commerce, and a very successful one at that, given the cut and quality of his suit, the way he stood, and the gold and diamond ring catching the light as he lifted his champagne glass to his lips. It was well known that Churchill had a fondness for Americans. His mother had come from that country to marry his father, and in so doing—with her not inconsiderable dowry—had shored up the fortune of the third son of the then Duke of Marlborough.

James mingled easily, his hand on Maisie's elbow, steering her to meet people he knew, introducing her to Lady this and Lord that, to the heir of this title, the politician from that party. Words seemed to carry on the air, and Maisie thought that a guest at such a party was rather like a bee, buzzing from one bloom to the next in search of nectar, whether it be the sweet devilishness of gossip, the gravity of politics, or the weight of opinion. And everyone had an opinion.

"And she was wearing red. I mean, who's wearing red this season?"

"I tell you, old chap, if I were you I'd keep an eye on those stocks; it's not over yet."

"Mark my words, that man Hitler has his eye on the whole of Europe, and we're not ready for it. Not ready at all."

"Put your money in land, that's what I say. Land."

"I do think it's about time the prince settled down, don't you?"

"And what about those Mitford girls? Can you imagine!"

On and on it went, like water tumbling across rocks in the riverbed.

And like a river, the groups and couples were soon on the move, funneled through double doors into a dining room that could quite easily have accommodated one hundred guests, thought Maisie.

She was surprised to find that she was seated to John Otterburn's right, at one end of the table. His wife, Lorraine, was at the opposite end, with Winston Churchill to her left, and James to her right.

James smiled at Maisie and gave a subtle wave. She smiled in return. In truth she was not sure how she felt at that very moment, and each time doubt threatened to undermine the depth of consideration she'd given the matter while at her flat the previous evening, she pressed it back again. Her thoughts were lingering on the subject of their relationship when she felt a hand on her arm.

"I said I'm pleased to meet you, Miss Dobbs—James has told me a lot about you." John Otterburn cut an impressive figure; Maisie thought he looked not so much like a man of business as a film star, though she suspected his hair might have been dyed to hide the onset of gray. His suit was of an elegant cut, and his demeanor gave him an air of confidence and power, as if he were a king in his castle and those gathered around him at table were his court.

"Oh, Mr. Otterburn. I'm so sorry. I was distracted."

"Probably by your amour at the other end of the table. I'm not sure he trusts me."

"I am sure he does, Mr. Otterburn—why wouldn't he?" Maisie picked up her water goblet to quench her thirst, then, without awaiting a reply, continued. "You've gathered an interesting assemblage of guests this evening."

"You make me sound like a collector of butterflies. Actually, I rather like watching people, flitting here and there, wondering what they're thinking—don't you?"

Maisie nodded thanks to a footman who filled her wineglass, and turned back to Otterburn. "I rather believe everyone does that at times."

"Certainly private inquiry agents have a tendency to more inquisitiveness than the average person."

Maisie gave away nothing in her demeanor, nor did she take up the point with Otterburn. "Well, I would imagine so. How else would someone in that line of work get along, without healthy curiosity and something of an imagination?"

"Imagination?"

"I would say that in such a profession, one has to have an imagination, if only to grasp the full extent of what human beings are capable of, and to what purpose."

Maisie was grateful when the woman to Otterburn's left interrupted and firmly asked what he thought of the Prince of Wales and his current paramour. "It's common knowledge," she exclaimed, and asked if the newspaperman didn't think the subject was worthy of a column or two, as people had a right to know.

"I say, I don't know what Compton must find to talk to Churchill about over there," said the man seated on Maisie's other side, as he listed towards her in a waft of whiskey. "Everyone knows he's got nothing better to do than pen his thoughts and then try to get them published."

"I've heard he's a very good writer," said Maisie, leaning back a little to avoid the downdraft of alcohol fumes.

"Oh, I suppose he is, but there are others, and much better, too. Surprised there aren't a few more here, but then Johnny's keeping his stable of opinion-makers under wraps."

Maisie was about to ask what the man meant when Otterburn interrupted them.

"Miss Dobbs, I see you've been set upon by my ne'er-do-well brother-in-law. Is he bending your ear with one of his stories?"

"No, not at all," replied Maisie.

"Just making sure. He tells a tall tale and must be regulated at times—isn't that right, Jonty?"

The man looked half asleep as he leaned forward, almost into his soup, and Otterburn rolled his eyes.

"Always the way. Don't listen to anything he says—not all there, you know."

Maisie nodded and picked up her spoon.

Conversation continued with Otterburn and the woman who had been so taken with the activities of the Prince of Wales, touching mainly upon the news of the day and the social calendar. Maisie looked down the table at James, who remained in deep conversation with Churchill, leaning behind Lorraine Otterburn, who was, in turn, cupping her ear to listen to the woman on the other side of Churchill. Her thoughts were interrupted when the port was brought in and their hostess stood up and indicated that it was time for the ladies to adjourn and leave the men to their cigars and politics. Maisie sighed, allowed Otterburn to pull out her chair so that she could exit the room with the other women, and felt a dread in her stomach at the next half hour or so in the company of women whom she did not know and who likely had little more to discuss than a new hat purchased at Derry and Tom's, or a gown from Paris.

Her fears came to fruition as the women were led to the drawing room, where Lorraine Otterburn directed the positioning of her female guests without appearing to tell anyone where to sit. She was as striking as her husband, with fair hair tied back in a chignon so tight it appeared to pull the skin across her high cheekbones. Her gown was of a black and gray silk blend that seemed to shimmer in the low light, and Maisie thought she looked like a Greek goddess in the midst of her handmaidens; it seemed she wielded a power no less potent than that of her husband. The women, arranged in clusters, proceeded to gossip about who was doing what with whom, and the trouble one had in hiring trustworthy household staff, especially as everyone wanted more these days. Maisie whispered to the woman seated next to her on a leather chesterfield—though she couldn't remember her name—that she had need to "powder her nose." She left the room and made her way along an endless hallway hung with paintings of gentry she suspected were no relation to John Otterburn. She thought she might delay returning until she heard the men leave the dining room to join the ladies for coffee.

She reached a door left ajar, and, when she looked closer, could see the lights had not been switched off. Curiosity—she almost laughed when she remembered the conversation with Otterburn about the curiosity of an inquiry agent—fanned the flames of interest, and she pushed against the door, only to realize that this room was a study and library. At once she was reminded of her nighttime excursions into the library at Ebury Place when she was a maid on the bottom rung of service. In the early hours she had tiptoed into the library to read and to learn, and she had never lost her love of libraries, of places of learning. Now she crept alongside Otterburn's bookshelves, her head to one side as she scanned the titles. Indeed, it was an enviable collection. Tapping her fingers against the leather spines, she stopped when she reached the two volumes of *Mein Kampf*, written by Adolf Hitler. She was at once surprised, then not, for this was the house of a leading newspaperman, and the German Chancellor was nothing if not newsworthy. She took down the first volume and began to read, skipping from one chapter to another as she drew upon memories of German classes from her student days. Then, with the book in hand, she walked across the room and took the liberty of seating herself at John Otterburn's desk.

Fifteen minutes later, she looked up at the mantelpiece clock and realized that time had indeed passed, and the men had likely finished their port and cigars and withdrawn from the dining room to join their womenfolk.

"Oh, heavens!" she whispered into the silence of the room.

Standing up, Maisie felt her foot catch on the carpet and began to stumble. She reached out for the desk to steady herself, knocking a pile of papers—which had been neatly stacked—onto the floor.

"Blast!" she said as she set the book on the desk and knelt down to gather the folders and pages.

She came to her feet slowly, leaning across towards the desk lamp to better see what was in her hand, but before she could read the words on the top page, she was interrupted.

"What the hell do you think you're doing, Maisie?"

James stood before her, his expression open, questioning.

"I was reading this book—you know what I'm like with a library, James, and when I saw the light on, I couldn't resist. Mr. Otterburn has a copy of *Mein Kampf*, so I began reading a few pages, and when I realized how much time had gone by, I started to hurry and knocked all these papers across the floor. I am so terribly sorry—I must have embarrassed you by not being in the drawing room with the other women."

James looked at the floor and at the papers in Maisie's hand.

"If I had no knowledge of your profession, I might be more inclined to believe you without question, but—oh well, look, let's put it all back and then join the other guests. I had to insist upon coming to find you when you weren't there with the women—frankly, I suppose I feared you might be up to something." James squared the papers on Otterburn's desk, while Maisie returned the book to its place. "There's more drinking going on in the drawing room, Maisie. I don't know if I want to stay long now, in any case."

They walked together towards the staircase.

"You seemed to be having a lively conversation with Mr. Churchill."

"Yes, he's an interesting fellow. I can't say you did as well, what with that woman who's obsessed with the Prince, and that drunk lolling all over you." He put an arm around her shoulder. "Come to think of it, no wonder you made a run for the library."

Maisie laughed, relieved that another row had been averted.

"Perhaps we should go home now, James."

"Mine or yours?"

"Either will do."

James pulled her to him and kissed her tenderly.

"Oh, I see you found your love, James." Otterburn walked along the hallway towards them.

"She was in the library, John." James took Maisie's hand. "If Maisie's missing, it's where I'll always find her, you know."

"Anything to interest you on my shelves, Miss Dobbs?"

"You have an impressive collection, Mr. Otterburn. I saw that you have the two volumes of *Mein Kampf*, so I started to read and . . . well, it's what always happens with me when I've a book in my hand; I forget time, and that's it."

"And what do you think of Hitler?"

"I didn't read very far into the book, just dipped here and there, but if I add what I read to what I know from the newspapers— your newspapers, actually—I would say he's someone to be worried about."

"You've got that right." Otterburn paused, extending his hand to James. Maisie thought it was the first time his Canadian accent had been evident in his speech. "In any case, my main collection is at our country home in Surrey. It's where I do most of my serious thinking—

and talking—at the week's end. In fact, it's unusual for us to entertain so many guests during the week, but Lorrie insisted it would be the most convenient day for our guests here tonight." He turned to James. "See you again soon, James. Looking forward to it."

James caught Maisie's eye, and it was clear that he had confirmed their presence at the Easter gathering at the Otterburns' Box Hill estate in Surrey.

John Otterburn escorted Maisie and James to the drawing room, where a few guests were making ready to leave, but others seemed to be settling in for an evening of convivial company.

On the way back to Ebury Place, James once again reached across to Maisie.

"Everything all right? You seem distant."

Maisie shook her head. "Oh, sorry. Nothing. Just thinking."

"Of me, I hope!"

"Yes, James—I think of you all the time." She smiled, teasing, and squeezed his hand in return.

The earlier arguments were buried for now. But Maisie had not been thinking of James. She was wondering if it was so unusual to find Bartholomew Soames' name on a file among the papers in John Otterburn's study—after all, the man was a reporter. More interesting was a file entitled "Douglas Partridge."

But most intriguing was the sheaf of papers she had glimpsed while she was on her knees gathering them from the floor where they had fallen. On these pages were drawings—quite sophisticated drawings, each accompanied by detailed notes—of aeroplanes. She was not familiar with aviation, her experience limited to the wood-and-cloth contraptions that buzzed overhead like moths in the wind during the war, and, more recently, when she'd boarded an Imperial Airways

Armstrong Whitworth Argosy aeroplane and flown from Paris to Croydon Airport with Maurice. She wished James had waited just a few more minutes before coming in search of her, for she remembered being told that Eddie had talked about aeroplanes. It was a recollection that chilled her.

CHAPTER TWELVE

◈◈◈

Maisie and James breakfasted together at Ebury Place, then each went their separate ways to work. Little was said about the events of the previous evening, as if each wanted to steer clear of the matter now that a measure of oil had been poured on the troubled waters of their relationship. For her part, Maisie was anxious about the day ahead, knowing that she would be seeing Billy, and also accompanying Evelyn Butterworth to the writers' studios at Lancaster Gate. She anticipated Evelyn's nervousness at seeing the place where Bart Soames had worked.

Leaving at the same time, the lovers turned to each other and kissed.

"Will I see you this evening, Maisie?" asked James. He seemed to be avoiding eye contact with her, looking at his watch while asking the question.

"I think we should talk, James. Don't you?" Maisie sensed a resignation in his manner. She went on. "I think we must be honest with each other, and look at how we can best be a light for each other. I've been . . . well, I've been giving it all some thought, and—"

"Me too. Yes, you're right. How about a quiet supper at your flat?"

Maisie smiled. "Oh, yes, James. Yes, that would be lovely." She rested her hand against the side of his face. "You're a good man, James."

He covered her hand with his, then pulled her to him and kissed her forehead. "See you later then."

"Yes, later. I'll go straight to the flat after work."

"See you then, my love."

Maisie slipped from James' grasp. "Well, we'd better be off, hadn't we?"

"Wouldn't do to be late at the office, eh?"

They parted, each walking to their separate motor cars, waving to each other as they drove away.

Pushing all thoughts of James to the back of her mind, Maisie recollected in her mind's eye the moment she began to pick up the papers that had fallen from John Otterburn's desk. She could see the pile of manila folders and a sheaf of loose pages, and, as if time had slowed, she could again feel her shoe catch the carpet and her hand reach out, sending the papers cascading onto the floor. In her imagination she could see the words and drawings, and could feel the tremor of shock as James entered, looking at her as if he had come upon a common thief. She could see the images in front of her, as if she were still holding the pages in her hands. What was going on? The pieces of the puzzle were at odds: Douglas Partridge a friend of Otterburn; Bart Soames' name among his private papers; and then detailed drawings of aeroplanes, the like of which she had never seen. Beyond what she already knew about him, who was Otterburn? And what had happened with Eddie Pettit that seemed to link him with Soames? James had said that Otterburn had a finger in many pies, intimating that he was a linchpin in the marriage between business and politics. One only had to cast a glance around the supper table at his Park Lane mansion to see the diverse walks of life represented. What strings was he pulling? And if there were strings being pulled, was he doing it to benefit himself, or another?

Evelyn Butterworth was waiting outside her friends' flat as Maisie pulled alongside the curb. She reached across and opened the passenger door for Evelyn, and as soon as her passenger was settled, Maisie negotiated the MG out into traffic and drove in the direction of Bayswater and Lancaster Gate, one of London's most prestigious addresses.

Decelerating as they approached a terrace of white stucco mansions alongside Hyde Park, Maisie slowed even more, to better see the properties, and Evelyn rolled down the side window.

"There, I think that's the one. Can you stop here?" said Evelyn.

"It's probably best to go around the corner and park by the church."

With the MG left close to Christ Church, the women walked back to the mansion owned by Douglas Partridge. As they walked, Evelyn told Maisie that, according to Bart, two floors had been designated as a place of retreat for writers who needed peace and quiet to accommodate the needs of their craft.

Evelyn pushed against the main door, which was unlocked.

"That's a stroke of luck!" she said, turning to Maisie. "I wouldn't know where to find the key."

A sweeping staircase led from the ground floor to the first floor, then narrowed as it snaked to the upper floors, where a series of private residences were rented out to gentlemen and women of means. A door at the first landing opened out into an expansive sitting room with a series of less ornate doors around it, each offering entrance to a small office for a working writer. A man sat in front of the fire, reading and smoking his pipe. He was dressed in corduroy trousers and a tweed jacket with leather elbow patches. Though his clothing seemed well cared for, it also showed age, with a shine to the trouser fabric and a line of darning at one edge of the jacket.

"May I help you, ladies?" inquired the man.

"Yes," replied Maisie. "Would you direct us to Bartholomew Soames' studio?"

Holding the bowl of his pipe in his right hand, he waved the stem in the direction of the last office on the right. "Over there. Haven't seen him in a while, though. Mind you, I've been away. India, you know. A lot going on there."

"Has anyone else been to visit his office?" asked Maisie.

The man put on a show of thinking, closing his eyes and tapping the lip of his pipe against his temple. "I'm wondering who you could ask. Despite the professional envy from which we all suffer when someone sells an article or, heaven forbid, a book to be published, we tend not to invade each other's havens, so any visitors would most likely have come from outside." He cleared his throat and was about to draw from the pipe when he frowned. "Look here, are you supposed to be going in there?"

"I am Mr. Soames' wife, sir," said Evelyn. "My husband passed away several weeks ago, and this is the first opportunity I've had to come collect his things. I asked my friend to accompany me."

"Bart? Dead? Oh good Lord, whatever happened to him? As I said, I've been away and this is my first day back."

Evelyn pulled a handkerchief from her handbag and pressed it to her eyes. Maisie put an arm around her shoulder.

"She's quite upset, if you don't mind. We'll go in now," said Maisie, leading Evelyn in the direction of Soames' office.

As they entered and closed the door behind them, Evelyn straightened her spine and looked around the room.

"Right then, let's get on with it."

"You're very good, you know," said Maisie.

"My heart's been broken, I've wept a thousand tears, and I've cursed every deity you can think of. And now I have to galvanize. Someone broke into our flat, into my home, my castle—small though it might be—and I am absolutely livid about it. So, let's get on with what has to be done; I'll do whatever I can to help you in your quest to get to the bottom of all this."

Maisie suggested to Evelyn that she go through the bookcase, take out each book, shake the pages, and check to see if anything had been written inside, other than marginal notes on the text itself. In the meantime, Maisie would search the desk, which was very much like that of a bank clerk, with a series of drawers on each side and a single wide drawer in the middle. Papers were stacked neatly on top, along with a pile of six or so books, leather markers lolling out from between the pages, like the tongues of dogs on a hot day.

"Remember to go slowly, Eve. Don't rush, just in case you miss something." She looked around the room. "Then we'll look at the piles of papers and books on the floor."

"Bart always was one for keeping things in piles on the floor. When he ran out of space on his desk—which, by the way, is worryingly tidy—instead of making more room, he would just start to pile things on the floor."

"I'll bear that in mind about the tidy desk—but people are sometimes like that: untidy at home, yet neat at their place of work, or vice versa."

Evelyn began taking down the books as instructed by Maisie, who opened the top drawer of the desk. Pencils, a blade for sharpening, an eraser, and a ruler. Drawing pins, several unused notebooks, a hole-punch, a small box of paper clips. Instead of closing the drawer, she eased it out and laid it on the floor.

One by one, she checked each of the other drawers, reading through correspondence, files of clippings of articles and essays written by Soames, and going through his notes. And as she finished with each drawer, she removed it, until finally all the drawers had been taken from the desk. She peered inside the wooden shell. Nothing. On her hands and knees, she stretched one arm in as far as she could and felt around the inside of the desk. Nothing. She even pulled the Anglepoise lamp from the top of the desk and directed the beam onto the dark interior wood, checking top, sides, and corners. Nothing. And as she replaced each drawer, she lifted it up to check the under-side, to no avail.

"Anything yet, Eve?"

"No. And I'm not feeling terribly confident either."

"Still too tidy?"

"Yes." Evelyn Butterworth turned around. "Those books on the table each have a proper marker. Now, I've seen Bart when he's working, and let me tell you, he rips off bits of paper all the time—from newspapers, usually—to place between pages he wanted to come back to—and he scribbles in books too. Here, look at this one—here's where he's made notes in the margin about something he's questioned. That's Bart. His mind was too active, and he learned that if he didn't put in a makeshift marker while he thought about it, he would be onto something else and forget there was a question unanswered. And it's not as if he didn't have proper bookmarks in his desk—but his mind was often working too fast to do things properly." She sighed and looked around the room while pushing back her hair with fingers dusty from handling books. "A big unanswered question—bit like this."

Maisie followed her gaze. "At the moment, yes, it is. But the answers will be found, you can mark my words."

Evelyn went back to taking book after book from the shelves as Maisie leafed through pages of manuscript on the desk. After turning each page so that it was face down on the desk, she would square it with the others. One by one, she turned the pages, reading a paragraph here, a sentence there. Bart Soames had been writing a novel, yet instead of being set in the present or even the past, it was a fantasy set in a mythical kingdom with an overpowering, godlike monarch; it was a story which, had she time to linger, might have intrigued her. As she lifted a page close to the end, however, she discovered that the following page was not part of the novel at all, but a list of fifteen names. "Douglas Partridge" was listed two-thirds of the way down the sheet of paper, and Maisie immediately recognized the others as being well-known novelists, for the most part, although she recognized the names of a playwright and a poet.

"Eve, I've found a list of names here—did Bart know these people?" She took out the page and passed it over to Evelyn. "I mean, did he know them well, or was he connected with them in some way?"

Evelyn looked down the list. "Hmmm, well, I recognize them, and certainly Bart knew *of* every one of them, but I don't think he knew any of them well—I don't think he'd ever met Partridge, even though he owns this place."

"You don't recall Bart talking about any of them?"

"No."

Maisie tucked her hair behind her right ear. "I think I'll hang on to this."

"Do you think it's important?"

"You know, I have a feeling it might be. Anyway, let's get on—and when we're finished, we should go and ask someone if there are spare boxes around here. For two women who've come to clear out someone's office, we are suspiciously bereft of boxes."

The women spent another hour and a half going through papers, which in the main amounted to transcribed interviews that had no connection to either Eddie Pettit, Douglas Partridge, or John Otterburn. They searched through the books, and they checked under a carpet and behind the picture frames, even going so far as to remove the back of each frame to check inside. Finally, they sat down—Maisie on the desk chair and Evelyn on a small button-back leather chair—and studied the room.

"It's very quiet, I will say that," said Evelyn. "No wonder Bart liked working here."

"Are you still planning to try to take it over?"

"I've been thinking about it a bit more, and, what with the distance, it's probably best for me to just work at the flat—it's not as if there's someone else there to disturb me." She shrugged. "Anyway, word went around my friends about the break-in, and people are dropping off bits and pieces for me over the next few days. I'll probably end up with more than Bart and I started with, and I'm going to make sure I have a desk."

"And you're sure you won't find other accommodation?"

She shook her head. "I suppose it's my way of keeping him close, being at the flat. In fact, the burglars, whoever they were, probably did me a favor, because it won't look like it did when Bart was there, when we were there together—but I'll still feel him there." She paused and closed her eyes. "I feel him here, too."

There was a faint aroma in the air that Maisie thought might remind Evelyn of Bart. Perhaps it was the soap he used, or hair oil, or the polish from his shoes; indeed, it was likely all three were blended to give an impression of Bart's unique presence.

As if woken from a dream, Evelyn looked up. "It looks like we're finished here, doesn't it, Maisie?"

"Yes, I think we've gone over everything."

The two women stood up, and as they did so, Maisie brushed against a photograph on the desk, catching it as it was about to fall. "Oh dear, not again. That's the second time I've knocked something off another person's desk in less than twenty-four hours."

"Is that a photograph?" asked Evelyn.

"Yes. I noticed it when I first looked at the desk—I think it's Bart's mother, though it must have been taken a while ago. I took the photograph out of the frame and had a look."

"Let me see." Evelyn took the photograph. "Yes, it's Pauline. It was taken before she was married—that's the school behind her." She looked up at Maisie. "But Bart always kept this at home. He must have brought it here just before he died. I wonder why?"

"Perhaps he wanted to write something about his mother and the photograph inspired him in some way," suggested Maisie.

"Yes. Yes, perhaps you're right." Evelyn placed the photograph on the desk. "Well, I don't want it. Anyway, I'll nip out to see if I can scrounge some boxes, or at least let someone know I'm coming back with them."

As Evelyn left the room, Maisie was already removing the back from the photograph a second time. Again, nothing. She replaced the cardboard behind the photograph and within another minute it was as if the photo had never been tampered with. There may have been nothing but an old photograph of the woman who had been Eddie Pettit's teacher held within the simple frame on Bart Soames' desk, but both the image of the young schoolmistress of yesteryear and its recent presence in the room among benign piles of papers and rows of books told Maisie something she knew already—that she would have to make another visit to Brighton as a matter of some urgency. When she visited Pauline Soames the first time, she could not escape the thought that something was being kept back. Now she felt she wasn't wrong in the least. It was as if, in positioning that specific photograph on the desk when he did, Bart Soames had left a message of some sort, and she thought she knew what it might be. She also had to consider Douglas again, for she could not help but wonder if it was he who had come into Bart Soames' quiet retreat after his death, and if he knew what he was looking for as he left the desk tidier than it had ever been during the younger man's tenure.

After dropping Evelyn at the flat, Maisie returned to the office.

"Hello, Sandra. Off to work for Mr. Partridge?"

"Yes, Miss. I've two messages here for you, and the invoices typed up from yesterday, and the letters." Sandra handed Maisie a leatherbound ledger with blotting-paper pages; a document awaiting signature had been placed between each page. "There was a telephone call from a Mr. Buckle, who said he was the head gardener at Chelstone. He told me he was using your father's telephone as he wanted to find out about a man called Mr. Dawkins who had just been to see him about a job."

"Oh good, at least that's one question answered." Maisie removed her gloves and hat, placing them on the desk. She pulled up a chair and sat down opposite Sandra. "I wondered—" She shook her head. "No, not to worry. Thank you for the letters. I'll put them in the pillarbox myself as soon as I've signed them. You should be on your way now—you've a busy week ahead, what with the move."

"Is everything all right, Miss?"

"Yes. In fact, I'm just going to clear up a few matters here and I'll be on my way to see Billy. He's fully conscious and he wants to see me. I just hope Doreen takes it well when she learns I've visited."

"I'm sure she will, Miss." Sandra gathered her own coat and hat, and picked up a cloth bag full of books.

"Goodness me, Sandra, that looks fit to break."

"Oh, it does the job, Miss. It's good enough." Sandra smiled and waved. "See you tomorrow then."

"Bye, Sandra."

Maisie listened to Sandra's footsteps as she made her way downstairs, then the door opening and closing as she left the building. Maisie leaned forward at her desk and rested her head in her hands. She had caught herself just in time, stopping herself from launching in and organizing Sandra's books. "You need a nice strong leather bag," she had almost said, already thinking of the lovely leather shop in Burlington Arcade where she would order a briefcase for her secretary. Indeed, it was as if Sandra had known exactly what was coming, had intuited that Maisie was about to come to her aid, and in that moment had staked a claim for independence. *It does the job. It's good enough.*

She drew the ledger towards her, uncapped her fountain pen, and began going through the letters and invoices, putting her signature to each document, often with a brief note thanking the client for their business. Having returned the ledger to Sandra's desk, she put on her hat and gloves again—she hadn't bothered to remove her jacket—gathered the letters to be posted, and left the office, taking care to lock the door.

Billy, you're looking . . . yes, you're looking well. There's a bit of color in your cheeks."

Maisie set a small bunch of daffodils on top of the locker at the side of Billy's bed, which were soon whisked away by a nurse.

"There's a bit of color all over my face, if you're telling the truth, Miss. There's the blue and black around my eye, the purple going on yellow around my jaw, and as for this scar down here—" He used his bandaged hand to indicate a scar across his scalp above his right ear. "It's a very nice shade of raspberry and blue."

"Oh, Billy, it's all my fault. I am so sorry. I am so very sorry."

"Just joshing, Miss. You weren't to know, were you?"

"I think the fact that Eddie Pettit was dead should have told me a lot more than it did. How do you feel?"

"Me head hurts at times, but I try not to take anything for it—I don't want trouble with that morphia again, not like I had before. But I've been worried about my nippers, though, and Doreen."

"She'll be at home by now, I should imagine. She was discharged today, so I daresay she wanted to see the children, and will be back here to see you in next to no time."

"I don't know how my mum coped."

Maisie was quiet, looking down at her hands. "Billy, I know it was probably not my place, and I realize that now, but your mother had help. As luck would have it, Mrs. Partridge was able to send her boys' nanny, Elinor, over to help—Sandra had been lending a hand for a day or two, but Elinor knows more about caring for a baby. So everyone is well, and in good heart. I know that's what you wanted to hear, but I also understand that I probably overstepped the mark a bit too. I'm sorry."

Billy nodded, his movement slow, his eyes showing pain. "You always take care of things, Miss. I don't know what we'd do without you. Don't know how I can ever repay you."

"You don't need to. Doreen was rightly very upset and angry with me. You shouldn't have been at that pub, should not have been at the mercy of Merton, or anyone else who would do you harm."

"Well, it weren't Jimmy Merton, for a start."

"I beg your pardon?"

Billy squinted at Maisie through swollen eyelids. "I just don't think it was Merton. I mean, I was talking to him all right, in the pub. I went in and got into a bit of conversation, said I was looking for work—it's all a bit hazy, to tell you the truth, but a little bit comes back to me every day. Anyway, I was asking him about the union, how there isn't one, and he told me that they ain't allowed there, but then, the company looks after its own, so they don't need one anyway. He said it was his job to look out for agitators, looking to make trouble."

"Did he think you were looking for trouble?"

Billy shrugged, wincing as he moved his shoulders. "I forget myself, at times. I forget what hurts and where—then I move and it's agony." He sighed. "Anyway, I don't think he thought that at all. Well, he might've wanted to keep an eye on me, if I'd gone to work there. But cosh me and turn me over like that? No, I don't think so. But I reckon he knew who'd done it, or that I'd been set upon. You see, it's a bit like fog at the moment, the memory sort of goes in and out, like a sound you think you've heard in the night, only the more you listen the more you can't hear it. I sort of remember lying there, with this taste of blood in my mouth, and my head pounding and knowing I was slipping away somewhere else, like one of them mornings you just can't open your eyes for the tiredness, only it was worse. And I thought I heard him shaking me. It sounded like him anyway, saying, 'Billy Beale. Beale, wake up. Come on, mate, get up, open yer eyes.' Then this voice, if it was him, said, 'Oh, what've they done? What's been done to you?' Then he said, 'I'm sorry for this, mate, but I've got to leave you, got to get out, before they find me.'"

Billy's eyes filled with tears. "It probably wasn't exactly like that, Miss, but that's sort of how I keep remembering it. And to think he left me. Left me for dead, and me with three nippers and a wife at home. What would have happened then, eh? What would have happened to them?"

"Shhh, Billy, don't make it harder on yourself than it already is. You're on the mend. You're going to get well again—you'll be amazed how quickly you pick up, now you're awake and talking."

"But I keep thinking about it all."

Maisie touched Billy's arm. "Hush. Hush now. As soon as you think one of those thoughts, put your mind to something else. There will be plenty of time to recount what happened, and when you're better, that's the best thing to do—get it out of your system. In fact, you might have to tell the story a few times, to bring it from the darkness and into the light, so you can see it and not be scared by it anymore. But in the meantime, help your body to heal—think of your children playing. Think of Doreen at home with little Meg. Get well, Billy. That's your job now."

"I should tell you something, Miss."

"What's that?"

"That Caldwell told me Jimmy Merton was dead, that he'd taken his own life. And I didn't tell him what I thought, that Jimmy might not've been the one to do me over. I reckon I just wanted to keep quiet about it, because I wasn't sure what I was remembering, even yesterday."

"That's all right. I'll get to the bottom of it all. You just get better."

"Thank you, Miss."

"No need to thank me, Billy—you've done a lot for me, and for the business. You almost gave your life."

Billy smiled, a crooked black-and-blue smile. "Got nine lives, I reckon. Trouble is, between this and the war, I reckon I've run through a few."

Maisie shook her head. "You're one of a kind, Billy, and that's a fact. Take care, now."

Maisie sat in the MG for some minutes after leaving the hospital. She was wondering if she had the courage to go to John Otterburn's Fleet Street offices, march in, and demand to know exactly what was going on, and what Eddie Pettit and Billy Beale had ever done to upset him. And as soon as the thought had crossed her mind, she examined it again, for it had come to her almost unbidden. She had been trying not to leap to conclusions, trying to keep the line of questioning open, so she could better see how Eddie Pettit and John Otterburn might be linked, and how Jimmy Merton fitted into the picture, with Bart Soames' shadow behind them—but now she knew that she had been veering in Otterburn's direction since her visit to Bookhams.

She checked the time on Big Ben as she crossed Westminster Bridge. It would take her nigh on three hours to get to Brighton at that hour, so instead she decided to pay a visit to Douglas Partridge. Brighton could wait until tomorrow. They had elected to drive down to John and Lorraine Otterburn's Surrey estate on Saturday. If she had more pieces of the puzzle in her hands, perhaps she could have that conversation with him then.

Douglas was not at his office when she arrived, and it appeared that Sandra had already left for the day. Stopping at a telephone kiosk, she placed a call to the Partridge home, and was informed by the house-keeper that the couple were out for the evening, although if she wished, a message could be inscribed for them to read upon their return.

Frustrated, she reconsidered the drive to Brighton—she was anxious to act upon her suspicions and obtain answers to her questions, but she knew the true need was to feel as if she were doing something instead of waiting, to make use of her time, to be in control, instead of marking time. Given the hour she would arrive in Brighton, she would have to stick to her plan to go tomorrow morning first thing, and be back in London by mid-afternoon. There was James to consider, and she knew it would cause more ill-feeling if she had decided to cancel their evening together.

She found it hard to put the day behind her when she arrived back at the flat. Thoughts still swirled around in her mind, though she welcomed the silence, the peace that seemed to envelop her. She had stopped at a small grocery shop on the drive back to the flat and bought ingredients for a soup of vegetables and chicken, some bread, sharp cheddar cheese, and liver pâté. It would be their favorite supper—a picnic of sorts, but indoors, with a glass of wine.

Having made a cup of tea, she fried cubes of chicken, chopped the vegetables, made a stock and brought the soup to a boil before lowering the flame to simmer. At that moment the doorbell rang. Sighing, she turned off the gas and ran to the door, wondering who might be calling on her.

"James—why didn't you use your key?"

James Compton shrugged. "I didn't feel I ought," he explained. "Just in case you weren't in the mood to see me after all. I thought I would leave it up to you whether you answered the door or not."

"Oh, come in. Let's not act as if we've only just met each other." She looked up at him and took his hand in hers. "We might have had a row, James, and I spoke harshly, I know, and for that I am sorry—but let's not harbor fear of each other."

"Maisie, I believe that's exactly what we've been doing."

"Come on. Hang up your coat and hat. I've soup on the hot plate, a fresh loaf, and some very nice pâté."

James smiled. "I wouldn't want for more, at this moment."

Maisie laid the table with a cloth and cutlery while James put out two glasses and poured from the bottle of wine he had brought with him. Soon they were seated, each with a bowl of soup and slices of toasted bread.

"Not much soup left in the saucepan, but I can make enough toast to plug a leaking ship if you're really hungry."

"This is plenty, Maisie." James took a spoonful of soup. "I think I've made a terrible mess of everything. I shouldn't have made such demands of you. I've no excuse, except perhaps that I'm at my wits end, Maisie, not knowing how we might go on together, how we might, well, make a life . . . or not, because I just don't know what you want or what I want or if we want the same things, and . . . I feel I'm floundering, and I don't want to do that anymore. I've done it before, after the war, and I don't want to flop around like a fish out of water, and I had such hope . . ."

Maisie reached across the table to cover his hand with her own. "James, hush. We're both at fault, and yet we are neither of us at fault. I feel dreadful about my behavior, and feel as if I have failed you in so many ways. But I have thought long and hard about our recent conversations, at those times when we've struggled for honesty—with ourselves as much as each other—and I believe we are both beginning to realize that at the moment we just want different things."

"What do you want, Maisie?" He grasped her hand. "I would do anything for you."

"I know, James. Truly, I know. I wish I could tell you what I want, but I have come to realize that I don't really know. I know only what I don't want."

"Sort of like Oliver Cromwell."

"Oliver Cromwell? James, you flummox me at times," said Maisie.

"One of the few things I remember from that period in history—in fact, from any period in history. 'I can tell you, sirs, what I would not have, though I cannot what I would.' That's Oliver Cromwell for you."

"I wish I could say I was in good company, but wasn't he rather a killjoy?"

James laughed, though it was not a happy laugh.

Maisie set down her spoon and lifted her wineglass to her lips, taking a sip and keeping the glass in her hand.

"Tell me about being a farmer, James. Tell me about the places in Canada that made you want to have land there."

James sighed. "I suppose it was when I first went to Alberta, probably ten years ago, something like that. I had business there, and one of the men I met—he'd been born on a farm, and when I say farm, nothing we have here can compare to the sheer expanse available there—well, he'd found out I'd been in the Royal Flying Corps during the war and asked if I'd like to go up in his aeroplane. As you can imagine, I jumped at the chance, and on his part, I think he fancied himself as some sort of barnstormer." James refilled both his and Maisie's glasses. "But of course, I hadn't been up since the war and it took my breath away. There I was, on a day filled with sunshine, looking out at fields upon fields of wheat as far as the eye could see, and I could not help but imagine—right here, in my mind, as if it were happening there and then—men fighting below me, the dreadful killing, as if they were thousands of ants warring with each other. Then it sort of faded, that memory, and I was left with the sun going down, splashed across the landscape like raw egg, and I felt calm again, soothed." He sighed. "Oh, what a lot of rot. Listen to me rambling on."

"James, you're not rambling. I could see everything you described.

I—I know this might sound strange, but I think you've found a place where you belong, and it probably explains why you've gravitated back to Canada so many times."

"You could be right."

"Then why don't you do it, James? Go. Buy your farm. I am sure you can do something for the company while you're there. Or perhaps not. Hand the running of the Compton Corporation over to that second cousin, or whatever he is."

"I can't just abdicate my responsibility, Maisie. What kind of man would do that? In any case, not only are those same prairies beset with problems at the moment—dust storms, locusts, an onslaught of biblical proportions—but I would want you at my side."

They sat in silence for a few moments. Both sipped more wine, and then Maisie spoke again.

"James, I am sorry to tell you this, but I don't think I can see myself as a farmer's wife in Canada. Or England, or France, or anywhere else. But I will do all I can to help you when you're certain of your path."

"I know. That's something I'm sure of, that you will help me if that's what I choose." He blew out his cheeks, a mannerism Maisie had come to regard with affection. "But can we be together until we both know what we're doing?"

"Yes. Yes, I think we can. But let's promise we'll agree to part, as friends, and with respect, if and when one of us knows definitely."

James raised his glass. "To us, then."

"To us. And to raw-egg sunsets everywhere."

They laughed as their glasses touched.

CHAPTER THIRTEEN

❖

J ames was still sleeping when Maisie left the flat the following morning. They had talked long into the night and, as she reflected during her drive down to Brighton, a new intimacy had been forged between them, a pact that might not be understood by anyone else but which brought with it a mutual empathy that had perhaps not existed before. She wondered if either of them were harboring false hope that the end, when it came, would be without sadness; she suspected James might still be nurturing a faint glimmer of expectation that she might, after all, agree to become the wife of a man of commerce who would have preferred being a farmer. Oh, who knew what was going to happen in the world? She might change her mind next week and decide that fighting dust and locusts was all she'd ever wanted to do.

She arrived at the home of Mildred Taylor at ten o'clock. It was later than she had planned to arrive—she had been anxious to see Eddie Pettit's former teacher again—but, thinking twice about arriving too early, she had stopped to walk on the South Downs. Having parked the MG close to the downs above the village of Plumpton, Maisie changed from her town-dweller's footwear to her sturdy leather walking shoes, and strode out along a path well traveled by hikers. She remembered walking the downs years ago, with Simon. It was during the war, at a time when they were both on leave from their service in France. Now she pulled her coat around her as if to protect herself from the memories as much as from the strong breeze catching at her collar and her hat, which she took off, allowing her hair to be blown around her face. There was barely another soul to be seen when she set out on the path, which surprised her. After the war, however, in the early 1920s, the government had launched a series of advertisements aimed at getting the population out into the fresh air, encouraging people to go hill walking, which some master of the slogan had abbreviated to "hiking." Soon it seemed as if footpaths everywhere were filled from Friday to Sunday with men, women, and children walking as if their lives depended upon a thumping good, heart-pumping pilgrimage towards better health.

Today Maisie intended to walk for only an hour, and in that time passed several people making their way across the escarpment: two men appraising the day, using binoculars to better identify a bird or simply to view the landscape. A woman struggled along with a small wooden easel under her arm and a rucksack on her back; she could hardly see beyond her straw hat tied with leather cord under her chin. Maisie suspected the artist was probably somewhat optimistic regarding the day's weather outlook.

Maisie's thoughts of Simon—the love who had died long after the war, of wounds sustained in the conflict—brought not the searing pain that once caught at her chest with such power she thought her heart was truly breaking, but instead a sweet ache of remembrance for one who has passed and who was much loved. She no longer asked herself, "What if . . ." while wondering how their lives might have been different had there been no war. She might not be completely at peace with the past, but rubbed along with it because it was part of who she had become. And part of her life had converged with that of Eddie Pettit, with Maud, with the men who had come to her, caps in hand, asking for her help so that the memory of a simple man could be laid to rest. Now she must confront the mother of another man whose life was lost, a man she believed might have exploited the gentle giant who had a way with horses.

Returning to the MG, Maisie changed into her town shoes and, once inside the motor car, brushed her hair, applied a little lipstick, and went on her way. She parked the motor car outside The Lillies and, after knocking, waited for footsteps to approach along the passageway extending from the front of the house to the kitchen. It was Pauline Soames' voice that came from beyond the door.

"Who is it? Who's there?"

"Mrs. Soames, it's Maisie Dobbs. Do you remember me?"

The door was unlocked in three places, and opened only as far as a chain would allow.

"Good morning, Miss Dobbs." The woman did not open the door to its fullest extent, instead pressing her head against the frame to peer at her caller.

"I wondered if I might speak to you, Mrs. Soames. I'm alone, just me."

The door was closed to allow the woman to draw back the chain, and then opened again.

"Come in. My sister's gone to the shops, and I don't like to open the door to strangers."

"I understand, Mrs. Soames. Shall we go into the kitchen?"

"Yes. I was sitting in there, reading a book."

When they reached the kitchen, Pauline Soames pulled out a chair and moved a book and some papers to one side. She offered a cup of tea, but Maisie declined.

"What can I do for you, Miss Dobbs?"

Maisie inclined her head, as if wondering what indeed she wanted from the woman. In truth she knew exactly what she wanted, but understood there was a need to choose her words with care.

"Mrs. Soames, I have come because I want to see Bart's papers. You have his notes, you have drawings done for him by Eddie Pettit, and also in your possession, I believe, is a notebook belonging to Eddie that held within it details of his clients." She paused. "I am not here to admonish you, Mrs. Soames, and I am not here to intimidate you. You are probably correct to fear the stranger at the door, but I assure you, the strangers in question would not allow three locks and a chain to stop them, if they wanted to enter this house. The papers might be better off in my possession—strictly speaking, a good number of them belong to Mrs. Pettit, if truth be told, because they are Eddie's."

"I—I don't know." The woman kneaded a handkerchief she'd taken from her sleeve and pressed it to her tear-filled eyes.

"I think we both suspect Bart did not take his own life. He was murdered because of certain knowledge he'd sought out." Despite the fact that she had tried out words and phrases as she walked on the downs, Maisie still felt as if she were treading upon hot coals, trying to parse the truth in a way that might minimize the woman's pain. "It was not right, was it, that Bart asked so much of Eddie? But in his defense, his life was sacrificed in the pursuit of the truth, and he was following the trail of a story that he believed should be known by all. I'm still unsure of what that truth might mean, but I know he sailed close to the wind, and that he soon learned there are those who would do anything to prevent release of the information he had acquired."

Pauline Soames drew the handkerchief across her reddened eyes, pulling at the sore, inflamed skin.

"I told Bart, I told him he shouldn't be so strong with Eddie, that he was like a young boy, really, and you wouldn't ask that of a child, to go creeping around someone's property, drawing this and writing down secret things. It wasn't fair, and it wasn't right, but Bart—you had to know him, Miss Dobbs, he was a very determined man. He was my son and I loved him, and in so many ways he was good to Eddie; he listened to him, he talked to him as if he was a man. You see, so many people just patronized him—'Oh, good old Eddie, come on over and see to my horse,' and when they were done with him, that was it, no more 'good old Eddie' anymore. No, they just wanted him off their property until they needed him the next time."

"Mrs. Soames, I don't doubt that there were people like that, but don't be blinded in your grief. You cannot deny that there were people who loved Eddie, who looked out for him and would have done anything for him."

Now Pauline Soames clenched her fists. "There was more to Eddie than people thought, and, God love her, Maud did her best. But he had a gift, you know, every child has a gift, but with some it's hidden." She pushed back her chair and stood up. "Wait here, and I'll show you."

Maisie sat at the kitchen table, listening as Pauline Soames climbed the stairs, went into the bedroom at the front of the house. It sounded as if she were pulling things out from under the bed.

"Oh dear," whispered Maisie to herself. "That's the first place anyone would have looked."

The woman returned to the kitchen with a box in her hand. It was no deeper than a shoe box, but wider, to accommodate papers.

"Bart gave this to me, for safekeeping. To tell you the truth, I was too scared to look inside; and it wasn't my place to snoop, anyway. It's his private papers." She set it in front of Maisie. "Go on. You wanted to see what he'd left, so here you are."

Maisie stood up, looking down at the box. She pulled back the string and lifted off the lid. Each of four folders bore a white label with a blue border, inscribed in handwritten capital letters:

OTTERBURN & CHURCHILL: AERONAUTICAL DRAFTS
OTTERBURN: PROPAGANDA
OTTERBURN: PATRIOT? NATIONALIST?
OTTERBURN: PROCUREMENT AND POLITICS

Maisie sat down, taking out the first folder. She frowned as she turned the pages, each of them bearing a drawing of an aeroplane, with engineering dimensions scribbled alongside.

"These are Eddie's drawings, aren't they?" Maisie held one up to show Pauline, who glanced at the drawing, then turned her head.

"I really would rather not know what's in there—it could be me dead next." She dabbed her eyes with the handkerchief again.

"I think you must have looked already, to know I'd find excellent examples of Eddie's dexterity in the art of copying. In any case, I'll take them with me, but I want to go through them here. Just in case."

"Just in case of what?"

Maisie looked up. "Just in case I part company with the papers on the way home." She faced Pauline until the woman felt Maisie's gaze and was compelled to meet her eyes. "Tell me about Eddie's skill with pencil and paper. How could he do this?"

"What most people didn't know about Eddie was that he could copy drawings. In fact, he could look at something—a bridge, a building, a row of houses, a boat—and then down at a sheet of paper, and with a pencil in his hand he could just draw it. He could do the same thing with letters, if he had a mind to, and that's why I had to be very careful with him, to make sure he was writing something down that he'd thought about, and not just copied. But as you can see, he'd laid his eyes upon these drawings somewhere and copied them."

"So, let me see if I have this right—Bart realized, indeed, perhaps you told him, that Eddie had a gift for copying letters and images. Yes?"

The woman nodded.

"Right, so Bart then asked Eddie to copy down anything he found interesting—perhaps, for example, Eddie had been called in to meet John Otterburn, who was impressed by the way he worked with one of his horses and wanted to meet the young man who had calmed the animal. Oh, and I think Eddie might have accidentally left his book, the one with all his customer names in, when he came for his lesson—and Bart found it. That might have been the beginning of everything. Does that sound about right?"

"Yes, that's about right—I would imagine."

"You would imagine? All right, so let's imagine Eddie standing in Otterburn's study at his home—perhaps Otterburn had heard from the groom that Eddie had worked miracles with his favorite horse and wanted to meet him—and Eddie sees a pile of drawings on the desk, of aeroplanes, only John Otterburn hasn't bothered to move them because Eddie came in while he was working and as far as he's concerned, Eddie is a simple man who can barely hold a conversation, let alone a memory, in his head. Yes? So they have a chat, but instead, Eddie's mind has gone click-click-click, like a camera, and soon he's sitting at your kitchen table with Bart—his friend, Bart, who treats him like an equal—drawing pictures of aeroplanes because he wanted to please Bart, to show how much the gift of his friendship meant to him, because as far as Eddie's concerned, he's found a big brother and he would do anything for him. And you were there, weren't you, Mrs. Soames?"

The woman began shaking with tears. "Yes, yes, that's right. I was there. I knew it was wrong, but Eddie was so happy to do something for Bart, and Bart was such a friend to him."

"But let me guess, Bart began pushing, not because he was bad, or ambitious, but because at heart he was a good man who simply wanted to know the truth about Otterburn. He asked Eddie if he could search out more papers, more pictures, only this time the images were words on the page. But soon it began to tell on Eddie, and he became morose, perhaps. He wanted to continue his lessons with you, because Maud was pleased with him and of course he wanted his mother to be proud. But Bart was pushing him well beyond his emotional capacity to deal with the demands upon him. Am I right?"

"I told him about that. I said to Bart, 'You shouldn't push him, son. He's very sensitive.' But, you know, it was as if someone else had taken over—he said to me, just before Eddie died, 'I only want him to do one more run for me.' That's what he called it, a run. He was asking Eddie to sneak into the house after he'd visited the stables, and of course, as you yourself said, there were people who were good with Eddie, and all he had to say was that Mr. Otterburn had wanted to see him. Because Otterburn had asked for Eddie to come to his study that one time, and because he sometimes came down to the stables to watch Eddie with the horses, no one really cottoned on. It was as if, because he was seen as simple, a slow man, he was invisible. And it wasn't as if he did it a lot, probably only a couple or three times."

Maisie leafed through the folders, looking at each page in turn.

"Do you know what it all means, Miss Dobbs?" Mrs. Soames looked across the table at Maisie.

"No, not really. But I know someone who will understand. The other folders are more obvious, and don't concern Eddie as much. But it amounts to the fact that your son was investigating a very powerful man, and in all likelihood he paid the highest possible price for his curiosity, though I fear it could never be proven in a court of law."

"Oh dear."

"You know that, though, deep down. You knew Bart was really taking chances, not only with his own life but with Eddie's."

"He said no one would touch Eddie because he wasn't all there, that there was nothing he could tell anyone because people knew he was slow."

Maisie looked away. She had said enough. Her anger at Bart Soames' willful use of Eddie Pettit was obvious and had led her to upset a grieving mother. But Pauline Soames was party to the abuse of Eddie—and that's what it was, an abuse of power. She rolled the words around in her mind. They would remain with her for a long time.

"I'll be leaving now," said Maisie. "I think you and your sister ought to go on holiday, perhaps cross the Channel for a bit. No harm will come to you, but it might serve you to put some miles between you, London, and Brighton. Cornwall can be nice at this time of year, too."

Mrs. Soames nodded as Maisie gathered the folders and placed them back in the box, making ready to leave. At that moment the door opened and a voice could be heard in the hallway.

"Very nice little motor car outside, dear. Did you see it?" Soames' sister came into the kitchen, her shopping basket over her arm. She looked from Maisie to her sister. "What's she doing here? And where's she going with that box?"

"It's all right, Millie. She knows everything, and she's taking the box away with her."

Maisie smiled at the woman, who was still clutching her shopping basket. "Your sister has just been telling me how much she would love to visit Cornwall, especially now that spring is just a little closer. I hear there are some lovely guesthouses in Penzance, and it's a nice run down on the train. You should stay a while. Let this all blow over."

"Let what blow over?" asked the woman.

Maisie held up the box. "This. Now then, I must be on my way. I have much to do in London today."

Few words passed between the three women as Maisie departed the house, and she would have laid money on the sisters' swift departure from Brighton, bound for Cornwall or even the Continent. She was less sure about information held within the box of files; there was nothing there that would blow over quickly.

Though she'd originally planned to return to London without delay, instead Maisie drove across Sussex and into Kent. She felt it might be safer to have the box with her at Chelstone. Time and again she checked behind her as she drove, to ensure she was not being followed. From the ancient town of Lewes, she made her way on towards Tunbridge Wells, then through Pembury, before reaching Chelstone. She went straight to The Dower House.

Instead of parking at the front of the property, she maneuvered the MG around towards the side entrance, and left it under an oak tree. The kitchen was warm when she walked in, the yeasty smell of fresh bread baking in the oven, and on the kitchen table evidence that two people had just eaten a midday meal. She walked through the house feeling like an interloper, stepping with care towards the conservatory, which had been Maurice's favorite room, and was now hers as well. When at the house, she would often pull a chair into a shaft of sunlight, to sit and watch the countryside greeting the morning. She would drink her coffee black and strong, and would imagine her mentor in the same room, advising her or listening to her recount work on a case, or perhaps they would discuss the latest news or a book both had read. The voices grew louder as she approached the sun-filled room, and she smiled upon seeing her father and Mrs. Bromley enjoying a cup of tea together. Frankie Dobbs had maintained, to the point of argument, that he would not consider moving up to The Dower House. And in the wake of Priscilla's brutally honest assessment of her behavior, she had sworn to herself that she would never mention the subject again—where her father lived was his business, and not a matter for her to dictate.

She stood at the threshold between the drawing room and the conservatory and cleared her throat.

"Hello, Dad." She smiled as she walked towards her father and kissed him on the forehead. "I'm sorry, Mrs. Bromley, I should have telephoned to let you know I was coming—it was a rather spur-of-the-moment decision."

Frankie and Mrs. Bromley spoke at once, with the woman coming to her feet quickly, and reaching for the teacups.

"We were just having a spot of lunch, weren't we, Mr. Dobbs—I'd have made more if I'd known you'd be coming."

"And I must be getting on—work to do," said Frankie, flustered.

"Oh, let's not go through that again, Dad. Come on, have another cup of tea."

"I'll get a cup and saucer for you," said the housekeeper, still blushing as if she were a schoolgirl with a crush. "Would you like a sandwich? I made some haslett meat loaf yesterday; it's very tasty sliced with tomato. Would that suit you?"

"It sounds delicious, Mrs. Bromley."

Maisie sat down and looked at her father. "This is a lovely place to sit back for a while, isn't it, Dad?"

"Yes, it is, love." He picked up his cup and saucer again, then pointed down towards part of the manor's garden visible from the conservatory. "See that young man there, that's the new under-gardener. Just been taken on—and mainly because he knows you. I suppose that's why you're here, to check up on him."

Maisie looked up, her hand above her eyes to shield her vision from the sun as she gazed in the direction indicated by her father. In truth, the matter of the young policeman had slipped her mind. "Oh, yes. Is he getting on well, do you know?"

"I think this is only his second day, perhaps third. He's lodging in the village at the moment. Mind you, it's a wonder he's got that far—should've seen the state of him when he arrived here."

"What sort of state?"

"Had a shiner on each eye and a cut along here." Frankie pointed to his jawline. "Said that it was the reason why he'd had enough of London and the job he did, that there were thugs all over the place. You couldn't help but feel sorry for the lad. Anyway, from what I know, he's already showing he's a worker—it never takes long to get the measure of someone when they're working with livestock or the land: either they put their back into the work or they don't." He looked at Maisie. "Anyway, what're you doing here—come for a bit of a rest until Monday morning?"

Maisie knew her father wanted to ask about James, but at the same time he was always reticent when it came to her personal affairs. As Mrs. Bromley returned with a tray bearing another cup, a jug of hot water to freshen the tea, and a sandwich thick with haslett, tomato, and pickle for Maisie, the thought crossed her mind that she should be more like her father when it came to the personal business of others—but wouldn't that be nigh on impossible with her job?

The three sat together for as long as it took for Maisie to finish her sandwich and a cup of tea, at which point Frankie declared that sitting about all day would never get any work done, and Mrs. Bromley agreed, listing the many jobs she'd lined up for the afternoon.

Maisie took another cup of tea with her to the library, where she unpacked the box she had taken from Pauline Soames and laid out the folders on Maurice's heavy oak desk.

Again she went through the drawings of aircraft, one by one, only this time with greater scrutiny. There were eight drawings, penciled with a heavy hand. Eddie had likely taken only a brief look at the original drafts, then committed them to his unusual memory until able to copy them out in his deliberate manner. She tapped the fingers of one hand with a pencil she held in the other, then went along to the kitchen.

"Mrs. Bromley, do you by any chance have any of that really thin paper you use for baking?"

The housekeeper looked up from creaming thick rich butter together with sugar in a large buff-colored earthenware bowl.

"Are you really needing tracing paper?"

"Well, yes, that's exactly what I need."

Mrs. Bromley smiled. "Dr. Blanche was just the same—always came in here to steal my baking parchment, so I ordered some special tracing paper for him. I'll show you where to find it."

The woman bustled into the library, pulled out a drawer in a chest next to the desk, and took out several sheets of the fine, almost transparent paper.

"There you are. You know where to find it next time."

Maisie laughed, thanking Mrs. Bromley as she left the room. Soon she was copying each drawing onto the tracing paper. She placed her own drawings into another folder, and replaced Eddie's copies back in the box. Then she began to read through Bart Soames' notes, which amounted to an investigation of John Otterburn. As she read each sentence—and many were only a few words long, perhaps ending with a question posed by Bart, creating his own assignment as he went along—it was with a deepening sense of dread. How could he not see that he was effectively picking a fight well above his weight? Though the notes were inconclusive, it seemed to her that Otterburn was less a businessman with a "finger in a lot of pies" than a powerful manipulator first and foremost. Against the list of authors and artists—which included Douglas Partridge—were questions pertaining to their work, along with titles of articles, essays, and novels that seemed to be out of their familiar subject matter. Maisie could not help but see the pattern identified by Soames. And then there was a history of Otterburn's relationship with Churchill and with other politicians—and his dislike of certain other leading lights in society. Maisie recognized the common denominator—John Otterburn's personal war was against fascism. She chewed her lip. That was all very well—she had her own deep concerns, a foreboding that had intensified in recent months—but what were these drawings all about? And was any of this worth the life of Eddie Pettit? What was she missing? She rubbed her neck to alleviate the fatigue she felt throughout her body.

Maisie did not make any further notes but packed up the box and placed a folder with the copies she'd made in her bag. She walked through to the kitchen.

"Mrs. Bromley—gosh, they smell lovely, by the way."

The woman was turning a batch of hot cross buns onto a cooling rack.

"I thought you wouldn't be staying long this time—would you like some to take back with you? It's not Good Friday without hot cross buns."

"Yes, please! I almost forgot it's Easter. And I'm sorry it's been such a short stay; but I think I might be back earlier next week. I'm planning . . . well, I thought I'd take a few days off and come here. Just for some peace and quiet."

"Right you are. Just let me know and I'll get your favorite things to eat brought in." Mrs. Bromley put a half-dozen hot cross buns in a bag and wrapped a plain round loaf in a sheet of paper. She pushed them across the table towards Maisie. "There. Nice with a bit of cheese, that cottage bread," she said. Then, as Maisie was loading the MG, the housekeeper came out of the kitchen, rubbing her hands on her pinafore as she approached Maisie.

"He worries about you, your father," said Mrs. Bromley. "He doesn't say much, but he worries all the same. And he misses you. I thought you should know. Especially at his age."

Maisie nodded. "I know, Mrs. Bromley. I'm glad he has you as a confidante, and I'm grateful to you for staying on to be my housekeeper. I don't know what I would do without you."

"Oh, and what would I do on my own? Twiddle my thumbs and do my tatting? Better to be here. I keep an eye on your father, you know, and we're good company for each other. You can't ask more than that, can you? Than for two people to be good company."

Maisie felt a lump in her throat as she nodded. "Yes. Yes, I think you're right."

And in a moment that could have embarrassed them both but didn't, Mrs. Bromley reached forward and rested her hands on Maisie's shoulders. "I heard Dr. Blanche once telling you not to take it all on your shoulders. Remember that, Maisie. Remember. Some things you just can't change—about people or things, or the way of the world. And some are not yours to change."

Maisie nodded. "I—I don't know what to say."

The woman shrugged, her cheeks reddened by the familiarity she had assumed. "I don't know why I said that, but it just occurred to me. Perhaps it was thinking of Dr. Blanche, and how much he's missed."

"Thank you, Mrs. Bromley. Thank you."

Maisie waved as she drove alongside The Dower House, and decided that she would spend more time at Chelstone. Perhaps when the case of Eddie Pettit's death was closed, and her load became lighter.

Her solicitor, Bernard Klein, agreed to be responsible for the safe-keeping of the box of folders, and together he and Maisie went to his bankers so that the box could be placed in safe deposit. From there she went to Ebury Place, to await James' return from work. She would have liked to see Douglas, but time was not on her side; however, on the way back to Belgravia she stopped at Victoria Station, where she bought several newspapers from a vendor, and asked if any were available from the previous day. Fortunately, he had several days' worth in piles ready to send back for pulping. She was careful to choose only Otterburn-owned newspapers.

She was in the library, the newspapers spread out across the desk, when James came home.

"Hello, darling—oh dear, that doesn't look like a quick look at the day's news. What are you up to, Maisie?" James eased the knot in his tie and unbuttoned his collar as he approached the desk and kissed Maisie on the cheek.

"I'm looking at John Otterburn's newspapers."

"Not trying to gather information with which to impress him tomorrow?"

She shook her head. "I don't think I will impress him at all." She looked up at James. "I know I've asked you this before, James, but how well do you know Otterburn?"

"Funny you should ask, but I seem to know him a bit more these days. We've lunched a couple of times recently, and last week—I think you were in Brighton—I rode out with him early one morning in Hyde Park. He'd telephoned and invited me, so I went along."

"What does he talk about?"

"Politics, mainly. And he wanted to know my opinion on several matters, mainly to do with business in North America. And he was interested in my thoughts on how Herr Hitler is received in the United States, what they think of him, in my view." He scratched his head. "Let's see. He's also interested in aviation, such as it is. Wanted to know what I thought about transatlantic flight—how far we've really come since Alcock and Brown, and what I thought about the airships, that sort of thing. I told him I was no expert, just a simple old aviator washed up from the war, but he said my experience alone would give me more right to an opinion than many people he knew. All very flattering and jovial an exchange—and he has some smashing horses here in London, as well as those he keeps at Box Hill. I'm looking forward to going down there, actually—how about you?"

Maisie chewed her lip. "Yes, I am. It'll be a welcome break."

James nodded towards the newspapers. "So what's this about?"

"Do you know there's a distinct difference between Otterburn's newspapers and others you might read—probably with the exception of Rothermere's *Daily Mail?*"

"I didn't, but I know you're going to tell me about it."

"Every single edition of his newspapers includes items about the country: what is to be protected, what might be threatened—everything from our green fields to the humble cup of tea. Now, it's not overt—I mean, look at this piece, on the ritual of afternoon tea, and how our small land is the envy of the Empire. And look at this here, about a village green in Norfolk, and the summer cricket table. I'm all for a love of country, but this interests me."

"Oh, Maisie, come now. Let me see these papers. This is not serious journalism and you know it. Otterburn was telling me: the way people read the papers is changing. They have to cater to women's tastes, as well as to the fact that the working man is reading his newspaper every day—it's not just the educated or the man of commerce who wants to know what's going on." He turned pages, bringing his attention to those columns Maisie had outlined in red pencil. "Hmmm, well, I suppose I see what you mean, but I wonder how it compares to other newspapers."

"It amounts to more columns on what must be protected about our way of life here than I've encountered in any other paper."

"Well, if that's the way of the future for the press, Otterburn is going to be at the forefront, without doubt." He reached out and put his arm around her. "I know your job means you have to look closely at things, but don't make a mountain out of a molehill, Maisie."

She tapped the table, then took out a folder from underneath the newspapers.

"I don't know whether I should show you these, but, well, you're the only person I know intimately who's been up in an aeroplane." She opened the folder and fanned the sketches across the table. "What do you think of these?"

James removed his arm and, resting his knuckles on the table, leaned forward to look at the drawings. "Where did you get these, Maisie?"

"They're second-round copies, these tracings in front of you being my attempt at copying from sketches of what I think must have been original engineering drafts."

"But where did you get them?" James faced her, repeating his question with more vehemence.

"Funny, I thought your first comment might have been regarding the aircraft depicted here, perhaps something along the lines of 'I've never seen the like of it before.' But instead you act as if these designs are not new to you."

"Maisie, you're dealing with information that could be explosive if it went beyond this room." With haste he gathered the sketches and walked across to the fireplace. "I'll save us both grief and do the right thing here and now."

Maisie stood back and watched him, first crumpling the papers, then taking them to the fireplace, where paper, kindling, and coals had been set to light later. He took a match, lit a spill, and held it to the paper. Flames leapt up, illuminating James' face as he stared into the fire and set alight the drawings. Maisie met his eyes as he turned around.

"James, when I said those sketches were second-copies, it means I know where the first round of copies are, and they are held in very safe keeping. I have knowledge of those sketches and could probably lay out a passable copy right now. But what is your part?"

"My part is insignificant and only to the extent that I know classified information when I see it—and in my job I see more than you might imagine, though from a commercial perspective. No, those drafts are better off as ashes. I would guess that they were never meant to be seen, especially not by those who have no idea what they are looking at."

Maisie drew back. There was no point in going on, in pushing

James to reveal anything more—if there was more to reveal. She knew he could be intractable on matters he considered serious, and clearly this was serious to him. Tomorrow they would travel down to the Otterburns' country estate. There would be time then to pull at the threads again and see if they led to the same skein of wool.

CHAPTER FOURTEEN

◆◆◆

hey had not planned to leave until around noon, allowing for
a stop on the way for lunch, perhaps somewhere near Epsom,
followed by a leisurely drive to Box Hill for arrival at the Otterburn estate just before tea. At breakfast, Maisie told James of her plan
for the morning.

"Look, I know you've some work to do, so would you mind if I went
to see Priscilla? I'll be back in time to leave at twelve, and I'm packed
already."

"Of course. Aren't they out of London, though?"

"No, the boys are having some friends from school to stay, so I
daresay Priscilla will be planning all sorts of things to keep them
amused," said Maisie.

"I would have thought just having more banisters for them to slide
down would be sufficient."

Maisie smiled. "You're right there—those boys keep everyone on their toes." She looked at the clock. "I'd better be going then. See you around half-past eleven-ish."

She stood up and leaned forward to kiss James on the forehead. He turned and pulled her onto his lap.

"Methinks you might be up to something. Are you sure you're going over to Priscilla's?"

"Oh, yes. In any case, I always love to see the boys, terrors though they are."

"All right then, see you later."

Though Maisie was indeed on her way to the Holland Park mansion where Priscilla lived with her husband and sons, it was Douglas Partridge whom she was now determined to see. If she could just place one more piece of the puzzle, she would feel more confident about confronting Otterburn. The problem was, she needed something concrete to put to him, other than her speculation that it was at his direction that Eddie Pettit lost his life.

The housekeeper opened the door.

"Miss Dobbs, how very nice to see you. But I'm afraid Mrs. Partridge is out at the moment—she and a troop of boys have gone to Exhibition Road, I think to the Natural History Museum, to look at Dippy, that dinosaur thing."

"Is Mr. Partridge with them?"

"Oh no, he's working in his study upstairs." She pointed towards the ceiling, as if Douglas might be floating above her.

"Would you let him know I'm here to see him, and would love to talk to him if he has a moment?"

Having been shown into the drawing room, Maisie waited by the long narrow windows and looked out at the garden. The weather had remained unseasonably fine for some days, and already cherry trees in the garden were in full blossom.

"Maisie. How lovely to see you."

She turned as Priscilla's husband approached her. Douglas Partridge walked with a profound limp, using a cane to balance as he put one foot in front of the other.

"Hope you don't mind me dropping in on you like this," said Maisie.

"Priscilla will be so upset to have missed you. How are you?" Douglas kissed her on both cheeks, then pointed his cane towards the plush sofa, waiting for her to be seated first.

"I'm very well, thank you. It's been a busy few weeks, actually."

"Anything interesting?"

"Well, that's why I'm glad I caught you. You see, I've crossed paths with someone known to you; in fact, I'll be seeing him later today. John Otterburn." Maisie looked at Douglas, who at once appeared uncomfortable and glanced towards the window.

"Yes, of course. I know Otterburn," he said. "Mind you, he and his wife are quite active socially, so I think half of London must know them."

"Douglas, forgive me for being so overt with my question, but I do believe you might know him better than most. In fact, aren't you working for him at the moment?"

"Did Sandra tell you something?"

"Oh, good Lord, no. Sandra is a stickler for confidentiality, and would no more tell me about your business than she would confide in you about mine. No, I gleaned the information from a couple of sources, most particularly in notes left by a young man by the name of Bartholomew Soames. In fact, I think you know him—he was a resident at the rooms at Lancaster Gate that you let out to writers."

"Oh, yes . . . yes. Took his own life, didn't he?" Douglas shook his head. "A great waste, for he knew how to write and could turn out a thumping good article, the sort of work that was approachable both to the common man and the expert reader alike. In fact, I heard that one of his articles on the hunger marches inspired a heated debate in the Commons. But he had notes on me?" Douglas looked at Maisie, then away, once again as if unwilling to meet her gaze.

"Yes, he did. Your name was on a list of writers—some poets and playwrights, as well as authors of essays and fiction."

"Well, how about that."

"Douglas, if I may stick my neck out, because I must rush back to Belgravia in a moment, and I have a desire to sort a few things out in my mind—I wanted to say that I know you're writing for Otterburn, and I believe you and the other men of letters are all composing your work in such a way as to sway public opinion, to make them more—how shall I put it?—yes, to make them more aware of the wonder of this country of ours, whether it's our countryside, our city streets, our King and Queen or our Empire. His regular reporters are doing that already." She rubbed the back of one hand with the other. "I can't put my finger on it, but I think you are all, effectively, engaged in some sort of propaganda—and that just doesn't seem like you, Douglas. I've always thought of you as being above the influence of men such as Otterburn."

"I think you might be surprised about Otterburn."

"Why would you say that?"

"Maisie, I know you very well indeed, and I know how you can hold on to suspicion like a terrier with a bone. But you cannot ask me about this matter. My acquaintance with John Otterburn is not one of friendship, though I have a certain respect for him, and—believe it or not—I hold him in some regard. He has the courage not to look away when others find it expedient to remain indifferent to affairs that might affect our country."

"What's going on, Douglas?" Maisie leaned forward.

Douglas turned toward her. "I can't be the one to tell you, Maisie. If you're going to confront Otterburn anyway—and I'm sure you are—you might as well ask him about me at the same time, because I can neither confirm nor deny that I am working for him."

"Oh, you've already done that, Douglas. But I wonder if you know the sort of man you've thrown in your lot with. He may well be a well-positioned businessman, but he's also someone to be feared. I have reason to suspect he may have taken steps to have an innocent man killed—his name was Eddie Pettit, and he would not have harmed a fly. So you see, although I am waiting to be proven incorrect in my summation, I believe John Otterburn is a master of manipulation."

"I think you'll find he's a man of vision, Maisie. The trouble is that others do not believe what he can see. He's the sort of man we need in this country, and he may prove to be the salvation of us all." He looked at his watch. "I'm sorry if I can't help you any more, but that's all there is to it. I always hope that in a small way, perhaps, my work will make a difference, either now, or at some point in the future."

Maisie regarded Douglas—his posture, his manner of speaking—and once again she considered how very fortunate Priscilla had been to have fallen in love with him, and he with her. He was a man of integrity, and even now, as he deflected her concerns, she respected him. But she had more questions.

"Did you visit Bart Soames' office after he died?"

"Yes, I did. I can't deny it. I know I shouldn't have, but I'd learned his death was somewhat suspicious, and I thought I'd check to see if there was anything in his office that might throw light on what might have inspired him to commit suicide. The desk was terribly untidy, so I moved a few things around as I was looking; straightened things up a bit."

"He didn't take his own life, Douglas. He was murdered. Someone killed him because he knew too much about John Otterburn."

They sat in silence for a few moments.

"You're sure?" asked Douglas.

"I have a very strong feeling about it. Let's assume that much."

"Here's what I have to say to you, Maisie. That there are times—funnily enough, more often during the war—when I have found that I must disregard my personal feelings about a person's conduct and look to something else about them. There were men I would not have given a thank-you for in civilian life, but fighting alongside them in the trenches, I discovered what it meant, truly, to be among the brave. If Otterburn has done what you say, then I believe that one day he will be brought to book. But at this moment I know I will continue with the task in hand, which I see has merit. I am not a killer, though I am sorry to say I have killed. Not one man goes to war thinking himself a murderer, and we go forward with honor in our hearts. But in truth, there is—too often—that searching of the soul, where we realize that if we had killed that same person on the street and not on the battlefield, we would go to the gallows for it. Thus I am a killer who does not sanction killing. With this news you've imparted, I find I am at odds with myself—and I probably sound it, too."

Maisie reached out and put her hand on his shoulder. "Thank you, Douglas, for being so frank with me. I am sorry if I've upset you with my questions, and to have challenged your decision to do whatever it is you're doing for John Otterburn. One thing I know, Douglas—you are a man who will always do the right thing."

They sat for some moments longer. Maisie asked about the boys, and Douglas proudly recounted their recent accomplishments and seemed equally pleased to reveal their mischief.

"There's something about the life in them, Maisie. There's this devilish energy that gets into them, as if they've drunk their weight in fizzy Whites lemonade and they're about to pop. Of course I reprimand them, but I'm secretly pleased. You see, I fought for them to have the freedom to laugh, to tease each other, to climb trees, and to run headlong into the world. And I've come to realize that everything I do—especially in my work—is another step towards protecting that freedom."

Maisie felt a lump in her throat and picked up her bag. "I have to be on my way. James will be waiting for me. We're off to Box Hill—to the Otterburns until Monday morning."

"They're wonderful hosts, you know."

"Yes. I'm sure they are."

James was driving a new Swallow SS1 coupe, and for the first half hour of the journey to Box Hill he extolled the virtues of the motor car, which was considered a very good buy, with an advertising slogan touting that it was an automobile worth one thousand pounds for the price of just three hundred and ten.

The day had become quite warm, though showers were expected. As planned, they stopped for lunch in Epsom, then drove on towards Dorking, and then to Mickleham, where Maisie read out directions to the Otterburn estate, which commanded views across the North Downs; indeed, from a vantage point it was said one could look across the land for miles on a clear day, and see the South Downs in the distance.

"This is it." Maisie pointed to double cast-iron gates that bore a warning to the effect that trespassers would be prosecuted.

"Look, there's the gatekeeper," said James. "That's handy—I wouldn't want to have to creep around looking for a way in."

"You wouldn't have to do that," said Maisie. "There's an electric bell—see it at the side of the gate. Very expensive, I would say."

The gatekeeper walked to the motor car, a clipboard under his arm.

"Good afternoon, sir, madam. You are expected?"

"Yes. James Compton."

The man tapped a page on the clipboard and smiled. "Very good, sir. Please follow the drive along to the front of the house, where the footmen will take your luggage and your motor car will be put away in the garage."

James thanked the man, who touched his cap before moving back to open the gates and wave them through.

"I wonder how many guests they have at the house this evening—I think I saw quite a few names on that board," said James. "I know John wanted to hack out tomorrow morning, and there was that talk of a hunt. I'm looking forward to seeing his stable of horses."

She looked across manicured gardens towards a grand mansion that was, she thought, quite new when compared to a property such as Chelstone Manor. The Otterburn home was built in the style favored by William Morris; in fact, she thought it looked like the artist's home, which had been named Red House, for the color of the brickwork. The roofs were steep in pitch, and even from a distance she could see windows embellished with stained glass. It was a mansion in every sense of the word, and she thought it must have many, many rooms.

As promised by the gatekeeper, a veritable battalion of footmen was at the ready to unload luggage before a chauffeur stepped into the motor car, to park it in the garage. The butler and housekeeper welcomed James and Maisie, and it was left to the housekeeper to show them to their rooms—in diplomatic country house fashion, they had been assigned adjoining quarters. The housekeeper informed them that tea would be served at half past three in the orangery, allowing for some relaxation before drinks at seven in the drawing room and supper at eight.

"Shall we go for a walk, darling? I don't know about you, but I think the ride was a bit less than smooth." James rubbed his neck.

"Smoother than the MG," said Maisie. "I think a walk would be lovely, especially as the showers may have passed. Come on, let's get our walking shoes."

Soon they were out on the downs, with a sharp breeze reminding those venturing out that it might be a sunny day, but summer was still a long way off. Birds caught on the wind seemed to fly in place, and the trees bent this way and that, swept back and forth by the wind. A boy and his father struggled with a kite, and James ran to their aid when it crashed into the ground before them. Maisie watched as he took the kite, helping the boy to hold on to it while the father wound the string, ready to try again. Whether it was a kite or an aeroplane, James adored flight. She wondered how much he might know about the sketches she'd taken from Pauline Soames. Had he prior knowledge? Or did he warn her based upon his understanding of aircraft and a sense that the aeroplanes depicted represented something new by anyone's standards? Perhaps the drawings were intimidating to someone who had an understanding of aviation. This is what she had come to find out, and she believed the only way to accomplish this was to talk to John Otterburn alone.

More than one person had warned her about him, and now she was gripped by the feeling that she was fighting above her weight. But she had no choice. Because of Bart Soames, Eddie had been fighting well above *his* weight, and it had led to his death and that of Bart, his so-called friend. Maisie was ashamed at the anger she felt at Bart Soames, wishing he were still alive so she could take him to task for duping a man who could not answer for himself.

"I used to love kites when I was a boy," said James, rejoining Maisie. "The trouble is, I wasn't actually much good at it, always ending up in a tangle with the kite in a tree. If you walk around Chelstone, you'll see the wooden carcasses of kites I lost in childhood, hanging in the branches of the tallest trees." He smiled at Maisie, putting his arm around her and kissing her on the forehead as they continued their walk, making their last stop when he just had to show her the very spot where a man had suffered a fatal fall from his horse, and was reputedly buried head-down in the ground, in the manner of his fall.

"And you want me to hack out tomorrow, James? No, I think not," said Maisie.

"I can't understand how a man who knows horses like Frankie Dobbs has a daughter who cannot ride." James pressed his hand to his forehead in mock dismay.

"Oh, I can ride, James. I just choose not to."

"Seems to me there are quite a few things you choose not to do," said James.

Maisie brushed the hair from her eyes, ignoring the comment. "I think it's time to be getting back for tea. I'm looking forward to meeting the other guests—aren't you?"

"Yes, I suppose I am." They started walking back towards the estate. "Do you think they have ginger biscuits?"

"You and your ginger biscuits!" said Maisie

orraine Otterburn presided over tea, making introductions and ensuring that everyone knew everyone else. The Churchills were there, though apparently leaving after supper to return to their home, Chartwell, close to the village of Westerham, in Kent. There were a couple of writers present, and some men of commerce and their wives, whom Maisie had met at other engagements on the social calendar. Though she might have seemed adept in such company, she felt like a fish who'd jumped too high in the water and landed in the wrong pond. It was the old conundrum, one she was now familiar with and which, she thought, she was still struggling to master after all this time.

She was aware that John Otterburn had cast his eyes towards her several times, and she wondered if she might be imagining his attention, especially as he seemed to be assessing the room, as if ready to change everyone around like pieces in a game of chess, just to see what might happen. But at the end of tea, Maisie felt rather flat. It was another social marathon, as far as she was concerned, one of many such races that had been run since she and James began courting, and since renovation at Ebury Place had been completed. Invitations arrived each week, though she considered it fortunate that James only ever wanted to accept two or three each month—and even that represented a leap for her. Now this one would drag on in the same way until she could speak to Otterburn alone, and she wasn't yet sure about the optimum timing for such a confrontation. Perhaps there was no good time, and she would just have to make her move when she could. She suspected that after supper might be a good idea.

Maisie had bought a dress for the occasion. There came a point where she realized she could not keep arriving at various functions having rotated the same three evening gowns passed on to her by Priscilla. She could not bring herself to spend good money on an expensive creation, so she bought the gown of pale lilac silk at a Dickens and Jones sale, adding a pair of shoes in the same color to her discounted purchase.

She was seated between a politician and an actor, and saw that James had been seated close to both Churchill and Otterburn, as well as a man called Hugh Dowding, whose presence gave her pause. As far as she knew, he did something important with the government in connection with aircraft. Where had she heard that? She put her hand to her head, as if in doing so she might remember. Yes. That was it—James had mentioned him months ago; Stanley Baldwin had announced that "The bomber will always get through," and James had commented that Dowding—who was Air Vice Marshal at the time—was incensed by the assertion, and considered it shortsighted. She hadn't thought much of it at the time, and was more interested in the fact that the poor man had been widowed when his son was only two years of age. She looked at the men again, and though she could see that private conversation would be prevented by the women seated between them, she was curious about the fact that they had been brought together at the same time. James smiled at her, and at once she wished they could have been neighbors, rather than again having to find common ground with people she did not know. Fortunately, a rather overdressed woman opposite had taken a shine to the actor and engaged him in loud conversation across the table. The woman seemed to have been caught in an earlier age, with all the embellishments one would have expected to see on a female guest at a dinner graced by the womanizing King Edward VII. The politician, the Member of Parliament for a Surrey constituency, talked about the area, encouraging Maisie to ride out the following day to gain a greater appreciation of the region.

Talk droned on and on around the table, and again she found the image of bees came to mind, but this time they were not going from flower to flower in search of sweet pollen; instead it was as if they were in the hive, buzzing about their business. If gossip were toil, then the guests around her were hard at work.

Course followed course, and after the savory, when footmen began bringing in port for the gentlemen, Lorraine Otterburn once again stood up to lead the women to the drawing room, so that the men could engage in talk considered too important for the ears of the gentler sex. They would be joined by the men later.

Maisie added to the conversation when she could, but found she had little to offer on the subject of Paris fashion, or the best finishing school for a daughter, or, indeed, the goings-on in the royal family and of socialites about town. However, the atmosphere changed when the overdressed woman, whose name was Cynthia Tomlinson, cut in with a topic of greater gravity.

"I really don't see why the men are in their own world, talking—as they must be—of what's going on in Germany, when we're all sitting here like stuffed ducks ready for the table."

Maisie could see that Lorraine Otterburn was a seasoned hostess, for she countered with a calm tone.

"Oh, Cynthia, we know exactly what they're talking about, and I am sure every single one of us could hold her own, if not improve on that conversation, but we know better, don't we? We know that whatever happens in this country as a result of anything else going on in the world, it will be women who are called to take care of matters behind the scenes. So let us not speculate, and just be confident in our ability to cope with whatever we are charged to do—and that our vote counts for something now."

"Oh, well done, Lorrie," said a woman with very blond hair.

"Very good, spot-on," added one of the older women.

Maisie realized that Lorraine Otterburn was looking at her, so she nodded her accord and smiled.

Mrs. Otterburn continued to hold court. "Speaking for myself, I can only say that I would rather be among a *monstrous regiment of women*—and thank you, John Knox, for giving us that description, it's quite wonderful in its way, I think—than be jawing along with men who believe they control the strings of political puppetry."

The women applauded, and Maisie found that she, too, was clapping, though her support was for Lorraine Otterburn herself, whom she thought to be a rather more interesting woman than she had imagined.

Later, after the men had joined them for coffee and mints, Maisie touched Otterburn on the sleeve as the guests mingled.

"Might I have a word in private, Mr. Otterburn?"

"John. Do call me John, Maisie—we're friends here. Of course, let's go to my study. Will James come? I don't want him to think I'm making off with his true love."

"Not to worry—he's deep in conversation with Mr. Churchill."

"Right then. Follow me."

Otterburn led Maisie up a wide staircase, then a short way along a dimly lit corridor until they reached his study. He opened the door to a room that was lined with oak panels interspersed with bookcases. A leather-inlaid desk was positioned close to a window, and there were two modern leather chairs in front of a fire. A table was surrounded by eight chairs—this was, no doubt, a room where Otterburn conducted business with men gathered at his estate on matters of commercial and political importance; the table was topped with multiple copies of the most recent Otterburn newspapers.

"Make yourself at home, Maisie." Otterburn held out his hand towards the leather chairs. "Now then, what can I do for you?"

Maisie had formulated a script in her mind, so that she would know how best to begin, but at once the imagined dialogue failed her.

"Maisie?" John Otterburn prompted.

She felt her breath become short and realized she was nervous. To still her mind, now racing, she placed her hand on her heart.

"I wanted to see you about a man named Eddie Pettit. I believe you know him—knew him—Mr. Otterburn. I also believe you knew Jimmy Merton, and that he was working for you when he caused the death of Mr. Pettit."

Otterburn did not rush to defend himself. Instead, he reached across to a humidor, took out a cigar, and went through the process of clipping and lighting. Maisie stilled her breathing, and with it her heartbeat. She could play the game. In fact, she only had to bring the costers to mind, and the leather pouch filled with coins that they had tried to press upon her at their first meeting, and she knew she could stand for them against a powerful man such as John Otterburn.

"Mr. Otterburn? I am sure we cannot be too long, and I have other questions."

"Oh, you do, do you?" Otterburn looked at the smoldering end of his cigar, as if well satisfied with his choice. "Well, why don't you tell me a bit more about this Eddie Pettit, and Jimmy Merton, and about the other items on your agenda."

Maisie smiled. She remembered seeing a film at the picture house. It was an American western, and there was a scene where two cowboys faced off against each other, both men with their hands wide by their hips, ready to be the first to draw his gun and fire. Should she go full-bore, or attempt to blow off pieces of smugness one by one?

"Right you are. I know that Eddie Pettit was murdered. His death was not an accident, though here's what I think—I believe he wasn't meant to be killed. I have a feeling that he might have been warned verbally, perhaps by a groom here, that he shouldn't snoop around. I think there might have even been some leeway, given his obvious . . .

his obvious problems in understanding, which always became worse if he felt himself to be under some sort of pressure. Perhaps Jimmy Merton was supposed to deliver Eddie's demise, or perhaps just a warning. But all the same, I believe the instruction—however it was carried out—came from you."

Otterburn nodded. "Go on."

Maisie felt her heart lurch. She was slipping further out of her depth, and she felt it in every fiber of her being, but she knew she was in too far to draw back.

"Eddie's eyes saw too much. And it was discovered that he had a friend—admittedly, a rather overbearing friend, who exploited a man who had not the reasoning to see how he was being used. Eddie saw the drafts of aeroplanes—and though I am far from being an expert on aviation, I believe those drawings are of aircraft to be used in battle. They are not for pleasure or transportation, that much is clear, and there are few other reasons to design aircraft."

Otterburn was silent. Maisie noticed he was not attending to his cigar, but staring at her, his eyes catching the flickering reflection of the fire's flames.

"I have seen copies of the drawings. And I also know about your coterie of writers. I may not be right, but here's what I think—I think you are, in some way or form, in the process of influencing public opinion. I believe you are working in ways invisible to most of us, to change how the population is thinking." She paused, drawing her gaze to the fire, then back to Otterburn. "But where I am having difficulty, is that I am not sure whether you are working in the best interests of those people or not. But Eddie Pettit is a different matter. I believe he was an innocent caught up in something he had no means of comprehending. He was a man who asked no more than to bring calm to horses whenever he could—he was born among them,

he understood them, and they him. And I cannot forgive his death."
She leaned back.

Otterburn nodded slowly, and had his eyes not been open, and his
cigar gripped tight between his fingers, Maisie thought it would have
been easy to believe him to be asleep.

"You are indeed an observant woman, Maisie. And I believe a formidable foe, if someone's on the wrong side of you. But in this matter,
what saves you from complete naïveté is that you admit you do not
know whether my work is for good or evil." He paused, looked at his
cigar, which was no longer lit, and pressed it into an ashtray on the side
table next to his chair; he stood up, went to a drinks tray, and poured
whiskey into two crystal glasses. He returned, held one out to Maisie,
and sat down again.

"I'm not going to sit here and deny your accusations as if I were
a common felon, Maisie," said Otterburn, running his hand through
hair brushed back in a way that made him seem as debonair as a mati-
nee idol. "Frankly, I have neither the time nor the temper for it. There
are more serious matters to consider. Instead, I will indulge your curiosity, and I will also add that I have no compunction when it comes
to sacrificing one—or two—lives to save thousands, perhaps millions.
I'm sure I make myself clear, without further description." He sighed,
and Maisie thought he seemed at once tired. "Eddie Pettit should have
stuck to what he knew and not gone snooping around. He may have
been simple, but he knew what he was doing. And he could be very
quiet. He was warned—and sympathetically, I might add—but he
didn't listen. It was therefore left to those who work for me to ensure
another warning was given. That's where it leaves my hands. I ask for
a job to be done, and I expect my instructions to be carried out; I don't
expect to have to say another word about it. If I make it known that a
certain activity must be stopped, then that activity had better bloody

well stop. Down the chain it goes. So, my dear, don't even consider giving your chums at Scotland Yard a call. In any case, by the time I've finished, I believe your perspective may have changed."

Maisie lifted the glass to her lips and sipped, feeling the whiskey scald her tongue and catch in her throat. She took a second sip.

"For whatever reason, Jimmy Merton went too far. He'd been chosen to have a word with Eddie because he came from the same streets and was about the same age—we knew that much. Merton had worked for my company in the past, and was taken on again after his absence—and, yes, I know full well why he was absent. He was a bad seed, but he could get things done that needed to be done. I don't know what ax he had to grind with Eddie Pettit that led to Pettit's death, but my lawyers have made overtures to the deceased's mother to ensure her well-being for the rest of her life. You know that already, though, don't you? Anyway, Merton had another job—to keep organized labor out of my factory. And how I run my business is no business of yours—my employees are paid over the odds and have working conditions as good as any other factory, so we don't have dissent, and they don't need a union. That's not up for discussion with the likes of you."

Maisie felt the insult, and though the knot in her stomach almost caused her to make a snap retort, instead she gave a half smile. It would not do to be abrasive with such a powerful man, especially if she wanted to learn more. She tempered her response. "Please continue, Mr. Otterburn."

Otterburn was silent. He drained the rest of the whiskey in his glass, went to the drinks tray, and came back with the whole decanter.

"I am going to tell you some things, and you, Miss Dobbs—and I am very aware of your current profession, by the way—you will not do so much as whisper about anything you hear in this room. Do I make myself clear?"

Maisie stared at Otterburn. "You have my word." She sipped again from the glass of whiskey. Otterburn leaned forward and poured more of the amber liquid into her glass, once again catching the fire's reflection. Maisie shivered, though the air in the room was warm.

"All right." He looked at Maisie. "You have shown yourself to be an intelligent, observant woman, so I assume you've been paying attention to the news—ideally from my papers—and I am hoping you have seen reason for concern in developments in Germany."

"Of course."

"Good. That's a start. Let's look at a very brief list of Herr Hitler's dubious achievements since becoming Chancellor." Otterburn held up his right hand, raising a finger with each point made. "Germany once boasted more newspapers than any other country. Now those newspapers are being closed down one after the other. Truth—whatever complexion the truth may have—is being suppressed. Never mind your accusation that *I* am a manipulator, in Germany news is stopped to prevent the people knowing what's going on." He paused, holding up another finger. "Next. You've been reading *Mein Kampf*, so you know that Hitler has it in for the Jews. If they don't think they're in trouble in Germany, then they have their heads in the futile sand of hope. Already families are getting out in droves, many leaving everything behind. It's been on the cards for years—at least, ever since that damn book was written—so a few with a bit of foresight started transferring their valuables out of the country, so they had something if they had to run."

Maisie nodded. She'd seen evidence of this in a previous case.

"You know what I'm talking about. That's a help."

She could see his anger rising.

Otterburn barely paused. "Now, let's consider the power being given to his henchmen, his thugs. The Sturmabteilung—Storm Troopers—are murdering Socialists, Communists, and Jews. They are torturing people in dark and isolated places, and they are feeding on their own notoriety. There are believed to be tens of thousands of previously free men and women now in jails across Germany." His eyes seemed enflamed as he spoke. "In fact, they're so overrun with these prisoners that a compound known as a concentration camp has just been completed in Dachau, for the incarceration of people picked up by the Sturmabteilung. It will be the first of many such camps, I am sure." Another pause, more whiskey, and Otterburn continued. "Three months. He's been in power three months. Think what that man will do given years of dictatorship. And what are our esteemed politicians doing, both here and across the Atlantic? Nothing. They're sitting on their hands, whistling to themselves, and hoping it will all go away— with the exception of one man who can see that it will not go away, who knows it's going to get worse before it ever gets better, whether it takes five, ten, fifteen, or twenty years."

"And who is that man?"

"The portly little fellow with his cigar out there. Oh, they always cast the prophets aside. 'Go forth into the wilderness and into the barren desert, get out of our sight so we can pretend everything in our garden is rosy.' But what they don't know is that he's not waiting for them. Mark my words, his time will come, but in the meantime, he is not a man to twiddle his thumbs until permission to act is sent down from on high." Otterburn waved his whiskey glass towards the door. He was not drunk, Maisie could see that, but he was on fire. "And so help me, I will do everything in my power to provide whatever he needs to do the job before him."

"Tell me what you mean, John." Maisie leaned forward, towards Otterburn.

He shook his head, as if not believing what he was about to say. "For a start, Herr Hitler, darling of too many of our so-called aristocracy, is a warmonger. I—we—Churchill and a few others— believe that his intention is to move into Europe and across the Channel. He is a man with a hunger for power and for revenge; it's so deep it has eaten his soul. Yet we are a country in no mood for another conflict. The war seemed to take our spirit, along with a generation of young men. We may have been the victors, but we are still half comatose in our corner; we're spent, unable to summon the will for another fight. Just two months ago, the Oxford Union carried the debate 'That this House will in no circumstances fight for its King and Country.' Everyone just wants to get on with their lives; they take what they have—what little they have, in most cases—and they are just going on from day to day. And they think their politicians will save them. But they won't, because they have limited vision. So, we have to change the national mood. We have to inspire the people to take pride in their country, to have something here." He pressed his hand to his chest. "They have to believe there is something worth protecting, worth fighting for. And they have to understand that there is a true and genuine foe on the horizon."

Maisie was on the edge of her seat. "And you're doing that through your newspapers, aren't you? Those articles about Britain, about our historical greatness. About the Empire—Canada, especially, I've noticed."

"Very good, Miss Dobbs. But that's just the beginning. Novels, poems, travel guides, books of recipes—we can get people thinking again through all sorts of reading matter. And not overtly; it doesn't have to be a story of us and them, of the Hun and the brave Tommy. No, we approach it with more subtlety, with the very best of our authors penning work that will first touch the spirit of the nation, then the ego. We have to inspire every man, woman, and child, or we will have those same Storm Troopers throwing their weight around on our high streets, marching us into the ground."

Maisie felt the bile rise in her throat, but forced herself to speak. "And what about the aircraft? I don't quite understa—"

"The prophet can see far into the future, Maisie. War will come to Britain's shores, but mark my words, it will also come in the air. We were bombed in the last war, and we'll be bombed again. Under the terms of the peace treaty, Germany is restricted with regard to the expansion of its airpower, but we have information to suggest that there are a number of flying schools being founded to promote taking to the air as a sort of recreation for young men. Do you know what that means? It means that at the snap of a finger there will be an air force ready to go into action. They don't need to be in uniform, they just need to know how to fly. And while our government, in its wisdom, is being pressed to increase our bombing capability by our Prime Minister, there is a wide-open loophole in what will one day be seen as a crucial prong of defense—the ability to take on the enemy in the air, before he reaches our shores. We saw it in the last war, and we will see it again. But at this moment, Britain has almost nothing, and Britain will have nothing unless plans are on the table for powerful, nimble, and, above all, deadly aircraft, ready to go into production. So my point is—why wait? I am a man of connections, I can get the machine going, and Winston and I, if we have people like James Compton—" He stopped speaking, his lips trembling, as if there were much, much more to say. "But never mind," he added. "I daresay you can now see the bigger picture."

"Yes, I can," she answered, her voice barely above a whisper. "And I confess, though it causes me great pain, Mr. Otterburn, I can see how events might well unfold as you have described, but I hope to God they don't."

"And so do I. In heaven's name, so do I."

CHAPTER FIFTEEN

❖

S uch was the chatter when Maisie joined the other guests in the drawing room that only one person noticed her entrance or her drawn expression. James excused himself from a conversation and, taking her by the elbow, led her to a quiet place by the grand piano that graced a corner of the room.

"Is everything all right, Maisie?" He kept his voice low.

She looked at him. "You know what's been happening, don't you? About Otterburn's plans?"

He shrugged. "Not as much as you might think. I know about the aircraft designs because John asked me to look at them early on. I flew in the war, Maisie, but since that day I told you about, being taken up over the prairie, I've been up a few times on my own, and I've taken an interest in aircraft design, and the way the business is growing— I've even invested in a couple of companies. Otterburn knew this, and took me into his confidence. I should have told you."

"No, you shouldn't. You've no obligation to tell me about your business, any more than I have an obligation to tell you about mine. But I want to know if you had any idea, while I was working on the Eddie Pettit case, that it was Otterburn's word that led to the deaths of two men."

James looked around, to see if anyone was within earshot of their conversation. "No, I didn't. I promise you. In fact, from information I've since gleaned, those men were never meant to die, but simply warned."

"Simply? Simply warned? And what sort of violence would be used in the simple warning—eh, James? I don't know how you can use the word *simply* as if you were talking about bumping your motor car into another. 'I simply came round the corner, he was simply there, and I simply didn't mean to bump him, honestly, constable.' James, we're talking about human beings."

James sighed. "I know. I chose the wrong words. Seems to be my stock-in-trade. Look, I can't condone what happened. But I can understand the need to keep this aircraft business under wraps, though of course I can't support taking such violent steps to do so." He sighed. "As you might have gathered, I've asked a few of my own questions in the past several days, and in John's defense, his instruction was to ensure the men kept quiet—for a start, the newspaperman was a troublemaker, Maisie. I've since read his articles. They were very well written, but his intention seemed to be to upset the applecart at every opportunity. As a writer he was something of an anarchist." He glanced around again to ensure that no one could hear them. His voice was just above a whisper. "And he had his sights on John ever since he'd been sacked from one of the newspapers, mainly due to his underhanded methods of reporting—and John has so many businesses to run, he didn't even know him." He took a deep breath. "Maisie, I am not aware of the ways in which John Otterburn keeps knowledge of his work secure, but it's clear the information this reporter gathered simply could not be allowed to reach a wider audience. The ability of our country to be impenetrable to invasion depends upon the highest levels of secrecy." He paused. "In any case, regarding Pettit, perhaps you should ask why the man whose hand is stained with blood went so far."

"He's dead. An apparent suicide."

"That should tell you everything you need to know, shouldn't it?"

"But it doesn't, James. It doesn't. Which means I'm going to have to use my imagination." She ran her fingers across the piano keys, the light touch barely sounding a note. "You know you said you wanted to go to Canada to be a farmer. That wasn't quite the truth, was it?"

James colored. "No, not quite. Well, it is—was—but it's moved on from there. Very recently, in fact."

"Are you going to tell me?"

He looked around the room. "Yes. But not here." He put his arm around her. "Do you want to stay, Maisie?"

She shook her head. "Let's leave tomorrow morning, first thing. Let's go down to Chelstone and stay at The Dower House. If we stop on the way tomorrow, I can telephone Mrs. Bromley to let her know we'll be there for a couple of days. I suppose eyebrows will be raised all around, but I am past caring. You can go for a hack out on your stallion in the afternoon."

"Will you ride with me?"

"You know, I might. Let's see." She pulled away and took his hand. "But I must know the truth, James. I've not yet decided whether those two men—Otterburn and his so-called prophet, Mr. Churchill—are truly the visionaries they think they are, or if they're men who would bring war to our shores simply by being ready for it. It's like a boxer putting on his gloves long before the fight, and punching the air. Someone might walk in unexpectedly, end up with a black eye, and just have to hit back."

They lingered for a while longer, moving back into the room to speak to a businessman and his wife, who were known to James. They were joined by other guests and were soon able to draw away from the party. Before they left, they informed their hostess that they would be departing after breakfast the following morning. They gave no reason, and no reason was sought, though regrets at the early end to the sojourn were voiced by both parties.

Maisie felt lighter as they approached Chelstone. They had come down to the dining room before other guests appeared and, wanting to be on their way as soon as possible, had taken only a cup of tea before departing Box Hill. The sky seemed almost transparent in its morning newness, and the green undulating landscape bore the sheen of nighttime dew. They had stopped at a telephone kiosk in Sevenoaks, where Maisie placed a call to The Dower House, and informed Mrs. Bromley that they would be arriving soon, probably within the hour.

Maisie was relieved, at last, to enter the house, with shafts of sunlight beaming through the windows.

"Oh, I am so glad to be here," said Maisie.

"And so am I," said James.

"May we have some coffee, Mrs. Bromley? We'll be in the conservatory." She turned to James. "I know why it was Maurice's favorite place—one feels so much calmer looking out across the land."

James followed Maisie into the conservatory, which was already warm. She sat down in an armchair and kicked off her shoes; James took the chair next to hers. They sat in comfortable silence; there was no need to speak, yet. Maisie wanted to sit with her recollections of the previous evening, and she wanted to weigh up what she now knew with what she might learn from James. While she had not been surprised by anything revealed by John Otterburn, she had been sickened while listening to him outline his predictions. She might have already felt Europe beginning to slide, as if it were a heavy lorry caught in ice on a hill, but it was different when she heard Otterburn lay out what he—and clearly many others—predicted would be an inevitable conflict. It was as if in outlining what might come to pass, he was lifting the lid on Pandora's box. And she was numb with fear.

Mrs. Bromley bustled in, bearing a tray with coffee and croissants.

"I know you've probably had breakfast, but I thought you'd like a bite to eat. I learned to make these on account of Dr. Blanche—loved his morning croissant, he did, and I must say, I miss making them. I must have known you'd come today, because as soon as I got up this morning, early, I set to making the pastry and letting it rise. I think even a Frenchman might be fooled after eating my croissants. There's homemade jam there, too."

"Oh, smashing, Mrs. Bromley. If you're not careful, I will have to steal you, simply to get my hands on a plate of these every day." James picked up a croissant, smeared a thick layer of strawberry jam across the pastry, and dipped it in his coffee before taking a bite. "This is as good as anything I've ever had in Paris," he said, wiping crumbs from the side of his mouth.

Mrs. Bromley blushed. "There's more where they came from, if you're that hungry."

"We might well polish off the lot—thank you, Mrs. Bromley, that was so thoughtful of you." Maisie tore half a croissant and dipped it in her coffee.

The housekeeper left the room, leaving Maisie and James alone once more. After a few moments had passed, Maisie spoke again.

"James, it's time to talk. Tell me what Otterburn has asked of you."

James did not answer immediately, instead gazing out towards woodland where he had played as a boy. Then he began.

"I've come to know John Otterburn quite well over the past months. I suppose I didn't let on how well, because I was still thinking about the way he very quickly seemed to get the measure of me—or of someone he believes me to be, I suppose. It was as if, once he'd made a decision about who I was, he went into action, and that came in the form of a proposition. No, that's not right—it was rather like being in the flying corps; you're given the opportunity to take on an exciting assignment, but one that comes with higher risks. Even though you're asked if you want to do it, you know you're not at liberty to turn it down; the request is really a command. That's how it felt."

A woolen wrap had been left across the back of Maisie's chair, and she pulled it around her.

"He took me into his confidence, and he showed me the plans," said James. "Churchill had been in the room at one point, but left with two other men; I've since felt he left at that point so that he wouldn't be implicated in the conversation that was to follow. Anyway, I looked at the plans, and asked how they were ever going to build such aircraft, and test them, all without word getting out. I was told that the parts would be built in different locations to very tight specifications. They would then be shipped to Canada, again separately, at staggered intervals, and through several ports of entry in both the United States and Canada. They would be assembled there, and then testing would begin. There's a lot of wide-open space in places like Alberta and Saskatchewan, Maisie, where you never see a soul, and you could conduct flying trials with little risk of being discovered."

She looked at him, burning to ask a question, but he saw her eyes, and answered without her having to say a word.

"Yes, I would be doing a lot of the flying. I know it's a gamble—it's a new design. But there are two other younger aviators—Otterburn's son and, believe it or not, his daughter. They're eighteen and twenty, respectively. They're the ideal people to test the aircraft, and they would never tell a soul, given who their father is. I've met them both, informally, at the house, and frankly, I've heard that the daughter, Elaine, is the better aviator of the two." He stopped, as if gathering his thoughts. "They have all the reflexes of youth on their side, and to be perfectly honest, they're the right age—it's the younger men who will fly those planes if there's war, not older chaps like me."

"Oh my God." Maisie rested her head in her hands.

James came to her, knelt down alongside her chair and put his arms around her. "I know. I'm so sorry. I'm so sorry I lied."

She shook her head. "It's not that. It's just the thought of it happening again. I can't get it all out of my head. I just can't get rid of it, and now there you all are, making these plans for when war comes—not even *if*, but *when*. Otterburn is planning for *when*. I know he's to be lauded for his foresight, and that he's taking steps to ensure our country is not left standing on the wrong foot if the worst happens, though I can't help but feel we're all just pawns in a game."

"War's like that, Maisie, as we both know only too well."

They sat together in this way for some time, with James holding Maisie in his arms. Then James spoke once more.

"And I have to tell you, too, that there's something else Otterburn wants of me, though I pray that time will never come."

Maisie looked at him; she was becoming settled, yet her eyes betrayed her sadness.

"He believes that if another war is waged in Europe, our success will depend upon an alliance with America. The average man and woman over there would be as against war as most of Britain, and John has predicted that no president of the United States will allow his country to be dragged into another scuffle on the other side of the Atlantic. If at any point war seems inevitable—and I mean in the very near future, which, thank God, doesn't seem so at the moment—he intends to begin his system of under-the-wire propaganda in America, and he has asked me if I would go there, perhaps take up temporary residence, along with a few other British subjects of his choosing. Our remit would be to socialize, to do business with Americans in the centers of influence—Washington, New York, places like that. It would be a job of persuasion, of pulling public opinion in our direction, from the top down. And we would in turn provide information to Otterburn—his idea is that we would be mixing with politicians, an ideal position in which to garner intelligence informally. You'd be surprised what people will tell you if they like you, and they've had a drink. The whole plan would make the leap smoother for the power brokers over there—from looking on while Europe burns, to helping Britain, should Herr Hitler's reach grow unchecked. Maisie, I don't know if John Otterburn told you this, but there's already evidence to suggest Germany is building munitions again at an alarming rate. If the unthinkable happens, with Otterburn's plan we stand a good chance of having our American cousins on our side sooner rather than later, along with their military might."

Maisie shook her head. "I truly don't believe what I'm hearing. No—no, that isn't so. I believe every word of it. Every single word. But there is one thing John Otterburn has very wrong—it's not Churchill who's the prophet, no, it's him."

"I think the imagination is Churchill's, the preparation is Otterburn's. Churchill is an orator and a strategist, but he cannot be seen to be acting upon his predictions—he's a politician, first and foremost. I believe Otterburn is one of his men behind the scenes—perhaps the most important at this point. I am sure he has more than one man who can procure and put ideas into some sort of action. And he's only ever seen socially with Otterburn; from my observations, he measures evidence of their partnership with care. He's never been present in any meetings I've had with Otterburn, nor does he let on that he knows I've been taken into Otterburn's confidence, or what has been asked of me. We have had conversations about Germany; he's solicited my opinion on all sorts of matters, actually."

Maisie topped up their cups with still-warm coffee. She sipped with both hands clutched around the cup. They were quiet again for some moments.

"What are you thinking, Maisie?" asked James, who had taken his seat once again.

She looked across the land, where mist was lifting from the fields of nearby farms, and caught sight of her father with his dog at heel, leading a willing old horse out to pasture.

"I'm thinking about Eddie Pettit."

Maisie and James spent a quiet, if somewhat melancholy, Sunday at Chelstone. They went for a ride in the afternoon, with Maisie borrowing an old pair of Lady Rowan's jodhpurs. She was comfortable around horses, but during her childhood in London, horses were beasts of burden and not a means of recreation for those of her station. She knew exactly how to care for a horse and was at ease in the saddle—she'd spent too much time with her father to be otherwise—but though Frankie had put her on a horse when she was younger, and she would sometimes ride Persephone, bareback, around the streets, the opportunity to ride was not something available to her in adulthood.

Frankie picked out an older gelding for his daughter and helped her mount. He reminded her to keep her heels down and her hands quiet, and cautioned James not to exceed a gentle canter. It occurred to Maisie that her father might enjoy the fact that improving her riding was something he could teach her. She wondered why it had never occurred to her before.

Having exhausted themselves with talk of John Otterburn, they avoided mentioning his name again for the remainder of the day. They enjoyed the ride, trotting along a bridle path through the woods, crossing a stream and cantering up the hill on the other side. Soon they were at a vantage point from which they could see the village of Chelstone, with its steepled church and a cluster of houses scattered around, from beamed workers' cottages to terraced houses built in Victoria's reign for the men who laid down the railway lines. Chelstone Manor, which had been in the Compton family for generations, was known locally as "the big house." Each year, on the first Saturday in August, James' parents opened the grounds to the villagers with a tea party laid on for one and all. Men, women, and children dressed in their Sunday best, and Lady Rowan held court, complimenting mothers on their children, farmers on their crops, and the young men on their luck in bringing the most beautiful girl in the village to the party.

Now, as they gazed at the village in the distance, it seemed that both Maisie and James were taken with the same thought.

"It's Easter, James, and so peaceful. It's supposed to be a time of new life. I can't imagine it being pulled apart again—such a small village, and such a long list of names on the war memorial, so many local lads lost in the war. I can't stomach the thought that—" She turned her head. She did not want James to see more tears.

"I can't bear it either, but it's thinking that this way of life, these people and all we have here could be at risk again—one day—from those who would wage war upon us, makes me all the more determined to do what's been asked of me." He reached down and ran his hand along the muscled neck of his stallion. "Those aeroplane sketches could be well out-of-date by the time anything happens, if it does happen. In fact, if I had my way, they would be superseded time and time again, and Otterburn would lose his money on more designs because war never came."

"I just want him to be wrong," said Maisie. "But right here, in my heart, I fear he is right. I may not like him, and I detest his way of working, but I have to admit, I think his predictions ring true. And I know I'm like you—I would do anything asked of me if it helped keep us safe."

James looked at Maisie, then at her horse. "Uh-oh, your trusty steed is dozing off. Come on, let's get back. I should have tea with my parents—you don't have to come if you want to remain at home."

Maisie nudged the gelding, turning him in the direction of The Dower House. "Yes, I think I'll stay. Dad's in the stables today. I'll give him a hand. He'll probably tell me about all the things I did wrong as we rode off."

"He probably will. But you don't mind, do you?"

She shook her head. "No. It's time to let those gods of perfection have their day."

Monday having been a bank holiday, Maisie was at the office early to open up again on Tuesday morning, following a crack-of-dawn departure from Chelstone. James dropped her at the Fitzroy Square office, then went on to the City, so she was at the table by the window when Sandra came in at half past eight.

"Good morning, Miss. Did you have a lovely Easter?"

"It was busy, Sandra. How about you? How did the move go?"

"Oh, very well, thank you. I don't have much, and it didn't take long. We girls got ourselves settled in the flat, then ended up going out on Sunday—we took the train out to Whitstable, had a walk around and treated ourselves to afternoon tea. Didn't touch any oysters, though, slimy-looking things. Anyway, since then I've been catching up with my reading for college, and I went to a meeting yesterday evening."

Maisie looked up. "What sort of meeting?"

"It's a women's gathering. We talk about the inequities between what men and women are paid, working conditions, and how women are taken care of when they're old." She hung her coat and hat on the hook behind the door and continued speaking to Maisie as she uncovered her typewriter. "It's all men-men-men, you know. Women are treated as if we never did a day's work, and as if our money is just pin money, you know, a little bit on the side to help out. Well, it's just not true. We women have to look after ourselves, and we will show we mean it when we say we want equal rights—the same day's pay for the same day's work."

"Good for you," said Maisie. She smiled. Sandra, she had observed, was finding her voice. "Well, I'd better get back to this case map, Sandra. I've left a couple of letters to be typed on your desk, and also the file on another one of Mr. Beale's cases—I think I'd like your help on that one. Perhaps we can talk about it later today."

"Oh, yes, Miss," said Sandra.

Maisie returned her attention to the case map. She had made notes in red, and linked names together, and also listed a series of reasons why Jimmy Merton might have been murdered, and also why he might have taken the instruction to warn off Eddie Pettit further than was ever needed or requested by his paymaster. John Otterburn clearly had a level of employee who could only be described as a thug, his orders trickling down a chain of command so that his wishes could never be linked to the outcome. Men in the next link along might have ended Jimmy's life because his actions left Otterburn and his factory, Bookhams, under a cloud. Yes, that could have happened. But Maisie did not think events unfolded in quite that way, though she suspected that it was Otterburn's men who saw to it that Billy was attacked, either to throw blame on Merton, perhaps to scare him, or perhaps they were watching and didn't like the questions Billy was asking. But more than anything, she didn't believe Merton killed himself, either. And that was one loose thread she had to deal with.

Maisie remained in the office for most of the morning, reviewing pending cases with Sandra. She talked with the young woman about college and helped her with an essay that was troubling her—she had waited for Sandra to ask her for assistance, without first offering. Sandra left at noon to go to her job with Douglas Partridge, and by the time Maisie looked up from a series of invoices she was checking it was mid-afternoon. The costermongers would be back at the market, emptying their carts. As Maisie walked down the street towards the market, she saw Jesse in the distance, talking to another coster. She waited on the corner until they had finished, and waved to him as he was about to move on.

"Maisie. Ray of sunshine on a breezy afternoon. Lucky it's not too cold, that's what I say."

"How are you, Jesse?"

"Mustn't grumble. Had a nice morning, got myself a new customer, so everything in the garden is rosy, as they say." He grinned, revealing a gap where two lower teeth should have been. "I thought we was all done, Maisie. Do we owe you any more, girl?"

She shook her head. "No. You don't owe me a penny," she said. "But you do owe me the truth, I think."

"I don't catch your meaning, love."

"Then let's go somewhere private where I can explain. Are the others here?"

Jesse looked around. "There's Pete over there. Look, hold on, I'll see if I can find the lads."

Five minutes later, the group were standing together. Maisie made sure her eyes met those of each man. "There's a caff up the road, on Long Acre. Care to walk with me?"

She knew Jesse was just about to point out that Sam's was closer, but she wanted to go to a place of her choosing this time. It was a larger concern than Sam's, with wooden tables and ladderback chairs. A tea urn was on the counter, while glass shelves displayed an assortment of cakes and pastries, though the proprietress also offered sandwiches, toast, or a plate of egg and bacon.

"Tea all round." Maisie smiled at the waitress, who counted the men and scurried away behind the counter.

"What's happened, Maisie? Is it your Mr. Beale? Taken a turn for the worse, has he?" Archie Smith's concern was genuine as he leaned on the table to face Maisie.

"He's doing well, much better. And I found out it wasn't Jimmy Merton who had a go at him. It was someone else who didn't like the questions he was asking."

"I'd like to find him, whoever he is," said Pete Turner.

"So, what's this all about, Maisie?" Jesse Riley sat back in his chair, and Maisie could not help but smile, recognizing that he was putting literal distance between them.

"Jesse, it's like this." She looked at each man in turn. "You, Pete, Seth, Dick, Archie—are the oak trees of my childhood. You were giants to me, especially when my mother was ill. For that I will never forget you, and for that I will be in your debt. However—" She stopped speaking, as images of the men when they were younger, when she, too, was younger, flooded her mind. "However, you took the law into your own hands, and I cannot let you think I don't know. I cannot let you imagine for a moment that I would condone taking the life of Jimmy Merton, though I know exactly what sort of man he was."

"Now, look here—"

"Jesse, I was brought up to mind my manners, so it grieves me to have to tell you to button it until I'm finished." She pointed to her lips. "I may be a woman who lives on this side of the water now, but if you think I've forgotten the streets, you can think again."

"An eye for an eye and a tooth for a tooth, Maisie."

"But you could have been wrong, and you could've been on your way to the gallows. I don't know who did what, but I know that you're all responsible for the death of Jimmy Merton. You're guilty of removing his body, of taking it by boat to the Lambeth Bridge, and for hanging him there as if he'd taken his own life."

"What if we did?"

"I just want you to understand that I'm aware of what happened, and that, even though I know very well he was responsible for making Eddie's life a misery, two wrongs don't make a right."

"He would never have been taken in, Maisie. He would've got away with it."

She sighed and looked away, then back at Jesse. "You're right. So help me, you're right; he would most probably have got away with it. But what you did was wrong." She thought of Otterburn and his description of Storm Troopers beating ordinary people on the streets if they even looked foreign; how they were guilty of dragging innocent tourists through the busy thoroughfare because they had failed to salute when everyone around them was shrieking "Heil Hitler" as the brown-uniformed men marched past. "It's wrong because we have a procedure here, we have something to protect in our country, and that is our judicial system. It's part of what we fought for, Jesse, in the war. And you especially, Seth, Dick. It may appear broken, but we have to protect it." She looked away so the men might not see her emotions.

"There, there, love." Seth put his arm around Maisie. "You're all worn out, look at you. We shouldn't've burdened you with our worries about Eddie; though we were more than grateful you got somewhere with it all."

"She's right," said Pete, his voice low, because the waitress was clearing a nearby table. "We're responsible. We're not proud, but Eddie was one of us and we look after our own. It's not as if any of us makes a habit of that sort of thing, and we know what happened was wrong. So I reckon you've about said what needs to be said, about justice and all that." He paused, looking down at his hands. "You know, I've got to tell you, girl, I know you're right, but I can't say as I'm sorry about my part in what went on. I don't want to ever remember that night, and to be sure, we were that mad when we saw him. But Jimmy Merton's gone now, and good riddance. Whole bloody family can go, as far as I'm concerned."

The other men nodded.

"I have to be off now," said Maisie. "You'll be glad to know that Bookhams, through John Otterburn, who owns the company, will be providing Maud with a generous settlement. They've realized that they should be looking after her until she passes from this life, so she and Jennie will never have to worry about money again."

"Good on you, Maisie," said Archie.

"I'm going now," said Maisie.

"Don't be a stranger, love. Come down to the market, pass the time of day when you can."

"See you then," she said, and stepped towards the door. She did not look back as she walked in the direction of the underground station. It was in something of a daze that she made her way back to Pimlico, forgetting she'd promised James that she would see him that evening.

Maisie entered her flat, which was quiet but for the distant sound of foghorns on the river. She went into the kitchen and picked up the kettle, but found that at once she had no energy to make tea, so she walked into her bedroom, closed the blinds, and without taking off her coat or clothes she slipped under the eiderdown and slept.

It was dark when she opened her eyes, and though her lids were heavy and sleep tried to claim her back, she could hear noise somewhere close. There was a rattling of metal, and as she squinted in the dark, she thought she could see a shaft of light. Her eyes closed again, against her will; she fought to open them, battling to come to consciousness. Sleep still did not want to relinquish its grip. She dozed once more and opened her eyes, this time more wakeful. But she lay there on the bed and thought she heard music, faint though it was, playing in the distance. Was it in her flat or from above? She reached for the clock on the table beside her bed. Eleven o'clock. She had been asleep for perhaps six hours. Her face felt dry, her eyes sticky. Had she wept in her sleep? Rising from the bed, she walked over to the door, where she stopped to listen. The music was coming from the drawing room, and someone was in her kitchen. She tiptoed along the hallway at the same time as Priscilla emerged from the kitchen, an apron drawn around her waist, a glass of wine in one hand, and a basket with bread in the other.

"Oh, good. How are you feeling, dear friend?"

"Pris? What are you doing here?"

"Your error—should never have given me a key to use in emergencies." She sipped from her glass. "Excellent wine, filched from Douglas' secret stash of Montrachet. I'll pour you one—hang on a minute."

Maisie sat down at the table, which was laid for two.

"Here you are. Chin-chin, darling." Priscilla placed the glass in front of Maisie. "Your sweet amour telephoned me to say how worried he was about you, and that he thought it best if he didn't come to see you at the moment, though he did ask if I might drop along to check up on you. Douglas has taken the boys to see his mother. Not exactly my idea of a satisfying evening; and as they are staying until tomorrow morning—no school this week—I thought I would come over here. Your delightful little box room is all I need for a good night's sleep."

"Thanks, Pris."

"I doubt you've seen them yet, but Sandra left a lovely bouquet of flowers for you, with a note of thanks."

Maisie rubbed her eyes, and nodded. She was about to say, *Oh, really? She shouldn't have spent her money on flowers for me.* But instead she replied, "How dear of her—so thoughtful . . ."

"So, cassoulet for a late supper? It was made yesterday, so it'll be even more tasty this evening. Luckily I managed to chauffeur it here without spilling a drop. Good enough?"

"Good enough."

The two women finished the meal, their talk deepening as the minutes passed. Maisie felt an old comfort return, as if they were new at college and she and Priscilla were establishing their friendship again, through midnight feasts and marathon discussions.

"So, what's happened to you, Maisie? You look all in. Is the dragon awake?" Priscilla had often described her memories of war as "the dragon."

"I still can't seem to get things right, Pris. Today I wanted to let some people know I was aware that they'd done something dreadful, and how dangerous it had been; the consequences could have been unthinkable. I judged them and let them know it, but the fact is, I blame myself. I should have seen it coming. I know these people well, I know how they think, and I might have guessed what they would do—and if I had, I could have stopped it." She rubbed her forehead. "And I'm so terribly confused—there's a man who's doing something quite . . . quite alarming, but truly honorable at the same time. He's caused such pain while trying to keep it all under wraps, but at the same time I cannot dislike him, nor can I say he's making a mistake, because I think he might help us all in time, and—"

"You're talking about John Otterburn. I know. I can't see how Lorraine stands him for one moment, myself."

"Yes, I am talking about him, and—"

"Maisie, stop. You will drive yourself mad." Priscilla poured more wine. "You're suffering, and you're the only person who can help yourself. Don't worry, it's only a blip, you won't sink as you did before. But you have to get used to the fact that you have the intense vigilance of one who has seen some dreadful things in the war. We both do it. I feel as if I'm always waiting for the most painful thing in the world to crop up all the time. And I'm trying terribly hard to rid myself of the habit." She twisted her wineglass by the stem. "I don't know what's happened over the past week or so, but I do know something's going on with you. You can't stop the world, Maisie. You can't stop Billy Beale from getting hurt, you can't save Sandra from the grief of widowhood, and you can't stop your father from falling in the stables again if he chooses to do half the things he shouldn't do at his age. And if you can't do that, then you can't expect to have a hand in stopping all the other disasters happening in the world, no matter how vigilant you are."

Maisie nodded. "I suppose I've become tired with trying."

"Yes, I suppose you have." Priscilla took a sip of wine. "Do you have anything wonderful to report, Maisie?"

She thought for a while. "Against my better judgment, I had a lovely ride out with James yesterday, at Chelstone. It was quite beautiful."

"That's my girl!" said Priscilla. "And are you finished with this latest case now?"

Maisie shook her head. "No, not quite. Soon, though. I'll be finished soon. Just one more loose end to tie up."

CHAPTER SIXTEEN

❖

Maisie rose later than usual, and was woken again by Priscilla moving crockery in the kitchen. Putting her arms into the sleeves of her dressing gown as she walked towards the kitchen, she could already smell the pungent aroma of fresh coffee, with a hint of chicory.

"Good morning." Priscilla held up a coffeepot. "Luckily, I came prepared; I brought coffee from home, which was just as well, because like a poor old lady, when I looked there, your cupboard was bare."

They sat together in front of the gas fire, one at either end of the sofa.

"You've a busy day ahead then," said Priscilla, sipping her coffee, steam rising from the hot liquid.

"Probably more, well, intense than busy would be a better way to put it. Not as full as some days, but more intense."

"Right. I see." Priscilla sipped again. "And what about you and James?"

Maisie sighed. "I think we could best be described as going through a somewhat uneven tear, rather than a clean cut, in terms of parting. It's hard to explain. He loves me, and I have love for him, but it's just not all fitting into place, if there is such a thing. And frankly, I don't think I want to bumble along, as if someone has put a new part in my motor car that looks like the right part, and does the job it should, but it scrapes here and there, and the engine doesn't ever go properly again. I think we both want something more than that. Something that fits."

"He's not the one, then," offered Priscilla.

"I don't know if there is such a thing for me." She sipped her coffee. "But we've talked about it, and James is rather . . . rather busy with all sorts of things at the moment, and has plans to return to Canada soon."

"Has he asked you to go with him?"

"In so many words, yes."

"And you won't."

"I don't believe so, but you never know, do you, what might come to pass when the time comes?" Maisie looked at the clock. "I had better be off, Pris."

"Oh, heavens, me too. Where are you going this morning?"

"Lambeth," said Maisie.

Jennie was wiping her hands on the hem of her apron as she greeted Maisie at the door of the small, smoke-stained house. The curtains had not been drawn since Eddie's death, and would remain closed for some weeks as a mark of respect, and to let callers know the occupants were in mourning.

"Maisie, this is a surprise. Come in, come in. Maud was just talking about you—bet your ears were burning, eh? Go through, into the kitchen."

Maisie thanked Jennie and walked along the dark passageway that led to the kitchen. Maud was sitting at the table, a plate of toast in front of her, along with a cup of tea. She was dressed in black.

"Maisie! Did Jennie tell you? We were just talking about you, wondering how you were, and—don't get too big for your boots—we were saying what a lovely woman you turned out to be. Very proud of you, we are."

Maisie came to the woman, put an arm around her shoulder, and kissed her cheek. "You're a gem, Maudie."

"We're off to the cemetery, to lay some flowers on the grave, put fresh water down, make sure it's kept nice. What with that storm we had a few nights ago, we're hoping the vase I left there hasn't broken." Jennie put the kettle on to boil. "I'll make a fresh pot."

"Thanks, Jennie." Maisie turned to Maud. "I've come to talk about Eddie, and Jimmy Merton."

"I've got nothing to say about the man who killed my Eddie, though I hope for his sake he rests in peace," said Maud.

Maisie took a seat at the table.

Jennie pulled out a chair and sat down opposite her. "What's on your mind, Maisie?"

She looked from Maud to Jennie, considering how she might begin. She could, of course, leave words unspoken; she didn't have to pick at this particular wound, for she knew that even truth could bleed. Yet at the same time, she believed there might be healing for Maud, and for Jennie, if the story were brought out from the dark shadows of Maud's memory.

"Maud, everyone around here knew that Jimmy Merton hated Eddie. Most people looked out for your boy; and for all his slowness, he grew up to be a good man, and he was one of us. But it was different for Jimmy. They were in the same class at school, exactly the same age, give or take a few months, I would imagine. The other children accommodated Eddie—perhaps a bit of teasing here and there, and though it was difficult for Eddie, he coped with it well enough. Jimmy was a different kettle of fish, wasn't he? As if he was on a quest to make Eddie as miserable as he could; as if Eddie had to pay for something. Eh?"

Maud nodded, and took a handkerchief from her apron pocket. "He was a nasty, mean little boy, and an even nastier, meaner man."

Maisie took her time. "He didn't have a good life at home. Many of the children in these parts have it hard; they're out to work before they should be, and half of them haven't shoes on their feet or warm coats in winter—yet Jimmy had it especially hard, didn't he?"

Jennie spoke up. "He certainly did, there's no lie there. Poor little scrap, he was. I remember seeing him once with bruises all down the side of his face, and a few stripes on his leg from his father's belt."

"That don't excuse the way he treated my Eddie," said Maud.

"Maud," said Maisie. "Why do *you* think he was like that with Eddie?"

"I'm sure I don't know. How would I know, Maisie? What're you asking me that for?"

Maisie could see the woman was shaking and reached for her hand. "Maud, I think you know. And I think I know, too. You've never talked about it, and you can't keep it bottled up forever. You were just a young, young girl. It's not too late to shed a burden, ever."

Jennie looked at Maisie, her brow furrowed, concern giving an edge to her voice. "What are you talking about, Maisie? What's this all about?"

"Maud?" said Maisie.

The woman's breathing became faster, and tears began to fall. "Jimmy Merton hated my Eddie." Sobs came with every breath. "He . . . he hated him because he knew. He knew, even though he had never been told. Jimmy knew that Eddie was his brother. His half brother."

"What?" said Jennie. "Maudie, love, what are you saying? You always said you never saw the man who took you. How could you know . . . oh, dear." She clutched a handkerchief to her mouth. "Oh dear . . ."

"It was Jimmy Merton's father who had me as I was walking home in the dark. He was well in his cups, and I'd never even been kissed by a boy, never been with a boy. He grabbed me and dragged me up the alley, and he . . . he was . . . cruel to me." She folded her arms and began rocking backwards and forwards in her chair.

Jennie moved to put her arm around Maud but was pushed away.

"No, she's right," said Maud. "The girl's right, I've got to get it out and I can't have you stopping me with your concern. It's been eating me up. Ever since then, it's been eating me up. He took me, he took my girlhood, he took my . . . oh, Maisie, what's the word?"

"Innocence?"

Maud nodded. "He took my innocence. He was a brute and he made me bleed and he left me scarred, and he left me . . . with a baby. A lovely, precious, special little boy, who I loved so much, never mind how he came into the world, and all his slowness." She gasped for breath.

Maisie went to the sink and ran water into an earthenware cup, which she put in front of Maud, who was talking quickly now, her words breaking through the dam of silence she had begun to build, stick by stick, the night Jimmy Merton's father had raped her.

"And he told me, after he'd dragged me up that alley and was about to leave me, that if I ever said a word to a soul about what he'd done, I'd find myself at the bottom of the water. And I don't know how that poor little mite, Jimmy, ever cottoned on that Eddie was his brother, but I always thought he just knew; just knew because blood can recognize its own. It was as if he wanted to destroy Eddie for not being right, for him being slow, as if it would show up on him too, one day. And Eddie never took a swing back, he just turned away, as if he could feel it, as if there was something inside him, telling him that they were joined."

"Perhaps, Maud, Jimmy wanted to destroy Eddie because he was loved, and Jimmy wasn't," said Maisie.

"Oh, Maud. You've even kept it from me, all these years. You poor girl." Jennie went to the stove and poured water from the boiling kettle, scalding the tea and leaving it to brew. "You should have got that off your chest a long time ago."

Maud wiped her eyes. "I was scared, Jen. I was always scared of that man, and scared of his family. And even after he died, I was so used to the fear, I didn't know what it would be like to stop being frightened." She looked at Maisie. "It sort of wraps itself around your insides, like a snake, I reckon."

Maisie nodded. "I couldn't describe it better myself, Maud."

"And it's not as if we can all just up and go, is it? I mean, you're born on these streets, and this is where you stay, unless of course you get called up to fight like Wilf, God rest his soul. Or if you've got something about you—like you, Maisie—you can probably get away."

Jennie put three cups of tea on the table, and a packet of biscuits.

"We've had a man round, about money. So we spent a bit more this week—some nice biscuits."

"I hope you're being looked after," said Maisie.

"I reckon we are," said Jennie. "Tell her, Maud."

Maud's eyes were still red-rimmed, and Maisie knew there remained much to tell; much for the elderly woman to reveal of the snake that was now loosening its grip on her soul. "The man told us we'd be sent money regular—very nice, wasn't he, with his bowler hat and pressed suit? He said we could move somewhere nicer, if we wanted to, and he would arrange everything. He told us to think about it. But we don't know. This is far from being a palace, but we know these streets, and the people know us, so we'd never be short of someone to come in and lend a hand. You can't take a plant from the shade and put it in the sun, not if it's been used to the shadows and done all right there."

"I'm not very good at gardening, Maud," said Maisie.

"I bet you'd be good at anything you turn your mind to, young lady." She took Maisie's hand. "The only thing I won't mind never seeing again is that workhouse. Terrible, terrible memories—eh, Jen? And they say there's people pouring in again, not able to pay their way."

Jennie nodded.

"I reckon that when all's said and done, we'll think about moving. After all, you never know. It's not against the law to change your mind, is it?"

"No. And there's no need to rush into anything," said Maisie.

"The other thing is that we wouldn't want to leave Eddie," said Maud. "Not alone in the cemetery like that." She paused. "Reckon that Jimmy Merton won't have a proper burial, what with him taking his own life."

"I don't know what arrangements are being made, but he won't be buried in consecrated ground," said Maisie.

"I still hate him, and I don't think I'll ever forgive him. But I do reckon he had it hard, growing up. That don't make it right. But if he had half the snake, here, that's been wrapped up inside me, then I reckon he must've been a very sad boy. Sad becomes bad too easy, eh, Maisie?"

Maisie squeezed Maud's hand. "I think I'd better be off. I'm sure you've got a lot to talk about with Jennie."

"We've always got a lot to talk about, haven't we, Maud?" said Jennie. "I'll come to the door with you, Maisie."

They walked along the passageway again, and to the door.

"How did you know about Eddie's father?" asked Jennie.

Maisie shrugged. "I just thought about it a lot. Some things you can't know definitely, but you have a feeling that points you in a certain direction. And someone said something to me, about Jimmy Merton having an ax to grind as far as Eddie was concerned, and I remembered seeing him, his face, his way of walking, and I realized that it reminded me a bit of Eddie, though Eddie was bigger."

Jennie nodded. "Gentle giant, wasn't he?"

"One of the best," said Maisie. "Now, you get back to Maud. It'll have done her good to get that off her chest, but I think you should do something for the rest of the day. Go to the cemetery, then catch a bus across the water—there are lovely flowers blooming in Hyde Park, so a stroll would be just what you both need. Treat yourself to a bite to eat, somewhere posh. You've been given some money—enjoy it."

Once across Lambeth Bridge, Maisie drove along the Embankment, stopping when she saw a telephone kiosk. She dialed the office in Fitzroy Square.

"Sandra? Good. Look, I'm not coming into the office this morning. I'm going to be away for a few days, perhaps a week. So could you hold the fort? I'll keep in touch and let you know when I'm coming back, and you can telephone the house if something urgent comes in."

Maisie spent her days at The Dower House alone with her thoughts for much of the time. She joined the gardeners when they came to her house, and worked alongside them, asking questions about this plant and that shrub, and where it might be best to grow some vegetables. She had a few words with Dawkins, the new apprentice gardener. He was enjoying his job and did not mention the fading bruises on his cheek and around his eye, and Maisie did not ask.

Each evening she went down to the Groom's Cottage for supper, or she sat in the kitchen at The Dower House and thought about the ease with which they had fallen into habit whereby Mrs. Bromley was both a companion to her father and someone whom she could count on, not simply as an employee, but one who sometimes volunteered a point of view. It was an opinion that usually gave food for thought, and for that she was grateful. Maisie suspected the housekeeper had done the same for Maurice, and she was gaining a new appreciation of their relationship. Some people were at their best, she realized, when relating to each other in a manner that was not in line with the accepted norm.

Upon her return to London, she felt a growing warmth in her heart for James. They began to establish something neither had expected at the outset, when they came together with the excitement of new love. They no longer had a courtship, though they continued to present themselves as a couple, yet they had something more than friend-ship. Neither one was seeing anyone else, and it seemed to suit them both. They did not argue as they had, and found much to laugh about, to talk about, and they enjoyed a certain companionship that could not easily be pigeonholed. When she tried to explain to Priscilla how things were, her friend sighed and responded, "Sounds awfully like a marriage to me, Maisie. You slip into step with one another, you have someone to talk to, to be with, to socialize with, but neither of you gets crabby if one wants to do something else for a change—at least that's how it is with Douglas and me."

It was to be some time before Maisie felt ready to go back over the many notes she had made on the case of Eddie Pettit—an investigation she could never quite get out of her mind. She had no need to provide a formal report to her original clients, but she felt drawn to putting down her thoughts in writing, to recount the case and the many tribu-taries she'd followed to discover who was responsible for Eddie's death. She read through the pages again and again, making corrections and alterations, and soon realized she was ready to embark upon the ritual of her final accounting. She had learned the importance of this step when she was first apprenticed to Maurice. He had instructed her that it was important to reflect upon each stage in the process of solving a case, perhaps to visit certain people again, or to walk a given route that she'd followed during her investigation. The final accounting was key to coming to the next new case renewed and ready for another challenge. It was not a means of forgetting, but of assigning completed work its place, as if it were freshly laundered linen—starched, ironed, folded, and put away in the airing cupboard.

———

Her first stop was Bookhams, where she planned to drop in to see the manager, but as luck would have it, as she approached the door leading to the office, the secretary she had spoken to on her previous visit was just leaving.

"Good morning—Miss Marchant, isn't it?" said Maisie.

The woman looked up, startled. "Golly, you made me jump—I was looking down, not where I was going. Mr. Mills isn't here anymore, if it's him you want to see."

"Oh dear, nothing serious happened to him, I hope."

"No," said Miss Marchant. "Least I don't think so. He was moved to another factory, owned by Mr. Otterburn. Now we've got a new manager, only he's sort of higher up, and he's overseeing the modernization that's going on."

"Modernization? What are they doing?"

"They're shutting the factory down in stages, so as not to completely stop production, but they've got all these new safety measures, and new machinery going in, so that there's no accidents. We already knew that there was work on the cards, but they're doing something much bigger now—a brand-new, much wider conveyor system for a start. And they're spending a bit of money, making sure we're not operating with a short staff and that everyone on the shop floor is trained properly—especially for emergencies. It's on account of Mr. Pettit's accident that all this is happening." She shrugged. "So it wasn't for nothing that he died. At least it won't happen again. The horses are all gone now, though."

"That's a shame. I suppose it's all in the name of progress."

"There was a bit of an uproar, to tell you the truth, what with Mr. Pettit's death, and how he loved them horses. So the company had the horses taken away in a big lorry, and we was told they were going down to Surrey somewhere, to live in a big field that Mr. Otterburn owns. One of the blokes went with them, just to make sure there was no funny business, like taking them off to a man with a gun."

"I'm glad to hear it. Well, thank you, Miss Marchant. I'd better be going."

She turned to make her way onto the cobblestone street when Miss Marchant called to her. "I'm not sorry about Jimmy Merton, you know. Never liked that man. I saw Mr. Pettit once, just after Merton came to work here. Mr. Pettit went up to him and held out his hand, friendly, as if he knew him and wanted to be mates. But that guttersnipe just pushed him away. Makes you wonder what gets into some people."

Evelyn Butterworth answered the door, brush in hand and purple paint smeared across her forehead.

"Miss Dobbs—Maisie! What a lovely surprise. Do come in, but please mind where you stand. Let me put this down and wash my hands."

"I just thought I'd drop in to see how you're getting on." Maisie stepped through into the small sitting room cum bedroom and stood by the window, touching the windowsill first to ensure it wasn't wet.

Evelyn had painted the small flat and put up new wallpaper and curtains. She came back into the room, wiping her hands with a cloth. "I was refinishing the kitchen table. I thought I would give it a new lease on life with a different color." She looked around the room, then at Maisie. "What do you think?"

"I think you've done a grand job," said Maisie.

"Everyone pulled together to help, in fact, I could have probably furnished a house with all the offers that came my way."

"I thought I'd bring you a gift for the flat." Maisie held out a box.

"It's not quite your grandmother's china, but I think Susie Cooper's designs are quite lovely—a bit different. I hope it's all right, and you can exchange it for another design if—"

Evelyn pulled back the wrapping paper, the cardboard lid, and tissue. "Oh my, this is wonderful—so bright and modern! Thank you, Miss Dobbs."

"I should thank you, Eve. You helped me enormously, and you've lost an awful lot."

Evelyn Butterworth pressed her lips together, as if to stem her emotions. "Well, as my grandmother always said, 'You just have to get on with it.' And she was right—you can't wallow, can you? So, I got stuck in and sorted myself out. I miss Bart more than I ever imagined, but I've made this place so new, it's different. I don't think he would have liked it, if I'm honest."

"As long as you like it, that's the most important thing," said Maisie.

"I'd put the kettle on and invite you to stay, but the chairs are covered with a sheet and I've not even had a chance to nip out to the shops for milk today—but would you come back next week? Everything will be perfect then."

As Maisie stepped along the path, she turned back and saw Evelyn Butterworth standing by the window. She waved farewell, and received a wave in return. And as she made her way to the underground station, it occurred to her that Evelyn had wisely created a vibrant cocoon in which to heal. It would not be long before she spread her wings.

Billy had been discharged from hospital and was convalescing at home. Maisie had arranged for her solicitors to remit payment of his wages by messenger each week. She thought it best to draw back from delivering the money herself. She wrote one letter, wishing him a good recovery, and assuring him that his job was waiting for him as soon as he was well. She explained that she would love to visit, but understood they had a busy household and would wait to hear from Doreen, to see if it would be convenient for her to call.

The letter arrived one morning in early May when it seemed the spell of unexpected fine weather was about to come to an end. It was penned in delicate cursive handwriting on a vellum notecard; Doreen must have invested in good paper to write to her customers, who seemed to be increasingly well-to-do. Maisie had never taken account of Doreen's handwriting before and felt it revealed someone who took care to do things properly, who liked her house in order, and who had received a good education. In truth, she realized she knew little about Billy's wife, except that she came from Sussex and met Billy while he was convalescing from his wounds, towards the end of the war. The letter invited Maisie to tea on Friday afternoon. Maisie penned a plain postcard by return post, accepting the invitation.

Bringing a small toy for each child and a basket of fruit, Maisie spent the better part of an afternoon with the family. Billy's boys were as boisterous as ever, and were sent to play in the garden, where Billy's mother sat in a chair with a blanket across her knees and tapped a wooden spoon on the side of the chair every time a boy threatened to misbehave. Maisie suspected the spoon would never be used to mete out discipline, though it proved a powerful deterrent.

Billy looked well, if a little more unsteady on his feet than usual. He promised to be back at work in a couple of weeks, perhaps sooner.

"I can't keep taking money for nothing, Miss."

"It's not for nothing. It's my obligation to an employee who was injured while working. But I'll be glad to see you back when you're ready."

At that moment, Doreen came back into the room. Little Meg had just woken from a nap; her eyes were half open, her cheeks peach-pink with sleep. Billy's wife had said little to Maisie since she arrived. There was a greeting and gratitude expressed for the gifts; she asked questions about how Maisie was keeping, and how she would like her tea. But now Doreen Beale walked straight towards Maisie and held out the baby for her to take, placing the beloved new daughter in her arms with pride.

Maisie cradled little Meg Beale and looked into her eyes. "She's like her mum, isn't she?" she observed, and was comforted by Doreen's radiant smile. It was a smile that matched her own, which was not just for the warmth of a dear child held close to her heart, but for the knowledge that she was forgiven.

She wanted to go to Box Hill, but rather dreaded a walk on her own, so she suggested to James that they could take Priscilla's sons down for an afternoon of kite flying.

"You do realize that this means we won't have the energy to go out for a week, don't you?" said James. "The Beale boys may be rascals, but Priscilla's toads are demons!"

"Come on, you'll love it, you know you will," said Maisie.

"Yes, yes, I know. It'll be great fun."

The previous visit to Box Hill had been one that opened Maisie's wounds. The planned day of kite flying was, she thought, something that would lighten the dark shadow left by John Otterburn's predictions. The boys ran back and forth, chasing downed kites, screaming at one another to keep a kite aloft, or simply running around making noise.

"I'd forgotten those boys have such big voices," said James. "This reminds me of school."

"Don't worry, they'll sleep on the way home."

"So will I. You're driving, Maisie."

"Your new car?"

"Any car that I fall into, my dear."

Maisie called out to Tarquin to pull in his kite, and ran to help him untangle his fingers from the string. And as she felt the smaller hand in hers, she thought of his father, and the lengths Douglas would go to to make sure his sons were at liberty to run, to yell, to play, and to know joy. She remembered his words by heart:

I fought for them to have the freedom to laugh, to tease each other, to climb trees, and to run headlong into the world.

The journey home to the Holland Park mansion where Priscilla and her family lived was as James predicted: Maisie drove while James slept in the passenger seat next to her, the boys curled together like puppies in the back of the motor car.

"Douglas and I have had the most wonderful day, and Elinor has enjoyed a brief respite from the fray. You must stay to supper—oh dear, if you can remain awake, that is." Priscilla looked from Maisie to James.

"I'm starving, actually," said James.

"Me, too. We'll stay to supper, but probably make it an early night—the boys have worn us out."

"You've got color in your cheeks, though. Come on, let's get some drinks. I think our trusty cook is preparing rainbow trout this evening."

With the boys in bed, Maisie and James enjoyed an informal supper with Priscilla and Douglas. It was as they were lingering over brandy that Priscilla announced that she would rather like to show Maisie a new gown that had just arrived from Paris. The women left the table and went to Priscilla's sitting room upstairs.

"I thought I would never get you alone," said Priscilla.

"Pris, I believe James and Douglas could see through that gown ruse with ease," said Maisie. "What's wrong?"

"Nothing's wrong, except I have to say, things seem to be going rather well between you and James, despite your predictions of an end to it all."

"I think we may have found our place with each other," said Maisie.

"Is he still going to Canada?"

"Yes, but we're not sure when—perhaps before Toronto is engulfed in snow."

"And you're not going with him?" asked Priscilla.

"I'm not sure where I'm going, yet," said Maisie.

"What do you mean? 'I'm not sure where I'm going, *yet*.' What are you up to?"

"I feel like a criminal, being asked all these questions." Maisie smiled at Priscilla and took her hand. "I think I might go abroad on my own for a while. Who knows? James might join me, or I might join him until I want to move on—or we may never see each other again, though I believe we will. I want to see more of the world while I can. And I want to be . . . unpredictable. I want to learn something, Priscilla. I want to learn how to just let things happen sometimes. I think I want to find out what it's like to approach a corner without constantly trying to be prepared for what I might encounter when I round it."

"Yes, it does make the load rather heavy if you carry tools for every eventuality. Where might you go? You could start in Biarritz, if you like—the villa's there at your disposal."

"We'll see. I'm not sure where, or when. It might be years. Or I might go somewhere just for a couple of weeks. I don't know. I am only sure it's something I must do."

On the following Monday morning, she parked in Horseferry Lane, north of the river, stopping at a flower stall on her way to Lambeth Bridge. She bought a large bouquet of spring flowers for Maud and Jennie, and a second smaller bunch. Halfway across the bridge, she leaned over and looked down into the swirling grayish-black water. She thought of Bart Soames, and of Jimmy Merton, and whispered the words, "May they know peace." She allowed the small bunch of flowers to fall into the river, to be carried along, past Parliament, past the pontoon where she'd spoken with a young police constable, past the docks, past plenty and poverty, past factories and fields.

Walking around Covent Garden market was, for Maisie, like meandering back into her childhood. Once again the porters ran to and fro as the lorries jockeyed for position with horse-drawn carts. There were calls back and forth between the costers, and men waving to each other, crying out prices.

It was a fine May day, one of those afternoons when, in the sunshine, a coat might be taken off, or a gentleman could be seen lifting his hat to wipe his brow or a costermonger pushing back his cap to run his fingers through sweat-dampened hair. In time, she made her way to Sam's café and asked Sam if she might take a couple of chairs out onto the flagstones, to sit in the sun.

"Course you can, Maisie," said Sam. "What can I do for you today?"

"Thank you, Sam. I'm waiting for someone; we'll decide what we'd like then."

"Just you sit there in the sunshine and give me a shout when you're ready, love."

She watched a coster bring his horse to a halt across the road. He jumped down from the cart and went to the horse, running his hand down the sturdy feathered left front leg of the piebald Welsh cob, and lifted the foot. He brushed off the hoof with his hand, then pulled a pick from his back pocket and popped a stone caught in the shoe. The man released the horse's leg with a gentleness that belied his gruff appearance, then rubbed his hand across the beast's thick neck, and was nuzzled in return. He fitted a nose-bag of oats and the horse was left to eat while the man went to talk to a friend.

Maisie thought she saw, in the market before her, the world in miniature: people going about their business, the horse and the motor car sharing the road, as if past and future were trying to get along. There were rich and poor and people in between; jobs to do and mouths to be fed; schools to be attended, lessons to learn and unlearn; and life went on its way, like the river. Everyone was doing what they had to do to maintain or better their lot, to stop themselves sliding, or to earn a few more pennies.

Her thoughts turned to John Otterburn and his predictions. When her investigation ended, she had asked Jack Barker if he had copies of old newspapers going back to the beginning of the year—and he didn't disappoint, bringing a boxful to her office one afternoon. She added them to those procured and read throughout her work on the case, and one day went through each newspaper, cutting out columns of news and strips of headlines, laying them out like daisy chains across the table by the window in her office. Every story was another brushstroke in an image of terror.

At the end of March, Germany's Herr Hitler had been given powers of dictatorship, and since that time decrees to disenfranchise the Jewish population had moved on apace, with Jewish men and women barred from government work, then from owning businesses and from the practice of law. Since the *Manchester Guardian* had printed an article in early April entitled "The Terror in Germany," recounting ways in which the Nazi government was hiding the truth of its actions, even more worrying revelations had come to light in the weeks to follow. John Otterburn had been quick to unleash a torrent of inflammatory headlines in every one of his newspapers.

But now, as the sun shone on an ordinary spring day in London, her thoughts turned to Eddie once again, and how he must have felt, how his confusion upon suffering a manipulation he was ill equipped to understand must have darkened his simple days. And it occurred to her that perhaps they were all like Eddie; perhaps they were all unknowing, influenced to think in a given direction by men who believed themselves visionaries—she had not decided whether such a thing was wrong or right or fell somewhere to the center of those two bookends of morality.

"There you are!" James called to Maisie as he walked towards her, his black pin-striped suit looking out of place in the market. He sat down beside her, leaning back into the chair. "If you hadn't told me about this café, I would never have found it. Lovely out here in this bit of sunshine, isn't it? What are we having, by the way?"

"Ice cream," said Maisie.

"Ice cream?" He began to laugh. "Sometimes you surprise me, Maisie."

"Sam has the most delicious flavors. He makes them all here, at the back of the shop—my father would bring me here when I was a child, for a special treat. I particularly like the hazelnut with a little chocolate sauce on top. Sam will put it in a cornet or a bowl, whatever you want."

"That's good enough for me. I'll never make it back to the office, though."

Maisie shrugged. "Does it matter? The Compton Corporation won't collapse if we go for a walk, will it?"

Maisie called out to Sam, who brought two cornets, each with chocolate rippling across a rounded ball of ice cream.

"Isn't this lovely, Maisie?" said James. "Watching the world go by while dripping chocolate down a new tie and my favorite suit."

"And my chin, and my blouse," added Maisie.

Then they sat back in silence, eating ice cream. Each with their own thoughts. Watching their world go by.

ACKNOWLEDGMENTS

To my father, Albert Winspear, for sharing with me the extraordinary true story of the man who was born in a brewery stable and from that time had a magical communication with horses—he inspired the character of Eddie Pettit. Thank you, Dad, for your stories, and for passing on your love of horses to me.

Once again, my friend Holly Rose fanned the flames of another novel with her insightful reading of the early chapters and huge helpings of encouragement.

To my agent, Amy Rennert, and my editor, Jennifer Barth—thank you for your enthusiasm for my work and your wise counsel. I am deeply grateful to you both.

To Andrew Davidson, the enormously talented artist and craftsman who designs the covers that grace the Maisie Dobbs series—thank you, Andrew, for your commitment to my books and for listening so carefully when I try to describe my own vision of each cover. Deepest thanks to Archie Ferguson at Harper, who pulls everything together.

Also at Harper, much gratitude to Jonathan Burnham, Josh Marwell, Virginia Stanley, Kathy Schneider, Katherine Beitner, Jennifer Hart, Nicole Judge, and Mark Ferguson—your support, hard work, and attention to detail is so very much appreciated by this author.

And deepest appreciation, as always, to my husband, John Morell, who knows the importance of breaking out the champagne when I reach The End.

About the author

About the book

Insights,
Interviews
& More . . .

Meet
Jacqueline Winspear

JACQUELINE WINSPEAR is the author of the *New York Times* bestsellers *Elegy for Eddie*, *A Lesson in Secrets*, *The Mapping of Love and Death*, *Among the Mad*, and *An Incomplete Revenge*, as well as four other nationally bestselling Maisie Dobbs novels. She has won numerous awards for her work, including the Agatha, Alex, and Macavity awards for the first book in the series, *Maisie Dobbs*, which was also nominated for the Edgar Award for Best Novel and was a *New York Times* Notable Book. Originally from the United Kingdom, she now lives in California. ∽

Lee Child Talks with Jacqueline Winspear

This interview was conducted by Lee Child and originally appeared on Amazon.com.

JACQUELINE WINSPEAR, like her interviewer, the iconic, bestselling author Lee Child, originally hailed from the United Kingdom. *A Lesson in Secrets* is her eighth novel featuring psychologist-investigator and former WWI nurse Maisie Dobbs. Here she talks with Child about her work on the series and her enduring interest in the aftermath of World War I.

Lee Child: *People are often surprised that I'm a huge Maisie Dobbs fan, because Jack Reacher is all about a kind of Spartan American masculinity, and Maisie Dobbs is all about a kind of feminine English refinement. But they're both strong, unconventional people. Perhaps that's the cross-genre appeal? Do you find that Maisie attracts an unusual mix of readers?*

Jacqueline Winspear: I'm thrilled you're such a Maisie Dobbs fan—and you can count me among those millions of Jack Reacher fans. Maisie and Reacher are both unconventional, but I believe another factor in their cross-genre appeal is that both have endured life- ▶

Lee Child Talks with Jacqueline Winspear
(*continued*)

changing challenges. Maisie attracts
diverse readers: men and women, all
age groups, veterans, nurses, college
students, people who have faced troubles,
and people interested in the era.

Lee Child: *And in fact your novels
are driven by violence far worse
than mine—off the page, granted,
but there's no getting around the fact
that at the heart of your books is the
aftermath of a horrendous war, with
its attendant violence and death. How
do you see the role of violence in your
novels?*

Jacqueline Winspear: I think you hit
the theme there with "aftermath." The
violence in my books is that searing,
painful residue left by the passing of
a terrible time, when people were also
crushed emotionally by the deep losses
over a four-year period. In addition,
there's that element of violence that
lingers—in *Among the Mad*, for
example—when war's tentacles will
not let go. We see that again today in
the stories of veterans who are still
fighting their wars, but the conflict
is raging inside them.

Lee Child: *As a kid in England I
remember seeing hundreds of maimed
old men, and hundreds of lonely old*

women. My grandfather was an example of the first, and two great-aunts examples of the second—sad reminders of a terrible time. Was it something similar that drew you to the First World War and the "Between the Wars" era that followed?

Jacqueline Winspear: I have the same memories—my grandfather was wounded at the Battle of the Somme, and my grandmother was partially blinded at the Woolwich Arsenal, in an explosion that wounded her sister and killed several girls working alongside her. There were the elderly spinsters in my neighborhood, and for each there was that old sepia photograph on the mantelpiece, of a sweetheart or brother lost to war. Those childhood memories led me to think a lot about what happens after war is done. As a character says in *Birds of a Feather*, "That's the trouble with war; it lives on inside the living."

Lee Child: *I was introduced to Maisie Dobbs by my wife, who passed through an airport and picked up the first in the series. She loved it, and urged me to read it, and I'm glad I did. It's one of the very, very few series we both love equally—in fact, perhaps the only one. Is this typical of your readers?* ▸

> " There were the elderly spinsters in my neighborhood, and for each there was that old sepia photograph on the mantelpiece, of a sweetheart or brother lost to war. "

Lee Child Talks with Jacqueline Winspear
(continued)

Jacqueline Winspear: I receive so many emails from fans who tell me that the books are read by all members of the family. And many women tell me that it was their husband who first discovered Maisie. The books are as accessible to readers aged about fourteen as they are to seniors. There are few things today that all age groups within a family can engage in, discuss, and get excited about, so it's lovely when I hear that family members are awaiting the next book so they can all read it.

Lee Child: *Maisie is definitively feminine, but she's running a business, and poking around in a "man's world," which is true to the times, and indicative of the early stages of feminism in the West. Was that something you wanted to explore?*

Jacqueline Winspear: It would have been difficult to introduce a character such as Maisie and not explore the fact that the Great War left so many women to forge a life alone. If there was one thing I wanted to do, it was to bring the spirit of that generation to the character of Maisie Dobbs. Of course, some women floundered and lived lonely lives, but there were a great many who blazed a trail. I believe an archetype was born at that time—the stoic British woman who

66 I receive so many emails from fans who tell me that the books are read by all members of the family. 99

is independent and more than a little opinionated, with a heart of gold under a tough exterior, and who knows what it is to endure. Dame Maggie Smith has played that character in several films.

Lee Child: *Maisie understands human psychology in a way that seems to be an early and experimental pre-echo of what we'd now call criminal profiling. It's a huge part of both her process and her appeal. Where did that come from?*

Jacqueline Winspear: That developed in a very organic way. Having established her as a "sensitive," I wanted to give her real expertise—and there are historical underpinnings to this aspect of her character. Maisie studied the Moral Sciences curriculum at Girton College when psychology was in its infancy. I have the prospectus from 1913, and about one-third of the course was the study of modern psychology. It was a time of great experimentation, so Maisie's processes have their roots in real practices considered innovative at the time.

Lee Child: *One of your decisions I admire is the way you have moved the series forward in time so firmly. Most writers would have continued mining the same immediate post-war seam* ▸

66 I believe an archetype was born at that time—the stoic British woman who is independent and more than a little opinionated, with a heart of gold under a tough exterior. 99

Lee Child Talks with Jacqueline Winspear
(continued)

forever. What was your thinking behind that? And how do you keep the character fresh as the series itself develops?

Jacqueline Winspear: I once heard you say at a conference, "The reader comes back to a series, not to find out what the sleuth does with the case, but what the case does to the sleuth." I agree. We are all impacted not only by our past, but by our current circumstances and those around us. You always put Reacher in a new area, be it small town or big city, and through his wandering we learn a lot about him. I work with the geography of time. Not everyone likes change and many readers would like Maisie Dobbs to stay as she is in a given book. But life's not like that—the goalposts tend to move when we are at our most comfortable, and I want to keep the series fresh.

Lee Child: *I'm often asked if I have a favorite book within my series, so now I'm turning the tables: Do you have favorites among your novels?*

Jacqueline Winspear: That's such a difficult question, because each book not only represents a different place on my journey as a writer, but has been inspired by something that touched me. I think *Maisie Dobbs* will always be very tightly

66 I once heard you say at a conference, 'The reader comes back to a series, not to find out what the sleuth does with the case, but what the case does to the sleuth.' 99

held in my affections, because it was my first book and was written at a difficult time in my life, when I was recovering from a horrible accident. The other choice would be *The Mapping of Love and Death*, because it was inspired by the true story of a soldier whose remains lay under Belgian soil for some ninety years until unearthed by a farmer. I learned more about him when I became involved in the quest to discover his origins. When I look at that book, I think of a young man lost to war who was never identified and who was eventually laid to rest as "A Soldier of The Great War, Known Unto God." I ache for the parents who never knew where their son died, for he had probably been listed as "Missing, Presumed Dead."

The Story Behind
Elegy for Eddie

THE INITIAL INSPIRATION for *Elegy for Eddie* was a true story my father told me many years ago about a young man known to everyone in the neighborhood when he was a boy. My father was born in 1926, and this man would have been a teen in 1933, the year in which the book is set. Though a little "slow," the young man—let's call him Eddie, though that wasn't his real name—was held affectionately by the locals, who looked out for him and protected him, as far as they could. His story almost seems the stuff of legend. Eddie's mother was only sixteen years of age when, pregnant and unwed, she went into labor while working as the night cleaner at the brewery stables. Up until that point she had disguised her pregnancy very well—the clothes of the day had helped. She had been working since the age of twelve, and cleaning at the brewery was not her only job. With the baby about to be born while she was at her work, she lay down on the low, hay-filled manger in a horse's stall and gave birth to her son. And in the days and weeks that followed, though she now had a baby boy, she could not afford to give up work, so she continued to be the night-time cleaner at the brewery stables, keeping the baby in a basket inside one of the stalls while she toiled. So young

Eddie grew up around horses, knowing it was important to keep quiet as his mother's job depended upon it. There was some talk, at the time, that his mother might have tried to stop him crying when he was born, and through fear of being discovered she had unwittingly caused a degree of brain damage in the boy. But no mother could have loved her son more. And the son grew up to love horses, and they always took to him. Even as a child he could gentle a troubled horse, so much so that he earned his money in this way, along with taking other odd jobs—remember, this was the time when horse-power meant something; all the factories used horses, food was delivered by horse and cart, and even in the early 1930s, you didn't have go far from central London to find streets where a motor car had never passed.

Eddie died under suspicious circumstances at a local paper factory, where he would go to run errands for the workers—perhaps to the shop to buy cigarettes or newspapers. I overheard my parents talking about him one day, wondering about his death and saying what a shame it was, as everyone had a soft spot for him. I was fascinated by my father's stories of how this man could just talk to an aggressive or out-of-control horse, perhaps lay a hand on him, and the horse became as quiet as a lamb and would do the man's bidding, whether it was to follow him without a ▶

66 The son grew up to love horses, and they always took to him. Even as a child he could gentle a troubled horse. **99**

The Story Behind *Elegy for Eddie* (*continued*)

halter or go into a stall for a wound to be treated. I was determined to write about him one day, but had to wait until the story was formed in my mind, and a reason developed for the death of a simple man who could make the most tempestuous horse settle. I hung the story of Eddie on the peg of history and, needless to say, the heart of the murder in the story goes well beyond a local south-London neighborhood. ∾